Books by Jonathan Kellerman

FICTION

ALEX DELAWARE NOVELS

Bones (2008)
Compulsion (2008)
Obsession (2007)
Gone (2006)
Rage (2005)
Therapy (2004)
A Cold Heart (2003)
The Murder Book (2002)
Flesh and Blood (2001)
Dr. Death (2000)
Monster (1999)
Survival of the Fittest (1997)
The Clinic (1997)
The Web (1996)
Self-Defense (1995)
Bad Love (1994)
Devil's Waltz (1993)
Private Eyes (1992)
Time Bomb (1990)
Silent Partner (1989)
Over the Edge (1987)
Blood Test (1986)
When the Bough Breaks (1985)

OTHER NOVELS

Capital Crimes (with Faye Kellerman, 2006)
Twisted (2004)
Double Homicide (with Faye Kellerman, 2004)
The Conspiracy Club (2003)

Billy Straight (1998)
The Butcher's Theater (1988)

NONFICTION
With Strings Attached: The Art and Beauty
of Vintage Guitars (2008)
Savage Spawn: Reflections on Violent Children (1999)
Helping the Fearful Child (1981)
Psychological Aspects of Childhood Cancer (1980)

FOR CHILDREN, WRITTEN AND ILLUSTRATED
Jonathan Kellerman's ABC of Weird Creatures (1995)
Daddy, Daddy, Can You Touch the Sky? (1994)

BONES

JONATHAN KELLERMAN

BONES

AN ALEX DELAWARE NOVEL

Doubleday Large Print
Home Library Edition

BALLANTINE BOOKS

NEW YORK

Copyright © 2008 by Jonathan Kellerman

All rights reserved.

Published in the United States by Ballantine Books, an imprint of The Random House Publishing Group, a division of Random House, Inc., New York.

BALLANTINE and colophon are registered trademarks of Random House, Inc.

ISBN 978-1-60751-094-9

Printed in the United States of America

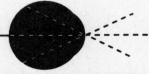

This Large Print Book carries the Seal of Approval of N.A.V.H.

To Lila

Special thanks to
Larry Malmberg and Bill Hodgman

BONES

CHAPTER
1

Everyone does it is not a defense!
Wrong.

If everyone did it, that made it normal, right? And after Chance did the research he knew he did *nothing* wrong.

Googling *high school cheating* because writing an essay was part of the punishment.

Finding out four out of five high school students—that's eighty frickin' *percent*—did it.

Majority rules. Just like that thing on his Social Action study sheet . . . social norms.

Social norms are the cement that holds societies together.

There you go, he was being a big help to society!

When he tried to joke about that with the parental units, they didn't laugh.

Same as when he told them it was civil rights, no way could the school force him to do community service outside the school property. That was against the Constitution. Time to call the ACLU.

That got Dad's eyes all squinty. Chance turned to Mom but she made sure not to give him any eye contact.

"The ACLU?" Big wet Dad throat clear, like after too many cigars. "Because we make a significant monetary contribution to the ACLU?" Starting to breathe hard. "Every goddamn *year.* That's what you're saying?"

Chance didn't answer.

"Cute, extremely cute. That's your point? Well let me tell you something: You cheated. Period. That is *not* the kind of thing the *ACLU* gives half a *shit* about."

"Language, Steve—" Mom broke in.

"Don't *start,* Susan. We've got a goddamn fucking serious problem here and

I seem to be the only one who fucking *gets* it."

Mom got all tight-mouthed, started plucking at her nails. Turned her back on both of them and did something with dishes on the kitchen counter.

"It's his problem, Susan, not ours and unless he owns up to it, we can kiss Occidental—or any other halfway decent college—fucking *good-bye.*"

Chance said, "I'll own up to it, Dad." Working on what Sarabeth called his Mr. Sincere look.

Laughing as she undid her bra. *Everyone buys Mr. Sincere but me, Chancy. I know it's Mr. Bogus.*

Dad stared at him.

"Hey," said Chance, "at least give me credit for hand-eye coordination."

Dad let out a stream of curses and stomped out of the kitchen.

Mom said, "He'll get over it," but she left, too.

Chance waited to make sure neither of them was coming back before he smiled.

Feeling good because his hand-eye *had* been cool.

Setting his Razr on vibrate and positioning it perfectly in a side pocket of his loosest cargo pants, the phone resting on a bunch of shit he'd stuffed in there to make kind of a little table.

Sarabeth three rows up, texting him the answers to the test. Chance being cool about it, knowing he'd never get caught because Shapiro was a nearsighted loser who stayed at his desk and missed everything.

Who'd figure Barclay would come in to tell Shapiro something, look clear to the back of the room, and spot Chance peeking into his pocket?

The whole class doing the same exact thing, everyone's pockets vibing. Everyone cracking up the moment the test started because Shapiro was such a clueless loser, the whole semester had been like this, the asshole would've missed Paris Hilton walking in nude and spreading.

Everyone does it is not a defense!

Rumley looking down his big nose and talking all sad like at a funeral. What Chance wanted to say was, *Then it frickin' should be, dude.*

Instead, he sat in Rumley's office, squeezed between his parents, his head all down, trying to look all sorry and thinking about the shape of Sarabeth's ass in her thong while Rumley went on forever about honor and ethics and the history of Windward Prep and how if the school so chose they had the option of informing the Occidental admissions office and causing dire consequences for his college career.

That made Mom burst into tears.

Dad just sat there, looking angry at the world, didn't make a move to even give her a tissue from the box on Rumley's desk so Rumley had to do it, standing up and handing it to Mom and looking pissed at Dad for making him stretch.

Rumley sat back down and moved his mouth some more.

Chance pretended to listen, Mom sniffled, Dad looked ready to hit someone. When Rumley finally finished, Dad started talking about the family's "contributions to Windward," mentioning Chance's performance on the basketball team, bringing up his own time on the football team.

In the end the adults reached an agreement and wore small, satisfied smiles.

Chance felt like a puppet but he made sure he looked all serious, being happy would be a *ba-ad* move.

Punishment 1: He'd have to take another version of the test—Shapiro would make one up.

Punishment 2: No more cell phone at school.

"Maybe this unfortunate event will have positive ramifications, young man," said Rumley. "We've been thinking about a schoolwide ban."

There you go, thought Chance. I did you guys a favor, not only shouldn't you punish me, you should be payin' me, like some sort of consulting deal.

So far, so good, for a second Chance thought he'd got off real easy. Then:

Punishment 3: The essay. Chance hated to write, usually Sarabeth did his essays, but she couldn't do this one because he had to do it at school, in Rumley's office.

Still, no big deal.

Then came Punishment 4: "Because substantive accountability has to be part of the package, Master Brandt."

Mom and Dad agreeing. The three of them going all al-Qaida on him.

Chance pretended to agree.

Yes, sir, I need to pay my debt and I will do so with industrious alacrity.

Throwing in some SAT vocab words. Dad staring at him, like who are you kidding, dude, but Mom and Rumley looked really impressed.

Rumley moved his mouth.

Community service. Oh, shit.

And here the frick he was.

Sitting in the Save the Marsh office on night eleven of his thirty-night sentence. Shitty little puke-colored room with pictures of ducks and bugs, whatever, on the wall. One dirty window looking out to a parking lot where no one but him and Duboff parked. Stacks of bumper stickers in the corner he was supposed to hand out to anyone who walked in.

No one walked in and Duboff left him by himself so he could run off to investigate how global warming got up a duck's butt, what made birds hurl, did bugs have big dicks, whatever.

Thirty frickin' nights of this, nuking his summer vacation.

Five to ten p.m., instead of hanging after school with Sarabeth and his friends, all because of a *social norm* four out of five people did.

When the phone did ring, he mostly ignored it. When he did answer, it was always some loser wanting directions to the marsh.

Go on the frickin' website or use MapQuest, Rainman!

He wasn't allowed to make outgoing calls but since yesterday he'd started to hook up with Sarabeth for cell phone sex. She was loving him even more for not ratting her to Rumley.

He sat there. Drank from his can of Jolt, now warm. Felt the Baggie in his pants pocket and thought *Later.*

Nineteen more nights of supermax confinement, he was starting to feel like one of those Aryan Brotherhood dudes.

Two and a half more frickin' weeks until he was free at last, doing his Luther King thing. He checked his TAG Heuer. Nine twenty-four. Thirty-six minutes and he'd be good to go.

The phone rang.

He ignored it.

It kept going, ten times.

He let it die a natural death.

A minute later, it rang again and he figured maybe he should answer it, what if it
was Rumley testing him?

Clearing his throat and getting Mr. Sincere ready, he picked up. "Save the Marsh."

Silence on the other end made him
smile.

One of his friends pranking him, probably Ethan. Or Ben or Jared.

"Dude," he said. "What's up?"

A weird kind of hissy voice said, "Up?"
Weird laughter. "Something's *down*. As in
buried in your marsh."

"Okay, dude—"

"Shut up and listen."

Being talked to like that made Chance's
face go all hot, like when he was ready to
sneak a flagrant in on some loser on the
opposing team, then get all innocent when
the dude wailed about being nut-jammed.

He said, "Fuck off, dude."

The hissy voice said, "East side of the
marsh. Look and you'll find it."

"Like I give a—"

"Dead," said Hissy. "Something real real
dead." Laughter. *"Dude."*

Hanging up before Chance could tell
him to shove dead up his . . .

A voice from the door said, "Hey, man, how's it shaking?"

Chance's face was still hot, but he put on Mr. Sincere and looked over.

There in the doorway was Duboff, wearing his *Save the Marsh* T-shirt, geek shorts showing too much skinny white thigh, plastic sandals, that stupid gray beard.

"Hey, Mr. Duboff," said Chance.

"Hey, man." Duboff gave a clenched-fist salute. "Did you have a chance to check out the herons before you got here?"

"Not yet, sir."

"They're incredible animals, man. Magnificent. Wingspread like this." Unfolding scrawny arms to the max.

You've obviously mistaken me for someone who gives half a shit.

Duboff came closer, smelling gross, that organic deodorant he'd tried to convince Chance to use. "Like pterodactyls, man. Master fishers."

Chance had thought a heron *was* a fish until Duboff told him different.

Duboff edged near the desk, showed those gross teeth of his. "Rich folk in Beverly Hills don't like when the herons swoop in during hatching season and eat their rich-folk koi. Koi are aberrations. Mutations, people messing with brown carp, screwing up the DNA to get those colors. Herons are Nature, brilliant predators. They feed their young and restore nature to true balance. Screw those Beverly Hillbillies, huh?"

Chance smiled.

Maybe it wasn't a big enough smile because Duboff suddenly looked nervous. "You don't live there, do I recall correctly?"

"No, sir."

"You live in . . ."

"Brentwood."

"Brentwood," said Duboff, as if trying to figure out what that meant. "Your parents don't keep koi, do they?"

"Nope. We don't even have a dog."

"Good for you guys," said Duboff, patting Chance's shoulder. "It's all servitude. Pets, I mean. The whole concept is like slavery."

Keeping his hand on the shoulder. Was the guy a fag?

"Yeah," said Chance, inching away.

Duboff scratched his knee. Frowned and rubbed a pink bump. "Stopped by the marsh to check for trash. Musta got bit by something."

"Providing food for the little guys," said Chance. "That's a good thing, sir."

Duboff stared at him, trying to figure out if Chance was messing with his head.

Chance brought out Mr. Sincere and Duboff decided Chance was being righteous and smiled. "Guess you're right . . . anyway, I just thought I'd stop in, see how you're doing before your shift ends."

"I'm fine, sir."

"Okay, check you out later, man."

Chance said, "Uh, sir, it's kinda close to the end."

Duboff smiled. "So it is. At ten, you can lock up. I'll be by later." Walking to the door, he stopped, looked back. "It's a noble thing you're doing, Chance. Whatever the circumstances."

"Absolutely, sir."

"Call me Sil."

"You got it, Sil."

Duboff said, "Anything I should know about?"

"Like what, sir?"

"Calls, messages?"

Chance grinned, flashing perfect white chompers, courtesy five years of Dr. Wasserman.

"Nothing, Sil," he said, with utter confidence.

CHAPTER

2

Bob Hernandez needed the money.

Nothing but money would get him out here this early.

At five a.m., Pacific Public Storage was a fog-shrouded dump—like one of those gloomy places they used for serial killer and drug shoot-out movies. Twenty-four-hour facility, but most of the bulbs supposed to light up the passageways between the units were out and the auctioneer had to use a flashlight.

At this hour, no one was fully awake except for the Asian guy. Lousy turnout compared with the other auctions Bob had attended. Just him and four other people and the auctioneer, a white-haired guy named Pete in a suit and tie. The suit was cheap and brown and the tie needed Viagra. Guy reminded Bob of those shabby lawyers hanging around the downtown court building, waiting to be assigned to a case.

L.A. law but nothing like *L.A. Law.* Or *Boston Legal,* for that matter.

Bob would've loved to get hooked up with a good-looking girl attorney like on those shows, real passionate about defending him. Passionate about other stuff, too, after she saves his butt, the two of them . . .

Instead he got Mason Soto from the PD's office, guy went to Berkeley, let that fact slip into the conversation three separate times. Trying to bond with Bob, like they were homeboys, talking about immigration, La Raza.

Mason Soto had grown up in San Francisco and thought the country should open its borders to everyone. Bob had been raised in West Covina by a third-generation Mexican American ex-marine firefighter dad and a fourth-generation

Swedish American police dispatcher mom and both his brothers were cops and the whole family, including Bob, thought people should play by the rules and anyone who didn't should get their ass kicked out.

He told Soto, "I hear you," hoping that would get Soto to put out some extra effort, get him totally clear of the traffic warrants as well as the failure to appear.

Soto yawned through the trial and Bob ended up with a massive fine and ten days at County Jail, cut to five. Then reduced to an overnight stay because of overcrowding but, man, one day in that hellhole was enough.

The fine was a more enduring problem. Thirty-five hundred bucks that he needed to come up with in sixty days and none of his landscaping jobs had come through and he was already behind on his rent. Not to mention the child support. If Kathy decided to make trouble for him, he was screwed.

He missed the kids living in Houston with Kathy's folks.

Truth be told, he missed Kathy.

His own damn fault. Screwing around with women he didn't even care about,

he still didn't understand why he kept doing it.

He'd borrowed five hundred dollars from
his mom, telling her it would go toward the
fine. But the city wouldn't take partial payment and he needed something to gener-
ate income so he could square up his rent
as well as the fine.

Yesterday, the tree-moving company
out in Saugus had called back, told him to
come in, fill out forms, maybe that would
pan out.

Meanwhile, he was doing what he could.

Up at four a.m., making sure he'd sail
on the drive from Alhambra to Playa Del
Rey, be at the storage facility when it
opened.

He'd read about abandoned property
auctions on the Internet a few months ago,
forgot about it until being slapped with the
fine. Not stupid enough to think he was
going to come up with one of those trea-
sures that made the papers—a Honus
Wagner baseball card or a rare painting—
his hopes were pinned on eBay.

Because people bought anything on
eBay. You could sell a *stool* sample
on eBay.

So far, he'd attended four auctions, driving as far as Goleta—which turned out to be a total bust. But striking gold—silver, actually—right close to home.

Pasadena facility, seven-by-seven room piled high with neatly sealed boxes. Most of it turned out to be old moldy clothes that he ended up tossing in a Goodwill box, but there were also some jeans full of holes and a wad of rock-concert T-shirts from the eighties that eBayed pretty good.

Plus the bag. Little blue velvet Crown Royal drawstring full of coins, including buffalo-head nickels and a few silver dollars. Bob took all that to a coin dealer in Santa Monica, walked away with two hundred twenty bucks, which was a fantastic profit, considering his bid on the entire contents had been sixty-five.

He thought of paying his mom back, but decided to wait until everything was squared up.

A yawn overtook him and his eye blurred. Pete the auctioneer coughed, then said, "Okay, next unit: fourteen fifty-five," and everyone dragged themselves up the murky tunnel-like hallway to one of the padlocked doors that lined the cement-block walls.

Flimsy doors, flimsy locks, Bob could've kicked any of them in. The storage facility got two hundred a month per, talk about a good scam.

"Fourteen fifty-five," Pete repeated unnecessarily. Rubbing a rummy nose, he fiddled with a ring of keys.

The other bidders worked hard at looking disinterested. Two were chunky old women with braided hair, looked like sisters, maybe even twins. They'd gotten a sealed steamer trunk for forty-eight bucks. Behind them was a tall, skinny heavy-metal type wearing an AC/DC tee, fake leather pants, and motorcycle boots, veiny arms more tattoo-blue than white skin. He'd just won the last two lots: a room full of dirty-looking, mostly creased paperback books for a hundred and fifty and what looked to be rusty junk for thirty.

The last participant was the Asian guy, midthirties, athletic-looking, wearing a spotless royal blue polo shirt, pressed black slacks, and black loafers without socks. So far he'd bid on nothing.

Freshly shaved and aftershaved, the guy looked sharp in the Beemer convertible he drove up in. Bob wondered if he was some kind of art dealer, had the *nose.*

Worth keeping his eye on.

Pete found his key to 1455, released the lock, opened the door.

"Stand back, folks, private property," he said. Saying the same darn thing every time.

Due to some weird state law, abandoned goods belonged to the owner until the moment they sold. Meaning you couldn't approach them or touch them until you'd bought them. Then poof, the owner's rights disappeared like a minor fart.

Bob had never understood the legal system. When lawyers talked at him, it might as well have been in Martian.

Pete ran his flashlight over the contents of the cell-like space. Bob had heard of people jerry-rigging electricity and bunking down in storage units, but he didn't believe it. You'd go nuts.

"Okay," said Pete. "Let's start the bidding."

The Asian guy said, "Could you please illuminate it one more time."

Pete frowned, but obliged. The space

was mostly empty, except for half a bicycle frame and two black garbage bags.

Pete coughed again. "See what you need to?"

The Asian guy nodded, turned his back on the unit. Maybe a fake-out, planning to jump in at the last moment. Or maybe he really didn't want it.

Bob didn't see any point in bidding on this one. So far he'd found that garbage bags held mostly garbage. Though he needed *something* to eBay, so if no one bid and it went cheap enough . . .

"Let's hear a bid," said Pete, not waiting before adding: "Fifty, do I hear fifty, fifty dollars, fifty, fifty dollars."

Silence.

"Forty, forty dollars, bargain at forty dollars, metal on the bike is forty dollars." Running the spiel, but without enthusiasm. So far, his commission hadn't even added up to chump change.

"Forty? Nothing at forty? Do I hear thirty-five—"

Without turning around, the Asian guy said, "Twenty," and Bob sensed something in his voice. Not shifty, more like . . . calculated.

Figuring the metal on the bike was worth something—just the pedals might be valuable to someone who needed pedals—Bob said, "Twenty-five."

Silence.

Pete said, "Twenty-five, do I hear thirty, let's hear thirty, thirty dollars—"

"Sure," said the Asian guy. Shrugging, like he couldn't care less.

Bob waited until Pete spieled a bit more, then came in for thirty-five.

Asian half turned. "Forty."

Bob said, "Forty-five."

The old ladies started looking interested. *Uh-oh.*

But they just stood there.

Heavy Metal edged closer to the open unit. "Fifty," he whispered.

"Sixty," said Asian.

The mood in the passageway got alert and tight, like strong coffee kicking in for everyone.

Asian pulled out a BlackBerry, read the screen, turned it off.

Maybe the bike was super-rare and even half of it would bring serious bucks. Bob had heard of old Schwinns—like the one he'd ditched when he turned sixteen and got his license—going for crazy money—

"Sixty-five," said Heavy Metal.

Asian hesitated.

Bob said, "Seventy."

Asian said, "Seventy-five."

"Eighty," a voice awfully like Bob's nearly shouted.

Everyone stared at him.

Asian shrugged.

Pete looked at Heavy Metal, who'd already walked away and was massaging a tattoo.

"Eighty dollars for this trove," said Pete. "Do I hear eighty-five? Eighty-five dollars, still a bargain at eighty-five."

Going through the motions, not pushing it. "Going once, going twice . . . eighty it is."

Banging that little plastic palm-gavel against his clipboard. Scrawling on his sheet and telling Bob, "You're the lucky winner of the trove. Eighty bucks, cash on the barrel."

Holding out a mottled palm for payment.

Everyone smiling. Like there was some private joke and Bob was the butt. A cold, soupy feeling filled his stomach.

"Cash, sir," said Pete.

Bob dug into his pocket.

Later, out in the parking lot, loading the bags and the half bike into his truck, he caught the Asian guy before he got in his Beemer.

"You do this a lot?"

"Me?" Guy smiled pleasantly. "First time, actually. I'm an anesthesiologist, have to be at Marina Mercy by six, thought it might help wake me up. And it kind of did."

"What got you bidding on fourteen fifty-five?"

Guy looked surprised by the question. "I was going to ask you the same thing."

Back home by seven, flies buzzing around the yucca plants that fronted his apartment building, a cruel sun fizzing through his dusty windows, Bob unloaded the garbage bags onto the floor of his grubby little living room.

Figuring he'd catch some sleep before the first Bloody Mary of the day, then go through his haul, then call the tree farm in Saugus.

He collapsed in his bed, still wearing dusty auction clothes. Closed his eyes.

Thought about Kathy. His fine. What his brothers said behind his back.

Got up and fetched a kitchen knife and sliced through the first garbage bag.

Inside were game boxes—Monopoly, Scrabble, Risk. But cracked and messed up, missing everything except the boards.

Great.

The second bag—the heavier one—held crumpled-up newspapers. Period. Why would someone pay to store shit like this?

With a real bad stomachache coming on, Bob got down on the floor and pawed through weeks of L.A. *Times.* Nothing antique, no historic headlines, just newsprint and those stupid ad inserts that fell all over the place.

Oh, man, he should've stayed in bed.

He said "Idiot" out loud and examined the half bike.

Cheap, flimsy junk. *Made in China* sticker pasted to what remained of a crossbar that Bob could bend with his hands.

Disgusted, he mixed a Mary in the kitchenette, sat down on the floor, and drank.

Thinking about eighty wasted bucks made him more tired than ever, but leaving the bags around reminded him he was an idiot.

Time to haul the whole damn load out back to the Dumpsters.

Finishing his Mary, he labored to his feet, tossed the papers back in the second bag, lifted.

Something rattled. Bottom of the bag.

Probably his imagination. He shook the bag hard.

Rattle rattle rattle—like one of those maracas they sold on Olvera Street, Kathy had bought him a pair of those when they were dating. Figuring, what? He was half Mexican, so he'd half like it?

He pawed through the papers, reached bottom, found the source of the noise.

Wooden box, dark, shiny. Long as a shoe box but wider, with curly brass inlay, nice lacquer finish, little brass latch holding it shut.

EBay here we come! The box alone . . . he'd call it exotic, imported, whatever, maybe make up a story about it coming from . . . Malaysia? No, something more mysterious, where was Mount Everest—Tibet . . . *Nepal.*

Exotic box—exotic jewel *case—from the Nepal alps, made of solid choice mountain . . .* looked like mahogany, he could play that up—*solid choice rare Asian mahogany.* Maybe stick on a *Buy It Now* for a hundred, hundred thirty. Now, let's see what's inside. And if it was dry beans, who cared? The box alone meant he was No Longer An Idiot.

He freed the brass latch, raised the lid. Inside was a gold velvet tray.

Empty; the noise was coming from below.

He lifted the tray, exposed a bottom compartment. Inside were . . . little white knobby things.

He picked one up. Smooth and white, with a pointy tip, and all of a sudden Bob knew what it was without being told.

Even though biology had never been his strong point, he'd flunked it once in high school, repeated, managed a D.

A bone.

Like from a hand or a foot. Or a paw.

Lots of little bones, so many they nearly filled the compartment, didn't make that much noise.

Had to be what . . . three, four dozen.

Bob counted.

Forty-two.

He examined his own hand. Three bones on each of the four fingers, two for the thumb, making . . . fourteen per hand.

Three hands' worth. Or three paws' worth. No reason to think these weren't from an animal. Then he thought of something—maybe these came from one of those skeletons they used in medical schools, people willing their bodies to science.

Getting cut up and examined and reconstructed into skeletons using wires to hold it all together.

Nope, none of these bones had holes for wires.

Weird.

Bob picked up another of the smallest ones, held it alongside the top joint of his own index finger.

Not as big as his.

Maybe a small dog.

Or a woman.

Or a kid . . .

No, that was too . . . had to be a dog. Or a cat. How many bones in a paw or a claw?

Too small for a cat.

A medium-sized dog, like Alf. Yeah, this might fit Alf.

He missed Alf, living in Dallas with Kathy.

Was thinking about all that when he shut the latch.

The box rattled.

Bones.

He'd do a little research on the Internet. Maybe sell the collection as antiques—like from an Indian archaeology dig. Out in . . . Utah. Or Colorado, Colorado sounded more . . . exotic.

Antique collection of exotic bones.

Stuff like that eBayed great.

CHAPTER

3

Milo had a fancy job title, courtesy the new police chief: *Special Case Investigator, Lieutenant Grade.*

Or as he put it: "Hoo-hah Poobah Big-Ass Sitting Mallard."

What it came down to was he avoided most of the paper-pushing that came with his rank, kept his closet-sized office at West L.A. Division, continued to work his own homicides until Downtown called and pointed him elsewhere.

Two calls had come in over the last fourteen months, both Rampart Division gang-revenge shootings. Not even close to whodunits but the chief, still feeling his way in L.A., had heard rumors of fresh Rampart corruption and wanted liability insurance.

The rumors proved false and Milo had concentrated on not being a nuisance. When the cases closed, the chief insisted his assignee's name be on the reports.

"Even though I was as useful as a stone-blind trapshooter. Made me real popular."

Easy metaphor; the morning he came up with it, the two of us were blasting away at clay pigeons on a Simi Valley firing range.

Late June, dry heat, blue skies, khaki hills. Milo lumbered through all five positions of the voice-activated trap setup, hitting 80 percent without much effort. Last year he'd been the target of a shotgun-wielding psychopath, still carried pellets in his left shoulder.

I'd emptied an entire box of shells before accidentally nailing one of the bright green disks. As I racked the Browning and drank a warm soda, he said, "When you shoot, you close your left eye."

"So?"

"So maybe you're right-handed but

left-eyed, and it's throwing you off balance."

He had me form a triangle with both
hands, positioned my fingers so the space
between them was filled by a dead tree off
to the east.

"Shut the left one. Now the right. Which
one makes it jump more?"

I knew the eye dominance test, had run
it years ago as a psych intern, researching
brain laterality in learning disabled children.

Never tried it on myself. The results
were a surprise.

Milo laughed. "Sinister-eyed. Now you
know what to do. Also, stop rejecting the
damn thing."

I said, "What do you mean?" but I knew
exactly what he was talking about.

"You're holding it like you can't wait to
ditch it." Hefting the gun and handing it
over. "Embrace it—lean forward—yeah,
yeah, like that."

I've fired pistols and rifles in ugly situations. Don't enjoy firearms any more than
going through dental work, but I appreciate the value of both.

Shotguns, with their elegant lethal simplicity, were another story. Up till today, I'd avoided them.

Twelve-gauge Remingtons had been my father's playthings of choice. An 870 pump-action Wingmaster purchased at a police auction stood in a corner of Dad's closet, almost always loaded.

Like Dad.

Summers—late June—he'd make me tag along on squirrel and small-bird hunts. Stalking flimsy little animals with absurd firepower because all he wanted to do was obliterate. Using me to search the bloody dust, bring back a bone fragment or a claw or a beak, because I was more obedient than a dog.

Scared of his mood swings in a way no dog could ever be.

My other assignments were keeping my mouth shut and toting his camouflage-pattern gear bag. Inside, along with his cleaning kit and boxes of ammo and the odd dog-eared *Playboy,* were the silver-plated whiskey flask, the plaid thermos of coffee, the sweating cans of Blue Ribbon.

The reek of alcohol on his breath growing stronger as the day wore on.

"Ready, Dead-eye?" said Milo. "Shut the

right, open the left, and lean—more—even more, make yourself part of the gun. There you go. Hold that. And don't aim, just point." Eyeing the bunker. *"Pull!"*

Half an hour later: "You hit more than I did, pal. I've created a monster."

At ten thirty we were loading the trunk of my Seville when Milo's cell phone beeped the first six notes of "My Way."

He listened while following the ascent of a red-tailed hawk. His big, pale face tightened. "When . . . okay . . . an hour." Click. "Time to head back to anti-civilization. Drive, *por favor.*"

As we got on the 118 East, he said, "Body dumped in the Bird Marsh in Playa, some volunteer found it last night, Pacific Division's on it."

"But," I said.

"Pacific's shorthanded cause of 'gang suppression issues.' The only free guy is a rookie His Holiness wants 'augmented.'"

"Problem child?"

"Who knows? Anyway, that's the official story."

"Yet, you wonder."

He pushed a lick of black hair off a pocked

brow, stretched his legs, ran his hand over his face, like washing without water.

"The marsh is political, right? And the chief's a politician."

As I drove back toward the city, he phoned for details, got a sketch.

Recent kill, white female, twenties, evidence of ligature strangulation.

Removal of the entire right hand by way of a surgically clean cut.

"One of those," he said. "Time to keep both your eyes open, Doctor."

The Bird Marsh is a two-acre triangle of uneasy compromise half a mile east of the ocean, where Culver and Jefferson and Lincoln boulevards intersect. Three sides of the triangle face multilane thorough-fares, condominium-crammed bluffs loom over the southern edge, the LAX flight plan brings in mechanical thunder.

The bulk of the wetlands occupies a bowl-like depression, well below the view of passing motorists, and as I parked across the street, all I could see was summer-brown grass and the crowns of distant willows and cottonwoods. In L.A. anything that can't be appreciated from a speeding car doesn't count, and federal protection for the flora and fauna sandwiched between all that progress has remained elusive.

Five years ago a film studio run by a klatch of self-proclaimed progressive billionaires had tried to buy the land for an "environmentally friendly" movie lot, funded by taxpayer money. Shielded from public exposure, the plan progressed smoothly, the usual soul kiss between big money and small minds. Then a talk-radio dyspeptic found out and latched on to the "conspiracy" like a rabid wolverine, leaving spokespeople tripping over each other in the rush to deny.

The save-the-marsh volunteer group that formed soon after disavowed the shock jock's tactics and accepted two Priuses donated by the billionaires. So far, no sign of earthmovers.

I turned off the engine and Milo and I took a few minutes to soak in the long view. Cute little wood-burned signs fashioned to resemble summer camp projects were too distant to read. I'd visited last year with Robin, knew the signs granted

street parking—a generosity now ren-
dered irrelevant by yellow tape and orange
cones.

A larger white sign directed pedestrians
to remain on the footpath and leave the
animals alone. Robin and I had figured on
a hike but the path covered less than a
fifth of the marsh's perimeter. That day, I'd
spotted a scrawny, bearded man wearing
a *Save the Marsh* badge and asked about
the lack of access.

"Because humans are the enemy."

Milo said, "Onward," and we crossed the
street. A uniform stationed in front of the
tape swelled his chest like a mating pigeon
and blocked us with a palm. When Milo's
gold shield flashed, the cop said "Sirs" and
stepped aside, looking cheated.

Two vehicles were parked in a gap between the cones—white coroner's van,
unmarked gray Ford Explorer.

I said, "The body was removed last
night, but the crypt crew's back."

"Fancy that."

A hundred feet north, two other uniforms
walked out of some foliage and climbed up
to the sidewalk. Then a broad-shouldered,

stocky man in blue blazer and khakis appeared, brushing off his lapels.

Blazer seemed to be studying us, but Milo ignored him and peered up at the mountain of condos. "Gotta be a hundred units, minimum, Alex. All those people with a clear view and someone chooses this place to body-dump?"

"All those people with a clear view of nothing," I said.

"Why nothing?"

"No streetlights around the marsh. After sunset, the place is ink."

"You've been here at night?"

"There's a guitar shop in Playa Del Rey that runs concerts from time to time. A few months ago, I came to hear flamenco. I'm talking nine, nine thirty, the place was deserted."

"Ink," he said. "Almost like a genuine bucolic nature preserve."

I told him about my daytime visit, the limited access.

"While you were here, you didn't happen to see a slavering bad guy skulking around, wearing a large-print name tag and offering a DNA sample?"

"Sorry, never met O.J."

He laughed, checked out the bluff again. Turned and scanned the expanse of the marsh. The cops were still there but the man in the blazer was gone. "Birds and froggies and whatever, sleeping through the whole damn thing."

We slipped under the tape, walked toward a white flag waving from a high metal stake. The stake was planted five or so feet off the path, set in dirt solid enough to hold it still. But a few yards in, the soil melted to algae-glazed muck.

The path continued for a few yards, then took a sharp turn. Voices behind the bend led us to three figures in white plastic coveralls squatting in shallow water, partially hidden by saw grass, tule, and bulrushes.

Submersion in water could slow decomposition, but moisture combined with air exposure could speed it up. As would heat, and this year June was starting to feel like July. I wondered what state the body was in.

Not ready to think about who the body had once been.

The stocky man materialized around a second curve, walked toward us while removing a pair of mirrored shades. Young, ruddy, dirty-blond crew cut.

"Lieutenant? Moe Reed, Pacific."

"Detective Reed."

"Moe's fine."

"This is Dr. Alex Delaware, our psychological consultant."

"Psychological," said Reed. "Because of the hand?"

"Because you never know," said Milo.

Reed gave me a long look before nodding. His unshielded eyes were clear, round, baby blue. The blazer was square-cut, made him look boxier than he was. Pleats and cuffs on the khakis, bright white wash 'n' wear shirt, green-and-blue rep tie, crepe-soled brown oxfords.

Dressed like a middle-aged preppie, but late twenties, tops, with the short-limbed, barrel-chested build of a wrestler. The barley-colored buzz cut topped a round, smooth face the sun would ravage. He smelled like a day at the beach; fresh application of sunscreen. He'd missed a spot on his left cheek, and the flesh was heading toward medium-rare.

A car door slamming caught our attention. Two attendants got out of the coroner's van. One lit a cigarette and the other watched his partner smoke. Milo eyed the white-clad women in the water.

Detective Moe Reed said, "Forensic anthropologists, Lieutenant."

"The body was buried?"

"No, sir, left out on the bank, no attempt to conceal. Had I.D. left on it, too. Selena Bass, address in Venice. I went over there at seven a.m., it's a converted garage, no one was home. Anyway, in terms of the anthropologists, visibility was poor so I thought it would be a good idea to bring in a K-9 unit, make sure we hadn't missed the hand. We hadn't but the dog got all excited."

Reed rubbed his left nostril. "Turns out, there were complications."

The Belgian Malinois named Edith ("a search dog, not a cadaver dog, Lieutenant, but apparently it doesn't always matter") had arrived with her handler at one thirty a.m., sniffed around the dump site, then proceeded to race into the marsh. Stopping at a spot thirty feet south of the body, she dove into the outer lip of a pocket of brackish silt no more than six feet from the bank.

Freezing in place. Barking.

When the handler didn't get there fast enough, howling.

Ordered back on land, the dog just sat there. The handler asked for hip waders. Those took another half hour to arrive and the dog stayed in place for ten minutes, suddenly bolted.

Setting in another spot, farther up the marsh, panting.

"Like she was proud of herself," said Moe Reed. "Guess she should be."

By five a.m., three additional bodies had been confirmed.

Moe Reed said, "The others seem to be mostly bones, Lieutenant. Could be one of those Indian burial rights situations."

One of the crypt drivers had come over. He said, "Sure don't smell like ancient history."

"Maybe it's natural gas."

The driver grinned. "Or the chili someone had for dinner. Or frijoles growing in the marsh."

Moe Reed said, "I'll let you know when you can go," and led us toward the trio of anthropologists. Groin-high in brown-green

soup, the women conferred earnestly
around another staked white pennant that
drooped in the warm, static air. If they saw
us, they gave no notice. We kept going.
Around the next bend were the other two
flags. Like a weird golf course.

We retraced. Two of the scientists were
young, one black, one white. Both had
crammed ample coiffures into disposable
caps. An older woman with short-chopped
gray hair noticed Reed and waved.

"Hey, Dr. Hargrove. Any news?"

"Normally, we'd be setting up the angles
for trenching, but this is protected land and
we're not sure what the parameters are."

"I can try to find out."

"We've already got a call in to the volunteer office, someone should be here soon.
More important, the earth gets so soft in
spots—inconsistently so—that we're afraid
we'll do more damage than good in terms
of finding everything there is to find." She
smiled. "At least it's not quicksand, I'm
pretty sure."

The young women laughed. Small, metal
tools gleamed in their hands.

Moe Reed said, "What's the plan, then,
Dr. Hargrove?"

"We're going to need time to poke around. The best technique may be to eventually slide something under whatever's in here, raise it up very gradually, and hope nothing falls off. One thing I *can* tell you, we're not talking paleontology. There's soft tissue present under the mandible of this one, and possibly behind the knees. The skin we've been able to observe appears dark, but that could be decomp."

"Fresh?" said Reed.

"Not nearly as fresh as the one left out in the open, but I can't give you a fix. Water can rot or preserve, depending on so many factors. We're getting moderate pH for samples in the immediate area, despite all the detritus, but there could still be some kind of buffering effect due to specific vegetation that mediates the effects of acid rain, plant decay, all that good stuff. I really can't tell you more until I get everything out of here."

"Soft tissue," said Reed. "That's pretty recent, right?"

"Probably but not necessarily," said Hargrove. "A few years ago they pulled a Civil War vet out of a mass grave in Pennsylvania, poor fellow just happened to end up in a low-oxygen, low-humidity pocket near a series of subterranean caves and still had skin and muscle adhering to his cheeks. Most of it was mummified, but some wasn't. His beard looked freshly trimmed."

"Unbelievable," said Reed, catching the eye of the young black anthropologist and turning away. "No way you can guesstimate for me, Doctor? Off the record?"

"Off the record, I'll go out on a limb and say probably not decades. There is one thing: The right hand's gone from all of them. But we haven't started examining closely, there could be other parts missing."

"Animal scatter?" said Reed.

"Don't imagine coyotes or raccoons diving into this, but you never know. Some of the bigger birds—herons, egrets, even a pelican or a gull—might've picked out a tidbitortwo. Orahumanpredator—someone taking a trophy. We'll backtrack weather reports, try to find out if wind on water could've been a factor in terms of drift and alteration of surface temperature."

"Complicated," said Milo.

Hargrove grinned. "It's what we live for, but I'm sorry for you guys."

The young black anthropologist, pretty, with a heart-shaped face and a bow mouth, said something to Hargrove.

Hargrove said, "Thank you, Liz." To us: "Dr. Wilkinson wants you to know that all three bodies seem to be facing east. Was that true of the one left out in the open?"

Reed thought. "As a matter of fact, it was. Interesting . . ."

Dr. Wilkinson spoke up. "On the other hand, we're talking about an *n* of—a small sample from which to draw a significant conclusion."

Reed said, "Four out of four sounds significant to me, Doc."

Wilkinson shrugged. The other young anthropologist, freckled and rosy-cheeked, said, "East. As in facing the dawn? Some sort of ritual?"

"Facing Mecca," said Hargrove. She grimaced. "We won't even *go* there."

Reed had kept his eyes on Dr. Liz Wilkinson. "Thanks for being so observant."

Wilkinson tugged at her hair cap. "Just thought you should know."

CHAPTER

4

Reed, Milo, and I returned to the entrance of the marsh. The coroner's van was gone. Two uniforms remained on guard, looking bored. One said, "The ghouls went to catch a bite."

Reed said, "Any ideas, Lieutenant?"

"Sounds like you've got everything covered."

The young detective fiddled with his sunglasses. "Tell you one thing, I'm happy for the help."

"Why's that?"

"It's shaping up like a team case, right?"

Milo didn't answer, and Reed's sunburned

spot turned crimson. "To be honest, I'm not exactly Sherlock, Lieutenant."

"How long on the job?"

"Joined the department after college, made detective two years ago, started at Central GTA. I just got transferred to Homicide last February."

"Congratulations."

Reed frowned. "Picked up two cases since then. Besides this one, I mean. One closed in a week but anyone could've done it, total no-brainer. The second one's an icy-cold missing person I'm not sure will ever be solved."

"Pacific sends MP cases to Homicide?"

"Not generally," said Reed. "Rich connections, the kind you definitely want to make happy, but . . ."

"Cases have their own rhythm," said Milo. "Takes time to get your footing."

I'd seen him lose sleep, gain weight, and experience soaring blood pressure over unsolveds.

Reed studied the soft brown dirt of the marsh. A brown pelican soared, aimed its massive beak downward, changed its mind and flew back toward the Pacific.

Milo said, "Let's talk about Selena Bass."

Reed pulled out his pad. "Female Cau-
casian, twenty-six years old, five five, one
ten, brown and brown. One registered vehicle, a 2003 Nissan Sentra, it was at her
apartment, didn't look disturbed, so we're
not talking a jacking. No signs of obvious
forced entry. Maybe she went off with
someone she knew and things got nasty."

"Where in Venice?"

Reed read off an address on Indiana,
south of Rose, west of Lincoln.

Milo said, "Gang stuff going on there,
right?"

"Some. Banger snatches her, it
wouldn't be much of a drive from there to
here. So sure, we could be talking about
a convenient dump site. But those other
bodies . . ."

"They could also be vics from Bass's
neighborhood."

"A gang-hit thing?"

"Or," said Milo, "a creepo thing. He
watches them, stalks them, grabs them."

Reed frowned. "Stranger-on-stranger."

A bellowed "Hey!" made the three of us
turn.

A scrawny, bowlegged, bearded man in
a white T-shirt, high green cargo shorts,

and flip-flops strode toward us, pumping his arms.

Same fellow who'd snarled the surly remark about humans three months ago.

"Hey," he repeated.

No one answered.

"What's going on?"

Moe Reed said, "You are . . ."

"Silford Duboff, Save the Marsh. This is my place. I'm here to keep an eye on all proceedings."

"Your place," said Reed.

"No one else cares."

Reed extended a hand. Duboff took it reluctantly, as if fearing contamination. "What's going on?"

"What's going on, sir, is early this morning we removed the body of a young woman who was murdered and left on the banks of the marsh. While processing the scene, we found at least three other bodies."

Silford Duboff blanched. *"Processing? You're digging?"*

"Nothing extensive—"

"Out of the question." Duboff noticed the flag marking Selena Bass's dump site. "What's *that* doing here?"

"That's where we found the first victim,

sir. And as I said, three other women. All dead."

Duboff rubbed his beard. "This is a disaster."

Reed removed his sunglasses. Baby-blue eyes had narrowed. "I'd call four dead bodies a disaster."

"You said *at least* three more. Are you implying there could be more?"

"Three's what we've got so far, Mr. Duboff."

"Oh, crap—where are the others? I need to look."

Duboff started to head for the flag. Milo's big arm held him back.

"What?" Duboff demanded.

"No access yet, sir."

"That's absolutely unacceptable."

Milo showed teeth. "Sir, it's eminently acceptable."

Duboff said, "What's the reason?"

"Police personnel are working the scene."

"What do you mean *working*?"

"Examining particulars."

Duboff yanked on his beard. "This is a protected site, you just can't have cops parking their grubby—"

"Forensic anthropologists, sir."

"Anthro—they're *excavating*? I *absolutely* must talk to them, right now!"

"We appreciate your concern, Mr. Duboff. But these people are specialists and they respect every site."

"This isn't just a site, it's a—"

"Beautiful place," said Milo. "The only thing that will be removed is evidence."

"That's outrageous."

"So is homicide, sir."

"This is worse," said Duboff.

"Worse than four bodies?" said Reed.

"I'm not . . . I appreciate the fact that people have died. But when push comes to shove, all humans do is alter the balance—your murders are perfect proof."

"Of what?"

"We keep murdering the earth, then we wonder why life's so brutal."

I said, "Sounds like you don't have much use for people."

Duboff stared at me. Not a hint of recognition. "As a matter of fact, I'm a card-carrying misanthrope but I don't kill anything that breathes oxygen." Pointing to his flip-flops. "Organic rubber." He eyed the white flag. "What I'm saying is we need to ensure that this rare pocket of tranquility remains that way."

"Seems to me," said Reed, "that it's already been disturbed."

"Then let's not make matters worse. I *must* have a talk with those ditchdiggers."

Reed looked at Milo.

Milo said, "After you answer a few questions."

He loomed over Duboff, began peppering the increasingly flustered man with a mix of relevant and seemingly random questions. Eventually zeroing in on Duboff's whereabouts during the past twenty-four hours.

Duboff said, "You suspect *me*?"

"Sir, these are the questions we need to—"

"Who cares where I was last night? But fine, I've got nothing to hide, nothing. I was home. Reading." Jutting his chin. "Enjoying *Utne Reader,* if you must know."

"You live alone?" said Milo.

Duboff smiled. "Yes, but often a friend stays over. A bright, altruistic, sensuous

woman who just happens to be in Sebas-
topol at the Green Fiber Music Festival.
When did your murder take place?"

"We're still determining that, sir."

Duboff said, "It had to be after eight
o'clock because I stopped by the marsh at
eight and trust me, there were no bodies."

"How long were you here?"

"Briefly, to check for trash. After that, I
bought a sandwich at the all-night market
on Culver. Greens and tempeh, if you must
know. Then I dropped over at my office to
see how our volunteer was doing." He
huffed. "Rich brat, got assigned to us for
a community service punishment. He
was doing fine, so I left him and drove to
Santa Monica and ate my sandwich on
Ocean Front. Then I returned to the office at ten oh five to make sure the brat
had locked up. Which was fortunate, because he hadn't. By ten thirty, I was with
my *Utne.*"

"Find any trash at the marsh?" said
Milo.

"Not this time . . . oh, yes, Alma—my
companion—was due to call me from Se-
bastopol at eleven fifteen. And she did."

"Your volunteer," said Moe Reed. "What's he being punished for?"

"Something to do with school," said Duboff. "I didn't ask, couldn't care less. He's no asset but he doesn't cause problems."

"Alma," said Reed, taking out his pad. "Last name, please."

Duboff's eyes bugged. "Why would you want to talk to her?"

"Routine—"

"Unbelievable. I'm here to safeguard the marsh and you *storm*-troop me?"

Reed said, "That's a little harsh, sir."

"Is it? I think not."

Milo said, "Alma what?"

"Good God—fine, fine, Reynolds, Alma Reynolds." He recited a phone number. "Satisfied? Now you *must* let me through."

We followed Duboff's race-walk to the anthropologists' work site. Moe Reed caught up, asked Duboff if the name Selena Bass was familiar.

"The only bass I know and care about are the striped ones. Grievously overfished because of American flesh-lust."

I said, "People," wondering if he'd finally remember me.

He said, "That song is absolute nonsense. Barbra had it completely wrong."

Dr. Hargrove's team had removed a few small brown fragments and placed them on a blue tarp laid out on the bank. All three women were back in the water, heads close to the surface, sifting, peering.

Duboff said, "What is *that*?"

Reed said, "Human bones."

Duboff cupped his hand and called to the scientists: "Be careful, you!"

The women looked up.

Milo said, "This gentleman safeguards the marsh."

Duboff said, "Don't make it sound trivial."

"This gentleman safeguards the marsh importantly."

Dr. Hargrove said, "Sir, we're being extremely careful, making sure not to upset anything."

"Your very presence means the marsh has been upset."

Hargrove, Liz Wilkinson, and the freckled scientist stared.

Duboff took another look at the bones.

Milo said, "Sir, we need to clear out, let them do their job. Speaking of which, do you have one, Mr. Duboff?"

"What are you implying?"

Milo didn't answer.

"I most definitely did. Worked at the Midnight Run bookstore."

"They closed down last year."

"Ergo 'did,'" said Duboff. "Over the years, I made some investments, can afford to take my time looking. And no wisecracks about oil and gas stocks, okay? I don't own any."

"Boy," said Milo, "must be hard on the shoulders."

"What is?"

"Carrying around a chip the size of a redwood."

Duboff's mouth dropped open.

Taking hold of his arm, Milo said, "Nice meeting you, sir," and guided him back to the street.

Reed and I watched the two of them walk to Duboff's dusty Jetta.

Duboff shook a finger at Milo. Milo remained impassive. Duboff got in the car, still ranting. Drove off.

Milo returned, scissoring his hand to mimic moving jaws.

Reed said, "Weird and hostile, but I guess if he was guilty he'd have tried to be friendly. One part of his story is definitely true—stopping by the office after nine and talking to the volunteer. The kid's name is Chance Brandt, and he's part of how we found out about Selena in the first place—what I was about to tell you before Numb Nuts interrupted us."

"Tell away."

Reed looked at his watch. "Better yet, how about we meet the kid face-to-face, I can fill you in along the way? All I've had is phone contact with his father, want to make sure I get the facts right. I've got an appointment at their house in thirty, going to be tight unless we start out now."

"You drive, we'll ride along, Detective Reed."

Milo sat shotgun in Reed's blue-black Crown Victoria. I got in back.

"Moe short for Moses?"

"Yes, sir."

"Ah."

"You're thinking about a baby floating in the reeds, the whole marsh thing?"

"It did occur to me."

Reed laughed. "Back when I was born, my mother was kinda biblical." A beat later: "Moses never got to see the Promised Land."

Milo said, "Tell me about the Brandt kid."

CHAPTER

5

Good-looking kid, insolent eyes.

Chance Brandt sprawled on an oversized brocade sofa in the oversized great room of an oversized Mediterranean mansion on Old Oak Road in Brentwood. The house smelled of take-out pizza and expensive perfume.

Chance wore tennis clothes. So did his mother, a stunning, long-legged blonde with sea-green eyes and obviously dominant chromosomes. Some of her frosted lipstick had caked and her mouth was pale. She wanted to hold her son's hand but didn't dare.

Sitting on the boy's other side was Dad: dark, beefy, huge-chinned, bald, still in blue dress shirt and gold Hermès tie.

Enraged attorney, always a joy to behold.

"Unbelievable. Now this." Steve Brandt glared at his son as if Oedipus had materialized.

The boy said nothing.

Brandt said, "I do wills and estates, can't help you here, Chance."

Susan Brandt said, "I'm sure there's nothing to help."

Her husband aimed venomous eyes her way. She gnawed her lower lip rosy, folded her arms.

Moe Reed said, "Chance, tell us what happened."

Steve Brandt snorted. "Without benefit of counsel? I think not."

"Sir, if all he did was take a phone call, there's no need for counsel."

Chance smiled.

His father flushed. "Something's *funny,* genius?"

Susan Brandt's breath caught, as if snagged on barbed wire. Green eyes moistened.

Milo said, "As Detective Reed explained, we're investigating a homicide. If Chance is involved, he absolutely does need legal advice and we want him to have it as soon as possible. But we have no indication of that. Certainly, it's your prerogative to request a lawyer in any circumstance, and if that's the route you take, we'll have this conversation at the police station, in an interview room with videotaping, paperwork, et cetera."

"You're threatening me," said Steve Brandt. His smile was unpleasant.

"Absolutely not, sir. It's simply what we'd need to do. At this point, Chance isn't being looked at as anything other than a witness. To a phone call, at that. So I really don't see why you wouldn't want to cooperate fully."

Chance's eyes shifted to us. No more smugness, just confusion.

Steve Brandt folded his arms across his chest.

Milo said, "Okay, sir, please make sure Chance is here tomorrow at seven a.m. when we send a squad car for him. Or, if the paper clears sooner, it could be tonight."

He started to rise.

Steve Brandt said, "Hold on. Let me talk to my *son* in private. Then I'll inform you which way we're going with this . . . mess. Fair enough?"

Milo sat back down. "We work hard to be fair."

One hundred fifty-eight seconds later, father and son returned to the room, walking four feet apart.

Father said, "He'll tell you everything. But could you please let me know how things got to this point? So *I'll* know he's being straight with me."

Son stared at a window with a view of a black-bottomed pool.

Moe Reed looked at Milo. Milo nodded.

Reed said, "At eleven-thirty p.m. we received a call about a dead person in the Bird Marsh. The caller heard about it from someone who heard about it from Chance."

"How do you know that?" said Steve Brandt.

"Our caller said someone had phoned the marsh volunteer office earlier that evening, talked to Chance, told him to look for a body. Chance thought it was a joke. Our caller took it seriously."

"Who's the caller?"

"We're checking that out."

The boy's posture remained slack but sweat had popped on his forehead.

"Thirdhand gossip?" said Susan Brandt. "That doesn't sound like much."

Her husband glared. She began fooling with a French-tipped thumbnail.

Steve Brandt said, "Kids blabbing and fantasizing, that's the sum total?"

"Might've been," said Reed, "except we did find a body. And mode of death was homicide." Swiveling toward Chance. "We need to know *exactly* what happened."

The boy didn't speak. His father placed a hand on his shoulder, thick fingers digging into white pique, nothing tender about the gesture. Chance squirmed out of his grip.

"Tell them what you know and let's finish with this."

"Like you said, someone called," said the boy.

Reed said, "Who?"

"Some asshole with a weird voice."

"Language, Chance," said Susan Brandt, in a defeated voice.

Moe Reed said, "Weird how?"

"Um . . . like hissy."

"Hissy?"

"Whispery. Like one of those grinder movies. Some death-bot, whatever."

"Someone disguising their voice by hissing."

"Yeah."

"Can you imitate this person, let us know what it sounded like?"

Chance laughed.

"*Do* it," said his father.

"I'm not in Drama, Dad."

"You've caused plenty of drama in *this* family."

Shrug. "Whatever."

"*Do* it."

The boy's lips formed an "F." Steve Brandt's knuckles whitened.

Milo said, "Someone hissed at you, Chance. What did they say?"

"Like . . . uh . . . there's something down in the marsh. Something dead."

"What else?"

"That's it."

"Male or female?"

"Male . . . probably."

"You can't be sure?"

"It was like . . . hissy. Bogus."

"Faking," said Reed.

"Yeah. I thought I was being pranked."

"By who?"

"Whatever. Friends."

Milo said, "Prince Albert in a can."

Chance's stare was uncomprehending.

Milo said, "Something dead in the marsh."

"Uh-huh."

"What else did this hissing person say?"

"Nothing," said Chance. "It sounded stupid, that's why I didn't tell it to the guy who came in right after."

"What guy?" said Reed.

"Guy who runs the place, real tool. Always checking on me."

"What's the tool's name?" said Reed.

"Duboff. He's like a hippie you read about in History."

"Mr. Duboff came into the office right after you took the call."

"I didn't take it. I just listened and hung up."

"How soon after did Duboff come in?"

"Like *right*."

"Checking up on you."

"Yeah."

"And you told him . . ."

"Everything's cool."

"You made no mention whatsoever of the hissing call."

"I thought it was bogus," said Chance. "Ethan or Ben, Sean, whatever." Peering at us as he dropped the names. Trying to figure out who'd given him away.

Reed said, "What time did this hissy call come in?"

"Um . . . um, um—like um nine thirty."

"Like articulate," said Steve Brandt. His wife looked ready to cry.

Reed said, "Can you give a more precise estimate?"

Chance said, "It was like . . . oh, yeah, before I looked at my watch and it was like nine twenty something, so it was after that."

"Nine thirty or so."

"Uh, yeah, I guess."

"Jesus," said Steve Brandt, "it's not rocket science."

Chance's shoulders bunched. His mother had gnawed her lip scarlet.

His father said, "I think it's obvious math isn't his strong suit, that's how we ended up in this mess in the first place. The *indignity* of an algebra test that required *minimum* effort to pass."

Chance chewed *his* lip. More genetics? Or would living with Steve Brandt drive anyone to it?

Brandt loosened his tie. "We're still trying to figure out if he *has* a strong suit."

His wife gasped.

"Get real, Suze. If he hadn't cheated in the first place, we'd never be talking to the cops." To us: "Maybe as long as you're here we should set up some tough love for my son. One of those programs you put youthful offenders into? Working at the morgue, getting in touch with reality?"

Susan Brandt got up and hurried out on elegant, bronze legs. Chance's eyes were fixed on his father's florid face.

Brandt said, "You *bet* I'm pissed, kiddo. Work's piling up and I have to come home in the middle of the day for *this.* And you're playing *tennis*?"

"Mom said I should get some exer—"

Brandt waved the boy silent. To Milo: "Do you still run those morgue tours?"

"I'm not sure, sir. From what I recall they were for juvenile drunk drivers and such."

"So, once again, he skates completely."

Chance's lips moved.

"What did you just say?" his father demanded.

Silence.

Milo said, "Mr. Brandt, we understand
that you're frustrated with whatever acting-
out Chance has done in the past. But from
our perspective, he's being cooperative. If
all he did was talk about what he perceived
to be a gag call, there's nothing to 'skate'
on. If he's somehow involved in this homicide, a tour of the morgue won't cut it."

Some of the color left Steve Brandt's
face. "Of *course* he's not involved. I'm
just trying to prevent any more . . .
complications."

Chance said, "I'm complications?"

His father smirked. "Oh, you don't want
me to answer that."

The boy's turn to flush. "Do your thing,
dude—hook me up to one of those fucking lie detectors—"

"Shut your stupid, foul mouth and don't
use that snotty, stupid tone—"

Chance shot to his feet, fists balled.
"Don't call me that! Don't fucking *call* me
that!"

Steve Brandt's hands slapped brocade.
He panted.

Chance's respiration rate raced ahead of his father's.

Milo stepped between them. "Everyone calm down right *now.* Chance, sit down—over there, where your mom was. Mr. Brandt, let us do our job."

"I wasn't aware I was doing anything but—"

"This is a homicide case, sir—lots of long days for us. We need to make sure that after we leave we won't be called back on a domestic violence complaint."

"Ridiculous—have I ever hit you, Chance? *Ever?*"

No answer.

"*Have* I?"

Chance smiled. Shrugged.

His father cursed. "Serpent's tooth."

Chance was still on his feet. Milo said, "*Sit.*" The boy obeyed.

"Son, I want a quick answer to this: How soon after the call did Mr. Duboff appear?"

"Right after. Seconds."

That fit Duboff's story. Either he'd dumped Selena Bass himself or the killer had watched Duboff clear out before venturing forward.

Or the killer had gotten lucky and just missed Duboff.

Either way, the murder had been called in soon after the dump.

Someone wanting Selena Bass found. And identified quickly.

Burying three other bodies that he'd concealed, but growing confident and progressing to boasting?

Claiming the marsh as his turf. Duboff or someone like him?

Moe Reed said, "Who'd you tell about the hissing call?"

"Just . . . Sarabeth—who'd she rat me out to?"

"What's Sarabeth's last name?"

Steve Brandt said, "Oster. As in malls and shopping centers." When none of us responded: "They're big-time, live in Brentwood Park. Sarabeth's their only child. She comes across sweet and innocent but she's the one gave him the answers to that goddamn algebra test, so I'd take anything she says with a pillar of salt."

Chance growled.

His father said, *"Ooh.* I'm *shaking."*

CHAPTER

6

Steve Brandt walked us out to a faux-cobblestone motor court, used a clicker to hold his front gate open.

"So he's clear?"

"So far, sir."

"Trust me, Officers, he's too dumb to kill anyone."

Smiling with sour satisfaction, he walked back to the heat and light of his home.

Moe Reed's call to Tom L. Rumley, head-master of the Windward Academy, achieved a promise to "ascertain all the relevant information" about the call to

Chance Brandt at an "expedited rate."
The trade-off: no police visit to the school
at the present time, because "it's hiatus
time and we're entertaining visitors from
Dubai."

Reed put Rumley on hold. "Lieutenant?"

Milo said, "Most likely it will boil down to
a blab chain, so give him a chance to make
good. Either of you hungry?"

We returned to the marsh and picked up
the Seville. As Reed followed us to West
L.A., Milo said, "What do you think?"

"About the case or Reed?"

"Both."

"He seems thoughtful, eager to learn.
Plenty to learn about this case."

"Four bodies."

"That kind of appetite," I said, "no reason to stop at four."

"I can always count on you for good
cheer."

Café Moghul, on Santa Monica Boulevard,
blocks from the station, serves as Milo's
second office.

The bespectacled, saried woman who
runs the place beamed, the way she always

does when Milo steps through her door. Besides the gargantuan tips, she regards him as a human rottweiler. Reed's obvious cop presence following close behind brought her to the verge of ecstasy.

"Lobster," she announced, seating us at Milo's rear table, humming and smiling and filling glasses with cloved iced tea. "I'll bring fresh platters. Everything."

Milo said, "Everything's a good concept," as he removed his jacket and tossed it on a nearby chair. Reed took off his blazer, draped it neatly. His white shirt was short-sleeved. His biceps filled most of the sleeves.

The food parade began.

Reed said, "You must tip great."

Milo said, "Boy. Why does everything in this world have to be about money?"

Sometimes Milo talks shop over food. Other times, he views eating as a sacrament, not to be disrupted by worldly matters.

This afternoon was a Holy Day. Moe Reed watched him bolt and chew and swallow and wipe his face. Caught on quickly and bent over his own plate like a convict.

Heaps of lobster, rice, lentils, spiced eggplant, spinach with *paneer* cheese vanished quickly as the young detective out-ate Milo. His frame was thick but hard as teak.

Just as the bespectacled woman brought rice pudding, his cell beeped.

"Reed . . ." Eyebrows so pale they fought for recognition arched steeply. "Yes, sir . . . hold on while I get something to write on." Reaching behind, he retrieved his pad, printed neatly. "Thank you, sir. No, not at this time, sir."

Click. "Headmaster Rumley says he traced the gossip stream completely. The Brandt kid told Sarabeth Oster, who also thought it was hilarious. She told a girl named Ali Light and Ali told *her* boyfriend, Justin Coopersmith, and *he* thought it was so darn funny, he passed it along to his older brother, a Duke sophomore named Lance, home for the summer. Lance Coopersmith seems to be more moral than the others, he's the one who called us. Said he felt it was his duty."

"Should be easy enough to verify."

Reed nodded. "I asked for a trace this morning. Came in on the non-emergency,

so it takes longer than a 911 and there's
no audio. Want me to check now?"

"Go for it."

Moments later: "Verizon cell phone registered to Lance Allan Coopersmith, address in Pacific Palisades. Any sense
following up?"

"Not for the time being," said Milo. "Gonna
be a long day, have some lobster."

Pulling out his own phone, he requested
a warrant on Selena Bass's apartment.

I left the Seville in the Westside lot, returned to the back of Reed's unmarked for
the twenty-minute drive to Indiana Avenue.
Milo used the time to follow up on the warrant request.

Granted telephonically, with paper to
follow.

"You run her beyond DMV?" he asked
Reed.

"Yup. Nothing on the bad-guy sites. I
was planning to Google her today."

Milo logged on to Reed's Mobile Dis-
patch Terminal and got on the Internet.
"Nice talking straight to God . . . here we
go—two hits . . . one's an exact copy of

the other . . . looks like she's a piano teacher—introducing a student at a recital . . . named . . . Kelvin Vander."

An image search pulled up nothing.

Reed said, "Piano teacher isn't exactly high risk."

Milo said, "Nothing like a sad song to kick off the week."

"What about all those other bodies, Lieutenant?"

"Let's see what the bone pickers come up with. Meanwhile, we work with what we've got."

I tossed in my thoughts about someone with a thing for the marsh.

Milo said, "Could be."

Reed said nothing.

Selena Bass's converted garage was a double, set behind a white stucco, one-story duplex.

The front unit, blanketed by banana plants and mock orange, was occupied by the owner-landlady, an ancient eminence in a wheelchair named Anuta Rosenfield. A cheerful Filipina caretaker ushered us into a diminutive front room muffled by pink

velvet drapes and crowded with house-
plants and porcelain figurines on precari-
ous stands.

"She will be a *hundred* this January!"

The old woman didn't stir. Her eyes were
open but clouded, her lap too flimsy to
support one of her bisque dolls.

Milo said, "That's wonderful," and stooped
close to the wheelchair. "Ma'am, could we
have a key to Ms. Bass's apartment?"

The caretaker said, "She's deaf, can't
see, either. Ask me all the questions."
Pointing to her chest. "Luz."

"Luz, could we—"

"Of course, guys!" Out of her uniform
pocket came the key.

"Appreciate it."

"Is she okay—Selena?"

"You know her?"

"I don't really know her, but sometimes I
see her. Mostly when I leave. Sometimes
she's leaving, too."

"When's the last time you saw her?"

"Hmm . . . now that you mention it, not
for a while. And you know what, I haven't
seen lights on in her place for . . . the last
few days, at least." Deep breath. "And now
you guys are here. Oh, boy."

"A few days," said Reed.

"Maybe four," said Luz. "Could be five, I don't keep count."

"What's she like?"

"Never talked to her, we just smile and say hi. She seemed nice. Pretty girl, skinny—no hips, the way they are now."

Milo said, "What time do you usually leave work?"

"Seven p.m."

"Someone else takes over the night shift."

"Mrs. Rosenfield's daughter comes home at seven. Elizabeth, she's a nurse at Saint John's." Whispering conspiratorially: "Seventy-one but she still likes to work the neonatal ICU—little babies. That's how I met her. I'm an LVN, also did the NICU. I like the babies, but I like this better."

She patted her charge's shoulder. "Mrs. R. is a very nice person." A sweet smile tangoed across the old woman's lips. Someone had powdered her face, blued her eyelids, manicured her nails. The air in the room was close and heavy. Roses and wintergreen.

Milo said, "What else can you tell us about Selena Bass?"

"Hmm," said Luz. "Like I said, nice . . . maybe a little shy. Like maybe she doesn't want to have a long conversation? I never heard Elizabeth complain about her and Elizabeth complains."

"What's Elizabeth's full name?"

"Elizabeth Mayer. She's a widow, just like her mommy." Downturn of eyes. "We all three have that in common."

"Ah," said Milo. "Sorry for your loss."

"It was a long time ago."

Mrs. Rosenfield smiled again. Hard to know what that meant.

Reed said, "Who lives in the other unit?"

"A man from France who's almost never here. A professor, French, I think. Mostly, he's in France. He's in France now."

"Name?"

Head shake. "Sorry, you'd have to ask Elizabeth. I don't see him five times in two years. Nice-looking man, long hair—like that actor, the skinny one . . . Johnny Depp."

Milo said, "Sounds like things are pretty quiet around here."

"*Very* quiet."

"Ever see Selena with a friend?"

"A friend, no. Once, I saw a guy," said

Luz. "Waiting out by the curb for Selena and she got into his car."

"What kind of car?"

"Sorry, I didn't see."

"Could you describe him?"

"He had his back to me and it was dark."

"Tall, short?" said Reed.

"Medium—oh, one thing—I'm pretty sure he had no hair—shaved, like those basketball players do. Light bounced off his head."

"Was he a white man?" said Reed.

"Well," said Luz, "not black, that's for sure. Although I guess he could've been a *light* black guy. I'm sorry, it was just his back, I guess he could've been anything. Did he do something to Selena?"

"Ma'am, at this point, we're not even close to a suspect. That's why anything you did see is important."

"A suspect . . . so she's . . ."

"Afraid so," said Reed.

"Oh, no." Her eyes watered. "That's very sad, such a young one . . . oh, my . . . I *wish* I could tell you more."

Milo said, "You're doing great. Could I

please have your full name for the records? As well as a contact number?"

"Luz Elena Ramos—is it dangerous to
stay here?"

"There's no reason to think that."

"Wow," said Luz. "This is a little scary.
I'd better be careful."

"I'm sure you're fine, Ms. Ramos, but
careful's always good."

"When you showed up, I guess I knew
something happened. I work in a hospital
for eight years, know what bad news looks
like."

Selena Bass's four hundred square feet of
space couldn't shrug off its automotive ori-
gins.

Cracked cement floors had been
painted bronze and lacquered but oil
blotches peeked through the gloss and a
faint petro-reek lingered. A dropped ceiling of whitewashed drywall panels compressed the room. The same material was
used for the walls, tacked haphazardly to
the underlying lath. Tape seams were visible, nailheads erupted like prom-night
acne.

"High-end construction," said Milo.

Reed said, "Maybe the piano wasn't bringing in the bucks."

We gloved up, stood in the doorway, took in the entire space. No obvious signs of violence or disorder.

Milo said, "We'll call in the techies, but I'm not seeing this as the operating room." He stepped in and we followed.

A right angle of black Masonite cabinets sectioned off a tiny, corner kitchenette. Space-saver refrigerator, microwave, two-burner electric cooktop. In the fridge: bottled water, condiments, a rotten nectarine, limp celery, a single carton of take-out Chinese in a generic carton.

Moe Reed checked his gloved hands, inspected the box. Sweet-and-sour chicken, tinted Caltrans orange. He tilted the box. "Gelled stiff. Got to be at least a week old."

A queen mattress sat on the floor, sheathed by a brown batik throw and piled with too many overstuffed madras pillows. Milo peeled back a corner of the throw. Lavender sheets, clean, unruffled. He sniffed. Shook his head.

"What, sir?" said Reed.

"No smells—no detergent, body odor,

perfume, zilch. Like it was changed but not slept in."

He moved on to an almost-birch night-stand, containing lightweight sweats, a white flannel nightgown, a cheap digital alarm clock, a comb.

Milo peered at the comb. "No hair I can see but maybe the tweezer squad'll find something. Speaking of which, Detective Reed."

Reed phoned the criminalists and Milo continued his circuit of the room. He checked out a tall, yellow plastic garbage can. Empty. Additional pillows strewn ran-domly supplied extra seating. Plumped and firm, as if they'd never borne weight.

Storage came by way of a three-drawer plywood dresser and a six-foot steel closet painted olive drab. To the left of the closet was a lav barely wide enough for one per-son to stand in. Nylon curtain instead of a door, fiberglass shower, Home Depot sink and commode. A flimsy medicine cabinet sat on the floor.

Everything spotless and dry. The cabi-net was empty.

The exception to all the bare-bones aes-thetic was a wall devoted to a pair of electric keyboards, an amp, a mixing board, a twenty-inch flat-screen monitor on a black stand, two black folding chairs, and several waist-high stacks of sheet music.

Reed examined the music. "Classical . . . more classical . . . some indie rock . . . *more* classical."

Milo said, "No stereo, no CDs."

Reed said, "There's probably an iPod somewhere."

"Then where's the computer that makes all the other gizmos operative?"

Reed frowned. "Someone cleaned up."

The two of them went through the dresser and the metal closet. Jeans, T-shirts, jackets, underwear in small sizes. Tennis shoes, boots, black high-heeled sandals, red pumps, white pumps. One end of the hanging rack in the closet bore half a dozen dresses in optimistic colors.

No discs, laptops, anything related to computers.

Reed kneeled in front of the dresser, slid open the bottom drawer. "Whoa."

Inside was a leather bustier, two sets of fishnets, three pairs of orange-trimmed black crotchless panties, a trio of cheap black wigs, three enormous purple dildos.

Each of the hairpieces was shoulder-length with short bangs. A blue vinyl sewing box held bottles of white face makeup, black eyeliner, tubes of lipstick the color of an old bruise. When Reed pulled it out, a small, black leather riding crop rolled forward.

Milo said, "Dominatrix in her spare time? Maybe her real pad's someplace else and she used this dump for partying."

Reed seemed transfixed by the garments. "Maybe she also gave her music lessons here, Lieutenant."

"Doubtful, no real piano, no instruction books." Milo shut the drawer, took in the room. "If this *was* her main crib, she led a pretty bare life, even accounting for a cleanup. Five minutes inside and I'm ready to gulp some Prozac."

He returned to the metal closet, ran his hand over the top shelf. "Well, looky here."

Down came a cardboard Macy's box stuffed with papers.

On top was Selena Bass's tax return from last year. Income of forty-eight thousand from "freelance musical consulting," ten grand worth of "equipment and supplies" deductions.

Beneath that, he found thirteen monthly checks clipped together in a precise stack. Four thousand dollars each, written on the Global Investment Co. account of The Simon M. Vander Family Trust, address on Fifth Street in Seattle.

Same memo for every payment in block printing: *Lessons for Kelvin.*

Reed said, "The kid on the Web."

Milo said, "Nearly fifty K a year to teach Junior how to tickle the ivories."

"One student paying all the bills, maybe he's got serious talent, some kind of prodigy."

"Or someone thinks he does. How about going out to the car and running Simon Vander's name? The kid, too."

"You bet."

Milo resumed examining the papers in the Macy's box. A California I.D. depicted a thin-faced, big-eyed girl with a pointy cleft chin and dirty-blond hair. Short bangs, just like the wigs. Easy fit for dress-up time?

I said, "Why would she need that if she had a license?"

He said, "Maybe she moved here without a license, got this in the interim."

Beneath the card were receipts from a Betsey Johnson outlet in Cabazon, near Palm Springs, and a six-month-old credit card bill for five hundred dollars, recently paid off after six months of mounting interest at the typical usurious rate.

At the bottom sat a single e-mail, four months old, from engrbass345 at a Hotmail account. I read over his shoulder.

Sel, so glad you finally found a job. And a satisfying one, to boot. Be well, dear. Don't take so long next time.
Love, mom.

Milo sighed. "Notification time."

"Your favorite thing," I said.

"That and drowning puppies."

Reed charged back into the apartment, bright-eyed and waving his pad.

"Looks like Simon Vander's a *big*-time money guy. The investment account might be in Seattle but he lives here, the Palisades. He owned a chain of supermarkets in Mexican neighborhoods, sold out two and a half years ago for a hundred and eleven million. After that, he drops off the screen except for three more hits for Kelvin, all recitals. Kid's ten years old. Found one photo of him."

He flashed a grainy black-and-white shot of a good-looking Asian boy.

Milo showed him the e-mail from Selena Bass's mother.

Reed said, "Going to try her by computer?"

"If she's local, we'll do it in person."

"'engrbass,'" said Reed. "Maybe she's an engineer. Meanwhile, should we start with the Vanders, see if they know anything about Selena's personal life?"

Using the murdered woman's first name. Beginning of the bond.

Milo said, "That's what I'd do."

Reed frowned. "Like I'm inventing the wheel."

CHAPTER

7

Five vehicles at two addresses were registered to Simon Mitchell Vander.

At Calle Maritimo in Pacific Palisades: a three-month-old Lexus GX, a one-year-old Mercedes SLK, a three-year-old Aston Martin DB7, and a five-year-old Lincoln Town Car.

At a Malibu listing on Pacific Coast Highway, a seven-year-old Volvo station wagon.

Moe Reed ran map traces. "La Costa Beach and the north end of the Palisades. Pretty darn close."

"Maybe he likes sand between his toes,"

said Milo. "Middle of the week, I'm betting on the main house. If that doesn't pan out, we get a day at the beach."

The drive from Venice to Pacific Palisades was a slow drip along Lincoln, not much better on Ocean Front, followed by a quick drop onto Channel Road and a blue zip up the coast. A charitable breeze whipped the ocean into cobalt meringue. Surfers and kite runners and people who liked clear lungs were out in force.

Calle Maritimo was a snaky climb above the old Getty estate. As the altitude climbed, properties enlarged, soil growing pricier by the yard. Reed drove fast, clipping past bougainvillea hedges, rock walls, charitable glimpses of ocean.

A sign warned *Dead End: No Through Traffic.* Seconds later that promise was fulfilled by ten-foot iron gates.

Hand-fashioned gates, with stout posts resembling oversized stalks of coral and curving iron rods tangled like octopus tentacles. On the other side of all that foundry work was an oval motor court paved with precise slate squares. Recently hosed slate, still beaded in spots, and ringed by razor-cut date palms. Behind the trees, a surprisingly modest house.

Single story, dun stucco, red tile roof, enclosed courtyard hiding the front door. Off to the side were the four cars listed on Vander's reg forms. Reed punched the call box. Five rings on the intercom, then silence.

He tried again. Four more rings. A boyish-sounding male voice said, "Yes?"

"L.A. police here to talk to Mr. Simon Vander."

"Police?"

"Yes, sir. We need to talk to Mr. Vander."

A beat. "He's not here."

"Where can we find him?"

Two beats. "His last stop was Hong Kong."

"Business trip?"

"He's traveling. I can give him a message."

"Who am I speaking with, sir?"

More hesitation. "Mr. Vander's estate manager."

"Name please?"

"Travis."

"Could you please come out to the gate for a second, Mr. Travis?"

"Can I ask what this is—"

"Why don't you come out and we'll tell you."

"Uh . . . hold on."

Moments later, the courtyard door opened. A man in a navy-blue shirt, pale jeans, and a large gray knit cap squinted in our direction. The shirt was baggy and untucked, tails flapping like breakers. The jeans puddled over white sneakers. The cap was pulled down over the tops of his ears.

He walked toward us in an unsteady gait—uneven shoulders, a foot that turned outward every other step, on the verge of stumble. When he reached the gate, he studied us through iron tentacles, offered an iron-streaked view of long, gaunt face, hollow cheeks, deep-set brown eyes. A three-day stubble, mostly black, some gray, coated his face. Same for whatever cranium the cap revealed. His mouth was skewed to the left, as if set in perpetual regret. That and the rocky walk suggested some kind of neurological insult. I put him at thirty-five to forty. Young for a minor stroke, but life could be cruel.

Milo pushed his badge through the tentacles.

"Afternoon, Mr. Travis."

"Huck. Travis Huck."

"May we come in, Mr. Huck?"

A long-fingered hand pushed a button on a remote. The gates swung inward.

We parked in front of the nearest date palm and got out. The property was set well above its neighbors, at least five acres worth of king-of-the-mountain. Rolling lawns and beds of creeping geranium maintained a low profile. The punch line was a dead-drop bluff rimmed by an infinity pool that kissed the Pacific.

Up close, the house lost any claims to modesty. One story provided maximum ocean view, but horizontal sprawl chewed up land.

Travis Huck poked a finger under his cap, flicked moisture from behind his ear. His face was glossy. Warm day for wool. Or maybe he just perspired easily. "If there's a message I can give to Mr.—"

"The message," said Milo, "is that a woman named Selena Bass was found murdered and we're talking to everyone who knew her."

Huck blinked. His sad, crooked mouth straightened into a position of neutrality, at odds with the tension around his eyes.

He said, "Selena?"

"Yes, sir."

"Oh . . . no."

"You knew her."

"She teaches music. To Kelvin. Mr. and Mrs. Vander's son."

"When's the last time you saw her, Mr. Huck?"

"The last time? I don't—like I said, she gives lessons. When he needs them."

"To Kelvin."

Huck blinked again. "Yes."

"Same question, sir."

"Pardon?"

"Last time you saw her."

"Let me think," said Huck. As if genuinely requesting permission. Sweat rolled down his chin, dropped to the slate. "I want to say two weeks ago . . ." Tugging at the cap. "No, fifteen days. Exactly fifteen."

"You know that because . . ."

"Mrs. Vander and Kelvin left the day after Kelvin's lesson. Which was fifteen days ago. Kelvin played Bartók."

"Left for where?"

"Vacation," said Huck. "It's the summer."

Reed said, "The whole family's traveling."

Huck nodded. "Can I ask what happened to Selena?"

Milo said, "What we can tell you at this point is it wasn't pretty."

No response.

"So the last time she was here was fifteen days ago exactly?"

"Yes."

"What was her state of mind?"

"She seemed fine." Huck's eyes fixed on wet slate. "I let her in, saw her out. She was fine."

Reed said, "Do you know anyone who'd want to hurt her?"

"Hurt her? She came here to teach. Like the others."

"What others?"

"Kelvin is homeschooled. Specialists come in. Art, gymnastics, karate. A curator from the Getty's been tutoring him in art history."

"Kelvin doesn't like regular school?" said Milo.

"Kelvin's too bright for regular school."

One of Huck's legs buckled and he braced himself on the hood of the unmarked. His forehead was soaked.

Moe Reed said, "Bright *and* a good piano player."

"He plays classical," said Huck, as if that settled it.

"How long has Selena Bass been teaching him?"

"She . . . I want to say . . . a year. Give or take."

"Where did the lessons take place?" said Milo.

"Where? Right here."

"Never at Selena's house?"

"No, of course not."

"Why of course not?"

"Kelvin has a busy schedule," said Huck. "Wasting time driving would be out of the question."

"The piano lessons weren't on a set schedule."

"Correct, it depended," said Huck. "It could be once a week or every day."

"Depended on Kelvin's needs."

"If he had a recital, Selena would be here more."

"Kelvin give a lot of recitals?"

"Not too many . . . I still can't believe . . . she was a nice person."

"What else can you tell us about her, sir?"

"Nice," Huck repeated. "Quiet. Pleasant, she always showed up on time."

Moe Reed said, "She got paid well to teach Kelvin."

"I wouldn't know about that."

"You don't sign checks?"

"I just take care of the house."

"Who signs the checks?"

"Mr. Vander's accountants."

"Who's that?"

"They're in Seattle."

Milo said, "You take care of the houses, plural."

"Pardon?"

"There's also a place on the beach." Hooking a thumb toward the ocean.

"Oh, that," said Huck. "That was Mr. Vander's house before he got married. He doesn't use it much."

"He keeps a car there."

"The old station wagon? Battery's probably dead."

"A pad right on the sand," said Milo. "Pity not to use it."

"Mr. Vander travels extensively," said Huck.

"Part of Kelvin's homeschooling?"

"Pardon?"

"Enrichment—seeing the world, learning about other cultures."

"Sometimes." Huck's brow gleamed as if brushed with egg yolk. "This is really upsetting."

"You liked Selena."

"Yes, but . . . it's a matter of someone you know—and then they're . . ." Huck threw up his hands. "Mr. Vander needs to know about this. Kelvin and Mrs. Vander, too. They're going to be—where can I reach you?"

Reed handed over a card.

Huck mouthed Reed's name silently.

Milo said, "We're trying to locate Selena's next of kin. Any idea where we can find them?"

"No, I'm sorry," said Huck. "Poor Kelvin . . . he'll need another teacher."

We drove back down to PCH, traveled a few minutes to La Costa Beach, where Reed hung a U-turn and parked in front of a cedar plank wall.

Forty-foot lot, a few paces from the highway. To the right of the wall was a cedar garage. A pedestrian door was dead-bolted. Milo rang the bell. No answer. He left his card wedged under the handle.

As we returned to the city, Moe Reed said, "What'd you think of Huck?"

"Different kind of fellow."

"He sure sweated a lot. And something else . . . can't put my finger on it, but . . . like he was too guarded. Am I off here, Lieutenant?"

"Guy was definitely antsy, kiddo. But that could just be employee nervousness—afraid to upset the boss. Wanna weigh in, Alex?"

I voiced the nerve damage theory.

Reed said, "Wearing a hat on a hot day is what caught my eye. There didn't seem to be much hair under it. Medium-build white guy, he could be the shaved-head dude Luz Ramos saw with Selena."

Milo thought about that. Reached for the MDT.

No criminal record on Travis Huck, and his DMV photo showed him with a full head of curly black hair. The license had been renewed three years ago. He'd listed his address as the house on Calle Maritimo.

Milo kept typing. The Internet had never met the man. "Shaving his head and being a little off ain't exactly grounds for a warrant, but let's keep him in mind."

Reed said, "What about that loudmouth from the marsh, Duboff? He's got a thing for the place like you said, Doctor. Obsessive, even. What if it has some kind of sexual significance for him so he dumps his bodies there?"

Milo said, "Serial conservationist."

I said, "I'd keep him in mind, too, but like you said, Moe, he didn't try to avoid attention. Just the opposite, he got right in our faces, admitted to being at the marsh right around the time Selena was dumped."

"Couldn't that be reverse psychology?" said Reed. "Or just plain arrogance— thinking he's smarter than us? Like those idiots who mail messages? Or return to the scene to gloat."

"It's possible."

Milo's fingers were already dancing

along the keyboard. "Well, look at this. Mr. Duboff has a record."

Silford Duboff had been arrested seven times in ten years, every instance a confrontation at a protest march.

Anti-globalization ruckus at the Century Plaza, pay raises for hotel housekeepers in San Francisco, sit-in opposing the expansion of the nuclear power plant at San Onofre, resisting coastal development in Oxnard and Ventura. The seventh bust was fighting the billionaires' grab for the Bird Marsh.

Six of the arrests were for resisting, but at the anti-globalization fracas he'd been charged with assaulting a police officer, pled to misdemeanor battery, paid a fine. Conviction reversed two years later when an appeals judge hearing a class-action suit ruled LAPD at fault for the near-riot.

"I remember that one," said Milo. "Big mess. So the guy likes to sit in the middle of the street and chant. But there's no serious violence on his sheet. Doesn't even merit being called a sheet. More like a pillowcase."

Reed said, "Anti-globalization attracts

anarchists and those types, right? Which brings me back to Huck's cap. Those guys wear stuff like that. What if Huck and Duboff were protest buds and found out they had a common interest in nastier stuff?"

"They attend the same marches, Duboff gets busted, but Huck doesn't?"

"Duboff's an in-your-face guy, no subtlety. Huck's more the sneaky type. Maybe that's what I was smelling about him."

"An unholy duo," said Milo. "By day, they agitate for liberation, when the sun goes down they kill women and chop off the hands and toss the bodies in the muck."

Reed drove faster. "I guess it is far-fetched."

"Kiddo, at this point far-fetched is better than nothing. Sure, look into both of them. You find Señor Huck's name on the membership rolls of any group Señor Duboff marched with—any link between the two of them, whatsoever—and we'll go the kill-team route."

I said, "A pair of killers would make the dump easier. One guy parks, the other hauls the body. Or they both haul, are able to do it quickly and get out of there."

Moe Reed said, "Think I should also talk to Vander's accountant, find out about the other teachers making house calls?"

"Someone Selena met on the job did her in?" said Milo.

"More like someone on the job could tell us more than Huck did. Maybe we didn't find any evidence of an outside social life in her apartment because being on call for Kelvin Vander stopped her developing outside interests." Shaking his head. "Fifty grand to teach one kid . . . what if Selena's involvement with this family is what got her dead?"

"Selena and three other women with no right hands?"

Reed didn't answer. Moments later: "No outside social life but there was that bustier et cetera. Like you said, Loo, maybe she partied somewhere else. And so far, the only place we know she spent time was the Vander house."

"Drilling the kid on Bartók," said Milo, "then sneaking off to the pool house for a quickie with the karate coach."

"Or Huck. Or Mr. Vander himself, for that matter."

Milo said, "The plumber, the pool boy, the florist, the gardener."

Reed kept silent.

"Sure, call the accountants and get anything you can about the staff. Until we get I.D.'s on the other victims, we're freeze-dried, anyway."

"Fifty grand," said Reed, "could've led to expectations by the boss. Huck says Vander's out of the country, but the rich don't do their own dirty work, they hire out."

Milo said, "Rich, ergo evil."

"I just think those people can get entitled."

"To you and me, Moe, fifty K is serious money. Guy like Vander pays more to insure his pots and pans. But sure, go for it, see what you dig up. Also, check in with the anthropologists."

"Will do," said Reed. "Thanks, Lieutenant."

"For what?"

"The training."

"First of all, we've shared enough frustration for you to call me Milo. Second, I'll send you a bill for the training." Stretching and laughing. "Fifty K sound reasonable?"

CHAPTER

8

Back in his closet-sized office, Milo re-read the e-mail from engrbass345. Booting up his desktop, he plugged in *engineer* and *bass,* pulled up lots of hits but nothing that fit.

"Time to backtrack her e-mail address . . . bingo . . . website of Emily Nicole Green-Bass—looks like she owns a vintage jewelry store in . . . Great Neck, New York . . . here's a picture of her with shiny stuff. Family resemblance, no?"

Thin-faced woman in her fifties behind a display of bracelets. Big eyes, pointy

cleft chin. Short, white hair brushed forward in uneven bangs.

Selena Bass, at the middle age she'd
never reach.

"Genetics," I said.

"This is gonna be fun." Taking a deep
breath, he picked up the phone.

He hung up ten minutes later, yawning.

Nothing casual about the intake of air.
Exhausted.

Emily   Green-Bass   had   screamed,
sobbed, hung up. Redialing a minute later,
she'd apologized. Cried some more.

Milo stayed with her, chewing on an unlit panatela. When she grew silent, he began pressing for facts.

Selena was the only child from her second marriage. The first had produced two
sons, one of whom lived in Oakland. Which
is where she was now, visiting her brand-
new granddaughter.

"I thought this was the happiest moment
of my life," she said.

She hadn't seen Selena in five years.
The e-mail was one of a handful exchanged
recently.

Selena getting in touch. *Finally.*

Milo asked why it had taken so long and she broke into fresh sobs.

"I'll fly down tomorrow."

At four p.m. a deputy chief named Henry Weinberg called to find out how the marsh murder investigation was progressing.

Milo put him on speaker. "So far, nothing plus nothing, sir."

"Then it might be time to go to the media, Lieutenant."

"I'd rather hold off until the anthropologists have a bone to throw us."

Silence on the other end.

Milo said, "That way—"

Weinberg said, "I heard you, Lieutenant. Nice pun. We put you in front of the cameras, are you going to do stand-up?"

"God forbid, sir."

"God *and* the boss, Lieutenant. And don't ask me which is which. Call those bone pickers *now.* Make sure they're *hustling.*"

Dr. Hargrove was still at the marsh. Dr. Liz Wilkinson answered the phone.

"Oh, hi, Lieutenant. We've made some

progress on Jane Number One. From the nasal bridge, most probably a black female, age estimate between twenty and thirty-five." She could've been describing herself, but there was nothing but science in her voice.

Milo jotted. "Anything else?"

"She's probably had at least one baby and she suffered a fracture of her right femur severe enough to warrant a metal implant. We didn't find the titanium, but we did find the screw holes. I wouldn't be surprised if she limped."

"Recent fracture?"

"There's been substantial bone growth around it. Years, not months, and it happened when she was an adult. The only other interesting finding is a broken hyoid. And, of course, the missing hand."

"Strangled."

"Most likely. Our guess is she's been submerged for several months, but that's all it is: a guess. Eleanor—Dr. Hargrove is still there, working with Lisa—Dr. Chaplin—on the other two sites. But it's going to take time, too much disarticulation and we don't want to miss anything. I'm here because Eleanor asked me to write up what we've got so far. I'll e-mail you what I just told you."

"Thanks."

"One more thing, Lieutenant. Just as I left the marsh, that volunteer—the guy with the beard—showed up again. The officer on guard kept him out and there were some words. I'd like to begin early tomorrow—soon as the sun's up—and I'll be alone because Eleanor and Lisa can't make it until nine. It would be nice to avoid distraction."

"I'll make sure someone's posted before you arrive."

"Thanks. It's a beautiful place but it can get a little . . . ominous."

He logged on to the department's Missing Persons list, searched for black females in the age range Wilkinson had given him, found five disappearances, the most recent half a year ago. No mention of limps or broken legs, but he printed the data anyway.

"Time to start looking at other counties. Hopefully she's not a throwaway no one gave a damn about."

Lighting up, he clouded the tiny room with illicit smoke. Coughed and loosened his tie, spit a shred of tobacco at his waste-basket and missed, and grabbed for his keyboard.

Typing silently and furiously.

I left without a word.

Commuter traffic and lane closures for no apparent reason turned the drive home into an ordeal, and by the time I reached Beverly Glen it was nearly six.

The old bridle path that leads to my house was a sudden infusion of peace. My house, framed by pines and syca-mores, was welcome white simplicity.

I called out Robin's name, got no an-swer. Tossed my jacket, grabbed a Grolsch, headed down the kitchen stairs, and walked through the garden past the pond.

My footsteps caused the koi to storm the edges.

Twelve adults and five juveniles. Half of the babies had died before reaching an inch, but the survivors were nearly a foot long and perpetually hungry. I tossed pel-lets, watched placid water churn into a maelstrom as the fish gorged. Enjoying the illusion of omnipotence for a couple of minutes, I continued along the rock pathway to Robin's studio.

Sometimes she stays at her workbench until I distract her. This evening the bench was clear and she was sitting on the couch, curling and uncurling her hair with a lazy finger while reading a book about Renaissance lutes.

Blanche nestled in her lap, bunny-ears drooping, flat face compressed to wrinkled velvet.

The other female in my life is a twenty-pound vanilla-colored French bulldog with tidy table manners rarely seen in the breed, and a saintly disposition. Some of my patients request her presence during sessions. I'm still trying to figure out what her cut should be.

She and Robin looked up simultaneously. New Olympic event: synchronized smiling. I kissed Robin's cheek, pecked the top of Blanche's knobby head.

Robin said, "Pooch and girlfriend are on an equal footing?"

"*She* pants in appreciation."

"She also pees in the bushes."

"And the problem is . . ."

"Oh, don't tempt me." We kissed. I sat

down next to her. Her skin and hair were fragrant with cedar and Gio.

Cool fingers rested on the back of my neck. "Have a good day?"

"Better, now."

During the next clinch, Blanche observed, head tilted to one side, ears erect.

Robin said, "Getting an eyeful, girlfriend?"

Blanche smiled.

We cooked up a mushroom-and-cheese omelet and I asked her what she'd been up to.

"Didn't do much but loaf around. I might get used to it."

A week ago she'd completed a major commission: replicas of four vintage Gibson instruments for a dot-com gazillionaire who'd donated them to charity. She'd been talking about starting a new project but had limited herself to repairs.

I thought of a still-fragrant, sixty-year-old flamenco guitar brought in for a neck-set. "Finished the Barbero?"

"Yup, it was simpler than I figured, Paco picked it up a couple of hours ago. You must've been really tied up. Service just called, said you hadn't checked in. Some lawyer wants you for a consult."

She told me the name.

I said, "If he ever pays his bills, he might actually get someone to work for him."

I finished my beer, stretched.

"You look weighed down," she said.

"Milo's burden. I hung around and watched."

"Watched what?"

I hesitated, the instinct to protect rearing its paternalistic little head. Back in the old days, I'd avoided talking about police cases. A couple of breakups and makeups later, I had a new appreciation for sharing.

I gave her the basics.

She said, "The marsh? Where we tried to take a walk?"

"None other."

"You know, the place was kind of creepy."

Same thing Liz Wilkinson had said.

"How so?"

"It's nothing I can really pinpoint. Un-friendly, I guess. Where were the bodies left?"

"The most recent one was right near the eastern entrance. The others were submerged farther up the path."

"Drive up and dump," she said. "A car would've been conspicuous, Alex. And all that development looking down on it."

"Nighttime dump, turn off the headlights, you'd fade into the darkness. Including the view from above."

She pushed her plate away. Mixed herself a cranberry juice with a splash of Grey Goose. "Three sunken bodies and one left right out in the open. What does that mean?"

"Maybe a new level of confidence."

"Bragging," she said. "Like it's something to be proud of."

The dot-com guy had sent Robin a box of Audrey Hepburn movies. We'd made our way through most of the DVDs, had saved *Charade* for a long quiet night.

Ten minutes into the film, the phone rang. I ignored it, drew Robin closer. Seconds later, the clanging resumed. I put Cary Grant on pause.

Milo said, "You free tomorrow at ten, right? Selena's mom is due."

"Sure."

"Everything okay?"

"Absolutely."

"I interrupt something?"

"High intrigue featuring gorgeous people."

"A movie," he said.

"Ace detective."

"Sure ain't real life. Go back to Cinema Dreams. I'll tell you about the bones tomorrow."

"What about the bones?"

"Hey, far be it from me to take you away from Robin and Doggie and fictitious gorgeous people."

"What?"

"Dr. Hargrove got a quicker fix than she thought. All three of the submerged victims are complete skeletons, minus the right hand. Jane Doe Number Two is also a black female, same age range as Jane One with the broken leg, also probable strangulation. From the length of *her* femurs, at least five seven, and strain marks indicate she was probably significantly overweight. Hargrove is guessing burial for maybe half a year, but she won't commit. Number Three's a white female, older than the others—closer to fifty, average size, another broken hyoid, nothing much in the way of distinguishing marks. Could be the same TOD as Jane Two, or longer, hard to say. The other tidbit is San Diego PD has a missing black female named Sheralyn Dawkins. Twenty-nine years old, arrests for solicitation and dope, and she broke her leg in a car crash five years ago and limped."

"Hundred and twenty miles away," I said. "Our boy's a traveler?"

"Just what I need. I told Reed to find family, drive down, and notify. Give him a sense of accomplishment, boy's got low self-esteem, no?"

"He have any luck with the Vanders' accountants?"

"Not a lick. Global Investments referred him to Vander's lawyer where he got shunted to a secretary. Who sent him to *her* secretary. Who put him on hold, then informed him she'd get back to him. No nasty stuff on Travis Huck or Silford Duboff, either. And no links show up between the two of them."

I said, "The thrilling world of sleuthing."

"Let's see what Reed learns from Sheralyn Dawkins's family. Maybe she moved to L.A. and we can establish some kind of connection to someone."

"If she did move, here's something to consider: The marsh isn't that far from the airport, and the area around LAX is full of streetwalkers."

"Hmm . . . I like that. Okay, go back to your movie," he said. "Which one?"

"Charade."

"Cavorting in Paris and snappy dialogue. If only crime were that much fun."

"Want to borrow it when we're through?"

"Nah," he said. "Right now I can't afford fantasy."

CHAPTER
9

I arrived on time for the meeting with Selena Bass's mother. The civilian clerk told me, "They already started. Room D, upstairs."

The door was unlocked. The A.C. blasted. Milo sat opposite Emily Green-Bass. His tie was knotted neatly and his face was soft. I've seen him practice in front of a mirror before meeting with grief-stricken relatives. Loosening his muscles. Keeping the wolf-glare out of his eyes.

Emily Green-Bass's white hair was now long and French-braided. She wore a black mock turtle over a long gray skirt, and black suede flats. Jewelry dealer, but no baubles. Her features were laser-cut, too sharp for beautiful. A handsome woman during good times. Now she was icy statuary.

Two bulky men in their thirties sat at the side of the table. The older one wore a yellow golf shirt, brown slacks, deck shoes. Reddish blond hair was side-parted executive-style. Close-shaved, bullnecked, three-martini nose.

The younger one was darker, just as husky but with a bonier face. He wore a faded gray *David Lynch Rules* sweatshirt, wrinkled cargo pants, high lace-up boots. Wavy brown hair hung to his shoulders. A triangular soul patch was white-blond. A chromium chain drooped from a rear pocket, and when he turned to me it jangled.

Milo introduced me. "These are Selena's mom and brothers, Dr. Delaware."

Emily Green-Bass held out a long, white hand that felt as if it had just left the freezer. I encased it briefly with both of mine and her gray eyes got wet.

Polo Shirt said, "Chris Green."

Soul Patch muttered, "Marc."

"We were just going over Selena's life in

L.A. Marc had some contact with Selena after she moved here."

"She visited me in Oakland," said Marc. "Said she was doing fine. She e-mailed the same thing to Mom."

Emily Green-Bass hadn't taken her eyes off me. "I'm glad a psychologist is here. What happened has got to be psychotic. There hasn't been *anything* extreme in Selena's life. Not for a long time."

Marc Green said, "There *never* was. It was basic adolescent crap."

"If you say so, Marcus." Wan smile. "It sure didn't seem that way when I had to contend with it."

Marc's shoulders rose and fell. His chain jangled and he reached behind to quiet it. "I did the same crap and so did Chris. Only difference is we were better at covering up."

Looking to his brother for confirmation.

Chris said, "Uh-huh."

"Unfortunately for *Selena*," Marc went on, "she had a compulsion to *confess* everything. Right?"

Chris smiled sadly. "Like a Catholic thing. Except we're not Catholic."

"First she'd try out the script on us," said

Marc. "'I smoked a joint.' 'I watched an X movie on cable.' 'I lied about where I was to Mom.' We're like, don't tell us, stupid. And for *sure* don't tell Mom. So of course she did."

Emily Green-Bass began crying.

Milo said, "Typical teenage stuff."

Marc Green said, "This is a waste of time."

Chris said, "She *was* into the whole music thing."

"So what!"

"Chill, Marc. I want them to have all the facts—"

"The *facts* are she was in the wrong place, wrong time, ran into Ted Bundy's reincarnation."

No one spoke.

Marc Green said, "This may be news to all concerned but being into the whole *music* thing doesn't make her a freak. Her basic mind-set was conventional. When she met some of the people I have to hang with, she thought they were weird."

Milo said, "Which people are those?"

Marc said, "From work."

"Which is where?"

"That relevant?"

His mother said, "Marcus, he's trying to help."

"Good for him." To Milo: "I work wherever they pay me."

Emily Green-Bass said, "Marc has a degree in acoustical engineering."

"I do sound recording and amplification, mostly concerts and indie films. And as long as we're doing the official family bio thing, Big Bro Chris works for Starbucks. That's an obscure coffee company in Seattle."

Chris said, "Marketing and distribution."

I said, "When did Selena visit you, Marc?"

"A year ago and maybe six months after that. The first time, I was working on a picture and she trailed along. That's when she told me the people I hung with were bizarre. Which was true of that particular crew, I guess. Half the dialogue was in Italian, the rest was pantomime—some sort of tribute to Pasolini but nobody actually *knew* Italian."

His brother said, "And the Oscar goes to."

"Hey, we can't all ride the caffeine train."

Milo said, "Selena's second visit . . ."

"Was when I asked her up for the weekend so I could introduce her to Cleo—then
my lover, now my wife. We just had our
first baby. Which is why I should be home.
Can we move this along?"

Milo sat back and crossed his legs. "If
you've got nothing more to tell us, feel free
to go."

Marc rubbed his soul patch, shoved hair
behind his left ear. Blue and green ink
washed across his neck. *Cleo,* amid a wreath
of vines. I hoped the marriage lasted.

"What the hell," he said. "I'm booked on
a nine p.m., no sense changing it."

Chris said, "Selena saw you twice, huh?
That's two more times than she bothered
to call me back."

"Guess she was too busy for corporate
chitchat."

Chris turned away from his brother.

Milo said, "You called her . . ."

"Just to see how she was doing."

"When was the last time you spoke to
her?"

"I dunno . . . two years ago."

Marc said, "Obviously we're a close-knit
family."

Emily Green-Bass said, "Chris and

Marc's father and I broke up when the boys were one and three and he hasn't been heard from since." Frowning at her sons as if the fault was theirs. "I met Selena's dad a year later. Dan was good to you guys."

No argument.

"Dan passed away when Selena was six. I raised her alone and I'm sure there are some people would say I screwed it up."

Chris said, "You did fine, Mom."

Marc said, "Can we stay focused on Selena?"

Silence.

"Why get distracted?" he said. "Selena was talented, but as essentially straight as they come. I'm not saying she never puffed a doobie. But even when she and Mom were doing their hostility thing, she never did anything spiteful, like hooking up with someone iffy. Just the opposite. We used to call her Sister Cee. As in celibate."

"She'd call herself that," said Chris.

Milo said, "What about boyfriends?"

Marc said, "Nope."

"Mrs. Green-Bass?"

"No, I never saw anyone."

She covered her face. Marc reached out

to pat his mother's shoulders. She drew away.

"Oh God," she said, through her fingers, "this is so horrible."

Marc's lip trembled. "All I'm saying, Mom, is that Selena didn't bring it upon herself. Shit happens, life sucks. Like stepping off a curb and some asshole comes barreling down. That just happened to me. Right after Cleo gave birth to Phaedra. I left the hospital to get some champagne, was floating on air. I step off the curb and this fucking *San Francisco Examiner* truck comes out of nowhere, misses me by a millimeter."

"Marcus, don't *tell* me those things! I don't want to *hear* them!"

Milo said, "So no boyfriend anyone's aware of. What about friends? People she hung with here in L.A."

No answer.

Emily said, "She *did* seem to be happy about her work. That's what she finally e-mailed me about."

"Teaching that rich kid," said Marc. "She said it was a dream gig. She called to tell me because I'm into music, too. Used to play bass. Not that I was ever close to

Selena's level. I'm competent, she's brilliant. Sat down at the piano when she was
three and just *played* the fucking thing. By
five, she was doing Gershwin by ear. Give
her anything, she could play it. I watched
her pick up a clarinet cold and run off a
scale. She got the breathing right away."

"Sounds like a prodigy," said Milo.

"No one used that word, we just thought
she was amazing."

Emily Green-Bass said, "I was so busy
supporting us, I was happy she had something to occupy her."

Marc said, "One day I come in—I'm talking years ago, when Selena was eight or
nine. She's in the living room strumming
my guitar. The guitar was new, a birthday
present, I got pissed that she took it without my permission. Then I realize she's
actually making music on it. Never had a
lesson and she's taught herself a bunch of
chords and her tone's better than mine."

Emily said, "When she was eleven I
could see piano was something she
wanted to stick with, so I got her a teacher.
This was back when we lived in Ames,
Iowa. Ames Band Equipment had a pro-
gram for the schools. Selena outgrew the

first teacher they gave her, then two others. They said I needed to find someone with serious classical training. When we moved to Long Island, I found an old woman in the city who'd been a professor in the Soviet Union. Mrs. Nemerov— *Madame* Nemerov, she was ancient, wore ball gowns. Selena studied with her until she was fifteen. Then one day she just quit, said she hated classical music. I told her she was wasting her God-given talent, she'd never play again. She said I was wrong. It got pretty—that was one of our biggest . . . disagreements. It was a tough time, Selena had totally abandoned her schoolwork, was getting D's and F's. She claimed she was learning more from life than any stupid school could teach her."

Marc muttered, "No shit."

I said, "Did she stop playing?"

"No. I *was* wrong. She actually played *more,* just not a lot of classical pieces. Though every so often she'd do a little Liszt or Chopin, whatever." Sad smile. "The Chopin études. She liked the ones in minor keys. Or at least that's what she said, I don't know a thing about music. Selena got her talent from her father, he played

guitar, banjo, you name it. Did that blue-
grass stuff, he was originally from Arkansas. Madame Nemerov said Selena was
one of the quickest sight readers she'd
ever taught, had perfect pitch. In her view
Selena could've been one of the great
concert pianists, if she'd wanted to."

Marc said, "She thought touring around
and playing Beethoven for stuffed shirts
would rob her life of normalcy."

"So this was better?" said Emily. "Doing
absolutely nothing until she was twenty-
one, then packing up and moving to L.A.
without telling me? Without any job prospects?"

Milo said, "She ran away?"

"When you're not a minor they don't call
it that. I came home and she'd packed her
bags and left a note that she was moving
to 'the coast' and not to try to stop her. I
was frantic. She phoned a few days later
but wouldn't tell me where she was. I finally pried out the fact that she was in
L.A., but she refused to say where. She
claimed she was supporting herself with
'gigs.' Whatever that meant."

Marc said, "She got some club dates,
playing backup keyboard."

His mother stared at him. "Well, that's news to me, Marcus."

"Then it's good that I'm here to inform you."

Emily Green-Bass's hand rose and arced toward his face. She checked herself, shuddered. "Lieutenant, the fact that Selena and I weren't in regular contact was her choice, not mine. She shut me out completely. I have no idea what she's been doing all these years. It's been *hellish* not knowing. If I didn't have a business to run, I'd have come out here and tracked her down. I called the police but couldn't provide an address, so they couldn't tell me which station to contact. And since Selena wasn't a minor and she had left voluntarily, there was nothing anyone could do. Their big suggestion was I contact a private detective. Besides being expensive, I knew that kind of snooping would irritate Selena, so I minded my own business, kept telling myself she was all right."

Milo said, "When did you call the department?"

"Right at the beginning. Must've been . . . four, five years ago. I kept hoping she'd ask for money, at least I'd have an inkling what she was up to." Swiveling toward Marc. "Now you're telling me *you* knew all along what she was up to."

Marc Green squirmed. "It wasn't a big deal."

"To me it was."

"She didn't want you to know what she was doing. Figured you'd try to stop her."

"Why would I stop her?"

Silence.

"I *wouldn't* stop her," said Emily Green-Bass. "Now, you tell us everything you know, Marcus. *Everything.*"

Marc tortured his hair.

"*Now,* Marcus!"

"It's nothing. I'm sure—"

"Shut up and *talk,* Marcus!"

"*Fine.* She didn't want you to know because the scene she was in really *wasn't* her thing. She was just playing music."

"What are you *talking* about!"

"Mom, she swore me to secrecy, I had no reason to violate—"

"Now you do," said Milo.

"Okay, but it really boils down to *nothing.* Like I said, she was playing in clubs. And that led to parties." Turning to his mother. "Some were situations she didn't want you to find out about because she knew you'd freak out."

"What kind of situations?"

No answer.

Emily Green-Bass grabbed her son's wrist and put her face close to his. "Like I'm some kind of fossil, Marc? Like I'm out of touch with reality? I *like* rock music. Your sister's *dead*! These people need to *know*!"

Marc licked his lips. "I'm not talking about the music, Mom. These were . . . specialty   parties . . . swinger   parties, okay? Freaks wanting background."

Emily Green-Bass let go of his sleeve. "My God."

"You wanted to know, Mom, now you know. Selena was broke, totally busted, so she checked out the classifieds in the freebie papers, found an ad for a keyboardist to play a private party. She had her Korg, her Pro Tools, all that stuff you got her for her eighteenth."

Milo said, "All that stuff comes with a computer, right?"

"And a cord and plug," said Marc. "Of *course* it comes with a computer."

"There was no computer in her apartment."

"Everything else was there?"

"Appeared to be."

"That's bizarre."

Chris Green said, "Someone did this for a Mac?"

Marc Green said, "Or they wanted her data."

Milo said, "What kind of data would that be, Marc?"

"I don't know, I'm just saying."

"Saying what?"

"Those parties . . . maybe she took notes or something about what she saw and someone wanted to maintain their privacy."

"Freaks," said Emily Green-Bass. "Oh, Lord."

Milo said, "Tell us about the parties, Marc."

"All Selena said was freak parties at private homes. We didn't get into details. Tell the truth, I didn't want to know."

Emily said, "The *whole* truth, Marcus."

"That is the whole truth."

"You keep saying that, dammit, then you drop in new tidbits! You were *always* a tease, Marcus."

Marc gritted his teeth. "What I *know* is

Selena played music for people having open sex in private houses. What I *know* is she said they wanted live music while they were fucking because they were fucking exhibitionists and fucking in front of a live fucking musician was a fucking part of the fucking high."

"Don't be vulgar . . . my God, Lieutenant, what if someone got her to do . . . more than music?"

"She never came close to implying that, Mom. *Never.* She was playing music, that's all. Got paid well, was real happy."

Milo said, "She quote you a figure?"

"No, and I didn't ask." Marc swung his chain, fingered keys. "Now that we've micro-analyzed Selena and violated her privacy, can you guys go and do some detecting?"

Chris said, "Chill, bro."

Marc slumped.

Milo said, "When exactly did she tell you about these parties?"

"When I saw her the second time."

"Six months ago."

"She knew I was the only one in the family who wouldn't judge her. Basically, she was laughing at it. Naked old people fucking and sucking and she's playing Air Supply. Then she got the teaching job and that was even better."

"How'd she find that?"

"She didn't say."

Emily said, "Maybe one of those perverts went crazy."

"We'll definitely check it out, ma'am," said Milo. "She did tell you about her job with the Vander boy."

"She said she had a full-time job teaching a musical genius. She e-mailed *me* and I answered right away. I asked her to call and she did. But only once. We had one conversation. She sounded happy." Sniffling. "I thought she'd call again. I told her I was proud of her, asked her to come home, at least for a visit. She said she'd think about it, but she never followed through."

Milo said, "She saved a hard copy of your e-mail, ma'am. It obviously meant a lot to her."

"Thank you."

He turned to the brothers. "You guys have no idea how she met the Vanders?"

Chris shook his head.

Marc said, "In music, generally it's word

of mouth—oh. You're thinking they were freaks, heard her play at one of those screwathons and hired her? Makes sense."

"Why's that?"

"The filthy rich do what they want."

Emily said, "Oh, my God."

Milo said, "Jumping to conclusions is a real bad idea. All we know about the Vanders is that they hired Selena to teach piano. But this is exactly what we need— any possible links to people in Selena's life. So if anyone has any other ideas, please express them."

Marc said, "The whole rich-asshole thing makes *total* sense. Selena meets them at a freak show and they decide to co-opt her for—"

"Didn't you hear him?" said his brother. "It's way premature to—"

Marc wheeled on him. "Like you've had something to offer? Fuck *off.*"

Chris's complexion deepened to sugar-beet. "Fuck *you.*"

"Stop it!" said Emily Green-Bass. "I can't stand this, it's like everything's *rotting.*"

CHAPTER
10

We watched mother and sons drive away in three separate rental cars.

Milo said, "Nothing like togetherness. Sounds like Selena was alienated from all of 'em."

I said, "People come to L.A. to lose themselves."

"You referring to me or you or everyone?"

"If the shoe fits."

Back in his office, I said, "Private gigs at swinger parties could explain the sex toys. Selena started off supplying the soundtrack, evolved into a different type of entertainment."

"Nice-looking girl, the whole Little Miss Chaste thing could appeal to a libertine." Smiling. "Last time I heard that word was from Sister Mary Patrick the Cruel." He fished a panatela from a desk drawer, unwrapped it, twirled. "What do you think of Angry Brother?"

"He's the only one who had any kind of relationship with Selena, but a hot temper can lead all sorts of places."

He ran a records check on Marc. "Clean. So maybe we should trust his instincts and the Vanders were shelling fifty grand a year for more than piano lessons."

"With a kid who's a prodigy, you'd think the family would hire a famous teacher, not a starving musician who'd dropped out of formal training. On the other hand, what better cover for Selena being on call?"

"Tickle the ivories, tickle Daddy and Mommy."

"That would account for Travis Huck's overactive sweat glands. Same for the stone wall Reed bumped up against when he tried to talk to the Vanders' accountants. And the Vanders just happen to be traveling when Selena shows up dead."

"Lifestyles of the rich and lustful," he said. "Marc Green might be one of those peevish class-warfare guys, but that doesn't make him wrong."

He rubbed his face. "That house, end of the road, gated, no neighbors in sight. Ideal setup for interesting soirees. Selena told Marc she dug the money. What if she got bonuses for nonmusical gigs, then she saw something that made her want out."

"Or she threatened someone literally."

"Blackmail?"

"Big secrets, big money."

"Yeah, that's the recipe."

"On the other hand," I said, "the truth could turn out to be much more of a downer."

"What?"

"She reached her expiration date and got discarded. Which could be the link to Sheralyn Dawkins. Maybe the other Jane Does, if they also sold sex for a living."

"Used and tossed."

"The swinger scene thrives on novelty," I said. "The big downer is getting jaded.

Hiring pros worked for a while. Then Selena came along, outwardly innocent. That would kick things up a notch."

"Maybe inwardly and outwardly chaste," he said. "Twenty-six and never been nothinged until she ran into the wrong crowd. Those years of playing clubs, think it's possible?"

"Anything's possible," I said. "Makes both our jobs interesting."

A call to the crypt revealed that Selena Bass's autopsy was scheduled in three days. Milo's wheedling to jump the queue produced vague maybes. Just as he hung up, Deputy Chief Henry Weinberg rang in, wanting to know when he was planning to go public on the marsh murders.

Milo said, "Soon," sat for a long time, listened impassively.

When he hung up, I said, "Wild guess: Immediately's a whole lot better than soon."

"Brass has the script written and proofread, ready to be recited with wooden earnestness. Goddamn pencil-pushers love press conferences because it lets them pretend they're doing a real job."

I said, "At the risk of being contentious, two victims with no I.D.'s, the media could be helpful."

"The media's like a penicillin shot, Alex. Pain in the ass, sometimes helpful in small doses. It's always a double-edged sword: too much exposure, people rabbit. Lemme see if the bone ladies have pulled up anything."

Eleanor Hargrove was at the marsh. All the bones had been extracted and tagged, were being prepped for transport to her lab. Her guess was very little additional data would be forthcoming, though Jane Doe Three did have "some interesting dentition."

Milo said, "Interesting how?"

"Two baby canines still in place and she was born without wisdom teeth. If you ever get dental records, matching would be a snap."

He thanked her, called Moe Reed, confirmed the young detective's trip to San Diego tomorrow, set up a second lunch meet at Café Moghul in an hour.

I said, "He likes Indian food?"

"Like that matters."

Reed was drinking tea when we got there. Same blazer and khakis, similar shirt and tie. Hours in the sun had grilled him medium-rare. He looked worn.

The woman in the sari brought us everything she was serving that day.

Milo snarfed. Reed didn't touch a thing.

Milo said, "Don't like Indian?"

"Had a late breakfast."

"Where?"

"IHOP."

"German pancakes, the applesauce?"

"Just eggs."

"Kid, you gotta carbo-load for the long trek ahead." Patting the swell of his gut. "Got anything for show-and-tell?"

"Talked to Alma Reynolds, Duboff's girlfriend. She sounds as whack as him, kept going on and on about the marsh being sacred even though she's an atheist. That made me wonder about the missing hands being some kind of religious ritual, but I looked up all the major religions and not one's got anything like that, even Wiccans and Voodoos. Reynolds confirmed she was out of town when Duboff said she was and I still can't find anything psycho in his past. His old boss at that left-wing bookstore says he was nonviolent, carried spiders and bugs outside and let them go."

Milo said, "Hitler was a vegetarian."

The young detective's blue eyes studied him. "That so?"

"Der Führer und der Tofu."

Reed smiled. "In terms of Travis Huck, I also got a bunch of nothing. But something about him still bugs me, Loo. Nervous and evasive."

"Maybe because he's protecting the Vanders." Milo summarized what we'd learned from Marc Green.

Reed said, "Weirdo parties. We need to learn more about these people."

An open door brought in a rush of traffic noise. A good-looking black man had entered the restaurant.

Early thirties, six feet tall, closely cropped hair, athletic frame packaged neatly in a body-conscious charcoal suit. A peacock-blue silk shirt gleamed. So did black alligator loafers.

The woman in the sari approached him.

A few seconds of conversation got her to smile. The man headed for our table, gliding more than walking.

Milo said, "Blast from the past."

Moe Reed shifted in his chair. His face had changed, lips folding inward, eyes tight, pale irises barely visible between half-closed lids. One hand gripped his tea glass.

A cloud of light, grassy cologne preceded the man's arrival. He had the clean features and poreless skin of a young Belafonte. Grinning, he held out a hand to Milo. "Congratulations, recently promoted Lieutenant Sturgis." The suit was hand-stitched with peaked lapels and working buttonholes on the sleeves. *ADF* monogram on the blue shirt. The reptilian shoes looked brand new.

Milo said, "Long time, Former Detective Fox. This is Dr. Alex Delaware, our consulting psychologist, and this is—"

Moe Reed said, "I know him," and turned away.

The man stared at him for a moment. Tightened his jaw. Smiled at me. "Aaron Fox, Doctor. The world can use more psychologists." I shook a warm, dry hand.

Pulling up a chair from a neighboring table, Fox positioned it backward and straddled. Pouring himself tea, he sipped. "Ahh, nice and refreshing, tastes like there's some white tea in there, maybe a nuance of jasmine."

Reed gazed out the window. Both his hands were curled into fists.

Milo said, "So there's no need to introduce you two."

Aaron Fox laughed. "Not unless one of us has Alzheimer's." He placed a palm on Reed's beefy shoulder. "Your brain working okay, Moses? From what I can tell, mine's still functional."

Reed sat there.

Fox said, "Brain like yours, Moses, probably stay good in the foreseeable future."

Reed stared past him.

Fox said, "He's always been modest. Back when we were kids, I'd take every bit of exaggerated credit I could for the most trivial, picayune accomplishments. Marketing and promotion, right? It's not enough to have the product, you've got to sell it. Little brother doesn't believe in that. He's smarter than me. But he's never been one to toot his own horn."

Reed removed Fox's hand and set it down with exquisite care.

Aaron Fox said, "I'm always doing that. Embarrassing him. Older brother's prerogative."

Milo said, "You guys are sibs?"

"You didn't know?" said Fox. "Oh, yeah, two dips into the same gene pool, but X chromosome only—same mommy, different daddies. I've always suspected she liked him better. He'd probably claim the opposite. That right, Moses?"

Reed pushed away from the table and headed to the bathroom.

Fox said, "Didn't know I still had that effect on him."

He drank more tea.

Milo indicated the food. "You like Indian?"

"Nothing against it, Milo, but I prefer fusion cuisine. Chinois, Medi-California, Southwest sushi. Artistic mélange of cultures brings out the best in human creativity. Been to that new place on Montana? Wagyu beef from Japan, they massage the beasts before cutting their throats. Kind of like the department, huh?"

Milo smiled. "How long you been out of the job, Aaron?"

"Centuries," said Fox. "To be precise, three years this September. Maybe I should throw a party."

"Looks like private enterprise agrees with you."

"I don't argue with it so it's got no reason to *dis*agree with me." Touching a silk sleeve. "Yeah, it's great, Milo. Rewards for initiative and achievement, lots of freedom, the only bosses are the people who write the checks and they're entitled to make demands."

"Nice," said Milo. "Long as you produce."

"So far, so good," said Fox.

Moe Reed returned. Edged his chair away from Fox's and sat down.

Milo said, "Why'm I thinking you're not here by accident, Aaron? Or for the food?"

"Definitely not the food," said Fox. "Had a late breakfast. Hotel Bel-Air with a prospective client."

"Apricot crêpes, that sauce they have?"

"Nice, but too messy for a first date, Milo. Just eggs—shirred with chives."

Reed muttered, "Call the Food Network."

Fox said, "You're right, bro, no more small talk. Nothing small about my intentions, I'm here about Selena Bass."

"What about her?" said Milo.

"Got a suspect for you and asking nothing in return."

Reed snorted.

Milo said, "Who?"

"Guy named Travis Huck."

Reed said, "We've already run him through, no history."

Fox grinned. "No history under *that* name."

"He's got an alias?" said Milo.

"Been known to happen," said Fox. "Aka Edward Travis Huckstadter." Taking his time spelling the last name. "No one's going to write that down?"

"What's he running from, Aaron?"

"What else? His past."

CHAPTER
11

Aaron Fox put down his tea and reached into an inner suit pocket. A wad of newspaper clippings dropped on the table in front of Milo. Great tailoring had hidden the bulge.

Milo said, "Why don't you summarize for us civil servants?"

"Pleasure. Edward Travis Huckstadter grew up in Ferris Ravine, one of those scrubby ranch towns inland from San Diego. Daddy, unknown, Mommy, a crazy drunk. When young Eddie was fourteen he got into a shoving match with a classmate and the other kid died. Eddie got convicted of murder, spent some time in juvey lockup, then got shunted around the foster care system. That's some *psycho-logical* history, Doc."

"Fourteen," said Moe Reed. "He's thirty-seven. We're talking clean record for twenty-three years—"

"No arrests doesn't mean no bad be-havior, Moses. The relevant point is he killed one human being and now he's as-sociated with a homicide victim. On top of that, his whereabouts since he turned eighteen are a big blank. No Social Secu-rity card or tax returns until three years ago when he started working for a mega-bucks fellow named Simon Vander under the alias. Obviously, he lied to get the gig because I don't see Megabucks hiring some mope with a felony record. You guys met him. You're telling me he didn't set off any alarm bells?"

Milo said, "How do you know we met him?"

"I pick up things."

"You meet Huck yourself, Aaron?"

"Haven't had the pleasure yet, but I've been watching him for the last twenty-four hours."

"Why?"

"After your case hit the news, someone hired me to do so."

"Selena hasn't been in the news."

"Not on TV," said Fox. "Or the *Times*. But the *Evening Outlook* ran a paragraph. Want me to get you a copy?"

"No, thanks. You pick up anything watching him?"

"So far all he's done is shop for groceries, but he's got a mopey walk and a weird crooked smile."

Reed said, "You don't like his looks. There's evidence for you." Huck had been his choice for Prime Suspect but something else was at work here.

Fox patted the newspaper clippings. "He killed someone at a tender age."

"Twenty-three years ago."

"You have anyone better?"

Reed didn't answer.

"That's what I thought. I'm serving up a serious lead. What you do with it is your own business."

Milo said, "Juvey records are sealed. How'd you find all this out?"

Fox smiled.

Reed said, "That's *real* helpful."

Fox's gold-brown eyes flashed. Shooting a cuff, he glanced at a blue-faced Patek Philippe.

Milo said, "Sounds like you're pretty invested in Huck being our bad guy."

Aaron Fox took a nanosecond to decide upon an emotion. Settled for placid. "Not invested, just aware of the facts."

"Who hired you to research the guy?"

"I wish I could tell you."

Reed said, "We're supposed to ask for a warrant based on twenty-three-year-old information obtained illegally from an informant too chickenshit to come forward."

Both brothers' bodies tilted like lances.

Regressed, for an instant, to feuding children.

Fox broke the stare first, smiling and shrugging. "Moses, however Detective Sturgis deigns to utilize the data with which I am gifting him is not my concern." He stood. "I've done my civic duty. Have a nice rest-of-the-day, gents."

Reed said, "Your brain's so functional, you'll recall the statutes on obstruction."

Fox smoothed a silk shirt collar. "Little bro, you *get* like that and I *know* you're blowing more smoke than one of those clunkers

you insist on driving." To Milo: "Word has it
there are other victims in the marsh. And
that a press conference is on the horizon.
It was me at the podium, I'd like a few fac-
toids when those pesky questions start
flying."

Milo flicked the clippings with a big,
square thumbnail. "We'll be sure to pore
over every word, Aaron. You tell us who
hired you to scope out Huck and why, we
might give them some credibility."

"Their credibility isn't in question," said
Fox. "Only issue is whether you decide to
follow through." Peeling a twenty from an
alligator billfold, he let it float to the table.

Milo said, "Not necessary."

"Thanks but no thanks," said Fox. "I always pay my own way."

Snapping a quick salute, he left the restaurant.

Moe Reed remained canted forward.

Milo said, "Your brother, huh?"

Reed nodded. "Vice has nothing on
Sheralyn Dawkins but I'd better run over to
the LAX stroll, see if I can learn something
before I drive to San Diego."

Erupting from his chair, he charged out
before Milo could answer.

Milo said, "Ah, the joys of family life."

I said, "Huck's also from the San Diego area."

"Funny thing about that. But why give Fox the satisfaction?"

We examined the clippings in Milo's office. Three articles from *The Ferris Ravine Clarion* spaced a month apart, written by Cora A. Brown, the paper's publisher and editor in chief. One piece covered the tragedy. Two follow-ups added nothing.

The facts were as Aaron Fox had summarized: On a hot May afternoon, eighth-grader Eddie Huckstadter, considered a shy child and loner by his teachers, had finally responded to months of bullying by an outsized ninth-grader named Jeffrey Chenure. During the schoolyard confrontation, the much smaller Eddie had shoved his quarterback antagonist in the chest. Jeff Chenure stumbled backward, caught his balance, charged at Eddie, fists flailing. Before a blow could land, he cried out, fell flat on his back, lifeless.

Milo said, "Sounds like an accident or at

the worst, self-defense. I'm surprised Huck served any juvey time."

I ruffled the clippings. "This is what Fox wanted you to see. Maybe there's more."

The Internet brought up nothing on Eddie Huckstadter, nor did the name appear in any criminal data banks.

Milo said, "No surprise, there. If Fox had found any more dirt, he'd have *gifted* me with it." He stood. "All that tea, gotta take a detour."

During his absence, I phoned *The Ferris Ravine Clarion,* expecting a disconnected number. A female voice answered, "Clarion."

I gave her a capsule I.D., asked for her name.

"Cora Brown, I'm the editor, publisher, opinion-editorial columnist, classified ad clerk. And I take out the trash. L.A. Police? Why?"

"It's about a story you wrote several years ago. A boy named Eddie Huckstadt—"

"Eddie? Has the poor boy done something—I guess he'd be a man by now. Is he in trouble?"

"His name came up as a witness in an investigation. When we backtracked we came across your articles."

"Investigation into what?"

"A homicide."

"A homicide? You're not saying because—"

"No, ma'am, he's just a witness."

"Oh," she said, "Okay . . . but *has* he become a criminal? Because that would be tragic."

"How so?"

"The mistreatment he got turning him bad."

"Juvenile detention and the foster system?"

"Yes, but even before that," said Cora Brown. "That mother of his. So much of life is pure damn luck, isn't it? Poor Eddie never had much. If you want to know my opinion, he got railroaded from the get-go. That boy he pushed was the son of a rich rancher. The whole family were bullies, used to having their way, no questions asked. They were rough on their migrants, treated them like slaves. Raise a child in that environment, what do you think you're going to get?"

"Are the Chenures still around?"

"Oklahoma, last I heard. Sold out years ago to an agribusiness firm and went into raising Black Angus."

"How many years ago?"

"Right after what happened to Jeff. Sandy—the mother—was never the same."

"Rich family," I said. "Eddie, on the other hand—"

"Lived in a trailer with a lunatic lush of a mother. What happened that day was one of those schoolyard things, happens all the time." Pause. "Not that children die from schoolyard things. That *was* tragic. Jeff was a mean boy, but he was still a child. He must've had something wrong with his heart to pass out like that."

"Eddie didn't shove him that hard."

"Nope. That didn't stop him from going into juvenile lockup and being forgotten until he got liberated."

"By who?"

"You said you read the articles, I figured you meant all of them."

I read off the dates of the three pieces.

"No, there's more, I did a follow-up piece a year later."

"Follow-up on what?"

"Eddie's redemption. A public defender from L.A. got interested in the case, what was her name . . . Deborah something . . . hold on, let me get on the computer, my grandson's one of those technical geniuses, his science project was scanning and cataloging fifty years' worth of our issues for an online base, going back to when my dad was the publish . . . okay, here it is. Debora with no 'h' Wallenburg." She spelled the surname. "Give me your e-mail and I'll send it to you."

"Thanks."

"Pleasure. I do hope Eddie hasn't turned bad."

When Milo returned, I waved the attachment I'd printed. "Here's the part Fox left out. A PD was handling the appeal of another ward at the youth camp and one of the counselors told her about a kid who was being brutalized, had received several concussions."

"Huck's neurological symptoms."

"Quite likely. The guard said Eddie didn't belong there in the first place. The lawyer—Debora Wallenburg—looked into Eddie's conviction, agreed, and filed an emergency writ. A month later, Eddie was released and the charges were expunged, he got sent to foster care because his mother was unfit. I looked Wallenburg up on the bar association website and she's private now, practices in Santa Monica."

"Do-gooder lawyer actually does some good," he said.

"Maybe Fox never found the follow-up. Or he did and chose to withhold. What kind of guy is he?"

"Don't know him that well. He worked Wilshire Division for a while, had a rep as a hotshot, smart, ambitious. He transferred to West L.A. maybe . . . four or so years ago, but quit soon after."

"Quit or asked to leave?"

"I heard quit."

"Not much family resemblance to Reed," I said. "And I'm not talking about race."

"Tortoise and hare," he said. "No business like sib business. Fox sure loved goading ol' Moe. And Reed responded exactly like he was supposed to."

"Showing up Reed was a side benefit for Fox. Now he can go back to his client and say mission accomplished."

"Someone's paying to get us focused on Huck."

I said, "Paying well. Fox wears custom-made duds and a ten-thousand-dollar watch."

"Maybe someone in the Vander household knows we were sniffing around the manse and wants to make sure we look in a certain direction."

"Huck comes across odd, so he'd be a natural. On the other hand he really could be your guy. The first thing Cora Brown asked was whether poor little Eddie had become a criminal. Because of what he went through."

Shoving black hair off his brow, he read the articles. "Railroaded and vindicated, but he got stuck in the same place as serious delinquents and had his brains scrambled."

"Toss in maternal deprivation and drifting around the foster system and all kinds of things can happen."

"He stays under the radar until three years ago . . . yeah, that adds up to what you guys call high risk for deviant behavior."

"What do you call it?"

"A lead."

CHAPTER

12

The press conference aired on the eleven o'clock news.

Milo stood by woodenly as D.C. Weinberg made love to the cameras during a steely-eyed request for public participation.

The public facts were thin: Selena Bass and three unidentified bodies in the Bird Marsh, no mention of amputated hands. All four network affiliates topped off fifteen seconds of public-interest sop with rehashed coverage of the progressive billionaires' attempt to buy the land followed by stock footage of egrets, herons, and ducks.

Milo knew what was going to happen, and he pulled Moe Reed back from the trip to San Diego. The two of them split the phone chores. By one a.m. sixty-three tips had come in. The next half hour earned five more. By three a.m., every call but one naming Sheralyn Dawkins's "main man" had been classified as worthless.

Reed's request for surveillance on Travis Huck had been sent to Pacific Patrol. No answer, so far. He said, "Guess we should start with this guy, Duchesne."

"Pimp in the morning," said Milo. "Something to wake up for."

Joe Otto Duchesne rejected the job description.

"Think of me as a human resources manager."

Duchesne's stats put him at forty-three as of March. Emaciated, gray-skinned, white-haired, and gap-toothed, he looked old enough to be his own father. Vice said he worked four or five women along the LAX stroll, had high turnover.

Duchesne sat comfortably in the interview chair. Surprisingly articulate. Surprisingly shabby clothes. His record was a mundane twenty-year paean to heroin addiction, though he claimed "seven months of utter sobriety." Despite a hot morning, his shirt cuffs were buttoned at the wrist.

He'd come in voluntarily and Milo gave him plenty of space, pushing the table into a corner, keeping the whole thing low-key. Moe Reed and I watched on closed circuit from an adjoining room. The young detective followed every word, like a paid attendee at a get-rich seminar.

It was Reed who'd found Duchesne after six hours of grunt work: questioning local patrol, hookers working the periphery of the airport, other low-grade pimps loitering near hourly rate motels.

It was one of the women who remembered Sheralyn Dawkins and confirmed that the missing woman had worked for "that skinny white boy, Joe Otto, you gonna find him on Centinela."

Reed showed her a San Diego mug shot.

"Yeah, Sheri, the limp," she said. "Good for business."

"The limp?"

"There's guys be liking it," said the hooker. "Maybe I should get myself a dee-fect."

Duchesne was open about his "new business plan."

"Lately I've been using Craigslist to set up appointments."

Milo said, "Being business-like I'm sure you keep all the e-mails and phone numbers?"

Duchesne flashed ragged canines and black gaps. "Like I said, lately, just a few weeks."

"How do you fill vacant slots?"

Hesitation. "I supplement the old-fashioned way."

Milo said, "Sidewalk displays."

Duchesne fingered an empty tooth socket. "I like to think of it as real-time marketing." On top of his drug arrests, he'd been busted five times for procuring, considered jail time and fines "corporate overhead."

Milo said, "Joys of the business world."

"Got a degree in business administration, Lieutenant. University of Utah, graduated twenty-one years ago and worked for IBM, and that's the truth. Call them to verify."

"I believe you, Joe Otto. Tell me about Sheralyn."

"You really think it's her?"

"Can't be sure, but she fits the body we found."

Duchesne nodded. "The leg. I met her last winter—February, I think. Maybe January—no, February. She just got into town, was hanging around, cold, lonely. I took her in 'cause no one else did."

"Why not?"

"The leg situation. Poor thing had trouble being on her feet for stretches of time, cut down on her productivity. I got her all kinds of different shoes. Insoles, inserts, gel pads, you name it. Nothing really helped, but she wouldn't give up. Hard worker, nice girl."

"You liked her."

"Nice girl," Duchesne repeated. "Not the sharpest scimitar in the scabbard, but she had . . . personal warmth. I took her in to be kind, but the leg ended up working out okay."

"How so?"

"A certain consumer segment was attracted to it."

"Guys who like limps," said Milo.

"Guys who like vulnerability."

"Anyone ever take advantage of her vulnerability, Joe Otto?"

"No, sir," said Duchesne. "That's what *I'm* here for." Puffing a sunken chest and curling a scrawny fist, the embodiment of pretentiousness.

Watching the screen, Moe Reed shook his head.

Milo said, "No one ever got rough with her, Joe Otto?"

"Never."

"You're sure of that."

"Lieutenant, she only worked for me a month and it was a smooth month."

"What did she tell you about herself?"

"Just up from Oceanside. Military maneuvers, *heh heh.* Military police decided to crack down on fun, made her situation tense. Doesn't seem fair, right? We send those young boys over to fight for our liberties and they can't even enjoy a few moments of shore leave?"

"So she came up to L.A."

"Greener pastures," said Duchesne.

"She talk much about her life in Oceanside?"

"She said she had a kid and her mother was taking care of it."

"In Oceanside?"

"She didn't specify. Didn't say if it was a boy or a girl and I didn't pry." Duchesne's runny eyes tightened. "Keeping it business-like, you know?"

Milo nodded. "Give me something to work with, Joe Otto."

"That's it—oh, yeah, she said she'd been married to a navy man but he aban-doned her early on. Can't tell you if any of it's true, but I don't see the point of lying about details like that." Duchesne wiggled a loose canine. "Lieutenant, if it's her you found, I'm feeling wistful. Here I was think-ing she abandoned me. I should've known she wouldn't."

"She just up and left?"

"Here one day, gone the next," said Duchesne. "Last time I saw her, she was happy. I come back and she's gone, her stuff's gone, no note, no forwarding." Frown. "Truth be told, I was baffled."

"Why wouldn't she abandon you?"

"Because I treated her better than any-one she'd ever known. Still . . ."

"What?" said Milo.

"With girls, you can never tell. Could I trouble you for a Coke?"

"Sure."

Moe Reed got up. Moments later, he was back in the side room and Duchesne was guzzling from a twelve-ounce can.

"Joe Otto, what *do* you think drew Sheralyn away from you?"

"That's what *I* kept asking, Lieutenant. Maybe something to do with her kid, her mother. But I didn't have any numbers to follow up on."

"Could be a better gig came along."

Duchesne's mouth shut tight.

"That possible, Joe Otto?"

"Better like what?"

"You tell me."

"I'm a fair man and she was happy."

Milo watched him drink soda.

Duchesne put the can down, belched. "I took her in when no one else did."

"Do you have any idea who'd want to hurt her?"

"I'm sure there's *plenty* of people who'd want to hurt her. The world being what it is. Can I specify? Unfortunately not. When

she worked for me there were no problems."

"She have any regulars?"

Slow head shake. "Those take time to
cultivate. Truth be told, she worked for me
maybe . . . twenty nights."

"During that time where'd she live?"

"With me."

"Where's that?"

"Various places," said Duchesne. "I prefer not to be tied down."

"Motels."

"And such."

Milo pressed him for names. Duchesne
hesitated, ran off a few, asked for another
Coke. After he'd drained it, Milo slid a
six-pack photo display across the table.
Half a dozen shaved-head white men arranged in two rows, Travis Huck in the
bottom right-hand position.

"One of these guys did it?" said Duchesne.

"Recognize any of them?"

Duchesne studied the images, one by
one. Spending the same glassy-eyed ten
seconds on each. Shaking his head.
"Sorry."

"Do you recall any other cueballs on Sheralyn's customer list?"

"Cueballs." Duchesne was amused. "Nope, sorry again."

"Joe Otto," said Milo. "You liked her, you were the one took her in. Now someone's done her up really badly."

"I know, I know . . . truth be told, Sheralyn's professional activity was always after dark and I had other employees operating simultaneously."

"You never saw her johns."

"Not . . . always," said Duchesne. "There was a problem, I'd get beeped." He pushed out his thorax again. "And there was none."

His left leg began bouncing. Stopped.

Milo said, "Joe Otto, something's at the back of your mind right now. Maybe something to do with a bald guy?"

Duchesne's eyes sparked with alarm. "You're a psychic, friend?"

"I know when someone's troubled."

"Why would I be troubled?"

"Because you cared about Sheralyn, know she wouldn't just leave you, meaning someone snatched her and maybe that same person left her lying around like trash."

Duchesne's spider fingers squeezed the empty can, tried to crush it, ended up inflicting a minor dent. He placed it to the side, worked the tooth socket some more.

"Joe Otto?"

"There was a guy. But not with Sheralyn, before Sheralyn."

"Another girl."

Nod. "I got beeped because he got freaky. Like you said, cueball, she's all breathing hard and telling me to look out for a skinhead. Time I got to the room, he was gone."

"This girl get hurt?"

"Minor bruise. She was a big girl, could take care of herself."

"What was the guy's freak, Joe Otto?"

"Wanted to tie her up, we get that all the time, say no. When she said no, this one pulled a knife. Not a normal knife, looked like a medical thing. That's what *she* called it."

"A scalpel."

"He tried to shake her up by showing how it could slice paper." Miming an upward thrust.

"She got bruised but not cut?" said Milo.

"Thank God," said Duchesne. "She got that weird feeling, went to run out of the room. He went after her, made a reach for her. Hit her with the hand, thank God times ten not the knife. Caught her here." Rubbing his temple. "Got her with his knuckles, you could see the marks, the next day she was all swollen. Dark, big dark bruise. Even on *her* skin you could see it."

"Dark girl," said Milo.

"Big beautiful sister."

"Name?"

"We called her Big Laura."

"DMV called her . . ."

"Don't know," said Duchesne. "Big Laura was all we needed."

"Tall."

"And big. Two tons of fun."

"Where can I find her?"

Long pause. "Don't know, Lieutenant."

"Another fly-by-night, Joe Otto?"

Duchesne pressed his palms together piously. "These people have unstable lives."

Milo questioned him through a third Coke and two Hershey bars, inquired about white prostitutes of advanced age.

Duchesne said, "Not on my pay*roll,* I'm all about *soul.* Can I go?"

"Sure, thanks. Stay in touch if you learn something."

"Believe it, Lieutenant. This kind of thing isn't good for business."

Moe Reed and I entered the vacated interview room.

"Big girl named Laura," said Milo.

Reed said, "Fits Jane Number Two. Interesting that two victims were in Duchesne's stable."

"You smell something on him?"

Reed thought. "Hard to say. He didn't have to come in, let alone tell us anything. Unless you think he's cagey enough to be playing us."

I said, "Maybe someone smelled his weakness. Figured out whose girls could be exploited."

"Beta dog," said Milo. "Makes sense. My guess is Duchesne told us what he knows. You did good finding him, Moses. Time to get back to the stroll and dig some more. I'll take on finding Sheralyn's next of kin. In a perfect world, one of us will learn something that turned her into a victim. At the least, we can get a cheek scrape from her mom or her kid, match it to the bones. Not that I'm expecting Jane One to be anyone other *than* her."

"What about Big Laura?"

"I'll see what the moniker pulls up. In terms of Jane Three, she's probably been dead the longest and memories on the street are short. But maybe an older white woman will stand out in someone's mind."

"If she's from the area, we could have a bad guy concentrating geographically for a while," said Reed. "Then he wants a new level of thrill and shifts from pros to Selena. Her apartment's not that far from the airport. Or the marsh, for that matter."

I said, "Psychosocially, Selena's a big leap from the others. There could be transitional victims."

"Such as?" said Milo.

"Nonprostitutes perceived as lower class."

"Working his way up the social ladder."

Reed said, "The dog didn't find anything else in the marsh, but the K-9 search was limited to the east bank."

"Cheerful thought," said Milo. "With a normal dump we could get warrants, no problem, bring in the backhoe. Instead, we're stuck with hallowed ground."

I said, "Maybe the killer sees it that way, too."

As Milo extracted a cigarillo from his pocket, Reed's pale eyebrows rose. "Don't worry, kiddo, I'll keep your air clean . . . in terms of going through the hassle of getting permission to dig up other areas of the marsh, let's clear up the bodies we already have first. Time to hit the streets."

As we headed for the door, Moe Reed said, "Too bad Duchesne didn't recognize Huck."

"Idiot claims he never sees the johns unless there's a problem, and I believe him," said Milo. "He wasn't much use to Big Laura when she did get into trouble with that skinhead. Some business model."

"Bald man with a scalpel," said Reed. "You'd need more than that to cut off a hand, right, Doctor?"

I said, "Wrong kind of doctor, but yes. A limb saw would work fine."

"Any kind of saw, sharp enough," said Milo. "Goddamn Chinese cleaver would do it if he's strong and coordinated."

Reed said, "Maybe we're talking about someone with medical training."

"Twenty years ago," said Milo, "I'd be looking that way. Nowadays, the Internet, anyone can get anything anytime."

"Freedom," said Reed.

"Nothing else worth living for, kiddo, but it's a tricky concept." Unwrapping the cigar, he jammed it into the side of his mouth. "Gonna light up, kid. Fair warning."

We walked Reed outside, crossed the street to the staff lot. His drive was a shiny black Camaro.

Milo said, "That's no clunker."

"Pardon?"

"What your brother said."

"He thinks he knows everything," said Reed. He got in, revved loud, drove off, tires squealing.

CHAPTER

13

Milo and I walked south on Butler Avenue. The cold glare of government architecture gave way to postwar bungalows and apartment buildings and the sky grew bluer, as if in sympathy.

He said, "Any new thoughts about Huck? Or anything else?"

"Now we've got two bald-guy sightings—the date Luz Ramos saw with Selena, along with Mr. Scalpel—so I like him a whole lot better. But at this point, short of watching him, I don't see what you can do."

"Too early to invite him for a chat?" he said.

"With crimes this calculated, he's likely to lawyer up. I'd want ammunition before I shoot."

Half a block later, he said: "That Camaro that Reed just peeled out in was either borrowed or a rental. AutoTrack says his drive of record *is* indeed a clunker. 'Seventy-nine Dodge Colt hatchback, bought used ten years ago. Before that, he sported around in a '73 Datsun wagon."

"Doing deep background on the staff?" I said.

"Perish the thought." Since the arrest of a corrupt private eye and several cops for trafficking in official data, the rules forbade traces on anyone but suspects.

I said, "What got you curious about Reed's wheels?"

"It seemed to be an issue between him and Fox."

"One of many."

"Exactly. Last thing I need is personal drama impinging on the investigation." Small smile. "Such as it is."

"What does Fox drive?"

"Brand-new Porsche C4S."

"Tortoise and hare," I said.

He lit up, blew smoke rings at the heavens. Aiming for casual but cherries in his jaw said he was faking.

I said, "Fox and Reed bother you."

"I asked around. Fox's dad was a Southwest patrolman named Darius Fox, murdered on the job thirty years ago. Before my time but I know the case. Everyone knows it because it's used during training. As in What Can Go Wrong."

I said, "Domestic call or traffic stop?"

He removed the cigar. "You read tea leaves, too?"

"Just playing the odds."

"Routine early-morning stop, Caddy with a broken taillight, Thirty-seventh just west of Hoover. Car came up stolen, but not before Darius and his partner made a bonehead goof. Instead of running the tags first, the partner did it while Darius went over to check out the driver. We're talking way before MDTs, everything was called in over the radio, records weren't computerized, it could take time. All the more reason to be careful."

"Rookies?" I said.

"On the contrary, Darius had eight years, the partner six, nearly all of it worked with Fox. Maybe that was part of it—comfortable marriage, taking too much for granted. It was close to shift's end, maybe they were eager to sign out, got sloppy. Whatever the reason, Darius walks up to the Caddy, raps the window, down it comes, a gun sticks out and . . ." Cupping his hands, he clapped three times.

The noise assaulted the afternoon. An old woman tending her flowers looked over. Milo's grin caused her to grip her pruning shears as we walked on.

"Direct hit, point-blank," he said. "Darius left a widow and a tyke. Aaron was three. The partner called in the Officer Down, got behind his door, started shooting. He managed to score a hit on the Caddy's rear but couldn't prevent it from driving off. He ran over to help Darius but Darius was gone before he hit the ground. Big city-wide sweep for the car, everyone check-ing out hospitals, doctors, on the off chance the partner wounded someone. Nada, and two weeks later the Caddy shows up in a junkyard near the Wilming-ton docks. Windows busted out, seats ripped, bumpers removed, no prints, no nothing. Darius got a bagpipe funeral and the partner got investigated, reprimanded, and demoted. Soon after, he quit the force. What I hear is he worked construction for a while, got injured, lived off disability for five more years then died of liver disease."

"Driven to drink?"

"Or maybe he had a problem before, don't know, Alex." Inhaling deeply, he burned through half an inch of cigar. "Seven months after Darius Fox's funeral, partner marries the widow in Vegas. Two months after that, she gives birth to a kid."

He dropped the cigar, ground it into the sidewalk. Picked it up and carried it at his side. "Figure out the punch line, Dr. Wizard?"

"Partner was Moe Reed's daddy."

"Guy named John 'Jack' Reed. People do say he tried hard to be a good father to both boys."

I said, "Few years later, he's gone, too."

"And Momma marries twice again. She just buried number four."

"Talk about baggage."

"A planeload, amigo. Let's hope it doesn't ground us."

Back in his office, he found half a dozen new tip messages, began the callbacks, sat up straight when he connected to the fifth.

He said, "That's great, ma'am, really appreciate your taking the time, now if you'd be so kind as to give me your—"

Dial tone.

He held the phone at arm's length. "Must be my breath."

Pressing redial, he got no ring. Tried again, same result.

I said, "Someone worth listening to."

"Someone refusing to identify herself wanting me to know that one of the Jane Does in the marsh might be someone named Lurlene Chenoweth aka Big Laura."

He traced the caller's number, dead-ended at a prepaid cell.

I said, "A female tipster with a prepaid might mean a pro from the area. Word travels fast, the girls know Duchesne visited, they're making associations."

Typing in Lurlene Chenoweth's name brought up a scowling, ebony moon-face crowned by a cumulus of orange hair. Thirty-three years old, five nine, two seventy, no scars or tattoos. Four solicitation arrests, one cocaine possession, two drunk and disorderlies, three misdemeanor batteries, all bar fights pled down.

He said, "Big and scrappy."

"She managed to avoid Skinhead's knife because she moved to the door quickly. Maybe something about him tipped her off early in the encounter and she was careful."

"An obvious weirdo? Too bad he found her later." Swinging his feet onto the desk, he loosed the laces of his desert boots, flexed his toes. "Two of Duchesne's girls die. What if that boils down to some stupid turf war between pimps and Skinhead was just hired help?"

"If that was it," I said, "why's Duchesne still operating? He's not exactly an imposing figure. And how would Selena fit in?"

"Three street girls and a piano teacher. You're making a point."

"A piano teacher who played swinger parties."

"Like you said, rich folk moving from stale to fresh."

"Rich folk with secrets could explain hiring Travis Huck."

"He's also into the scene?"

"Or just a guy with a past."

"Tormented soul finally finds a legit job—with an ocean view. Yeah, that could inspire loyalty. 'Estate Manager' is rich-folk talk for gopher, right? Huck's basically a procurer, gets sent out to bring back the goodies."

I said, "Flowers, catering, victim of the evening."

His laughter was metallic. "Joe Otto has no idea how small-time he is."

Big Laura's mother lived in a beautifully kept house in the Crenshaw District. Tall, like her daughter, Beatrix Chenoweth was as skinny as a walking stick.

She wore a mint-green blouse, wide-legged black trousers, and ballet slippers. Her living room was Delft blue trimmed in white, set up with floral couches and no-nonsense chairs and hung with prints of impressionist masterpieces.

Her reaction to our presence was dry-eyed resignation.

"I knew it . . ."

"Ma'am, we can't be sure—"

"*I'm* sure, Lieutenant. How many girls are that size? And have taken that path?"

Milo didn't answer.

Beatrix Chenoweth said, "I've got four daughters. Two are schoolteachers like myself and the baby's a flight attendant for Southwest. Lurlene was the third. She took every bit of fight out of me."

"Ma'am," said Milo. "I'm not here to tell you something definitely happened to Lurlene and I really hope it didn't. But if you don't mind giving me a cheek scraping we can find out—"

"Oh, something happened, all right, Lieutenant. I've been dreading this moment for an entire year. Because that's how long it's been since I heard from Lurlene. And no matter what happened, she always called. *Always.* It would start off like a genuine conversation. 'How're you doing, Mommy.' But by the end it was always the same. She needed money. Money was the reason she *went* that way in the first place. More accurately, something that *cost* a lot of money."

Her voice had climbed but her face was impassive. "It started in high school,

Lieutenant. Someone gave her amphet-amines to lose weight. It didn't work, she never lost a pound. But that didn't stop her from getting addicted and that was the be-ginning of the end."

"I'm sorry, ma'am."

"Lurlene was my only heavy one. Took after her father. The rest of us girls never had problems in that area. In fact my sec-ond did some fashion modeling."

I said, "Must've been hard for Lurlene."

Her head dropped, as if suddenly too heavy. "Everything was hard for Lurlene. She was the smartest of the four, but the weight ruined her life. Being ridiculed."

She began crying silently. Milo found his stash of tissues and gave her one.

"Thank you . . . I didn't realize until later what a burden it was for her. All those ar-guments over too much butter on the bread . . . she was an eleven-pound baby. None of my others topped eight."

Milo said, "She started with amphet-amines."

"Started, yes," said Beatrix Chenoweth. "In terms of what else she got into, I don't know, you can probably tell me more than I can tell you."

Milo didn't answer.

"I want to know, Lieutenant."

"From what I can tell from her arrests, cocaine and alcohol were issues, ma'am."

"Alcohol, yes, I knew that. Lurlene got arrested once for being drunk."

Twice; Milo didn't correct her. "Did she get in contact with you after she got arrested?"

"You mean to help her with bail? No, she told me afterward."

"Someone else paid her bail."

"She said she'd paid it herself, Lieutenant. That was the point of the call. Bragging. I asked her how she got the money and she laughed and we got into a . . . discussion. I suppose I knew how she was supporting herself. I suppose I chose to pretend I didn't."

She cleared her throat.

Milo said, "Can I get you some water, ma'am?"

"No, thank you." Touching her neck. "It's not thirst that's caught in here."

"Ma'am, what can you tell us about Lurlene's friends?"

"Not a thing," said Beatrix Chenoweth. "She didn't expose me to her personal life and as I said, I didn't want to know. Does that sound uncaring, Lieutenant?"

"Of course not—"

"It wasn't. It was . . . an adaptation. I've got three other daughters and five grand-children who need my attention. I can't . . . couldn't . . ." Her head bowed again. "Every single counselor we spoke to said Lurlene would have to bear the consequences of her own actions."

I said, "Were there a lot of counselors?"

"Oh, yes. First from the schools. Then we went to a clinic our HMO recommended. Nice Indian man. Dr. Singh. He said the exact same thing. Lurlene had to want to change. He suggested Horace and I have a few sessions, to learn how to cope. We did. It was helpful. Then he died. Horace, I mean. A stroke. A month later, when I tried to contact Dr. Singh, he'd moved back to India." Frowning. "Apparently, he was some sort of intern."

Milo said, "Is there anything you can tell us about who Lurlene associated with?"

"Not since she took *that* path."

"How old was she when she—"

"Sixteen. She dropped out of school,

ran away, called when she needed
money . . . she was a fighter, Lieutenant.
You'd think she could've fought the damn
drugs."

"It can be really hard, ma'am."

"I know, I know." Beatrix Chenoweth's
long, bony fingers gathered black trouser
fabric. "When I say fighter, I mean it literally, Lieutenant. Lurlene bucked authority
for the *sake* of it. It got so her father had to
leave the house to cool off. One time she
hit her baby sister so hard, Charmayne's
head just about spun around and she had
pain for days. It got to the point where—God
help me for saying this—we were thankful
Lurlene stopped coming by."

"I can understand that, ma'am."

"Now someone hurt *her.*" She stood,
smoothed her pants. "I'm going to go off
by myself for a while and then I'll call
Lurlene's sisters and they'll have to figure
out what to say to their children. That's
their responsibility, all I want to do is have
fun with my grandkids . . . would you
please see yourselves out?"

CHAPTER

14

So much for Duchesne as a factor," said Moe Reed as we waited for the woman to return from the bathroom.

He and Milo and I sat in an orange plastic booth in a chicken-and-pancakes joint on Aviation near Century. The restaurant smelled of burnt feathers and hot fat. Jumbo-jet thunder shook the room at random intervals, thrumming cloudy glass and Z-Brick and threatening to shake asbestos loose from the goose-bump ceiling.

Three coffee cups in front of us, untouched brown surfaces skimmed with rainbow oil slick. The woman had ordered extra-sweet, extra-crisp thighs and wings, a double plate of cinnamon waffles, and a jumbo orange soda. She'd finished one plate of chicken, asked for another, made her way through most of the breading before needing "a woman break."

Her name was Sondra Cindy Jackson and she called herself Sin. Twenty-three-year-old black female, pretty face, wounded eyes, huge blue talon-nails, half of them inlaid with rhinestones. Her teeth were straight but her left incisor was a gold cap. A complex cornrow tested the boundaries of string theory.

She was the eighteenth prostitute Moe Reed had talked to in two days of canvassing the airport hot zone, and the first who was sure she knew the identity of Jane Doe Three.

Built like a dancer, her appetite was astonishing. So far she'd flirted, shoveled food down her gullet, played coy.

Reed was antsy. Milo emitted an odd Buddhic calm.

Over the same forty-eight hours, he'd contended with a continuing trickle of worthless tips, learned nothing more about Big Laura Chenoweth, failed to locate

Sheralyn Dawkins's family anywhere in San Diego, Orange, or L.A. County. That kind of fun often erodes his patience but sometimes it works the other way.

Reed eyed the ladies' room. Our booth was positioned so Sin couldn't leave without passing directly in front of us.

"When she gets back, I'll press her."

Milo said, "Sure. Or you can let it play out a bit longer."

The young detective had switched from jacket and tie to a gray polo shirt bisected by a wide red stripe, fresh blue jeans, snowy white Nikes. His eyes were clear, his ruddy face shaved glossy. Side-of-beef pectorals and massive shoulders strained the shirt.

Aiming to blend in, but he might as well have worn the uniform.

Sondra Cindy Jackson had known what he was right away. Sixty dollars and the promise of dinner had induced her to get into the Camaro.

Milo said, "Be sure to put in for reimbursement."

Reed said, "Eventually."

"I'm back!" came the cheery announcement.

Sin's pink velvet bra and white lace hot pants showed off her skin tone. Slender girl except for breasts enhanced to cartoon proportions. Somehow, she'd found the money.

"Welcome back," said Milo. "Bon appétit."

She flashed a gold smile, slid into the booth, got to work on the second plate of chicken.

Four swallows later, she said, "Y'all are so quiet."

"Waiting for you," said Reed.

"To do what?" Batting her lashes.

Reed blinked.

Milo said, "To take the lead."

"About . . . oh, yeah, Mantooth."

Reed said, "Mantooth?"

"That's her name, 'Tective Reed."

"Mantooth."

"Yup."

Reed opened his pad. "That a first name?"

"Last name," said Sin. "Dolores Mantooth but we jes' called her Mantooth because it was a good one for her." Wink wink.

Reed stared at her.

"Tooth. Chew. Like that song?" said Sin.

"We chewin' on it . . . what? Y'all don't listen to the blues?"

Milo said, "Musta missed that one."

"'We chewin' on it all day long.'"

I said, "Bonnie Raitt."

"Yeah," said Sin. "Nice dirty song. That
was Mantooth. She had a mouth."

Reed said, "Mouth as in . . ."

Sin said, "Huh?"

Milo said, "Who was her pimp?"

"Jerome."

"Jerome who?"

"Jerome Jerome," said Sin. "I'm not
kidding, same first name and last name.
I'm not claiming that's what his momma
called him but that's what he was called.
Jerome Jerome. Don't go asking for him.
Dead."

"How'd he get dead?"

"O.D." Lifting a wing, she held it daintily
between two fingers, nibbled voraciously
to the bone.

"When?" said Reed.

Shrug. "I just heard he was dead."

"From an O.D."

"What else?"

"You assumed he O.D.'d."

Sin's look was full of pity. "'Tective Reed,

'Tective Reed. Jerome was bagging all day, then he got dead. That sound to you like old age?"

Milo said, "Dolores never worked for Joe Otto Duchesne."

"No way. Joe Otto works black, never looks back."

"Tell us about Dolores."

Sin waved a chicken bone. "Old. White. Ugly."

"When's the last time you saw her?"

"Hmm . . . a year ago?"

"How old is old?"

"A hundred," said Sin, laughing. "Maybe a hundred fifty, she looked real *used*."

Peach-flavored ice cream disappeared between her lips. No new information made the reverse trip. Reed gave her his card and she looked at it as if it were an exotic insect.

After she left the restaurant, we walked to the parking lot and watched her sway south on Aviation. Reed's Camaro had no computer so Milo had brought a newer Chevy sedan from the staff lot that was fully equipped.

No Dolores or Delores Mantooth in the

system. A bit of LAPD Scrabble finally pulled up her I.D.

DeMaura Jean Montouthe. Blond and green, five five, one forty, DOB fifty-one years ago, thirty years of low-level arrests.

No mention of tooth anomalies but LAPD wasn't interested in the finer points of dentition.

Milo called Vice and had the name of her pimp within seconds.

Jerome Lamar McReynolds. The crypt confirmed his death fourteen months ago. Heroin-cocaine overdose, COD determination based on track marks and blood work, no autopsy.

"Guy speedballs," said Milo, "DeMaura's freelancing, vulnerable. Bad guy senses it, moves in."

"Perfect for some rich predators," said Reed, massaging a swelling biceps.

"The key," said Milo, "is to turn women into prey."

CHAPTER
15

Three days of not-so-happy hunting.

Milo and Reed's canvass of the airport stroll revealed no other prostitutes who'd encountered a knife-wielding, bald-headed john. A Vice detective named Diane Salazar had arrested DeMaura Montouthe several times and thought her family was from Alabama but wasn't sure. No one with the surname had come up in that state's tax rolls.

"You wouldn't happen to know her dentist, Diane."

"You bet, Milo. Her hairdresser and her personal trainer, too."

"What was she like?"

"Nice girl, not too bright, never fussed when we snagged her on decoy runs. Years ago, she was actually kind of pretty."

"Only mug shot I've seen is two years old."

"You know," said Salazar. "The usual."

No one had heard anything about De-Maura, Sheralyn Dawkins, or Big Laura Chenoweth working private parties.

"They'da done it, they'da bragged," said one pimp. "Big L especially, she like to challenge you, give you the eye. You not agreeing with her, she got herself a reason to go off on you."

"That happened to you?" said Reed.

"What?"

"Confrontation with Big Laura."

"Hell, no. That happened to me, she'da hurt."

"She did get hurt."

"Whatever. Got to go."

A hooker named Charvay, young, still lithe and unscarred and thinking she had a lifetime ahead of her, caressed her breasts and laughed and voiced the prevalent sentiment: "Them? With rich folk?

What kind of Westside pap*aratz* par-*tey*
would be wanting *that* old skin?"

During the ride back to the office, Milo was
sullen.

Maybe sensing it, Moe Reed drove fast.
"Could be the Vanders have nothing to do
with it and it's all about Huck being a solo
psycho."

Surveillance on the estate manager
had stalled. The top-of-the-hill, dead-end
placement of the Vander estate limited
vantage points on Calle Maritimo. The
watch from two blocks down had produced nothing: Huck never left the
house.

Milo decided to hold observation to after dark, told Reed they'd split the shift.

Reed said, "No prob doing all of it, Loo.
I really want to check this guy out."

"We go that way, kiddo, I'll be partner-
ing with the living dead."

"Trust me," said Reed. "With all due respect."

"You don't believe in sleep?"

"Don't need much. I'll move around, no
one'll spot me. I'm good at fading into the
background."

"Why's that?" said Milo.

"Second kid."

Most of Huck's adult life was a blank space and one person who might be able to fill in the details was Debora Wallenburg, the lawyer who'd sprung him out of juvey jail. No sense suggesting that; attorney–client privilege meant a stone wall, at best.

At worst, she'd alert Huck and if he was dirty, he'd split.

With no need for my services, I took on a custody consult that didn't look too fierce, had time for leisurely walks with Blanche, pleasant dinners with Robin.

In the midst of that, Emily Green-Bass phoned me from Long Island.

"I got your number from the state psychology board, Doctor. Hope you don't mind."

"Not at all. What can I do for you?"

"The reason I'm calling you and not Lieutenant Sturgis is—it's not really about Selena's case . . ." Her voice broke. "Can't believe I'm using that word."

I waited.

She said, "I've already spoken with Lieutenant Sturgis, I know there's been no progress. The reason I'm calling *you* . . . actually, I don't *know* why I'm calling you . . . I guess I feel . . . sorry for wasting your time, Doctor."

"You're not."

She said, "You're just saying that because . . . sorry, I don't know *what* I'm doing."

"You've gone through something most people can't come close to comprehending."

Dead air; when she finally spoke, her voice was low and hoarse. "I guess I—guess what I'm after . . . Dr. Delaware, I keep thinking about that meeting. At the station. My boys . . . we must've seemed like one big crazy dysfunctional family. That's not how it really is."

I said, "What happened was one hundred percent normal."

"Was it?"

"Yes."

"You've seen other people in my . . . situation."

"Lots of people. There's no road map."

Long pause. "Thank you. I guess what I want you to see was that we're really pretty normal—typical people—now that I'm out with that, it sounds ludicrous. Why would I need to impress you?"

"You're trying to get some control."

"Which is impossible."

"Still," I said, "sometimes it's good to try. What I saw in your sons was attachment and love. For you and Selena."

Sobs broke like thunder, rattling the phone's tinny speaker. I waited as the sound diminished.

She said, "I really don't know what I could've done differently. With Selena, I mean. Maybe if Dan would've lived. He was such a good father. He got a brain tumor. Nothing he did caused it, he didn't smoke, he didn't drink, he didn't—it just happened, the doctors said it's just one of those things that just *happens.* I guess I should've explained it to Selena. She was so young, I thought . . ." Sucking inhalation. "*She* lost her father and *I* lost the love of my life. After that, everything kind of fell apart."

"I'm so sorry you've had to go through that."

Silence.

"Ms. Green-Bass, what happened to Selena wasn't connected to losing her father." Maybe a lie, but who cared?

"What was it, then?"

"Another of those things you can't explain."

"But if she hadn't moved to L.A. . . ."

Harsh laughter. "If *this,* if *that,* if *only, should've, could've, would've*—she cut me off totally."

I said, "One way or the other, children move away. If not geographically, psychologically." Images of my own cross-country ride, at sixteen, flashed in my head.

Long hyphens of desert and railyard and hamburger stands. The shake-awake of city skyline. Prospects of a new life thrilling and terrifying.

"They do," said Emily Green-Bass. "I suppose it's necessary."

"It is. People who stay in one place are often stunted."

"Yes, yes—Selena was doing exactly what she wanted. She always did. Such a strong-willed child. She knew her mind and pursued it. That's why it's so hard to think of her as . . . overpowered. She was a little person with such a big personality, Doctor. A hundred ten pounds, it was easy to forget she was just . . . small." Tears. "She was my *baby,* Doctor."

"I'm so sorry."

"I know you are—you sound like a kind man. If you learn anything, anything at all, you'll call me?"

"Of course."

"Stupid question," she said. "I seem to have a lot of those."

I'd finished the consult, was writing my report when Milo called.

"Up for fine dining?"

Three p.m. "Kind of an off hour."

"Call it a snack. I'm meeting with Reed in thirty, his request."

"What's up?"

"He left the message on my machine, didn't specify. Lad does sound a bit excited."

"I'll be there," I said. "Curry and tandooried whatever?"

"Nope, pizza. The kid needs variety. Also, a place where his brother can't find him."

"Variety" was a barn-like Pizza Palazzo on Venice near Sawtelle. Seating was picnic tables and benches. Off-hour gourmandizing meant a nearly vacant room ripe with memories of stale cheese. The exception was a pair of long-distance truckers whose big rig took up half the parking lot. Extra-large pies for extra-large men.

Blinks and burps voiced by a bank of video games against the far wall broke the silence. Unused machines crying out for attention.

Milo and I arrived at the same time. No sign of the black Camaro in the lot, but Moe Reed was inside, back to blazer and tie, looking ill at ease as he nursed a mug of root beer.

"New wheels, kiddo?" said Milo.

"Pardon?"

"Nothing black, shiny, or Chevy out there."

"Oh," said Reed. "That was a rental. I exchanged it."

"Clunker in the shop?"

Reed colored.

Milo said, "Here's a guess: You've been renting cars so you can tail your brother. Did you at least fill out the forms so you can get reimbursed?"

Reed shook his head.

"Got a trust fund, kiddo?"

"I just don't care about stuff like that."

"Tsk, tsk, Uncle Milo is crestfallen—okay, how long you been following him?"

"Um . . . since that day he dropped in on us. It didn't get in the way of work, Loo, I promise. I used my own time. He expects me to drive garbage, so it wasn't any big challenge, he never noticed the Camaro. But I wanted to make sure so I exchanged it yesterday."

"Upgrade to Ferrari?" said Milo.

"Charcoal Caddy," said Reed. "Smoked windows, just in case. I figured with Huck never going anywhere, maybe I should try to figure out who paid to cast suspicion. Not that I don't think he's our best bet. I just wanted to know who wanted *us* to think that. Maybe they could tell us something else."

He stopped and examined the table's plank top. Fidgeted like a kid who'd just rattled off excuses to an irritated parent.

"Makes sense," said Milo. "Learn anything?"

"Actually, yeah."

Reed had watched Fox take numerous business meetings ("At the Ivy, Grill on the Alley, Jean-Paul, that's his thing"). Running the tags of Fox's dining companions—a sketchy move, at best—had produced the answer.

"New BMW 3 registered to Simone Vander, address on Breakthorne Wood. That's up in the hills, Beverly Hills P.O. The name tracks to a thirty-one-year-old white female, no wants, warrants, or priors, and the physical stats match the woman I saw him with at Geoffrey's."

"In Malibu?"

"Yup."

"Lives in B.H. but dines at the beach," said Milo. "Who is she, another ex-wife?"

"Daughter," said Reed. "I found her birth certificate. Born locally, Cedars-Sinai, father's Simon Vander, mother's Kelly. I looked Kelly up, too. Five-year-old Volvo, Sherman Oaks address with a unit number."

"Daddy and second wife live the high life, first wife gets an apartment."

Reed said, "But the daughter—Simone—has a pretty nice place. Gated, secluded, real woodsy."

"You drove by."

"This morning."

"Simon and Simone," said Milo. "Cute.

What's that, Alex? Bonding, emotional identification?"

I said, "Couple more like that, you score your own couch."

He turned back to Reed. "What kind of pizza do you want? I'm visualizing the XXXL deep-dish, grotesquely stuffed-crust, half-sausage, half-anchovy, half-meatballs, half-moose-head special."

Reed looked dismayed. "I was wasting my time?"

"Not at all, but first we dine. Name your pie, Detective Reed."

"Um . . . plain cheese. Couple of slices."

"Go crazy, kid. I'll have a medium sausage for myself, extra garlic and chili flakes. Go put the order in, then head over to the gum machine, get us some sugarless spearmint. Don't want to risk undue offense to Ms. Simone."

CHAPTER
16

Reed left his Cadillac at the pizza joint and we piled into Milo's unmarked.

Breakthorne Wood was a steep, carelessly paved road above Benedict Canyon. The curves, width, and flavor of an old bridle path; I felt right at home.

One thing Simone Vander shared with her father was a taste for dead ends. Her property was marked by a simple iron gate flanked by used-brick posts. The same masonry faced the shake-roof cottage visible through the slats. Dark-stained pine planks graced the façade where brick hadn't been applied. Diamond-pane windows, a hand-carved oak door, and a witch-on-a-broomstick weather vane added up to neo-rustic adorable.

A tomato-colored 335i convertible was parked in the flagstone motor court. Pine needles littered the car and the ground. Huge Aleppos shadowing the property, darkening most of the roof. Beyond the branches was a patchwork of brighter green and beige: ivy-colored hills.

Reed had been antsy during the ride over. Justifying the surveillance of his brother repeatedly though Milo never challenged him.

"Maybe it'll be nothing, but at least we can find out what she knows about Huck."

"Maybe she once lived at the house. Or she visits—even if she doesn't come out and tell us anything about Huck or parties or whatever, maybe we can still get a feel for whether or not weird stuff went on there."

"At the very least, we'll find out there's nothing to find out and won't have to spin any more wheels. Not that I'm saying there isn't something hinky about

**Huck, I still think there is. Otherwise why
would she pay to dig up dirt on him?"**

Now, facing Simone Vander's gate-call
button, the young detective jammed his
hands in his pockets and chewed his
cheek.

"Go ahead, this is your time to shine,"
said Milo, jabbing air with his finger.

"Anything you want me to concentrate
on?" said Reed.

"Follow your gut," said Milo.

Reed frowned.

"That's a reward, not a punishment, Moses."

Reed pushed the button.

Milo said, "You get good grades, I'll let
you spin the steering wheel. But only when
the car's in the driveway."

A young-sounding female voice said,
"Yes?" Another female voice sang sweetly
in the background.

"Ms. Vander? Detective Reed, L.A. police."

"Is something wrong?"

"We'd like a few minutes of your time,
ma'am. Regarding Travis Huck."

"Oh." The music receded. "Okay, one sec."

Several minutes passed before the carved door opened. The woman in the opening was medium height, pale, stick-thin and leggy, with a gamin face under a layered mass of long black hair. She wore a white-and-pink-striped boat-neck top, white knee-length cargo pants fastened with bows at the patella, backless pink sandals with stilt heels. Gold hoop earrings large enough to be visible across the motor court caught sunlight.

She studied us. Waved.

Moe Reed waved back. She clicked the gate open.

"I'm Simone. What's going on?" Soft, melodic voice, a vibrato that made each word sound tentative. She was one of those people who look better upon close inspection. Porcelain skin, gray-blue capillary mesh at the temples, fine features, graceful posture. Her eyes were brown and round with enormous irises. Dilated pupils implied curiosity. Her brows had been artfully plucked.

An ivory hand cradled the remote module. She smiled and looked younger.

Moe Reed reintroduced himself, identified Milo, then me. Leaving out my title. No
sense complicating matters.

Simone Vander said, "So many people.
I guess it's pretty important."

Before Reed could respond, an engine
growled behind us.

A silver Porsche cabriolet idled behind
the gate. The top was down, revealing
terra-cotta leather. Behind the wheel sat
Aaron Fox, wearing mirrored sunshades,
a beige linen jacket, a black shirt.

"Oh, good," said Simone Vander as she
clicked him in.

Fox got out of his car buttoning his jacket.
Perfectly cut linen pants made the outfit a
suit. Black snakeskin loafers were cut low,
revealing mocha shins.

"P.I. Fox," said Milo.

"Lieutenant Sturgis. In the neighborhood, so I thought I'd drop by."

He headed for Simone Vander. Moe
Reed blocked his way.

Fox said, "Excuse me?"

"Not a good time."

Simone said, "I called Aaron. Right after
you rang in. Boy, you got here fast."

Milo said, "Why'd you call him, ma'am?"

"I don't know—I guess I thought he should be here. He's the one who knows all about Travis."

Reed half turned to face her. Next to his lifter's bulk, she looked like dry twigs. "You paid him to learn."

Simone Vander didn't reply.

Aaron Fox said, "Ms. Vander has a perfect right to hire me to do anything legal. And as she just said, whatever she knows about Mr. Huck, I told her. So why don't we just—"

"We'll do what we need to do," said Reed, shoulders spreading as he tried to enlarge himself. He was wider than Fox but shorter by a couple of inches. Fox stood straight, aiming to widen the disparity.

Simone Vander stared at both of them.

Dominance duel.

Toss-up.

Milo said, "Aaron, we appreciate your loyalty to your client—"

Reed said, "Not to mention billing by the hour—"

"—but right now we need to talk to her alone."

Fox's smooth brown face betrayed no emotion.

Reed said, "*Alone,* Mr. Fox."

Fox's grin was too sudden and wide to imply anything close to cheer. Tugging linen lapels, he shrugged. "I'll stay close, Simone. Call me when you're through."

"Okay—thanks."

Still smiling, Fox clapped his brother on the shoulder, hard enough to echo. Reed's meaty hands rolled tight.

"Always great seeing you, bro."

Climbing back in the Porsche, Fox revved, shifted into gear. Twisted his head clear of the windshield. Gave the thumbs-up, focused on Reed.

"Nice touch, the Caddy."

Simone Vander's living room was cheerful and cozy and overfurnished, with chintz chairs, oak pieces that might've been old, floral prints in white distressed frames. A collection of Japanese dolls filled a hutch that bordered a bright red tile kitchen. Warming our feet was a lavender-and-cream Aubusson rug. The music wafting from a Bang & Olufsen entertainment center was Tori Amos, singing about a black dove.

A Chinese camphor-wood trunk served as a coffee table. Three gilt-framed photos stood on the top, along with flowers and candles.

Two shots were of Simone Vander: straddling a beautiful brown horse, and a close-up that had her holding a coffee cup, backed by the ocean.

The largest photo, positioned dead center, was a formal portrait: a tall, stooped, sixtyish bearded man with thin gray hair brushed forward in an awkward comb-over, a tiny, pretty Asian woman at least twenty years his junior, and an almond-eyed boy around eight holding both their hands. The boy and the man wore tuxedos, the woman a long red gown. Both adults smiled. The child's mouth was tiny and tight.

Simone Vander touched the frame with a French-tipped nail and smiled. "That's my brother Kelvin. He's a genius."

She switched off the music as Milo and Reed and I settled on the longest sofa. Our combined weight compressed fluffy down cushions a foot or so. Simone Vander asked us if we wanted something to drink and when we demurred, she took a hard-backed chair and crossed her legs. The

chair was high, and we had to look up to
make eye contact with her.

She fussed with a sleeve. One pink san-
dal dangled. "Sorry," she said. "For calling
Aaron. It's just that he's been really helpful
to me."

"Investigating Travis Huck," said Reed.

"Uh-huh." She pushed thick black hair
behind a flat, delicate ear. Another network of blue veins marked the juncture of
jaw and lobe, suggesting translucence.

She hugged herself. "I guess you'd like
to know why I hired him in the first place."

Reed said, "Yes, ma'am."

"Aaron came highly recommended," she
said. Searching our faces for confirmation
or debate.

"Who referred you to him, ma'am?"

"A man who's worked with my father—
doing real estate deals—had used Aaron
before, said he was the best. It wasn't
something I was sure about, the whole
thing felt kind of strange. Hiring a private
eye, I mean. But I just felt I had to. When I
heard about Selena."

"You knew Selena," said Reed.

"She was my brother's piano teacher.
Sometimes she'd show up at the house

when I was there, and we'd talk. She seemed like a really nice person. I was so upset when I heard what happened to her."

Reed said, "Talk about what?"

Simone smiled. "You know, casual stuff. She seemed sweet. Kelvin—my brother— really liked her. He's been through other teachers—strict, really stuffy—professors from conservatories. They leaned hard on him and Kelvin had enough. He's been playing since he's three, got tired of practicing six hours a day. Just because you're a genius doesn't mean you're a slave, right? He also had his fill of classical music, wanted to write his own songs. Dad and Nadine—Kelvin's mom—were fine with it. They're not like other parents in that situation."

"What situation is that?"

"Having a genius. A prodigy," said Simone Vander. "From what I saw, Selena was a great fit for Kelvin. She told me she'd gone through the same thing. Being real talented, expected to practice all the time." Frown. "This is horrible. Kelvin's going to freak *out.*"

Reed glanced at Milo.

Milo said, "So you liked Selena."

"There was nothing not to like." A hand pressed the side of her face, left a faint, rosy print. "The way I found out, just horrible. I was getting ready to go out and caught it on the news. Half listening, you know? I heard Selena's name but thought no, you're making a mistake. So I looked up one of the TV station websites but the story wasn't posted and I forgot about it. But the next morning, there it was. I couldn't believe it."

Moe Reed said, "What made you suspect Mr. Huck?"

"I can't say I *suspected* him. It's nothing that definite. I just . . . the *first* thing I did—when I learned what had happened to Selena—was call my father. His regular cell phone wasn't working so I got transferred to an international cell because he was in Hong Kong. He was in a meeting, but I told him. He was stunned, said he'd let Nadine and Kelvin know when he called them."

"They're not with him?"

"No, they're in Taiwan, visiting Nadine's family there. Dad's looking at some real estate in Hong Kong."

Moe Reed said, "About Huck . . ."

"Yes. I'm not saying I suspected him, but he always gave me a . . . weird feeling." Pause. "And I know for a fact that he was interested in Selena."

"Interested how, ma'am?"

"You don't need to call me that," said Simone Vander. "Ma'am."

"Mr. Huck was interested in Selena . . ."

"Physically. Not that I ever saw him do or say anything overt, but a girl can tell." Half smile. "At least I think I'm pretty perceptive."

"What did he do?"

"Looked at her," said Simone. "You know, *that* way. With a capital L." She toyed with her hair. "I don't want to get anyone in trouble . . . to be truthful, sometimes I felt he looked at *me* that way. No big deal, he never stepped out of line, and normally I'd never say anything. But . . . when I found out what happened—you won't tell him, will you? That I hired Aaron."

"Of course not," said Reed. "Guy acted creepy, you had every right."

She exhaled. "That's a strong word. I don't want to make accusations, but Travis has a way of making everything seem . . .

not sneaky, I guess the best word would be . . . covert? Like a spy?" She frowned, not satisfied with the choice of vocabulary.

"Furtive," said Milo.

"Perfect! Yes, furtive, like everything's in code. Like he's looking over his shoulder all the time and that makes you want to do it, too? I'm a really direct person so . . . but my dad likes him, and Dad's brilliant, so who am I to say?"

"What does your father like about Huck?"

"He never said, but you could just tell. Which is why I never made a fuss. Dad has a good feel for people. That's part of what made him so successful." She chuckled. "Who do you think bought me this house? My job sure couldn't pay for it and I'm the first to admit it."

"What do you do?"

"Work with kids. Nanny, preschool teacher, I've done some remedial tutoring. And . . . I probably shouldn't admit it but, yes, like everyone else, I wanted to act. But want's a long way from do. Right now I'm taking some downtime, maybe I'll transition to something totally different. Anyway,

Dad's not like you'd imagine, for a man in his position. He's a people person and his instinct is to trust. He always says he'd prefer to trust and end up disappointed rather than live his life as a cynic. 'A cynic understands the price of everything and the value of nothing.' That's his favorite saying."

Reed said, "Travis Huck hasn't disappointed him yet."

"Apparently," said Simone Vander. "Maybe because Travis doesn't have a life of his own, is always there to run some errand, whatever. I know that's helpful for Dad and Nadine, but maybe that's what bothers me. Maybe Travis is *too* involved?"

She sat forward, folding like origami. "Being an assistant is more than a job. He lives in that house." Exhaling. "That's why I hired Aaron. To find out if there is some reason to be worried. And you guys know what he found. Travis *killed* someone."

She hugged herself.

Moe Reed said, "Did Mr. Fox give you the details?"

"I know it was kids pushing and shoving.

But still. Someone died and he went to prison. Thinking about it last night, I didn't sleep very well."

Brown eyes drifted to Milo. "Aaron said you'd follow through, Lieutenant. That you never let go of a lead."

CHAPTER

17

We left Simone Vander standing just inside her gate. Milo drove down Benedict Canyon slowly.

Moe Reed said, "She's someone who knows Huck. Guess this puts more focus on him as a solo psycho, Loo."

Grunt.

At Lexington Road, Reed tried again. "It won't be a problem, Loo."

"What won't be?"

"Aaron and me."

"Never assumed it would be."

"One thing she gave us: Doesn't sound like the Vanders are running from anything.

What are we thinking about those sex parties Selena played at?"

"Good question."

"So they're still potential suspects?"

"No reason to eliminate them. Or anyone else." Milo smiled. "With an alternative
lifestyle. Whether or not that's what got
her—and the other women—killed? Who
the hell knows?"

I said, "Selena's missing computer says
there are secrets the killer wants to stay
hidden."

Reed said, "Or it's just the bad guy getting rid of any link between him and Selena. Meaning someone she knew. And
she knew Huck. And now we know he
had the hots for her. Toss in the baldie
Ramos saw and he's looking better and
better."

"Creepy guy," said Milo. "But not to the
Vanders. Simon's a sharp-eyed businessman. Trusting according to his daughter,
but she never said he was an outright
sucker. Why would he give Huck a job that
had him living in?"

"The weird—the alternative lifestyle?"

Milo didn't answer until we'd traveled
a mile on Sunset. "All right, we'll invite

Mr. Huck for an interview, keep it mellow, maybe he won't lawyer up immediately. But not today, give it a few more nights of surveillance. God's smiling at us, guy'll finally leave the house, head straight to Century Boulevard, solicit a working girl under your watchful eye, Detective Reed. Royal-*flush* scenario, he tries something nasty and you nab him heroically. That happens, you get to be at the press conference and I'll do the paperwork."

Reed said, "You think he'd be that stupid? With all those bodies turning up, he goes back there?"

"You're the one been itching to watch him, kiddo."

Silence.

Milo said, "Yeah, it would be stupid but without stupid criminals, the job would be as cheerful as cancer. And from Huck's perspective, there really isn't much heat. We had a two-minute chat with him, haven't been back, the press conference emphasized no leads. He's got to feel we know diddly. Which ain't far from the truth."

Reed said, "Feeling confident, so he strikes out."

I said, "The pattern of the murders implies a sequence of confidence-building. Start with women who could be considered throwaway victims and bury them out of sight. No one catches on, kick it up to someone bound to be missed, display her, call it in just to make sure."

"Mr. Hissy," said Reed. "And everything goes down at the marsh. What's that, staying in his geographic comfort zone?"

I said, "The marsh could be part of the thrill."

"The place turns him on? How?"

"Dr. Hargrove called it hallowed ground. Lust murders are often about control through defilement. What better place to showcase your handiwork? There could've also been a practical reason. There's limited public access to the marsh. If he'd stuck to stashing bodies in the muck, his crimes could've stayed undetected for years."

"Instead he decides to advertise." Reed gave a low whistle. "Life do get twisted."

Milo said, "First step toward being an ace detective, kid."

"What is?"

"Figuring out you're living in a different world."

Pigeons had partied atop Reed's rented Cadillac. He grumbled, "Story of my life," sounding uncannily like Milo.

His cell phone went off. "Reed . . . I'm so sorry, ma'am . . . yes, absolutely, ma'am." Pulling his pad out, he scrawled, hung up.

"That was Mary Lewis, Sheralyn Dawkins's mom. She lives in Fallbrook. What's more important, watching Huck or talking to her?"

"Her," said Milo. "Bring a scrape kit. At the very least we'll get a firm I.D. on Sheralyn. I'll watch Huck."

"Depending on what she has to say, Loo, I can start out now, do a turnaround, and be back at the Vander house in eight, nine hours."

"You start out now, you hit the crush, forget it. Get the DNA kit, pack yourself an overnight bag, leave when it's clearer. Take the coastal route, find yourself a bed in Capistrano, whatever. Eat a nice seafood dinner, watch cable, be ready for Ms. Lewis in the morning."

"Any suggestions where to stay?"

"Department's not gonna pay for the Ritz-Carlton, you'll be lucky to get a mattress and Cheez Whiz from a vending machine. And for God's sake, fill out the forms—no, forget it, I'll do it for you."

"I'll do it," said Reed. "Promise."

"Yadda yadda yadda."

The two of them drove off the Pizza Palazzo lot and I headed home.

I phoned Robin, asked if she wanted me to pick up dinner.

She said, "Beat you to it. Prime rib."

"What's the occasion?"

"Prime rib. I was thinking we could invite Milo and Rick. On the off chance Rick's free."

"Feeling hospitable?"

"Got my hostess gown and my martini shaker and I bought enough cow for eight, which should accommodate Milo. It dawned on me after he called you this morning. I haven't talked to him in ages—and we haven't seen the two of them socially for even longer."

"Nice thought," I said, "but Milo's doing surveillance tonight."

"Oh. Starting when?"

"After dark."

"Let's eat early."

"You feeling okay?"

"What?"

"Acute attack of sociability."

"I've been too isolated, darling. You get to go out, meet people. I talk to Blanche and pieces of wood."

"I'll call Milo."

"I'll call. He has trouble refusing me."

Pleasant surprise for both invitees.

Dr. Rick Silverman was off shift at the E.R.

Milo said, "Red meat. Public safety will just have to cool its goddamn heels."

Rick arrived first, wearing a maroon silk shirt, pressed jeans, and mesh loafers, bearing an enormous orchid arrangement for Robin. His silver hair was longer than usual, his mustache boasted of surgical skills. Robin took the flowers and kissed him. Blanche rubbed her head against his cuffs.

He kneeled, petted. "Gorgeous. Can I take her home as a party favor?"

"Love you, Richard," said Robin. "But not that much."

He played with the dog some more, eyed the roast, sizzling as it rested. "Smells fantastic, glad I took an extra dose of Lipitor. Can I help with anything?"

"Nothing to help with. Manhattan on the rocks, Maker's Mark, capful of red vermouth, dash of orange bitters, no cherry?"

"Impressive," said Rick. "Not that I ever stray from the familiar." He sat. Blanche settled at his feet. A long arm dangled; adroit fingers kneaded her flews. "Big Guy should be here any minute."

Robin said, "He phoned half an hour ago, said he got beeped by Downtown, would let me know if he couldn't make it. I haven't heard from him since."

"Downtown. That again."

"What again?"

"New chief's a hands-on administrator. Milo's never had to deal with anything like it. It's probably better than the old days— Siberia. But the personal attention cuts both ways. Right, Alex?"

I said, "Pressure to perform."

"Exactly."

Rick tried Milo's cell, got voice mail, didn't bother to leave a message.

Robin brought his drink, turned to me. "Chivas, baby?"

"Thanks."

As she poured, Rick carried his Manhattan to the kitchen window, looked out at trees and sky. "I forget how pretty it is." He sipped. "Sounds like this marsh mess won't resolve soon, Alex."

I nodded.

"Terrible," he said. "Those poor women. Though I'm thinking selfishly. Disgustingly narcissistic, in fact. I got invited to give a speech at an alumni meeting. Thought we both might make it. Do a New England thing afterward. Milo's never been."

Robin said, "Undergrad at Brown or med school at Yale?"

"Yale." He laughed. "No big whup, those things are always mind-numbing."

The front door shut. A voice roared: "I smell *carcass*!"

Milo stomped into the kitchen, hugged everyone, sucked up all the oxygen in the room. The look on Rick's face was pure relief.

Within three minutes, Milo had guzzled juice from the fridge, downed a beer, inspected the roast as if it were evidence, dipped a finger into a gravy spot on the counter and tasted. "Oh, this is going to be good. Where we going in terms of wine?"

The four of us ate lustily and polished off a bottle of New Zealand Pinot.

When Robin asked how Milo was doing, he took the question literally and reviewed the basics of the marsh murders.

Rick said, "Appetizing."

Milo ran a finger over his lips.

Robin said, "No, I'm interested."

Milo said, "*You* might be, but Dr. Rick is repelled and Dr. Alex is bored out of his skull. Whoever has custody of the potatoes, please pass."

Small talk commenced. Milo didn't contribute much, continued to shovel food like a combine. Rick worked hard at ignoring the rate of ingestion; he's still trying to get Milo in for a checkup.

Blanche toddled in from her nap. She's the only dog Milo's ever admitted liking, but when she brushed against his leg, he ignored her. Rick lifted Blanche onto his lap, worked her ears.

Milo said, "Arf," and stared into space.

Robin said, "Dessert?"

"I'm full, thanks," said Rick.

"Congrats," said Milo.

"For what?"

"Speaking for yourself."

We moved outside, to the pond, ate fruit, drank coffee, watched the fish, tried to identify constellations in the moonless sky.

Milo said, "Twinkle, twinkle," and lit up a cigar.

Rick said, "At least it's outside, you won't be poisoning the hosts."

Milo tousled his hair. "How thoughtful of me."

"What you're doing to your own lungs we won't talk about."

Milo cupped a hand near his ear. "Ey, what's that, sonny?"

Rick sighed.

Milo said, "I am beyond mere chemistry."

"Ah, the *theory.* Call the Nobel committee."

"What theory?" said Robin.

"He's been so long on the job that his internal organs are petrified and immune to toxins."

"Man of Granite," said Milo, smoking hungrily. Holding his Timex to a low-voltage spot bulb, he said, "Oops, it's that time," got up, stubbed the cigar on stone, hugged everyone, and left.

Rick picked up the butt, held it between thumb and index finger. "Where should I toss this?"

By midnight, Robin and I were in bed, under crisp, clean covers.

She fell asleep quickly. I dragged myself through the usual brain-sweep, working to quiet my mind. Was back in Missouri, mastering my father's Remington, feeling bigger than Dad—bigger than a bear—when the phone rang.

Dad said, "Hey, Al, you really caught on."

Ring ring ring ring ring.

Stupid; no phones in the forest. I pulled the covers over my head.

Stayed gigantic.

CHAPTER

18

Robin was up by six, working in her studio soon after.

I found her sliding a razor-sharp mini-plane over a pristine rectangle of spruce. From the size and thickness of the wood, the future soundboard of an archtop guitar.

"Stromberg copy. Going to try the diagonal brace, see if I can tweak it for some interesting nuances."

"Brought you coffee," I said.

"Thanks—you've got crust in your eye— there we go, gone. Feel rested?"

"I tossed?"

"A bit. Get the message from your service?"

"Haven't checked yet." I yawned. "When did it come in?"

"Two calls, actually. Twelve forty and then at five, both from Milo."

I reached him at his desk. "Huck did something?"

"Huck did the usual nothing. But there's another body in the marsh."

"Oh, no. Poor woman."

"Not exactly."

From seven thirty to nine p.m. the previous night, Silford Duboff and his girlfriend, Alma Reynolds, had enjoyed a vegan dinner at Real Food Daily on La Cienega.

"More accurately, *I* enjoyed it," said Reynolds, on the other side of the one-way glass. "Sil was grumpy the entire time. Preoccupied. With what, I couldn't pry out. I found the evening frustrating, but held my peace. Sil ordered his favorite item on their menu: the TV Dinner. Normally, that's palliative. This time, it wasn't. He closed up completely. So after a while I stopped trying, and we both simply consumed."

Telling the story to Milo with authority but curious detachment, as if teaching a class.

A tall, solid woman in her fifties, Reynolds had an eagle nose, a heavy jaw, piercing blue eyes, and waist-length gray hair plaited tightly. The lecturer's tone came honestly: For fifteen years, she'd worked as a junior college instructor in Oregon, teaching political science and economic history before retiring due to "budget cuts and apathetic students and fascist bureaucracy."

Now she sat across from Milo, straight-backed, dry-eyed, wearing last night's blue work shirt tucked into gray flannel trousers, hemp sandals. Tortoiseshell reading glasses hung from a chain. Turquoise-and-silver earrings livened her ears.

Milo said, "No idea what was on his mind?"

"Not a clue. He gets like that. Uncommunicative, like most men."

Milo didn't argue. Alma Reynolds wouldn't have cared if he had.

She said, "We had our dessert and left. After the way Sil had behaved, I decided to cut my losses with a good book. I asked him to drive me to my apartment, made it clear he was to proceed to his."

"Both of you live in Santa Monica."

"Two blocks apart, but any space can be a universe if one wants it to. This was one of the times I wanted it to."

"Were there lots of those times in your relationship?"

"Not lots," said Alma Reynolds, "but not a rarity. Sil could be difficult."

"Like most men."

"I put up with it because he was a *fine* man. If there's anything that emerges from this conversation, Lieutenant, that should be it."

She took a deep breath through her mouth.

"Oh, well," she said. "No sense fighting it."

"Fighting what, ma'am?"

"This."

Tears streamed down her cheeks. Embedding her hands in her thick, gray hair, she wailed.

Milo took his time, got her to repeat the story.

Rather than drive Alma home, Duboff

had veered south to the Bird Marsh. She'd protested, he'd ignored her. A "dispute" ensued, during which she told him to stop obsessing about the marsh. He said the place was his responsibility. She said the damn place was fine. He said don't refer to it like that. She said, you're being irrational, nothing the police did caused any serious disturbance, time to move on, Sil.

He ignored her.

Last straw; she blew.

Raising her voice in a way she hadn't done since her divorce. Letting him know her green credentials were every bit as good as his, he was confusing ecological consciousness with obsessive-compulsive neurosis.

He ignored her.

She ordered him to stop the car.

He kept driving.

If she'd had a cell phone, she would've used it, but she didn't, neither did he. Those towers, no matter what *they* wanted you to believe, were carcinogenic and disastrous for birds and insects and she'd rather be stranded in Timbuktu than capitulate to a toxic lifestyle.

She *insisted* he stop.

He drove faster.

"What's gotten into you?"

Pretending she wasn't there.

"Damn you, Sil! Talk to—"

"There's something I need to see."

"What?"

"Something."

"That's no answer!"

"It won't take long, baby—"

"Don't baby *me, you know I despise tha—"*

"Afterward we'll go home and brew some tea—"

"You'll go to your home and I'll go to my home, and any tea I drink will be my own damn tea."

"Suit yourself."

"You don't care what I want, do you?"

"Cool the drama, Alma. There's something I need to see."

"You're imprisoning me—that's psychologically toxic behav—"

"It won't take long."

"What won't?"

"Not important."

"Then why do you need to see it?"

"Not important to you."

"What the hell are you talki—"

"Someone called me. Told me the answer was there."

"The answer to what?"

"What happened."

"To who?"

"Those women."

"The women in the—"

"Yes."

"Who? Who called?"

Silence.

"Who, Sil?"

"They didn't say."

"You're lying, I can always tell."

Silence.

"Someone calls you out of the clear blue and you comply like a droid?"

Silence.

"This is absurd, Sil, I insist—"

Silence.

"Blind obedience kills the soul—"

"The marsh is what matters."

"The damn marsh is fine, can't you get that through your thick skull?"

"Apparently not."

"Unbelievable. Someone calls, you pant like a lapdog."

"Maybe that's what it takes, Alma."

"What?"

"A dog. That's how they found the women."

"Oh, so now you're a detective. Is that what you want to be, Sil? A uniformed droid?"

"It won't take long."

"What am I supposed to do while you nose around?"

"Just sit for a moment. It won't take long."

But it did.

Sitting parked on Jefferson, near the east-side entrance, she grew nervous, then scared. Wasn't ashamed to admit it. Because to be truthful, the place always spooked her, especially at night, and it was spooky on this night, a moonless night, the sky thick and tarry and black.

No one around. No one.

Those stupid condos, abominations of human-centric narcissism, looming down, some of *their* lights on, but little good did they do, so distant, could well have been on another planet.

Waiting for Sil.

Five minutes. Six, seven, ten, fifteen eighteen.

Where the hell *was* he?

Fighting her nervousness with anger, she'd learned the technique from a faculty buddy in Oregon who taught cognitive psych. Substitute an empowering emotion for a helpless one.

It worked. She grew hotter and hotter under the collar, thinking about Sil, so rude arrogant compulsive goddamn thought- less.

Leaving her stuck in the damn car.

When he got back, there'd be hell to pay.

Twenty-five minutes and still no sign of him and the anger began morphing back to nervousness.

Worse than nervousness. Fear, she wasn't ashamed to admit it.

Time for another strategy. Confront the helplessness with action.

She got out of the car, walked toward the marsh.

Encountered pure darkness and stopped.

Calling his name.

No answer.

Calling louder.

Nothing.

She took a step forward, encountered way too much darkness and stopped—where was Sil's penlight?—said, "You get your ass over here and take me the hell home and don't call me until I call you."

The impact sent her flying.

Hard, vicious fist in her belly, so much force it felt as if the hand were penetrating her innards.

Electric pain sparked through her body, captured her breath.

The second blow caught her on the side of the head and she went down.

A foot kicked the small of her back.

She curled herself tiny, prayed no more punishment would come.

Just as quickly as the attack had begun, it ended.

Footsteps fading into the night.

No sound of a car engine so she lay there thinking, He's watching. Waited for a long time, before being able to entertain the big question:

Was that Sil?

If not, where *was* Sil?

Duboff had been knifed on the pathway. Bloodstains splotched the dirt twelve feet past Selena Bass's dump site. Care had been taken to brush the surrounding soil all the way to the sidewalk, obscuring footprints. No errant hairs or body fluids that weren't Duboff's, no tire tracks along either side of the street.

A deep back wound had pierced Duboff's left lung, the blow driven with enough force to crack a rib. The follow-up was an ear-to-ear throat slash, with Duboff lying facedown.

"Bad guy probably lifted him by the head," said Milo. "Reached around and bam."

Sneak attack in the dark, it needn't have taken more than seconds. Alma Reynolds had sat in the car for nearly half an hour, ample time to clean the scene.

By calling out Duboff's name, she'd announced her presence to the killer. Subsequent speech had pinpointed her location and he'd charged her.

Assaulting a potential witness but making no effort to finish her off.

Too intent on making his escape.

He'd expected a one-on-one meeting, but Duboff, ever the contrarian, had brought along Alma Reynolds, put her in mortal danger.

Milo said, "You still all right, ma'am? From your injuries?"

The question offended her.

"As I told you the *first* time, there *are* no injuries. Except to my ego." She pushed herself upright, suppressed a wince.

"Bastard," she said, leaving the interview room stiffly "I'm going to miss him incredibly."

Milo and I moved to his office. I said, "Duboff was a misanthropic crank, but he trusted someone enough to meet in the dark. Alma Reynolds knew he was lying when he said he didn't know who'd phoned. The lure was solving the murders."

"Pretty flimsy," he said. "Why would he fall for that?"

"Dedicated activist shows up the cops and keeps the sacred grounds pristine?"

"Guess so."

"Being at the marsh after dark didn't scare him. Alma said he dropped in regularly—including the night Selena was found when he missed the dump by a narrow margin."

"Maybe too narrow, Alex."

"He was part of it?"

"Like you said before, two guys would make the job easier. And talk about someone with an intense attachment to the marsh. Plus the guy's weird. We considered him in the beginning, dropped him off the screen when we couldn't find any felony record or links to Huck. Maybe that was a big-time goof."

"He showed up to talk to his confederate?" I said. "Then why take Reynolds along?"

"He thought it would be a brief chat, like he told Reynolds. Got surprised."

"Be interesting if Huck's name shows up on any Save the Marsh mailing lists."

"Be interesting to know where the hell Huck was last night. Which was the point of sitting on my commodious butt watching the shrubbery. No sign of him leaving or entering the house, but that means squat. He coulda made his move before I arrived, returned after I left to take the call on Duboff."

"When did the call come in?"

"Right after midnight. But that was well past Duboff's murder. Ol' Alma wasn't wearing a watch but she knows they left the restaurant shortly after nine, guesses she got blindsided at ten thirty or so. Which would put Duboff getting gutted at ten or so. She lay there, out of it, for another half hour, finally got up and looked for Duboff, which was stupid, but adrenaline can do all sorts of things to your judgment. After she found him, she ran back out to the street, screaming. No one around to hear, like you said, it's a ghost town at night. So she got back in Duboff's car, drove to Pacific Division, and reported the murder. Pacific has her logged in at eleven thirty-two. They put her in a room, took her statement, dispatched a car to the marsh, confirmed the body, and phoned Reed. He was in Solana Beach, called me. I was taking a bladder break, saw the message, called back, cowboyed to the marsh. Leaving Huck plenty of time and opportunity to return home."

He rubbed his face. "I'm losing it, Alex. Shoulda driven up to the Vander house, leaned on the gate bell. If Huck wasn't there, maybe someone else was—a maid, whatever, and I'd know."

"You got called to a murder scene, you went."

"Guy was dead, what was the rush?" Cursing. "Yeah, it was the logical response. Aka utter lack of creative thinking."

"Unseemly," I said.

"What is?"

"Self-flagellation from the man of granite."

"Right," he said, "I'm thinking sandstone."

CHAPTER
19

An expedited search warrant of Silford Duboff's apartment produced nothing of value. The only surprise was philosophical: dog-eared copies of the complete works of Ayn Rand hidden under Duboff's mattress, like pornography.

"No knives, guns, garottes, sex toys, weird body fluids, incriminating notes," said Milo. "No computer, either, but Reynolds says he never had one. Damn fridge had fruits, veggies, whole-grain everything. Rah rah for the healthy life-style."

◆

Moe Reed returned from Fallbrook with cheek scrapes of Sheralyn Dawkins's mother and the dead woman's stunned fifteen-year-old son. The mother worked as a housekeeper on a rich man's avocado ranch. Devon Dawkins was an honor student, did farm chores during his spare time.

Reed said, "Nice lady, the way she described Sheralyn's leg break matches Jane One to a T. She wouldn't talk in front of Devon, but after she sent him out she poured it out. Sheralyn was a problem since high school. Low self-esteem, drugs, alcohol, bad men."

Milo said, "Same story Big Laura's mommy told us. Any bad men in particular?"

"She meant Sheralyn's teen years, but even back then she didn't know any names. That was the problem, Sheralyn kept her private life private, wouldn't give an inch to Mom. The two of them hadn't been in contact for years. I got the feeling Mom had been happy with the arrangement, wanted a shot at raising Devon properly. Really nice kid, it was tough giving him the bad news."

I said, "How long has the family been living down there?"

"They moved to San Diego right after Sheralyn's father got out of the military. His civilian job was school district custodial manager, he died twelve years ago. Sheralyn was born in San Diego, did a couple years of high school, dropped out. Her mom never heard of Travis Huck, and the six-pack with Huck's picture didn't jog her memory."

Milo said, "Why should life be easy?"

"She did tell me one thing that might be interesting. When Devon couldn't hear. Sheralyn had a thing for pain. Not causing it, experiencing it. Mom said when she was a teenager, she'd cut herself on the arms, pull her eyelashes out, once in a while she'd burn herself with cigarettes. Sometimes she'd come home from being with boys and have bruises on her neck and arms. Mom threatened to take her to a psychiatrist. Sheralyn yelled at her to mind her own damn business, ran out of the house, stayed away for a few days. What boiled things over was Sheralyn getting pregnant when she was sixteen and refusing to say who the father was. She was already into dope, so the parents worried about a drug baby. When Devon was born healthy they tried to get Sheralyn to let them adopt him. Sheralyn went ballistic, took the baby and left. No contact for three years, then Sheralyn shows up without warning, stays for a couple days, things seem to be going okay. All of a sudden, she sneaks out in the middle of the night, leaves Devon behind."

"Into pain," said Milo.

"And being squeezed around the neck," said Reed. "That would make her an easy mark for a sadist, right? They start off playing the choking game for what she thinks is money and fun, he turns on the pressure, she's caught off guard. Make sense, Doc?"

"Makes perfect sense," I said. "It could also be our link to Selena. The parties she played at got extreme and she joined in."

Reed said, "Thinking she was in control, but she got flipped."

Milo said, "Sheralyn's story also reminds me of Selena's. Bad feelings between daughter and mother, leaving home."

Reed said, "So what now?"

"Got a call from the chief," said Milo. "Caitlin Frostig."

Reed slumped. "Am I in some sort of shit?"

"No, you're fine. He wanted to know how we were doing on the marsh murders. I gave him the honest answer and he pretended to be understanding and patient. Then he brought up Frostig."

"Checking up on me," said Reed.

"His Fierceness takes a personal interest in the troops."

"Did he make like I'm supposed to be doing something on Caitlin? Because I did everything I could think of."

"He wanted to make sure you *ignore* Caitlin until we close the marsh murders. That was before Duboff. I'm sure it goes double now."

"Okay . . . any hint about a task force, Loo?"

"Why, you want one?"

"Hell, no," said Reed. "I was just wondering, another body and all that. I'm green, haven't exactly burned up the record books—"

Milo's hand clapped Reed's shoulder. "It's a *whodunit,* kiddo. Meaning no one burns up anything, we simmer slowly and hope something cooks. No one with half a brain—and the Sun King has at least that—expects resolution by the fourth commercial break."

"Okay," said Reed. "He actually mentioned Caitlin by name?"

"First and last."

"He probably got a call. Her father works for a big-time tech guy."

I said, "Caitlin's your missing person?"

Reed nodded. "College girl, left work thirteen months ago, hasn't been seen since. Cold as frozen fish sticks and they hand it to me, my second case. If I pissed someone off and it's punishment, I can't figure out who or how."

Milo said, "You solved your first one. That's batting five hundred."

"Unfortunately, this ain't baseball." Reed tightened the knot of his tie. "So when can we talk to Huck?"

Pools of water spread beneath Simon Vander's Aston Martin, Lincoln Town Car, and Mercedes. Moisture blackened the slate motor court.

Reed said, "Car wash day, either they

have a service or Huck does it himself. Lexus is gone, maybe he's out gassing it. Or the car wash dude is."

He pushed the call-box button. No answer from the house. Same for two more attempts.

Milo looked up the Vanders' landline and punched it, got voice mail, kept his voice even as he left a message for Travis Huck to get in touch. Cordial as an invitation to a poker game.

We loitered near the octopus gates. Twenty minutes in, the mailman drove up and dropped ad circulars and bulk mail into a slot on one of the gateposts.

Reed went up to him. "Know these people?"

The carrier shook his head. "Never see anyone around." His fingers brushed the gate. "I have packages, I just leave 'em here, no one signs."

"Private, huh?"

"Rich," said the mailman. "These kind of people keep you at a distance."

"What kind of packages?"

"Wine, fruit packages, gourmet food. The good life, right?" Hoisting his bag, he trudged down the road.

Milo waited, descended Calle Maritimo himself, far enough to disappear around a bend. He returned a few minutes later. "Nothing plus nothing, time to boogie. Leave your bona fides, Moses."

Reed dropped one card onto the mail pile, wedged another between the gate and the post. "Think Huck might've rabbited?"

"There's always that chance."

We drove to PCH. The sun was custard, the ocean a melting jigsaw puzzle of green and blue. No Lexus in front of the Vander beach house, no more success with the bell push there.

Moe Reed tapped the high wooden fence that blocked off the beach. "What's next, a moat?"

"That's what money buys," said Milo.

We cruised up and down the highway, scoped every filling station until Broad Beach for a sign of the Lexus. Gas in the Palisades was nearing five bucks a gallon for high-octane. That didn't stop motorists from lining up for a petrochemical IV. Huck wasn't one of them.

Milo said, "Let's get back, call the crypt,

get a time line on Duboff's autopsy, see if they've done a prelim, anything useful on the visual. Then we need to work on confirming that Jane Three is DeMaura Montouthe. Victim I.D. isn't likely to be a big deal on this one, but we can't afford to screw up and get it wrong. That working girl said DeMaura was from Alabama, but it could be Arkansas, anywhere down south. Hell, it could be Arizona or Albania. If we can locate some next of kin, maybe we'll get lucky and DeMaura talked to someone about an especially creepy john."

"Like the guy Big Laura escaped from."

"Like him," said Milo. "In a perfect world."

Back at the station, a civilian clerk I'd never seen before said, "I've been trying to call you, Lieutenant."

"Never got any message," said Milo.

"Well, I *did* try."

"Which number did you use?"

The clerk read off a number. The final digit was off by two.

"Well, that's what I was *given*," said the clerk, without remorse. "Anyway, someone came in to see you, went upstairs, is still there. So no big deal."

James Robert "Bob" Hernandez was a blue-eyed, muscular six-footer with slicked-back brass-colored hair and a four-inch Vandyke of matching hue. He wore jeans with rolled-up cuffs, weathered motorcycle boots, and a plaid shirt with short sleeves folded up high. Tattoos the color of swimming pool water ran from thick wrists to corded biceps. Tweety Bird, Popeye, smooching cherubs. On his right arm, devotion to *Kathy* was proclaimed calligraphically. Pro jobs, not prison art. Hernandez's record was minor. Drunk driving, traffic warrants, failures to appear.

After running him through the databases, Milo returned to the interview room and sat back down. During the brief break, I'd waited with Hernandez, the two of us talking about sports.

Moe Reed was out processing the pretty wooden box Hernandez had brought for show-and-tell. Phoning the crypt first and getting authorization to carry the box personally to Dr. Hargrove's lab.

"Human bones," said Milo.

"That's what they look like to me," said Bob Hernandez. "I mean, I'm not a scientist, but I looked them up on the Internet and they match human fingers. Enough for three complete hands."

"Doing research, huh?"

"Didn't want to waste your time, sir."

"We appreciate that. So go over again how you found them."

"Didn't find 'em, *bought* 'em," said Hernandez. "I mean not them, specifically. A whole bunch of stuff. Unclaimed storage, they have auctions, people not paying their monthlies. Like you guys do with confiscated cars." Hernandez smiled. "Lost an El Camino that way."

"What else was in the bin?"

"Garbage bags full of crap. Bicycle I thought might be worth something, turned out to be crap, some old board games, newspapers. I tossed it all except the box. Because the box was nice wood. Later I found out what was inside. I'm pretty sure they're finger bones 'cause they don't look like anything else. So I called Pacific Division and they sent me to Detective Reed and he said to come here. So here I am."

"Was the box wrapped?"

"Yeah, in one of the garbage bags. Turned out to be Brazilian rosewood, which is rare, endangered. Would've been better to find jewelry or coins."

"How long ago was this, Mr. Hernandez?"

"Two weeks. I tried to find something else they could've been, some other animal, but from what I can tell they're human. So I didn't put 'em up on eBay, that would be wrong."

"eBay accept that kind of thing?"

"I never got that far," said Hernandez. "Didn't even try. Probably coulda sold 'em, but then I heard about those murders. On TV." Peering at Milo. "Four women, and that marsh is pretty close to the storage unit. I know this is three, not four, it probably doesn't mean anything, but I just thought I should come forward."

"You did the right thing, Mr. Hernandez. Where's the facility?"

"Pacific Public Storage, Culver Boulevard just before it intersects with Jefferson."

"You live in Alhambra."

"Sure do."

"Bit of a drive to the auction."

"Not compared with other places I been," said Hernandez. "Did one in San Luis Obispo." Yellow smile. "Heck, I'd drive to Lodi you tell me there's bargains."

"Auctions are your main job."

"Nope, I'm trained as a landscaper, looking for work."

"Been looking for a while?"

"Too long." Hernandez sat back and laughed. "My brothers said it would be like this."

"Like what?"

"Personal questions. 'Come forward, be a good citizen, Bobby, but you're gonna be looked at like a suspect because that's what the job's like. We don't trust nobody.'"

"Your brothers are on the job."

"Gene's Covina PD, Craig's South Pasadena. Dad's a retired firefighter. Even Mom's into it, West Covina dispatcher."

Milo smiled. "You're the nonconformist."

"No offense, Lieutenant, but you couldn't pay me enough to be cooped up in a car or an office. Give me a backhoe and five acres and I'm sailing. Speaking of which, I'd better get going. Job interview out in Canoga Park. They're moving big palms and I know how to do that."

Milo took his information, thanked him again, shook his hand.

At the door, Hernandez said, "One more thing, sir. It's not the main reason I came in but I've got a court date on my warrants, so if you're of a mind to put in a good word . . ."

"Your lawyer told you to come forward?"

"No, it was my idea. But he thought it might help. So did my brothers. You can call either of them, they'll vouch for me. If I'm outta line, just tell me, and it never came up."

"Who's your lawyer?"

"Some fresh-out-of-school PD, that's what bugs me," said Hernandez. "Mason Soto, he's more into stopping the war in Eye-Rack."

Milo copied down Soto's name and number. "I'll tell him you've been a big help to LAPD, Bob."

Hernandez beamed. "Thank you, sir, appreciate it deeply—those bones, at first I thought they might be from one of those anatomical models. You know, what doctors learn from? But there's no holes drilled through them, like you would do if you were stringing them together. So they're just loose bones."

Short, hard tug at the Vandyke. "Can't see any reason for a mentally healthy person to want something like that."

CHAPTER

20

Pacific Public Storage was a city block of beige bunkers hemmed by twenty-foot chain link. Flagrantly orange ten-foot signage promised special deals. The company's logo was a stack of suitcases.

We drove past and clocked the drive to the marsh before circling back. Six minutes each way, at moderate speed.

Perched above the entry to the facility's parking lot was a security camera. A Quonset hut served as the office. One man worked the desk, young, chubby, bored. His orange polo shirt bore the logo. His I.D. badge said *Philip*. A biography of

Thomas Jefferson was unfolded facedown on the counter. Passionate sports talk blared from a radio.

Milo eyed the book. "History buff?"

"School. Can I help you?"

"Police."

The badge made Philip blink.

Milo said, "Some contraband was found in one of your units. Number fourteen fifty-five."

"Contraband? Like dope?"

"Let's just say something illegal. What can you tell me about that bin?"

Philip leafed through a ledger. "One four five five . . . that one's vacant."

"We know that, Mr. . . ."

"Phil Stillway."

"The contraband in question was obtained when the contents were auctioned off two weeks ago, Mr. Stillway."

"I've only been here a week."

Milo tapped the ledger. "Could you please check who rented the unit?"

"It's not in here, in here is just the occupied units."

"Occupied? You've got tenants living here?"

Philip gaped. "No, sir, I meant material.

Belongings. No one lives here, that's against regulations."

Milo winked and grinned.

"Oh," said Philip, "you were joking."

"Who rented fourteen fifty-five and when?"

Philip walked two steps to a computer, sat down, tapped keys. "Says here it's been in arrears for sixty days and that was ... two weeks ago ... um, yeah, there *was* an auction, everything got cleaned out." Tap, tap. "Says here the rental agreement was ... fourteen months ago. One year, paid in advance, sixty days in arrears."

"Paid, how?"

Tap tap tap. "Says here cash."

"Who's the renter?"

"Says here Sawyer comma initial T."

"Address?"

"P.O.B. 3489, Malibu, California, 90156."

Malibu's zip code was 90265. Milo scowled as he copied down the information.

"What other information did Sawyer, T., give?"

Philip read off an 818 phone number.

Malibu's 310 but with everything cellular, logic no longer pertains.

Milo said, "Okay, let's have a look at your security tapes."

"Pardon?"

"The camera out front."

"Oh, that," said Philip. "It's for when the gates close after eight p.m. and renters want access."

"You lock up after eight?"

"Yeah, but they can give a deposit and apply for a twenty-four-hour card key."

"When do the cameras get turned on?"

"When there's no one in the office."

"Which is?"

"At night," said Philip. "After eight."

"Did T. Sawyer apply for a card key?"

Philip swung back to his keyboard. "The box is checked. Yes . . . looks like we never got the card back, so the deposit was forfeited. Two hundred dollars."

"Okay," said Milo. "Let's see those tapes. Anything before two weeks ago would be best."

"It might be best," said Philip, "but it's also impossible. Everything's recorded over after forty-eight hours."

"Two days and gone? Tight security system you've got here."

"This contraband, was it dangerous? Like toxic waste, something hazardous? My parents aren't too cool with me working here, worried about the stuff people store."

"Nothing toxic or radioactive," said Milo. "Is there anyone in the company who can tell us something about Mr. Sawyer?"

"I can ask but I don't think so. Everything we need to know is here." Tapping the computer.

"Let's look at the last forty-eight hours of tape."

"Sure." Philip reached to his left and switched on a VCR. The feed went straight to the computer and the screen turned gray. Stayed that way. "Hmm," he said, tickling the keyboard and changing nothing.

"It's not showing much, I don't know . . ."

"Stay with it, Phil."

A perusal of the Help menu and several false starts later, we were staring at a grainy black-and-white close-up of the storage facility gate. Static shot, but for a time register playing bingo. The camera angle was tilted to give a truncated view of the lot, maybe fifteen feet of asphalt, well short of the parking slots.

I said, "All You Wanted to Know About the Driveway But Were Afraid to Ask."

Phil started to smile, saw the look on Milo's face and changed his mind.

The screen reverted to gray.

Error message.

Philip said, "Looks like it's broken. I'd better report it."

Milo said, "Fast-forward to make sure it's blank."

Philip complied. Nothing on the rest of the tape.

"Give us a key to fourteen fifty-five."

"I guess it's okay."

"Think of it this way," said Milo. "If there is something dangerous in there, we'll be the ones who get zapped, not you."

"I need to stay up here, anyway," said Philip, scrounging in a drawer. "This one should work. If it doesn't, I don't know."

On the way to the bin, I said, "T. Sawyer."

"Huck's buddy. Har dee har har."

The facility was laid out in a series of

dim, narrow hallways that right-angled and continued, a broken snake of cement block tunnel. Door after plywood door, a variety of padlocks, some of them serious.

Company key-bolt on the hasp of 1455. Milo gloved up, unlocked, pulled the door open on fifty square feet of unlit vacancy.

Floors swept clean, not a speck of dust. The smell of bleach floated to the hallway.

He rubbed his eyes, ran his penlight over every surface. "Do I bother wasting the techie's time?"

"Depends on how much butt-covering you need to do."

"I'll tell 'em to luminol, maybe we'll get lucky."

We returned to the front office. Philip was playing a game on the company computer, some floridly colored thing featuring ninjas and space aliens and sloe-eyed women whose chests defied gravity.

"Hi," he said, continuing to work the mouse.

Milo said, "Are vacant units generally cleaned by the company?"

"Uh-huh."

"With bleach?"

"It's a special solution we get from the home office," said Philip. "Kills anything. So the next person doesn't have to worry."

"How considerate," said Milo.

"Yup." Philip, encountering a lance-wielding demon materializing out of a massive, mauve cloudburst, squinted, hunched forward, and braced himself for battle.

Milo gunned the unmarked and played NASCAR on side streets all the way to the station. Itching to get back to see if a warrant on Travis Huck's quarters at the Vander house was feasible.

The assistant D.A.'s he'd talked to so far weren't encouraging, but he had a couple more to go. "John Nguyen's sometimes helpful."

"Lawyer-surfing," I said.

"Talk about toxic waste."

I left him to the legal system and drove home thinking about molars and incisors.

DeMaura Montouthe, the leading candidate for Jane Doe Three, was fifty-one, a fossil by street standards. The ten-year mug shot Moe Reed had unearthed showed a droopy-eyed, wrinkled, lantern-jawed visage crowned by a platinum bird's nest. The life she'd led was a road map to mental and physical breakdown and she looked well into her sixties.

Yet she'd held on to her teeth.

Lucky genetics? Or was full dentition her last shred of vanity, the result of special care?

I looked up free facilities offering dental services in L.A. County, found eight, began calling, using my title.

Success at number four, a neighborhood walk-in clinic run by the dental school at the U.

Rose Avenue, south of Lincoln. Walking distance to Selena Bass's garage digs.

Another brief car ride to the Bird Marsh.

I asked the receptionist when Ms. Montouthe had last visited. "Doctor" only went so far.

"She's on our files, that's all I can tell you."

"Who's her dentist?"

"Dr. Martin. She's with a patient."

"When will she be free?"

"She's busy all afternoon—can I put you on hold?"

"No need."

Western District Community Adjunct Dental Health Center was a converted storefront wedged between a designer ice cream parlor and a vintage-clothing shop. Pretty people flocked to both of the neighbors. A couple of homeless men hung out near the clinic's wide-open door, smoking and laughing. One guy's worldly belongings were piled on the sidewalk. The other held up a set of dentures and guffawed through a black maw. "They did me good, Mr. Lemon!"

Shopping Bag said, "Lemme try 'em!"

"Gimme a can of soup!"

"Yeah!"

The exchange was aborted when they saw me coming. Two cracked palms blocked my way as they panhandled me simultaneously.

"Breakfast money, Perfesser?"

"It's afternoon, Mr. Lemon. Pancakes for the *people*!"

"*Powder* to the people!"

High-fives and raucous, phlegmy laughter.

I gave them each a five and they whooped, stepped aside. When they tried the same routine with a woman in dance tights leaving the ice cream joint clutching a double cone studded with candy bits, she said, "Fuck off."

Inside the clinic's aqua-blue waiting room a heavy woman with fearful eyes clutched a squalling baby and snuck glances at a sunken-faced codger slumped, half asleep. His clothes were filthy. He could've turned the scene outside into The Three Amigos. Sitting upright in a corner was a skinny-flabby Mohawked kid around twenty, with branded arms, a missing frontal incisor, and vengeful eyes.

The receptionist was cute and buxom and blond. Whatever her black tank top revealed was smooth and tan. She remembered my name and that killed her smile.

"Dr. Martin's still busy, sir."

"I'll wait."

"It could take a while."

"When she takes a break, please let

her know DeMaura Montouthe may be dead."

"Dea—" Her hand jetted to her mouth. "What kind of doctor are you?"

I showed her my LAPD consultant badge.

Her lips worked. She looked ill. "Oh, my God. Hold on." She hurried through a back door.

The kid with the Mohawk drawled, "Everyone gets dead."

Faye M. Martin, D.D.S., was thirty or so and gorgeous, with ivory skin, a heart-shaped face framed by gleaming red-brown hair, liquid dark eyes, and a figure a white coat couldn't camouflage.

Stunning resemblance to Robin—she could've been Robin's younger sister—and, God help me, I felt a tug below my waist.

I worked at staying business-like as we shook hands. Her business-like manner and my thinking about DeMaura Montouthe helped.

As she led me to an unused treatment room, she asked what a psychologist was doing working with the police. I gave her the short version and it seemed to satisfy her.

The room smelled of raw steak and mint. Gum care posters, and ominous photos of what happened when gum care was abandoned, papered the walls. Canisters of free toothbrushes and paste shared space with chrome-plated picks and curettes and bottles of cotton balls. Off to one side was a bright red patient chart.

Faye Martin perched on a rolling stool and placed her hand on the chart. Crossing her legs, she unbuttoned her coat, revealed a black blouse, black slacks, a gold chain bearing chunky, free-form amethysts. Her figure was fuller than first impression. She seemed unaware of her looks.

The only other seating was the dental chair, still in full recline. She said, "Oh, sorry," got up and adjusted the tilt. I climbed on.

"As long as you're here, open wide and let's have a look at your bite—sorry, it's terrible about DeMaura, I shouldn't joke."

I said, "There's no better reason to joke."

Faye Martin said, "Guess so . . . I'm assuming it was a violent death?"

"If the body we have is her, it was."

"The body." She sat back down. "Poor DeMaura. Do you have any idea who did it?"

"Not yet. Confirming identity would be a big help." I described the dental irregularities Dr. Hargrove had listed.

"It's her," said Faye Martin. "Darn."

"You don't need to look at X-rays?"

"Before I swear to anything I'll need to, but it's her. That combination of anomalies is rare. DeMaura and I used to joke about it. Baby teeth. 'Guess I never grew up, Doc.'"

She picked up the chart, read for a few seconds, put it down. "She had a nice laugh. The rest of her was so . . . what you'd expect from her lifestyle. But her teeth could've belonged to a healthy woman."

An unpolished fingernail plinked a button of her white coat. "She was a nice person, Dr. Delaware. Almost always cheerful. Considering her situation, I found that pretty remarkable."

"Sounds like you knew her pretty well."

"As well as you can know anyone in this setting," she said. "Except for kids, we mostly treat a transient population. But DeMaura was pretty regular about her appointments."

She checked the chart again. "She's been coming in for three years. For the first six months she saw Dr. Chan. He retired and I picked her up."

"The patients get regular dentists?"

"When the workload permits, we try to make it as much like a private practice as possible. For DeMaura that was easy because all she needed were cleanings—oh, yes, and one replaced amalgam right at the beginning."

"Why would she need to be a regular just for cleanings?"

"She had some tendency to build up plaque, but nothing extreme." She played with the chart. "Dr. Chan had been seeing her twice a year but I put her on every three months. To keep tabs on her, not just dentally, for overall health. I felt the only way she'd get regular medical care was if I referred her."

"She trusted you."

"I took the time to listen. Truth is, I enjoyed talking to her. She could be funny. Unfortunately, she stopped coming in . . ." Flipping a page. ". . . fifteen months ago. When did she die?"

"Possibly around then."

"I should've known something was up, she was always so dependable. But the phone number she left was inactive and I had no way to contact her."

"I found it surprising that she'd held on to her teeth."

"She had super-long roots, lots of room for error," said Faye Martin. "She'd been told that by another dentist, years ago, and it became a point of pride for her. So did her name. 'Mon*touthe,* it's karma, Doc, I'm the Chomper Queen.' And she didn't have too many points of pride, healthwise."

"What physical problems did she have?"

"You name it," said Faye Martin. "Arthritis, bursitis, acute bouts of pancreatitis, liver issues, at least one episode of Hep A I'm aware of, the usual STDs. She wasn't HIV-positive, at least she'd avoided that. Not that it matters anymore."

"Where'd you refer her for those issues?"

"The Marina Free Clinic. I called over there once to find out if she'd followed through. She only came in to get her pre-scriptions, no follow-up."

I said, "No one she trusted there."

Faye Martin's long-lashed brown eyes locked in to mine. Her cheeks were pink. "Guess I practiced your profession without a license."

"Good thing. You're the first person we've found who knows anything about her. We haven't been able to turn up any relatives or friends."

"That's because she had no friends. Or so she claimed. She said she didn't like people, was happiest just walking around by herself. She called herself a lonely bad girl. Disowned by family back when she still lived in Canada."

"Where in Canada?"

"Alberta."

I laughed. "We were told Alabama."

"Hey, an A's an A," said Faye Martin.

"Why was she disowned?"

"They were farmers, religious funda-mentalists. DeMaura really didn't give out the details. She came in to have her teeth cleaned, would talk and I'd listen. That happens here more than you think." She brushed hair from her face. "I didn't get much psych training in dental school, sure could use some."

"Is there anything in the chart that could help us know her better?"

"The official record's just teeth and gums, anything else DeMaura told me stayed in Vegas. But I'll make you a copy. If your forensic odontologist has time, he or she can make the official match. If not, send me what you've got and I'll do it."

"Appreciate it. What stayed in Vegas?"

"What she did for a living. She wanted me to know right at the outset that she was a 'bad girl.' Made love only for money— that's not the terminology she used. But I don't want to imply that was a big part of our conversations. For the most part, it was just silly chat. She'd come in, kind of goofy, start laughing about some joke she heard on the street, try to retell it, mangle it, and we'd both crack up. For a moment I'd forget what—who she was—and it would be like hanging with a friend, chick-talk. But her last visit, fifteen months ago, was different. First of all, she *looked* better. Nice makeup, not the crazy stuff she wore for work. Decent clothes and her hair was clean and combed out. Nothing could erase all those years of hard living, but that day I caught a glimpse of what she might've looked like if things had turned out differently."

I said, "The only picture I've seen was a mug shot."

Faye Martin frowned. "One thing I know is facial structure and DeMaura's was well proportioned and symmetrical. She had the underpinnings of a good-looking woman, Dr. Delaware. That day, it shone through. I told her how pretty she looked, asked if she was going somewhere special. She claimed she had a date with her boyfriend. That surprised me, she'd never talked about men except as customers."

"She claimed. You had your doubts?"

"Even with her teeth and fixed up, De-Maura was far from ravishing. And the man she described was younger and good-looking."

"How much younger?"

"She didn't specify but she called him a kid. 'Gorgeous kid, I could be his momma but he likes 'em mature.' Honestly, I thought she was making it up. Or, at the least, exaggerating. After I finished doing her teeth and my assistant left the room, she started talking about the sexual side of their relationship and for the first time I saw a hint of . . . I guess it would have to be arousal. As if she could still feel. So maybe this guy, whoever he was—if he existed—maybe he turned her on. Though I also wondered if DeMaura had been the victim of some cruel joke. Misconstruing one of her business relationships as personal."

"Crush on a client," I said.

"What she told me next made it the wrong type of client. She said he liked to hurt her. And that she liked to *be* hurt."

"Hurt how?"

"I didn't ask. The prurient details didn't interest me, just the opposite—to be truthful, I was repulsed. I did warn her to be careful but she said they were just playing games."

"She used that word?"

"Yes, games. Then she placed her hands around her neck and stuck out her tongue and wobbled her head. As if she was being strangled."

Dark eyes narrowed. "Is that how she died?"

"There's evidence of strangulation, but all that was left of her were bones."

"My God," she said. "It wasn't her fantasy, it *happened.*"

"What else did she say about this boyfriend?"

"Let me think back." Massaging the smooth space between shaped eyebrows. "She said . . . now I'm sorry that I didn't press for details . . . okay, she said she liked rubbing his head, he was her good-luck charm. It was one of the games they played, she'd rub his head and he'd do what he wanted—her words, he does what he wants, whatever he wants. She said she loved his head, how smooth it was. 'Like a baby's ass.' So I guess he was bald." Frowning. "I gave her a new toothbrush and a pick and some Colgate Total."

She sprang up. "Let me copy this for you."

I said, "This has been helpful. You've got nothing to regret."

She turned, smiled. "At least someone has psych training."

CHAPTER
21

Assistant District Attorney John Nguyen rubbed a baseball.

Pristine Dodger ball decorated with lots of signatures. Three other orbs in plastic cases shared shelf space with law books and case folders. Nguyen was senior enough to get a corner-view office on the seventeenth floor of the Clara Shortridge Foltz Criminal Justice Center. Foltz had been the first woman lawyer on the West Coast. I wondered what she'd think of the soulless, twenty-story fridge that bore her name.

The vista was downtown rooftops and chrome-cold parking lots; square footage was minimal. Milo and Moe Reed and I crowded Nguyen's city-issue desk, leaving no room for dancing.

"That's it?" said Nguyen, massaging a tightly laced seam. "A possible victim has a possible john but he's just as likely to be an imaginary boyfriend without hair?"

Reed said, "Plus there's Big Laura Chenoweth escaping from a homicidal skinhead, and Selena Bass getting into a car with a baldie."

"Both stories were obtained from recollective third-person accounts, making it hearsay twice removed. Don't you guys follow pop culture? Bald is the new lush." Nguyen touched his own thick, black brush cut. "Sorry, no one will give you paper with that."

Milo said, "C'mon, John, it's more than that. Travis Huck's shown clear signs of evasion."

"Not being home when you drop in is evasive? Plus, he was wearing a hat, you can't be sure he's a cueball."

"What was visible beneath the hat was clearly skinned."

"What if he skins around the sides and on top there's a shaving brush? Like the freak in that movie David Lynch did years ago . . . you know the one I'm talking about."

Silence.

Nguyen said, "Eraserhead. Hell, what if you yank off the hat and out pops a one-foot Afro? You're relying on some dinkyshit physical description that's worth less than flea-spit. But I won't stop you, go judge-fishing. I just can't put in a good word with anyone, way too anemic."

His eyes dropped to Travis Huck's most recent DMV photo. "Here he's got surplus locks. But let's say he shaved his dome. You'd have to prove it happened during a time frame that matches him to the dude seen with Selena. No, even farther back—to Montouthe. Which was what, two years ago?"

"Fifteen months," said Milo.

Nguyen played with the baseball some more. "I'm sure your instincts are right about this guy, but what you've got is fee-ble. Let's stretch and say you dig up enough so Mr. Huck becomes a viable suspect. We've still got a problem getting into the house. It's not his residence, belongs to his employer. Who is *not* a suspect."

Moe Reed said, "Not yet."

Nguyen rolled the baseball between his fingertips. "Is there something you want to tell me? As in the full picture?"

Milo recounted the swinger parties Selena Bass had described to her brother, her subsequent hiring as Kelvin Vander's piano teacher. The fact that the Vander family had left town.

"Okay, she advanced from bad girl to Bach," said Nguyen. "So what?"

Reed said, "Or Bach was a cover to get her over to the house at regular intervals."

"Kinky rich people," said Nguyen. "Boy, that's a novelty in Hollyweird. Same question, guys: Who says 'swinger parties' is anything more than good, clean, adulterous fun? You've got absolutely no connection to the S and M stuff two of your hookers allegedly engaged in. And, frankly, your other hooker . . . Chenoweth, doesn't sound like she'd let anyone tie her up. Just the opposite."

"There was a riding crop in Selena's—"

"So she liked horses. Girls do." Nguyen

swiveled in his chair, placed the baseball on a plastic stand, placed the box over it with loving care. "I know I'm being an asshole but you'll get worse from the other side, so better to proceed with caution."

"Meaning?"

"Get better evidence."

I said, "If the Vanders gave permission to search, would it extend to Huck's quarters?"

Nguyen leaned back. "Interesting question . . . might depend on the nature of Huck's arrangement with the Vanders. Is his room a stipulated component of his salary? If so, it would be a legally contracted domicile, no different from any rented or leased space, and only the resident can grant permission."

"If the resident is still in residence."

Nguyen smiled. "You could've been a lawyer, Doc. Yes, if he's vacated and the Vanders grant permission, you're in. And if there was no formal agreement vis-à-vis the job and he just moved in, I suppose a case could be made that he's a guest. How long's he been there?"

"Three years," said Reed.

"Nope, no way that's a guest. One

more thing to be aware of: Even if you get someone to sign a warrant for the room, Huck's belongings won't fall under its provisions unless he's abandoned them. And you can't play fast and loose with that, they need to be obvious discards. It's exactly the kind of privacy issue the courts get picky about . . . though the exterior surfaces of *permanent* furniture previously owned by the Vanders might be . . . it's possible you can swab the furniture."

He scratched his head. "To be honest, I don't have a clue without doing some depth research. It's not the kind of thing that comes up." Smiling. "You could make case law but lose your bad guy."

Milo said, "If we get permission from the Vanders and see something creepy in plain sight—"

Nguyen covered his ears.

"What?" said Milo.

"That game might work on a brain-dead bar-murder mope. Plain sight, indeed. Huck hasn't answered your phone calls, so he's clearly opposed to cooperating. Who's going to believe he'd leave evidence around?"

"Stupid criminals," said Moe Reed. "Without them, the job's as funny as a heart attack."

Milo shot him a sharp look that took on amusement. Turned back to Nguyen. "Detective Reed makes a good point, John. What if Huck thinks he's all fortressed up and gets cocky? We get in somehow, use the element of surprise, there's no telling."

"If he's even there, Milo. Two days running, none of you have seen him coming or going and that Lexus is gone. You're the detectives. Doesn't that smell of bunny hop?"

"Running for president of the Pessimist Club, John?"

"I thought of it," said Nguyen, "but they're too giddy a bunch."

Moe Reed said, "He can't have it both ways. Guy rabbits with intention never to return, what he leaves behind is abandoned, right?"

Nguyen studied the young detective. "LAPD's growing them sophisticated, huh? Yeah, you'd be okay if it's indisputably obvious that he moved out permanently. And believe me, that's going to be challenged, they'll claim it was a vacation with expectation of privacy."

"Vacation from us?" said Reed. "That indicates guilt."

"Vacation from work, boredom, whatever he feels like getting away from, Detective Reed. The point is the Founding Fathers wanted people to be able to enjoy Yosemite without returning home and finding their house subjected to a police state ransack. And for this particular suspect a rabbit can be construed as something other than guilt. He was railroaded as a kid. What better justification for avoiding the cops?"

Reed's lips turned down. He ran a finger under his collar.

"Listen," said Nguyen, "you get permission from the Vanders, there's some latitude. But make sure it's in writing. At the least, you'll be able to go in, get a feel for the place, make contact with other people—maid, a gardener, whatever, see if they can incriminate Huck."

Milo said, "So far there's been no sign of any staff other than Huck."

Reed said, "But the place is huge, there's got to be someone."

Nguyen stood. "Always a pleasure, guys. Got a meeting."

As we reached the city parking lot, Reed got a call.

"Liz Wilkinson," he said, clicking off. Blushing. "*Doctor* Wilkinson. She wants to talk about the hand bones."

"Crypt's a ten-minute ride," said Milo. "Go for it."

"She's back at the marsh, studying those aerial photographs the chopper took this morning."

Reed had initiated the aerial scan.

"Anything from that?" said Milo.

Reed shook his head. Hurrying to his Crown Vic, he drove off fast.

We continued to Milo's unmarked. "Mind being the wheelman, Alex? Got some calls to make."

"Isn't that against regs?"

"Hell, yeah. I need something to cheer me up."

I directed the big, ungainly car westward as he called the forty-lawyer Beverly Hills firm that handled all of Simon Vander's legal interests. The first attorney who stonewalled was named Sarah Lichter but when Milo kept pushing her secretary, the fact emerged that Ms. Lichter had represented Mr. Vander on "a business matter some years ago," but Mr. Vander's primary attorney for "the majority of business matters" was Mr. Alston B. Weir.

Weir's secretary was amiable but no more helpful, referring him to Weir's paralegal, who put him on hold. He switched the phone to speaker, yawned, stretched, studied downtown streets.

The unmarked's alignment was way off, forcing me to wrestle the wheel. My appreciation for Milo's job performance kicked up a notch.

A cheerful, syrupy voice said, "Buddy Weir. How can I help the police?"

Milo told him.

"Travis? That's a bit shocking," said Weir.

"You know him?"

"I've met him. What I mean is the fact that anyone Simon or Nadine would hire being . . . I certainly hope that's not the case. In terms of getting into the house . . . I suppose, given the circumstances, that neither Simon nor Nadine would have a serious problem with a *supervised* visit. You really think that's necessary?"

"We do."

"Oh, my," said Weir. "If you're correct about Travis being involved in something criminal—this is *really* shocking—my assumption is Simon and Nadine will appreciate your assistance."

"Our job is to assist, sir."

"Thank you, Detective. Let me see if I can reach Si—Mr. Vander."

"Simone said he was in Hong Kong."

"Did she? Well that's helpful . . . one thing, Detective. Criminal law isn't my specialty but I'm not sure Simon or Nadine's permission to enter the house will indemnify you against legal roadblocks in the future."

"What kind of legal roadblocks, sir?"

"Defense attorney's tactics," said Weir. "If it gets to that."

"What comes to mind, sir?"

"As I said, it's not my field of expertise, but right off the bat I can see all sorts of tenancy issues. If Travis's living arrangement was a formal rental or lease, either directly or in the form of a perquisite . . ."

He spieled on, repeating John Nguyen's oration nearly word for word. Milo stayed silent, flapped his hand like a duck's bill.

When Weir finished, he said, "We'll bear all that in mind, sir."

Weir said, "Let's return to the crux: reaching Simon and Nadine in Hong Kong."

"She's in Taiwan with family."

"Oh," said Weir. "Good, that's helpful. If I reach anyone—let's think positive and say *when*—I'll have them fax me limited power of attorney. That way I can get you in there."

"Thank you, sir. Please include the beach house."

"The beach house," said Weir. "Can't see why not."

"One more question," said Milo. "Who else works in the main house besides Travis Huck?"

"I'm really not sure," said Weir.

"Maids, housekeepers, that kind of thing?"

"The times I've been there, I've seen gardeners but no regular staff."

"Big place like that?" said Milo. "Who cleans it?"

"Travis manages the estate, maybe he arranges things—one of those cleaning services you call, as needed? I really don't know, Lieutenant. We don't pay the bills, they're handled through a private bank up in Seattle . . . here we are, Global Investment."

He read off a number. "Oh, boy."

"What, sir?"

Buddy Weir said, "If Travis does decide when the house is cleaned he'd be in a position to obscure evidence, wouldn't he?"

"That's why we want to get in A-sap."

"Of course . . . Lieutenant, on a one-to-ten scale, how serious is this?"

"It's a homicide, Mr. Weir, but I can't honestly tell you Mr. Huck's definitely the perpetrator."

"But you suspect him."

"He's a person of interest."

"Wonderful," said Weir. "Just wonderful. I *need* to reach Simon."

CHAPTER

22

I took Beverly Boulevard west as Milo phoned Global Investment in Seattle.

Several underlings and one private banker later, he managed to cadge the fact that a Palisades-based service called Happy Hands cleaned both Vander houses on an as-needed basis.

"Who determines when it's needed?" said Milo.

"How would I know that?" said the banker.

Click.

Milo glared at the phone, stashed it. "So Huck does control the process. My gut's telling me he's split. But like I said, going public is always a double edge. With Huck living under the radar from the time he got out of juvey until three years ago, putting on the pressure could get him burrowed deeper."

I said, "Living underground can be an education."

"What do you mean?"

"He may have been innocent of what put him in juvey, but the experience and what followed could've taught him nasty habits."

"Strangulation and mutilation for fun and profit . . . How would a guy like that get in with the Vanders?"

"Maybe they're kindhearted."

"Gentle, nurturant rich folk."

"It happens."

"Think so?"

"You don't?"

"I'm sure there are some like that, but I have to wonder if the kind of ego it takes to amass all that dough excludes kindness."

"Ace Detective Vladimir Lenin."

"Power to the people." He thrust a clenched fist, had to bend his arm to avoid hitting the car's headliner. "Drive to Mo-ghul. All this failure is giving me an ap-petite."

"You say the same thing about success."

"Least I'm consistent."

We stashed the car in the staff lot, walked to the restaurant. The room was buzzing; two long tables filled with white-collar co-workers and a corner booth occupied by Moe Reed and Liz Wilkinson.

The two of them sat closer together than required for business. Serving bowls were untouched. Reed had his jacket on, but he'd removed his tie, spread his collar. Liz Wilkinson's unnetted hair was a wealth of glossy ringlets. A teal-blue dress worked well with her skin tone.

He smiled, she laughed. Their elbows bumped. They both laughed.

They saw us simultaneously, startled like kids caught playing doctor.

Reed shot to his feet. "Loo. Doc. Dr. Wilkinson's got interesting stuff to tell us about those finger bones. 'Bout time we got something, huh?"

Jabbering fast. Liz Wilkinson stared up at him.

Milo eyed a plate of lamb. "I converted you to curry, Detective Reed?"

"She—Dr. Wilkinson likes it."

Liz Wilkinson said, "It just so happens to be one of my favorite cuisines, so when Moses suggested it, I thought great. I'm adding this place to my list."

"Join us," Reed said, with more volume than necessary.

The bespectacled woman emerged from the rear of the restaurant. Today's sari was blood red. The sight of Milo made her glow. She hurried back to the kitchen.

"She sure looks happy," said Liz Wilkinson.

"He's a good customer," said Reed. "The lieutenant."

Moments later, a platter of lobster arrived with a flourish.

Liz said, "Whoa, someone's VIP. Thanks for letting us ride your coattail, Lieutenant."

"Milo's fine, Doctor. So what do you have for us?"

"We assembled the phalanges from the box and ended up with three complete sets. Given the dimensions of the left hands on all three of your buried victims, it was fairly easy to match everything up. Laura Chenoweth's digits were noticeably larger than those of the other two. And Number Three—Ms. Montouthe's— showed clear signs of arthritis. The other finding is the bones were subjected to an acid wash. Sulfuric acid, specifically, diluted to a level where it debrided—removed soft tissue but did no serious damage to the bone. I suspected some sort of treatment right off. The surfaces are much smoother—polished, really—than you'd expect from time and water and decomp. I did a scraping and found traces of sulfuric acid in the outer layer for all three victims."

Moe Reed said, "Shining them up fits with a personal trophy."

"So does placing them in a fancy box," I said. "The question is why go to all that trouble, then abandon the cache in a way that guaranteed discovery? That makes me wonder if they started as souvenirs but changed to something else: a taunt."

"'Look what I did,'" said Milo.

"It's consistent with the games Hernandez found in the storage unit."

"Playing with us."

Liz Wilkinson said, "What kind of games?"

Reed said, "Just the boards—Monopoly, Life."

"Money and basic existence," she said. "That's pretty primal."

Reed said, "Money, existence, ending someone else's existence." He shifted closer to her. She didn't mind.

I said, "Selena's murder also supports an exhibitionist angle. Up until her, the killer chose victims he considered throwaways, buried them where they could've remained indefinitely. Selena's murder was called in, her body left out in the open, with I.D. in her purse. He wanted us to know who she was and what he'd done to her."

Reed said, "And with her there, he was hoping we'd search the marsh, find the others."

"If you didn't, there'd be other prompts."

Milo said, "He stops paying for storage, knows the unit will come up just around the time he's gonna do Selena. Whole damn thing's a production?"

Liz Wilkinson grimaced. "Treating the fingers with acid means he kept the bodies. Maybe to play with them."

Reed said, "You okay?"

"Fine. I just usually don't see this side of it." As she moved to smooth hair from her face, her fingers brushed his cuff. "People ask me all the time if I get grossed out working with remains. When I tell them I love it, they look at me funny. But down at the tissue level, you can deny. Once I start thinking about a human being connected to what's on the table . . ." She pushed her plate away. "Guess I'd better be getting back. If you want, Moses, we can talk about that other stuff later."

"I'll walk you out."

When Reed returned to the restaurant, Milo said, "What other stuff?"

"Pardon?"

"What you'll be talking to the good doctor about."

Reed went scarlet. "Oh, that. She's putting together a forensics reading list. I figured it's something I should know."

"The power of education—you eating any of that lamb?"

"All yours, Loo. Guess I should also be booking."

"Why?"

"Thought I'd go by the Vander house, maybe I can catch Huck coming or going."

Milo shook his head. "I'll go through His Eminence, get some patrol officers into civvies to run shifts. You're meant for bigger and better."

"Like what?"

"Go nationwide on unsolveds featuring missing limbs, body parts treated with chemicals. Start with hands but don't limit yourself."

Reed said, "Legs, arms, whatever."

"Heads, shoulders, knees and toes. I don't care as long as something got cut off."

"You're figuring he could've switched techniques?"

"As Dr. Delaware likes to remind me, patterns are for fabric." He turned to me. "If the bodies were kept around to play with, the Vanders' property probably isn't the crime scene. Estate manager or not, setting up Dr. Frankenstein's lab in that place would be too risky."

Reed said, "Not if the Vanders are also involved in weird stuff."

"Even so, Moses. They've got a kid on the premises. Kinky parties after Junior's gone to bed is one thing—and even there, I'm doubtful because we've got no evidence saying these people are bizarre. But hacking up corpses in the manse with Junior around is over the top."

"So Huck has another place."

"Maybe that's why we haven't seen him, he's hiding out in his kill-crib. Check with the assessor, see if he pays property tax on anything. Rentals are a problem, no way we'll be able to trace unless we go public on him and I'm not ready for that."

I said, "When we were at Pacific Storage you made a crack about people living there and the attendant denied it. But I'm sure it happens."

Milo thought about that. "Worth checking out. Including back at Pacific itself. We never showed the clerk Huck's picture. Your plate getting too full, Moe?"

"Not even close," said Reed. "Give me more."

"Nothing more. Sure you don't want any lunch?"

"No thanks, let me get going."

After finishing Reed's and Wilkinson's food, Milo topped off his meal with the lobster and two bowls of rice pudding. He returned to his office. I went home and repeated searches on *Travis Huck, Edward/ Eddie/Eddy/Ed Huckstadter,* came up empty.

Keywording *Simon Vander* pulled up the eight-figure grocery chain sale and a couple of mentions of Vander and his wife on charity committees: the art museum, the zoo, Huntington Library. Your basic genteel philanthropy.

If Simon and Nadine Vander had a dark side, they'd hid that fact from cyberspace.

At four thirty, I logged off, talked to Robin about dinner. Pasta sounded good to both of us. She kept working and I made a run up to the market at the top of the Glen, called my service.

One message from Alma Reynolds.

The operator said, "She said if you didn't remember her name, she's Sil Duboff's lover."

"I remember her."

"Interesting way to label yourself, don't you think, Dr. Delaware? Someone's lover? Then again, you deal with all types."

Alma Reynolds's phone rang eight times. I was just about to hang up when she answered.

"Lieutenant Sturgis didn't call back, I figured I'd get the same from you," she said. "I'm running out to the mortuary. They're releasing Sil in a few days. He always talked about cremation, as long as it could be done in an eco-respectful manner. The ideal, of course, would be if all of us were just placed in the compost heap."

"What's up?"

"Anything new on the case?"

"Not yet, sorry."

"Well, I thought of something. Been ruminating about what could've gotten Sil over to the marsh that night. Not that he needed prodding, he was always going there. To clean up trash, make sure no one had trespassed. He had a thing for that place. Truth is, he was somewhat obsessed. I know why. His parents were beatniks who moved from Ann Arbor to a rural part of Wisconsin. The family lived in a cabin near a guess-what."

"Freshwater and reeds."

"A huge marsh, fed by one of the Great Lakes. Sil said it was perfect—idyllic, until a paper mill opened up nearby and polluted the hell out of it. All the fish died, the air smelled horrible, and eventually Sil's family had to move to Milwaukee. Both his parents died of cancer and he was convinced it was the toxic air and water. Even though his father was a three-pack-a-day smoker who got lung cancer, and breast cancer ran in his mother's family. But try telling Sil that. Try telling him anything."

I said, "I can see why the Bird Marsh would be important to him."

"Obsessed," said Alma Reynolds. "Sometimes it got in the way."

"Of what?"

"Us. We'd be relaxing and he'd jump up suddenly, say he needed to drive over, make sure everything was okay. It annoyed me, but I rarely said anything because I could see the psychology behind the idealism. But the night he was—that night, I really didn't want to go and he defied me. So it had to be something major."

"He told you the caller promised to solve the murders."

"And I believed him. When those bodies showed up, Sil took it personally, as if he'd allowed something to happen to his baby. He was also worried the murders would be used to say the marsh was no longer pristine and that would open the door to development. I know it sounds paranoid, but Sil didn't dance to anyone else's beat. Just the opposite, the world waltzed, he two-stepped."

I said, "With that level of anxiety, he'd follow any lead."

"Exactly. I'm glad I reached you and not Sturgis."

"Did Sil give any indication he knew who'd called?"

"No," she said. "I thought about that, trying to remember if he indicated one way or the other, and he didn't. You're thinking someone he respected might've gotten him over."

"Someone who supported his work. Do you have a list of Save the Marsh members?"

"Never saw one, don't know that one exists."

"Who's in charge of the office now?"

"Don't know, don't want to know," she said. "I wash my hands of all of it."

No one answered at Save the Marsh.

The group's board of directors listed the progressive billionaires who'd tried to build on the land, in addition to Silford Duboff, a woman named Chaparral Stevens, and two men: Tomas Friedkin, M.D., and Lionel Mergsamer, Ph.D.

Chaparral Stevens was a Sierra Madre–based jewelry designer, Dr. Friedkin was a ninety-year-old ophthalmologist, emeritus at the U.'s med school. Professor Mergsamer was a Stanford astronomer.

Not a likely bunch, criminal-wise, but I printed their names.

I looked for fund-raisers held for the marsh, found three Westside cocktail parties, no listed guests.

Backing away from the trees, I thought about the forest: *Why* had Silford Duboff been lured to his death?

Dispatching him didn't fit with the thrill-seeking aspect of a sexual psychopath. The only motive that made sense was he'd known too much—knowledge that came about innocently or otherwise.

More bones beneath the muck? Aerial photos had revealed nothing, but the earth had a way of swallowing and digesting death.

Or Alma Reynolds was right and Duboff's desire to play savior—to undo his childhood trauma—had led him to walk into a trap.

That felt analytically pat, but I turned it over and came up with nothing further. A soft rap on my office door snapped the tape loop.

"You look engrossed," said Robin.

"No, I'm finished."

"If you're not, I can cook."

I got up and we walked to the kitchen.

She said, "Co-Op-E-Ration, just like on *Sesame Street.* Want to be Bert or Ernie?"

"Maybe Oscar."

"That kind of day, huh?"

Blanche waddled in and smiled.

I said, "She can set the table."

CHAPTER

23

Head, arms, and legs in Missouri," said Moe Reed. "Head, hands, and feet in New Jersey. Three hands and feet only in . . ." He scanned his notes. "Washington State, West Virginia, and Ohio."

Milo said, "Nothing with just hands."

"Nope. And no acid wash. Plus, in three cases, they have a good idea who it is but don't have enough evidence to bring charges."

We were in a Westside interview room at the end of another draggy day. Milo's follow-up call to Buddy Weir had evoked a "still working on it" message from the

attorney's paralegal. Plainclothes surveillance of the house on Calle Maritimo had
revealed no movement, other than the entry of a gardener's crew.

None of the groundsmen had any idea
if Huck was inside the house, and when
Milo convinced one of them to ring the
front doorbell, no one answered.

Huck continued to refuse telephonic in-
vitations to talk with the police.

Reed said, "The one in Jersey, they're
sure is a mob deal. Victim was I.D.'d by a
surgical scar on the back."

"Some goombah with disk problems.
Anything else?"

Reed shook his head.

I said, "Any of the amputations spare
only one hand?"

"Nope."

"Because chopping was used to hinder
the investigation. Our case has nothing to
do with that. Our hands are symbolic."

"Of what?" said Milo.

"I'm good with questions, not answers,"
I said. "But maybe something to do with
Selena's piano playing?"

"People play piano with both hands,
Alex."

"The right hand plays the melody."

Both their expressions said thanks, but no thanks.

"An alternative," I said, "is someone's trying to make the killings appear bizarre."

"Psychosexual fake-out?" said Milo. "To hide what?"

"I keep coming back to Selena. She really stands out from the others. What if this is all *about* her and the other women were prep?"

Milo said, "Over a year of prep? What made Selena so important?"

"Something she knew turned her into a threat. Something serious enough to take her computer. Same reason Duboff got killed."

"Long-term planning is usually about money."

Reed said, "And the Vanders have big money—it keeps coming back to them. And Huck, who works for them."

Milo said, "If you're right about the other women, digging up background on them isn't a good use of our time."

I said, "The killer had to connect with them somehow, so it could still bear fruit."

Reed said, "I've been up and down the

airport stroll and no one remembers Huck."

"It's a transitory population. And people have short memories for all sorts of reasons."

Milo got up, paced, pulled out a panatela. Moe Reed relaxed when the cigar dropped back into a pocket. "A guy goes for hookers, who says he limits himself to one neighborhood?"

"Another stroll?" said Reed.

"Huck lives in the Palisades," I said. "For pure fun, he could stay on the Westside. But when he's trawling for victims, he travels to where he's less likely to be recognized."

"Maybe somewhere closer to his kill-crib," said Reed. "Which could be relatively close to the Vander house. Not that I've found anything in the assessor's files or anywhere else."

Milo said, "The airport, the marsh—that storage facility—they're *all* pretty close together. So the crib could be in that vicinity."

Reed said, "To find a rental we have to go public, hope someone tips."

"It may come to that, Moses, but not

yet. Let's stick with the second-stroll angle. If we can find other working girls Huck frequented, learn he's into rough sex, maybe even put his hands around someone's neck, it sets up cause for a warrant."

"I could do Lincoln Boulevard farther north."

"Good idea. That doesn't pan out, we move on to the Strip. In fact, we don't wait. Tonight, you do Lincoln then Sunset from Doheny to Fairfax. I'll take Sunset East to Rampart, then Downtown. I'll re-fax Huck's license to Vice, maybe someone's memory'll be jogged."

"What about surveillance of the house?"

"We continue to leave that to patrol. Huck doesn't show his face soon, I guess I'll have to talk to the brass about a press conference. In addition to the deep-burrow risk, we've really got nothing on the guy and he's already been the victim of official injustice. Can't you just hear the defense attorney's opening statement?"

He turned to me: "In terms of Duboff getting gutted by another marsh hugger, maybe, but making our way through the eco-crowd is low priority."

I said, "I'll see what I can find."

Reed said, "Might as well join the department, Doc."

Milo said, "He's my friend. Watch your mouth."

Save the Marsh: A Citizens' Committee was headquartered in a beige frame bungalow in Playa Del Rey, where that district turns into a cute little village of cafés and shops.

Two miles from the marsh, closer yet to Pacific Storage.

The building was shuttered. No cars sat in the three-space lot.

No ad hoc memorial to Duboff—no evidence at all he'd been murdered.

I walked across the street to an eatery called Chez Dauphin. White wood, blue shutters, screen porch, a handful of snackers. I ordered a roll and coffee, finished half before asking the Gallic proprietress if she knew who to contact at the bungalow.

She said, "Non, m'sieur, I have never seen anyone there."

I began phoning the people on the Save the Marsh board.

The voice-mail message at Chaparral

Stevens's jewelry business was sound-tracked by bird squawks, trickling water, and wind chimes. Stevens's voice was low-pitched and sultry, her speech slightly halting. The "tantric ecstasy" she claimed due to "my six-month spiritual retreat at the Monteverde Cloud Forest Reserve in breathtaking Coth-ta Ree-ca" came across like cannabis languor.

The secretary at the U.'s Ophthalmology Center told me Dr. Tomas Friedkin hadn't been heard from in years.

"At least, *I've* never seen him. In fact—I hope I'm wrong—I think he passed away."

"Oh, too bad," I said.

"Are you a colleague?"

"A student."

"Oh," she said. "Well, hold on and let me check."

Several beats later: "Yes, I'm sorry, he passed last year. One of his other students—Dr. Eisenberg—says the funeral took place on a boat. Ash-scattering, you know?"

"Dr. F. loved nature."

"We all should be like that, right? Go back where we came from, and stop making a big mess."

"Dr. F. was involved with the Bird Marsh."
"How nice. I love birds."

Professor Lionel Mergsamer was on full-year sabbatical at the Royal Observatory in Greenwich, England.

Everyone taking downtime. When was the last time I'd bothered? I tried the studio owned by the progressive billionaires, got exactly what I expected: long stretches on hold, an eventual hang-up.

An absentee board of directors implied ceremonial titles, meaning running the organization was left to anyone willing to shoulder the responsibility.

Meaning Silford Duboff.

Who else would know about the group . . . the volunteer kid who'd taken the killer's call . . . Chance Brandt.

No listing for the Brentwood residence but Steven A. Brandt's law office was in the book. Recalling his hostility, I figured him for a stonewall or a tantrum and called the Windward School. Fudging my police status and asking firmly to speak to Headmaster Rumley, I cajoled a secretary into forking over Master Brandt's cell number.

"Yeah?"

I told him who I was.

He said, "Yeah?"

"Chance, who did you see at the office besides Mr. Duboff?"

"Yeah?"

Female giggles and hip-hop bass thrum. I repeated the question.

"That place . . ." His words slurred. His girlfriend remained appreciative.

"What about it, Chance?"

"Yeah?"

Male laughter bottomed the girl's squeals.

"Who'd you see, Chance?"

"Yea—"

"Okay, we'll talk at the police station."

"Nobody, okay?"

"No one except Duboff."

"It's his *thing*. Marsh Man." Rising volume on the background hilarity. "Like he *fucks* it. All that mud."

Using the present tense; Duboff's murder hadn't hit the news. I thought of telling him about it, hung up instead.

Not to protect the kid's delicate sensibilities. Afraid he'd have none.

CHAPTER

24

Moe Reed burst into Café Moghul, wrestler's body canted forward, shoulders lowered. Aggressive surge, but smiling, as if charging toward victory.

First time I'd ever seen him happy.

Milo swallowed his tandoori chicken and wiped his mouth. "At least someone's having a good day."

He'd spent the night in a futile search for street girls who knew Travis Huck. The morning had been office-bound, filled with endless phone discussions, with an escalating series of higher-ups, of whether or not to go public with Travis Huck's identity.

The debate had reached the chief's office and the answer had just come down from the mount: Given Huck's history of judicial abuse, wait for more evidence.

Unless a new victim showed up. "Nothing like body-count politics."

I'd just finished telling him about Chance Brandt's bad attitude.

He said, "Generation N, for numb."

Reed sat down and waved his notepad. "Two hookers."

Milo put his fork down. "And the question is: 'What weekly perk comes with a congressional office?'"

Reed smiled. "Found 'em on the Strip, Loo. Forty bucks is what they charged Huck. They're both sure it was him, down to the crooked mouth. And guess what? He wasn't wearing a hat and he *is* totally skinned."

He flipped the pad open. "Charmaine L'Duvalier, real name's Corinne Dugworth, and Tammy Lynn Adams, that appears to be her righteous I.D. They both work Sunset, mostly between La Cienega and Fairfax. Huck picked Charmaine up right at Fairfax a month or so ago, Tammy Lynn hooked up with him two blocks west. She thinks it could be as recent as six weeks ago. Both times Huck was cruising at three, four a.m. in a Lexus SUV. Color and style match Vander's, guy gets to use the boss's wheels for recreation."

"Any unusual sexual habits?"

"They both recall him as super-quiet. Adams admitted he spooked her."

"Admitted?"

"These girls like to pretend they're street-hard, nothing scares them. I pushed her a little and she said, yeah, he kind of spooked her."

"In what way?"

"Being so quiet. Like he wasn't even pretending to make it friendly the way a lot of the johns do. Like he'd been paying for it for a long time and it was just another quickie business deal."

"As opposed to her," said Milo. "All the romance in her heart."

"What I'm seeing," said Reed, "is these girls need to feel in charge, so they come on tough. Makes a lot of johns nervous. Not Huck, sounds like he was totally at ease: Here's the dough, deliver the goods."

I said, "What did he pay for?"

"Oral sex."

"Anything aggressive?" said Milo. "Grabbing their hair, talking in a hostile manner?"

"Nope," said Reed. "I think he spooked both of them, but only Adams admitted it. She's been on the streets for five years, says she has a good sense for which guys are off. And Huck impressed her as one of them."

"But she took him on anyway."

"First impression he looked well groomed, was driving nice wheels. It was only after she got in that he started to get to her."

"By being quiet and business-like."

"Zero talk," said Reed. "Not making any sort of conversation."

"You get callback numbers for these girls?"

"Prepaid cells, for what they're worth. In terms of addresses, neither of them have driver's licenses and both claim to be looking for permanent residence."

"Ah, the glamorous life," said Milo.

"Yeah, it's b.s. but it's all I could get,

Loo. Both of 'em did agree to ask around about Huck. It sounds naive, thinking they'll cooperate, but maybe my asking about him kicked up the fear level. He tries to hook up with either of them again, I'm betting they'll let me know."

He spotted the woman in the sari, asked for iced tea.

She said, "No food?"

"No, thanks, just tea."

She walked off, shaking her head.

Milo said, "Excellent work, Detective Reed. Too bad I didn't know an hour ago." He summarized the debate about going to the press. "Not that I'm sure it would make a difference. Brass is really edgy about the whole thing falling apart due to lack of evidence, Huck suing the city."

Reed said, "They really think he'd have the balls to do that?"

"Best defense is a good offense, kiddo. We shine the spotlight on him without enough juice, he's in the driver's seat. Can't you just see him up on the stand, some lawyer guiding him through everything he went through in juvey?"

"What if he's named as a person of interest, not a suspect?"

Milo said, "That might buy us time, but Downtown isn't ready for it." His phone jangled Brahms. "Sturgis. Who? What about? Oh. Yeah, yeah, sure, give me the number."

He got to his feet. "Let's go."

"What's up, Loo?"

"Renewed faith in the flower of our youth."

The woman in the sari watched us leave, Reed's tea in hand. As we exited, she drank it.

The girl was barely five feet tall, seventeen, hard-bodied and glossy-tan, with luxuriant red hair, light freckles, and cornflower eyes.

Younger version of her mother. The two of them sat holding hands, a pair of pixies perched on a massive royal-blue damask couch.

The crimson silk sitting room gleamed like blood under a Swarovski chandelier. The fixture's long gold chain was wrapped in aqua satin, suspended from a twenty-foot coffered, gilded ceiling. Mullioned windows framed velvet acreage. Massive stone fireplaces graced both ends of the room. Renoir over one, Matisse over the other. Both paintings looked real.

We'd waited at the Brentwood Park gatehouse for several minutes before being allowed entry.

"I'm so proud of Sarabeth," said Hayley Oster. She wore a plum-colored Juicy Couture velour sweat suit. Hot day, but the manse was as chilly as a supermarket deli case. Her daughter's matching size 0 Juicy was moss green.

Oster, as in malls and shopping centers.

Milo said, "We're proud, too, ma'am." His smile caused Sarabeth to press closer to her mother.

Hayley Oster said, "You're sure I can't get you something to drink? It was extremely gracious of you to come down here and spare us a trip to the police station."

"No, thanks, ma'am. We appreciate your calling."

"It was the least I could do, Lieutenant. After Sarabeth became embroiled in that to-do with Chance Brandt at school, we made it clear that things had to change. Right, honey?"

Smiling at her daughter, but an elbow delivered a prod.

Sarabeth looked down and nodded.

Hayley Oster said, "The way my husband and I see it, Lieutenant, privilege is a blessing that should not be abused. Neither of us come from wealthy families and scarcely a day goes by that we don't thank our lucky stars for how far we've come. Harvey and I believe blessings should be repaid in kind. We do *not* tolerate poor character. Which is why we've always had reservations about Sarabeth associating with Chance."

The girl appeared ready to argue. Thought better of it.

"I know you think I'm being harsh, baby, but one day you'll see I'm right. Chance is *unsubstantial.* All looks, nothing beneath the veneer. Worse, he lacks moral fiber. In a sense, that makes me even prouder of Sarabeth. Though she found herself in the company of amorality, she chose to think independently."

The girl's eyes rolled.

Milo said, "Why don't you tell us about it, Sarabeth?"

"It's just what I said to Mom."

"Tell them," said Hayley Oster. "They need to hear it directly from you."

Sarabeth inhaled and shook out her hair. "Okay . . . okay. Someone called last night. Over at Sean's house."

"Sean who?" said Reed.

"Capelli."

Hayley said, "Another shallow young man. That school seems to breed them."

Milo said, "Someone phoned Sean?"

"Uh-uh," said Sarabeth. "Called Chance. We were at Sean's."

"Just hanging."

"Uh-huh."

"Tell us about the call."

"He said he was a cop—one of you guys. Asked if anyone else came into the office when Chance was there. Chance kept pranking, saying 'Yeah' over and over. He thought it was funny."

"The call?"

The girl didn't answer.

Another elbow prod made her say, "Ouch."

"Poor darling," said Hayley Oster, through tight jaws. "Let's get this over with, post-haste, Sarabeth."

"He lied," said Sarabeth. "Chance.

'Cause there was someone who *did* come in."

"To the office."

"Yeah."

"Who?"

"He just said that he knew him but he wasn't going to tell because he'd have to be pulled in by the cops again and his dad would get all up in his buttho—"

"Sara!"

"Whatever," said the girl.

"Whatever, indeed, young lady. Use language in a way that advertises your virtues."

Shrug.

Milo said, "Chance told you he lied to avoid getting involved."

"Yeah—yes."

Hayley Oster smirked. "Looks like *that* backfired."

We found the boy at the Riviera Tennis Club, playing singles with his mother. She nearly dropped her racket when we walked across the court.

"Now what?"

"We missed you," said Milo. "Your son, in particular."

"Oh shit," said Chance.

"Indeed."

The information came quickly, Chance sweating under full sun, wise-guy pretensions erased from his Polo-ad visage.

Not someone he *knew,* someone he *recognized.*

Milo said, "From a party."

"Yeah."

"Whose?"

"Theirs." Hooking a thumb at Susan Brandt.

She said, "What are you talking about? When's the last time we threw a party, your dad hates them."

"Not that," whined her son. "One of those fund-raisers—the boring shit you make me go to."

"Which boring shit in particular?" said Milo.

Chance pushed yellow hair out of his eyes. "One of 'em, dunno."

"You'll have to do better than that, son."

"Whatever . . ."

"For God's *sake,*" said Susan Brandt, "just tell them what they need and we'll finally be free of this."

Chance bounced a tennis ball.

His mother sighed. Switched her racket to her left hand and slapped him hard across the face with her right. Perspiration sprayed. Finger marks rouged the boy's cheek.

He had six inches and fifty pounds on her. Seemed to expand as his hands became fists.

She said, "You keep screwing around and I'll do it again."

Milo said, "There's no need for that, ma'am. Let's keep everything friendly."

"Do you have children, Lieutenant?"

"No, ma'am."

"Then you don't know anything."

"I'm sure I don't. Even so—"

Chance said, "A guy, okay? It was that Malibu thing, the lame bullshit thing where everyone wore Hawaiian shirts and pretended to be a surfer."

Susan Brandt said, "That one." To us: "He's referring to a Coastal Alliance benefit we attended last year—last fall. Despite what he says, we generally don't make him go to any of our charitable events, but that one, it was an outdoor barbecue, casual dress, other people brought their kids.

It was supposed to be a family affair, rock music and hot dogs." To her son: "You eat, you dance, you go home. Is *that* so bad?"

Chance rubbed his face.

His mother said, "We didn't know anyone there, only reason we went was Steve's firm donated and the senior partners were in Aspen, needed someone to attend."

"I saw the dude drinking beer."

Milo said, "Where did this party take place?"

"At the Seth Club," said Susan Brandt.

"Describe this person, Chance."

"Old." Smile. "Like Dad. Blond hair, bullshit hair."

"Dyed?"

"Yeah. Some old tool trying to look like a surfer. Bigtime Bondo job on the face."

"Bondo?" said his mother.

"It's putty used to patch cars," said Moe Reed.

Chance patted his cheek. The finger marks had begun to welt.

Milo said, "The guy had plastic surgery."

The boy snickered. "Ya *think*?"

"Chance," warned his mother.

The boy's eyes heated. "What, you're

gonna *hit* me again? In front of the *cops*? I could get you busted for *child* abuse, right?"

Milo said, "Easy now."

"You never *hit* me before, why you want to go *do* that?"

"Because . . ." Susan Brandt wrung her hands. "I'm sorry, I just didn't know what to—"

"*Right,* it's for my own *good.*"

She touched his arm. He shrugged her away ferociously.

Reed ushered her a few feet away. Eye-to-eye with Chance, Milo said, "Blond, tucked, what else?"

"Nothing."

"How old?"

"Like Dad."

"Middle age."

"Guy was a total tool—fucked-up hair."

"Fucked up, how?"

"Shaggy, moussed up. Retro-bullshit like . . . Billy *Idol.* All that shit in his face, like whoa, it's True Value Hardware."

"Tell us about this guy and Duboff."

"He showed up."

"How many times?"

"Once."

"When?"

"Dunno."

"Was it close to when you started volunteering or toward the end?"

The boy thought. "Start."

"So three, four weeks ago."

"Right at the start."

"So this guy comes in to see Duboff. Go on."

"Not *in, out.* The parking lot," said Chance. "I'm inside, bored fuckless, look out the window, there's two of them."

"Doing what?"

"Talking. I didn't hear what they were saying, didn't give a fuck. That's why I didn't say the whole thing to you when you called."

"When this guy and Duboff were talking, did it look friendly?"

Mental exercise strained the boy's eyes. "Dude gave Duboff something. Duboff looked happy."

"What'd he give him?"

"Envelope."

"What color?"

"Dunno—white. Yeah, white."

"Big or small?"

"A regular envelope."

"And Duboff looked happy."

"He shook dude's hand."

"Then what happened?"

"Dude drives off."

"In what?"

"Mercedes."

"Color?"

"Black? Gray?" said the boy. "Who the fuck remembers?" Staring defiantly and calling to his mother: "C'mon, Susie. Give it your best shot."

Susan Brandt wept.

Milo said, "We're going to show you some pictures, Chance."

As we drove away from the country club, Reed said, "One day, there's going to be a domestic violence call to their house."

Milo said, "Good bet . . . unfortunately, what the kid had to say boils down to nada. Blond guy who drives a Mercedes and who the kid swears ain't Huck."

I said, "Unless the guy was paying Duboff off for something."

"Like what?" said Reed. "Swimming privileges in the marsh?"

Milo laughed. "Congrats, Detective Reed."

"On what?"

"Bitter sarcasm, you have now achieved optimal workplace adjustment. My bet is the guy was making a donation to the herons and gulls. Chance saw him at an ocean benefit, we're talking eco-sensitivity."

"Water guy," said Reed.

"Meanwhile, we drown."

CHAPTER

25

A flurry of message slips crowded Milo's desktop.

Three halfhearted media follow-ups on the marsh murders, two deputy chiefs requesting confirmation that Milo had gotten the message about no BOLO on Travis Huck.

He played target practice with his wastebasket, kept reading. "All right, *here's* a keeper. Mr. Alston 'Buddy' Weir, and *another* one, Selena's brother Marc, up in Oakland."

"Brother probably wants follow-up."

"Grab yourself a phone in the main room and find out."

After Reed left, Milo called Weir, switched to speaker. "So we can share the misery."

The usual paralegal answered, but Weir came on quickly. "Lieutenant, thanks for getting back to me." Weir's smooth voice sounded higher, tighter.

"What's up, sir?"

"I'm getting concerned. Simon hasn't responded to my calls or my e-mails and when I phoned the Peninsula in Hong Kong, they informed me he checked out last week. I immediately got in touch with Ron Balter at Global, but he had no idea where Simon was. I got him to go through Simon's recent purchases and we found that Simon indeed flew back to the States. But he hasn't used his credit cards since."

"Back to L.A.?"

"No, San Francisco."

"Is that unusual for Mr. Vander?"

"Not really," said Weir. "Simon and Nadine love San Francisco, go for art fairs, that kind of thing. They generally stay at the Ritz, but there's no record of either of them checking in."

"Does Mr. Vander generally keep such a low profile?"

"He's a low-key person, no question about that. But he's generally good about responding to calls. And he always uses credit cards, carries very little cash. That's not all, Lieutenant. I tried to reach Nadine in Taiwan, was told by her family that she and Kelvin left around the same time Simon flew out of Hong Kong."

"Did her family say why?"

"No," said Weir, "but there's something of a language gap."

"So it could be a family vacation—wanting to be together."

"Yes, of course. But the credit cards, Lieutenant. Both Simon and Nadine charge everything. I phoned Simone to see if she knew anything about this. She didn't and she grew extremely upset . . . about Travis Huck."

"She thinks Huck's harmed her family?"

"She doesn't know what to think, Lieutenant."

"Would Huck know their whereabouts in San Francisco?"

"I really can't say. After I spoke with Simone, I felt I should do something, so I went over to the house and looked around. It does appear as if Huck's jumped ship. His room is empty, everything's been cleared out. I suppose that could be construed as guilt over something . . . I just don't know."

Milo mouthed a silent *Shit.* Rubbed his face. "How thoroughly did you search?"

"I opened some drawers, looked around. He's gone."

"You went by yourself?"

"No, with Simone. I felt that as a close family member, given exigent circumstances, she'd have a right to enter the premises. In fact, I don't know why I didn't think of that before, when you asked me for entry. What's your feeling about Huck clearing out?"

"Hard to say, sir."

"I suppose it's possible," said Weir, "that he got spooked after being questioned by you people. But still, if there's nothing to worry about, why flee? Or maybe he simply up and quit, the typical California thing."

"Flaky."

"Seems to come with the weather, Lieutenant."

Milo said, "When can we do our own walk-through?"

"Say when and I'll have someone from the office meet you there."

"How about in an hour?"

"An hour? I didn't realize . . . there are meetings all day . . . let me see here—more meetings until noon tomorrow. How about eleven a.m. tomorrow? I'll send Sandra, my best paralegal."

"Have you checked the beach house?"

"Simone and I had a brief look and it seemed to us no one had been there for a while. I'll make sure Sandra has keys to the beach house as well."

"Thank you, sir."

"I'm sure the family's fine," said Weir. "There's absolutely no reason for them not to be."

Milo phoned a source at Homeland Security and verified Simon, Nadine, and Kelvin Vander's flight schedules. All three had traveled first-class on Singapore Airlines, with Simon entering SFO a day before his wife and son.

The next call was to the Seattle money managers, where he cajoled a cagey

Ronald W. Balter, Certified Financial Planner, and confirmed that nothing beyond airfare had been billed to the Vanders' credit cards.

"Do they have a place in Northern California?"

"A home?" said Balter. "No."

"What about a rental property?"

"No."

"Any idea where they could be, sir?"

"Of course not."

"Of course?"

Balter said, "I manage their money, I don't get involved in their personal life."

"Mr. Weir seems concerned."

"I'm sure he is."

"Why's that?"

"He's more involved with their personal life."

Moe Reed returned to the office and gave a thumbs-up. "Marc Green didn't want follow-up. He recalled something else Selena told him."

"Sudden memory jog?" said Milo.

"My feeling is he didn't want to bring it up in front of his mother. Apparently, Selena had started dating someone a few

months before she died. Marc can't remember exactly when but he thinks it was
three, four months ago when she told him.
An older guy."

"How old?"

"She didn't say. Marc says she was embarrassed about it, so could be there was
a serious age gap. The juicy part is she
kept up that confession habit of hers, told
Marc the guy liked it rough. And so did
she, the two of them fit together like a
socket and a wrench. Her words."

"Sounds like something a guy would tell
her."

"I agree, Loo. So now we have a dominance thing consistent with Sheralyn and
DeMaura. Maybe on that level Selena
wasn't that different from the others. What
do you think, Doc?"

I said, "It does put things in a new
light."

Milo said, "An older guy into rough. She
say anything else about him?"

Reed said, "No, no, it's likely some
swinger she met at one of those parties,
right?"

Milo said, "Older. Simon Vander would
sure qualify. And so would Huck, he's

thirty-seven, which is eleven years older than Selena. The net does seem to be tightening. And things could be even nastier than we thought."

He summarized the news of the Vanders' return and disappearance.

Reed said, "Simon's sounding more like a victim than a bad guy. Unless he did bad things and needs to keep a low profile . . . to me, it still smells like Huck's our prime guy. We need to find him, we really do, Milo."

First time he'd addressed the boss by name.

Optimal workplace adjustment.

CHAPTER

26

At seven p.m. the following day, an LAPD press release offered Travis Huck's name to the media. The timing was fine-tuned: too late for the papers or the six o'clock news, early enough for a feed to the eleven o'clock broadcast. Or in D.C. Henry Weinberg's words, "a trickle, not a flood, we're vulnerable, Lieutenant."

Departmental spinners described Huck as a "person of interest" and included "a prior felony conviction." None of the four women found in the marsh was mentioned by name. The Vanders never came up.

In the interim, Milo and Reed and I did

walk-throughs of both Vander residences. We hit the beach house first, found no evidence the family had ever lived there. Soggy leather furniture sat on purple wall-to-wall. The smell was salt, rust, an old-paint sourness that shouted disuse. Oars and a man's wetsuit in the closet said the place hadn't progressed much past bachelor pad.

Heavy twin doors at the mansion on Calle Maritimo opened to a loose chain of high, broad vanilla rooms, tastefully if blandly furnished, floored with golden limestone. Family photos tilted on a couple of mantels, abstract art hung in the spaces where windows didn't dominate. A grand piano took up a corner of a cavernous back room. A spinet piano sat in Kelvin's sky-blue bedroom.

Travis Huck's quarters consisted of a smallish room past a vast caterer's kitchen and a lav. Twin bed, IKEA dresser, aluminum reading lamp. Monastic, but cheered by an ocean view. Placement in the service wing said the space had been designed as a maid's room.

No signs of struggle or body fluids there, or anywhere else, but Milo called for a crime scene team. The legal assistant Buddy Weir sent to keep watch looked alarmed, but she checked with the attorney and he told her to cooperate.

Given a huge backlog, the techs were expected "within days," and Milo's call to the crime scene office didn't change that. He tried the chief, couldn't get through, smiled grimly.

Moe Reed said, "Keeping it in low gear?"

"Heaven forbid, kiddo."

Reed smiled. "I'm learning."

I left the detectives to their frustration and drove home. The discovery of Selena's lover had scrambled my theories about the three other women being a rehearsal for her; the case was boiling down to another hideous pattern of sexual sadism.

A killer building up his confidence. Selena, the unlucky upgrade.

I phoned Marc Green to see if there was anything more to tease out.

He'd been hovering on the brink of rage. My voice pushed him over.

I waited until he stopped shouting. "I

know it's tough, but I still need to ask. Is there anything more you—"

"More? All that shit I just told them isn't enough?"

Slam.

I drove to the Crenshaw District and paid a second visit to Beatrix Chenoweth, Big Laura's mother. Ready to serve as an anger receptacle again. If anyone was trained for that, I was.

She saw me in graciously, served coffee and chocolate wafers. Waited me out as I approached the topic with as much tact as I could muster.

She said, "Let me understand this: You want to know if Lurlene liked being hurt?"

"We've found evidence of that in other victims, so—"

"The answer is yes, Doctor. I didn't mention it the first time because . . . because I was so stunned when you all dropped in. I've been thinking about calling, but talking about that kind of thing is hard. I won't pretend Lurlene and I were close, but she was my child. Imagining what happened to her hurts me terribly."

"I'm sorry."

"Any progress?"

"Not so far."

"But you've got other victims who . . . oh, Lord . . . Lurlene's time on the streets, part of me has been waiting for this." Thin, square shoulders rose and fell. Her hands shook. "Did she like being hurt? When she was a child, just the opposite, Lurlene was the one hitting other people and getting in trouble over it. I kept telling her being big meant she needed to be doubly responsible." Frown. "It wasn't until later, when I realized what a problem her weight was, that I knew I'd said exactly the wrong thing . . . did she like being hurt . . . apparently, yes. I'm talking about later, when she was out of the house. *Working.*"

She grabbed for a hankie, stanched a sudden burst of tears. "As if that's a *job.*"

Clearing her throat, she put steel in her voice: "A couple of times when she came by—for money—I noticed bruises. Here. Here." Fingering both sides of her own neck. "At first I wasn't sure they were bruises. Lurlene was dark, took after her father. And the first time she was trying to cover it, wearing a scarf. Which is exactly why I *noticed,* Lurlene *never* wore scarves. I spotted something purple beneath the fabric, put my finger there, and she slapped it away."

Wincing. "Hard, not just a love pat. But I can be as pigheaded as she can and I persisted and she got terribly angry and ripped it off—the scarf—and said, 'Happy?'

"I said, 'I'm not happy if someone hurt you, Lurlene.' She said, 'No one hurt me in any way I don't want to be hurt.' Then she smirked. I was appalled and that amused her. She rolled up her sleeves and I said here it comes, she'll show off her needle marks, what else does this girl have planned to disappoint me? But instead, she displayed more bruises on her wrists. I was repelled and turned away and that fueled her up. She told me people were willing to pay for extras and she had the confidence to handle anything. So of course, I got preachy. Told her dangerous ways led to— why bore you? She laughed at me and left."

Smiling. "That's the whole of it, sir."

I said, "You've been through a lot."

"My other girls are doing well. May I pour you more coffee?"

"Laura, too, now it's a hat trick," said Milo.

I'd pulled up to the station just as he stepped out the front door and began walking.

"All this exercise," I said. "I'm starting to worry about you."

"Afternoon constitutional at a non-aerobic pace," he said. "Walls tend to close in when I'm feeling useless. You probably jogged five miles this morning."

We passed the same houses and apartments. This time the sky stayed gray and the air was soupy and lazy.

He said, "Airport cops found the Vanders' Lexus in the LAX long-term lot, but we can't find evidence Huck flew anywhere."

"Oldest trick in the book."

"Young Moses and I have been canvassing nearby hotels and motels anyway. Same for fancy places from S.F. to Santa Barbara, looking for the Vanders. We also tried private charters. Zippo on all counts. This is smelling like a wild man on a rampage and he's long gone."

"Four sadistic sexual murders, playing

with the bones of three victims," I said. "Then Duboff, then the Vanders? Hard to see a theme there."

"Does there need to be?" he said. "That asshole in Kansas killed women, men, kids, whoever he found in the house. Same for Ramirez, Zodiac, blah blah blah."

"In those cases the males were collateral damage."

"The same could be true here. How about this for a theoretical: Huck works for the Vanders for three years, develops a letch for Nadine. Before he can have his way with her, he needs to get rid of Hubby and Kid."

"He manages to get them back from Asia?"

"He lied about something that got them back. These guys, it's all about control, right? Can you think of a better power trip than moving rich folk around like chess pieces? We come nosing around about Selena, he figures it's only a matter of time, so he splits."

I thought about that. "A family emergency might've worked as ruse. Simone's been hurt, or she's sick. Simon and Nadine trusted Huck, no reason to verify. But how does Duboff fit in?"

"When we nab Huck, we'll find out. Let's face it, Alex, when you cut through all the bullshit, this ain't a whodunit. We had the prime suspect in our sights right off the bat—he had good reason to sweat."

Ten steps later: "God only knows what Huck was doing all those under-the-radar years before the Vanders took him in. So, of course, he repays them in a metaphysi-cally consistent manner."

"No good deed," I said.

"I'm amending it," he said. "No good deed goes un-tied-up and bloodied and degraded and dumped like garbage."

"Too long for a bumper sticker."

CHAPTER

27

Limited TV exposure brought in thirty-four sightings of Edward T. Huckstadter aka Travis Huck.

Milo and Moe Reed spent two days chasing air.

A man who'd worked at the Youth Authority when Huck was in custody informed Reed that Huck had "given him the willies. Always crybabying about something, but those eyes of his . . ."

"Mean?" said Reed.

"Crafty, you know? Like when they're plotting something. I woulda never let him out."

"He do anything bad while he was in?"

"Not that I remember, but so what, I was right. Those types get all coiled up and wait like snakes."

Huck's name didn't show up on the passenger logs of trains and buses leaving L.A., but a Metro ticket paid for in cash would've provided easy escape. After some lawyerly hedging, Buddy Weir consented to have the Vanders' Lexus examined at the LAPD motor lab.

"But please, Lieutenant, no damage. I don't want Simon and Nadine returning home to that kind of thing."

No one was paying attention to Silford Duboff's murder, but I couldn't let go of it. I called Alma Reynolds, listened to the phone ring.

No voice mail, and she'd bragged about no cell for her or "Sil." Maybe no computer or TV either; I wondered if she'd heard about the search for Travis Huck.

She'd retired from teaching college, hadn't mentioned another job. I called Milo to see if the file contained a work number. He was over at the airport, re-scanning departure records, and I spoke to Moe Reed.

He said, "Let me check . . . here it is, doctor's office, West L.A. What are you figuring she can tell you?"

"Probably nothing."

"You do this a lot, huh? Helping out."

"When he asks."

"He ask you to check Reynolds?"

"Sometimes I improvise."

"Yeah," said Reed. "He told me that."

Given Alma Reynolds's lifestyle, my bet was on some sort of holistic practice for her employer. But her boss turned out to be a conventional ophthalmologist in a conventional building on Sepulveda near Olympic.

The waiting room was full. Small-print brochures for LASIK were the preferred reading material.

Reynolds's job title was office coordinator. The receptionist at the front seemed happy for a break in routine. About my age, with short dark hair and an easy smile.

"Sorry, she's gone to lunch."

"Two forty-five," I said. "Kind of late."

"We were swamped all morning, I guess she didn't have time till now."

"Any idea where she eats?"

"This about her boyfriend?"

"It is. She talk about him?"

"Just that she misses him. Wants to see whoever did such a terrible thing pay—you don't wear contacts, do you?"

"Nope."

"Thought so," she said. "Your eyes are that natural gray-blue, with colored lenses they tend to overdo the blue . . . Alma likes Mexican, there's a strip mall three blocks west."

The mall provided easy parking and six ethnic restaurants. Alma Reynolds was the sole patron of Cocina de Cabo, sitting in a blue, molded-resin booth, enjoying blue corn fish tacos and a can of Coke Zero. Despite the heat, she had on the same mannish wool slacks, below a white V-neck that made her look ten pounds lighter than the work shirt she'd worn at the station. Long gray hair was tied back in a ponytail, and I thought I spotted makeup around wrinkle lines. Bright blue eyes made me wonder about cosmetic lenses.

I waved. She slapped a hand on her chest. "Stalking me?"

"Only in the service of public safety. May I sit down?"

"Can I stop you?"

"If it's not a good—"

"Just kidding. *Sentarse.* I think that's the right word, when in Cabo, do as the Caboans do." Her big jaw jutted and the blue eyes lowered to her taco. "Sil was a vegan. I eat fish from time to time."

"I was wondering if you've come up with any other ideas."

Her mouth narrowed. "Citizen participation? The answer is no."

"One thing we're still trying to figure out is how Sil fits the other murders."

"Maybe he doesn't."

I waited.

"That's all," she said. "Maybe he doesn't. One of those lunatic copycats. Unless the scumbag who lured him over was trying to hide something about the first murders."

"Lured him with a promise to help him solve the other murders."

The hand on her chest shifted and I spotted a glint of gold. She moved her fingers back into position. "Yes."

"Do you think it could've been someone

who knew Sil well enough to push his buttons?"

"Such as?"

"A friend, even an acquaintance who understood his attachment to the marsh."

"His friend was me," she said. "Same for acquaintance."

"Limited social circle."

"By choice. People can be so tiresome."

"What about someone who knew him indirectly—through his work?"

"That's a possibility, but he never mentioned a name."

"We can't seem to find a membership roster for Save the Marsh."

"That's because it's not a real group. In the beginning—after Sil rescued the marsh from the B.S. boys, Billionaire Scum—a board was established. But that was just rich people trying to feel virtuous. No meetings were ever held. For all practical purposes, STM was *Sil*."

"Who paid the bills?"

"Said nine-figure scumbags. I told Sil it was risky, once he got too dependent on them they'd have complete control, like dope pushers. But he said he wanted to take them for every dollar they'd give, worry about consequences later."

Her lower lip shook and her hand wavered for a second before returning to her chest. Just long enough to reveal a huge pearl on a chain.

She picked up a taco, nibbled, put it down. "I'd like to be alone, if you don't mind."

"Bear with me, please. What was Sil's salary?"

"It was a stipend," she said. "So the B.S. boys could avoid payroll taxes. Twenty-five thousand. Sil said anyone could live on that if they simplified."

Her hand fanned out over the pearl.

"Pretty," I said.

Her neck turned red. "Sil gave it to me for my birthday. I hated it, told him I'd never wear it, too ostentatious. Now I wear it."

I nodded.

She said, "Don't pretend you understand, because you don't. People like Sil and myself are more than intelligent enough to play by the rules and live fat and sassy like every other urban droid. I've got master's degrees in two subjects and Sil had a B.A. in physics."

She leaned forward, as if offering a secret.

"We *chose* to embrace the core. But even Sil could be romantic. For our last anniversary, he wanted me to have something nice. Even idealists need some beauty in their lives."

"I agree."

"I told him I didn't want it, demanded he return it. He refused. We sparred. He outlasted me. Now I'm glad he did."

Her eyes traveled to the restaurant's wall of windows. "That your car? The green whatever it is."

"Seville."

"A Cadillac," she said. "Seville—nothing Spanish about it, what possesses corporate liars?"

"Sales."

"You're driving an egregious gas guzzler. What's your excuse?"

"We've been together over twenty years and I don't have the heart to trade her in for someone younger and prettier."

The hand dropped and her chest arched. Flaunting the necklace.

The pearl was outsized, creamy, unblemished. Too heavy for the chain, which looked flimsy, maybe plated.

I said, "So the billionaires paid all the bills and Sil ran the show. Did anyone else donate?"

"Sure, people would send checks in from time to time, but Sil called it petty cash. Without the B.S. Brothers, he'd have been out of luck. May I finish my lunch in peace? I really don't want to think about this anymore."

I thanked her and headed for the door.

She said, "You're not conservation-minded, but at least you're loyal."

The eye doctor's receptionist said, "You couldn't find her?"

"I found her, thanks for directing me. She seems pretty down."

"Wouldn't you be?"

"I'd probably be worse . . . maybe that humongous pearl will cheer her up."

"I doubt it," she said. "But it *is* something. She bought it for herself yesterday. We were all surprised."

"Not Alma's style?"

"Not hardly."

"Grief changes people," I said.

"Guess so . . . what else can I do for you?"

"Nothing." I turned heel.

"Then why'd you—"

"Just wanted to thank you for cooperating."

Before she could process the lie, I was gone.

CHAPTER
28

I drove a block west of the strip mall where Alma Reynolds lunched, circled a few times before scoring a parking spot with an unobtrusive view of Cocina de Cabo.

Reynolds left fifteen minutes later, walked back to work on foot, taking long slow steps, looking grim. I trailed her as slowly as I could, stopped half a block from the medical building.

She bypassed the front entrance, walked down the ramp to the sub-lot.

I didn't have to wait long before a dented, old yellow VW Bug putt-putted up the ramp. Reynolds slanted forward as if urging the little car faster. Dark smoke belched from the exhaust. Tsk tsk.

She headed straight for a pea-green apartment building on Fourteenth Street, just north of Pico. The numbers matched the home address Reed had given me. The place was ill maintained, half hidden by shaggy palms, the stucco molting.

The less glamorous side of Santa Monica. Even here, membership had its privileges: resident permit parking only. I hung back.

Alma Reynolds struggled a bit to wedge the Bug into a tiny space, bumped cars on both ends without apparent remorse. Slamming the door hard enough to vibrate the VW, she entered her building.

I stationed myself in front of a hydrant, listened to music. Thirty-five minutes later, I decided Reynolds was in for the day and drove home.

On the way, I tried Milo again, left a message. Just as I reached Westwood Village, my cell beeped.

"Hi, Doc, it's Louise from your service. A Dr. Rothman just called."

"Nathalie Rothman?"

"She didn't give a first name, said call

as soon as you had a chance. Something about a Mr. Travis."

I hadn't spoken with Nathalie Rothman in years.

She said, "I'm tied up with patients, Alex, but if you want we can talk later."

"You know Travis Huck?"

"Know? That's a bit—sorry, Alex, hold on . . ." After several moments of dead air: "One of the residents just had a baby and we're hellishly short-staffed and the moment I'm free I need to leave. I can spare you the time it takes me to wolf down dinner—say six?"

"You don't want to give me a hint?"

"Too complicated. Does six work?"

"I'll call you at the stroke."

"No, let's do it in person. Jarrod, my oldest, has a basketball game at seven, I promised him I'd absolutely attend this one. Are you still in the Glen?"

"I am. This is a lot of intrigue, Nathalie."

"Right up your alley, no? I'll meet you anywhere near Jarrod's school."

"Where's the school?"

"Brentwood," she said. "Windward Academy—how about a Thai place I like?

Bundy off Olympic. Pad Palace. Know it?"

"I'll find it."

"Quality, low-fat grub," she said. "I get takeout there. Way too often."

Another strip mall; maybe one day real estate would be too expensive to make them viable.

Pad Palace made the most of what it was: a storefront with a limited design budget. Screens and pine tables aimed for elegant simplicity. Walls were painted in variants of honeydew green. Slender, shy young Asian women waited on loud, cheerful Anglo hipsters.

The menu was vegetarian with eggs, vegan on request. Lots of virtue making the rounds in L.A. I half expected Alma Reynolds to bop in. Or maybe she'd always been into the pound of fish-flesh.

Nathalie Rothman's white BMW ragtop pulled in five minutes after I'd settled with a pot of tea. She entered like a bullet: tiny, fast, direct.

All of four ten and ninety muscular pounds. Her face was soft and smooth as a teenager's under a cloud of careless brown hair. Forty-two and the mother of four boys, she was married to a developer who owned chunks of Wilshire Boulevard, had been in charge of emergency services at Western Pediatric Medical Center for a decade. I'd met her when she was a brand-new Yale-educated resident. Then chief resident, then fast-track to faculty.

A lot of important people at the hospital considered her curt and abrasive. I could see their point, but I liked her.

She waved a finger at me, bounced over to one of the waitresses. "I'm Dr. Rothman. Is my food ready?"

By the time the girl's head stopped nodding, Nathalie had plopped down opposite me. "I call beforehand. Hi, Alex. You look handsome, the criminal side of life must be agreeable. Ever think of coming back and doing your real job?"

"Good to see you, too, Nathalie."

She laughed. "No, I'm not on Ritalin, yes, I should be. That smidge of gray is flattering. I tell Charlie the same thing, but he doesn't believe me. Okay, cut to the chase: I happened to be watching the news, saw the broadcast on Mr. Huck, called the number like a good little citizen.

Some police-type named Reed said he was interested in talking to me but I don't think he really was."

"Why not?"

"Because when I told him why I'd called, he said he was out in the field, would get back to me. What crops do cops grow in the field? I actually asked him that. He didn't appreciate my humor. Do you know him?"

"Young rookie detective."

"Well, he's got some learning to do in terms of how to treat law-abiding sources of potentially helpful information. He started grilling me: who I was, why I'd called. Like *I* was under suspicion. When I told him I was a physician at Western Peds, it was like a light going on. He relaxed, told me someone who used to work at Western just happened to be consulting on the case, did I know you. I said sure, we went way back. He said, good, how about I talked to you. No offense, Alex, but I felt I was being shunted. He was supposed to tell you I'd be calling. Did he?"

"Not yet."

"Figures. Well, *I'm* following through. Rookie Detective Reed may not want to deal with cognitive dissonance but too bad."

"Dissonance over what?"

"Mr. Huck."

"You do know him."

"That's too strong a word," she said. "I met him once. But that was enough for me to see him as a hero."

A plate of cellophane noodles and tofu chicken arrived. Nathalie ate a few bites, fidgeted with a diamond ring. Big, square stone. Jewelry wasn't my thing, but Alma Reynolds's mammoth pearl had gotten me paying attention.

Nathalie said, "We're talking ten years ago. I'd just taken over outpatient as well as inpatient, was doing the late shift to prove I was of the people. Three a.m. or so, the triage nurse pulls me over. Someone's brought in a blood-covered infant. At first everyone thought it was going to be an incredible horror story but when they cleaned the little thing up there were no wounds, not a pinprick anywhere. Little girl, seven months old. Except for being cold and agitated, she was fine."

She chopsticked a cube of tofu. "The good Samaritan was your pal, Mr. Huck.

He never gave his name but I'm sure it's him, that face is hard to forget. He was gaunt, almost feeble, not in good shape at all. I distinctly recall some sort of neuro damage, maybe an old closed head injury or a minor stroke."

"Off-kilter mouth," I said.

"Yes," she said, flashing a victory V. "I *knew* it was him. His walk was unsteady, at first the triage nurse thought he was drunk, in danger of dropping the baby. Meanwhile, the baby's wailing, all that blood, it was some scene. The news said Huck was a person of interest for those killings. What does that mean?"

"It means the department's being ambiguous."

"Why?"

"Too complicated, Nathalie."

She gave me a long look. "Fair enough. But off the record, is he a suspect for those murders?"

I nodded.

"Wow," she said. "I have to tell you, Alex, I never got any ominous vibe from him. He was nervous, timid, probably more scared than the baby. He said he'd found her on the sidewalk while taking a walk, heard the squalling, thought it was a wounded animal. When he saw it was a baby, he grabbed her up and hand-carried her to us. We're talking from Silverlake to East Hollywood, a good two miles on a chilly night. He'd taken off his jacket to keep the baby warm, had on a T-shirt and these cheap plaid pants—funny the things you remember. Probably thrift-shop stuff, tied at the waist with a rope. His teeth were chattering, Alex."

"Any reason he didn't call 911?"

"Maybe he felt he could get her there faster, I don't know."

Or he knew that his history would make him an immediate suspect.

Nathalie said, "Did he scare us at first? Of course he did. He had blood all over himself, it was something out of those disgusting movies my kids like. We didn't want to confront him, but we did try to keep him there until the cops arrived. Once he saw the baby was okay, he bolted past our guard. You remember the caliber of our security."

"Old, weak, lazy, myopic."

"On a good day. On top of that, the cops took a long time to arrive and our attentions were focused on the baby. Which is somewhat alarming, now that I think about it. What if Huck really had been a psycho killer?"

"How do you know he wasn't?"

"Because the case closed right away. That's the official term, right? Closed, not solved."

"You've been doing your homework, Nathalie."

"Charlie likes those crime shows."

"How'd the case close?"

"We directed the police to where Huck said he found the baby, they found the blood trail, followed it, discovered a body lying in some bushes. Turned out to be the baby's mother, seventeen-year-old girl named Brandi Loring. She lived a few blocks away, alcoholic mother and stepfather, half sibs, stepsibs. The baby's name was Brandeen, miniature Brandi, I guess. The family knew who the killer was. Brandi's ex-boyfriend, another kid, one year older than Brandi. Apparently, she broke up with him before the baby was born and he'd been stalking her. Soon as the police showed up at his house, he broke down, confessed to beating her to death. He had a broken hand and raw knuckles to prove it, plus they found his blood on Brandi's face and neck and chest. When the cops asked him why he left the baby there, right out on the sidewalk, he gave them a stupid look. Like, oops, I forgot about that."

"Who gave you all the details?"

"The detective who did the paperwork. That's what he called it. 'Doing the paperwork. This ain't Sherlock territory, Doc.'"

"Remember his name?"

"Leibowitz," she said. "Jewish detective, who knew?"

Before we parted, I asked her how her son was enjoying the Windward School.

"Interesting place," she said.

"Interesting how?"

"It's really two schools—sociologically. Smart rich kids and not-so-smart *really* rich kids."

"I'm sensing a common theme."

"Forty grand tuition makes it common, Alex. Charlie thinks it's ridiculous and I guess I do, too. As to which group Jarrod falls into, depends what day you catch me. You know adolescents, no impulse control—look at what happened to poor

Brandi Loring. I wouldn't have minded sending him to public school and Charlie definitely wanted that. But our *prince* yearned to play varsity baseball and was sure he'd never make the grade in public school. I guess that makes him one of the smart ones. Knowing his limitations."

I phoned Hollywood Division and asked for Detective Leibowitz. The clerk had never heard of him and neither had the desk officer.

"Detective Connor, then."

"She's out."

I tried Petra's cell. She said, "Barry Leibowitz, he left shortly after I came on. And don't be making any causal connection there. Barry was in his sixties."

I laughed. "Any idea where I can find him?"

"Sorry, no. Can I ask why?"

I told her about Travis Huck rescuing the baby.

She said, "Your bad guy did something good? Ted Bundy worked a suicide hotline."

Milo said, "Doesn't mean a goddamn thing. BTK was president of his church."

Moe Reed said, "That's what I figured when she called, Doc. I was going to let you know, but I got swamped, going over bus and train records and checking out car rental contracts."

Milo said, "So there's no doubt the boyfriend killed the baby's mom."

I said, "That's what Detective Leibowitz told Dr. Rothman."

"Leibowitz . . . don't know him."

"He retired right after Petra came to Hollywood. I was going to look for him, but if you think it's a waste of time, I won't."

"What would be the point?"

"If Leibowitz managed to find Huck and interview him, it might give us some insight into Huck's personality."

"The insight *I'd* like is what Huck was doing walking a dark, deserted street at three in the morning in Silverlake, but sure, go ahead."

Reed said, "That time frame, we know he trolls for street girls. Maybe when he can't connect, he stalks houses, peeps windows, or worse."

Milo said, "Least now we know where he was ten years ago. Street guy, no Social Security number, so ten to one he was supporting himself illegally. Let's see what Records can give us on hot-prowl burglaries back then, especially in East Hollywood and Silverlake. I'll do it, Moses, you keep working the transport angle and taking phone tips."

"You got it."

I said, "Huck said he'd walked the baby to the hospital. If it's true, he didn't have a car. That could mean his home base wasn't far from where he found her."

Reed said, "He stays on the boulevard for fun, crawls back to some hole up in the hills."

Milo said, "Could be, but forget about canvassing the boulevard. No one from ten years ago is gonna be around. The residential neighborhood could be a different story. We go back to where the baby was found, we might turn up someone who remembers Huck."

"Better yet," I said. "Huck remembers and returns there to hide."

Milo chewed his cheek. "Home is where the heart is, huh?"

Reed said, "Back to the old comfort zone. Might sound appealing when you're rabbiting from *la policía*."

CHAPTER
29

Brandi Loring's body had been found on Apache Street, near the western edge of Silverlake, up four sloping blocks north of Sunset.

The neighborhood was meager frame houses, some no larger than shacks, more generous structures sectioned into rentals. The spot where Travis Huck had reported finding Baby Brandeen was a cracked, buckling sidewalk on its way to being trashed by the roots of a gigantic banyan.

An hour and a half of door-knocks up and down Apache produced quizzical looks and declarations of ignorance, mostly in Spanish. A woman named Maribella Olmos, ancient and withered but bright-eyed, remembered the incident.

"The baby. Nice person to do that," she said. "Brave."

"Did you know him, ma'am?" said Milo.

"Wish I did. Very brave."

"Saving a baby."

"Saving, taking to the doctor," she said. "All those gangbangers riding around, shooting? It's better now, but back then? *Hoo.*"

"The bangers were out at three in the morning?"

"Anytime they want. Sometimes, I'm sleeping, I hear gunshots. It's better now. Much better. You guys are doing a good job."

Snatching Milo's big hand, she pressed it to wizened lips.

One of the few times I've seen him caught off guard. "Thank you, ma'am."

Maribella Olmos let go of his hand and winked. "I'd give you another one right on the lips, but I don't want your wife getting jealous."

Next stop: the last known address for Brandi Loring's mother and stepfather.

Anita and Lawrence Brackle had lived in a pink two-story prewar, divided into a quartet of apartments. No one on the block had ever heard of the family, Brandi, or the baby-saving incident.

The rest of the afternoon was spent cruising Silverlake, showing Huck's picture to people old enough to be of potential use.

Blank stares and head shakes; Milo dealt with failure by stopping at a street cart for two glasses of iced tamarind soda. Other vendors had set up bins of clothing on the sidewalk. He eyed the illegal display with amusement, drank with fervor as cars bumped by on the pothole-afflicted stretch of Sunset.

Back in the car, he said, "It was a long shot. You still wanna find Leibowitz, be my guest. I'm going back to the office, expanding the real estate search to neighboring counties, just in case Huck did manage to hitch a ride on the real estate train. Then it's old Hollywood hot-prowls. Maybe I'll find a severed hand."

"Any word on the Vanders?"

"Not yet, and Buddy Weir keeps calling, guy's starting to sound hysterical."

I said, "A lawyer who cares."

He snorted. "All those billable hours down the tubes."

Thirty seconds of Internet search brought up a Barry Leibowitz who'd come in fourth at a charity pro-am golf tournament held last year. Tres Olivos Golf Club and Leisure Life Resort in Palm Springs.

The desert could be an affordable place for an ex-cop to retire. I pulled up a group photo. Golfing Barry Leibowitz was a white-haired, mustachioed man of the right age standing in the back row. Further Web-surfing produced a follow-up piece in the club bulletin, with capsule bios of the four top amateurs.

Two dentists, one accountant, and "Detective Leibowitz, our law enforcement duffer. Nowadays, he captures trophies, instead of criminals."

I phoned Tres Olivos, used my real name and title but made up a story about calling on behalf of Western Pediatrics as the hospital searched for Mr. Leibowitz's current mailing address.

"The trophy he won in our recent Nine Holes For Kids tournament was returned by the post office and we'd really like to get it to him."

At worst, the club secretary would be cautious, verify with the hospital, learn I was on the staff but that no such award existed.

She said, "Here you go, Doctor."

No desert air for Det. III (ret.) Barry Z. Leibowitz.

He lived in a one-bedroom condo on Pico west of Beverwil. I called, got no answer, set out anyway.

The address matched a gated complex called Hillside Manor. Not much of a development, just a hundred yards of driveway lined with sand-colored boxes that bordered the northern edge of Hillcrest Country Club's verdant eighteen holes.

The club was a nice fit for Leibowitz's interests, but I couldn't see an ex-detective making the membership fee.

A call box to the right of the gate listed thirty residents. I entered Leibowitz's code. A bass voice said, "Yes?"

I started to explain who I was.

"You're putting me on."

"Not at all. I'm working with Detective Sturgis. It's about Travis Huck—"

"Hold on."

Five minutes later, the man I'd just seen pictured in the tournament photo appeared on the west side of the truncated street, wearing a gold polo shirt, black linen pants, and flip-flops. Taller and broader than the picture had suggested, Barry Leibowitz supported a wine-barrel torso on short, stumpy legs. The white hair was thin. The mustache was full and waxed.

His look of amusement recalled the jaunty, monocled fellow from Monopoly.

When he reached the gate, I showed my consulting badge.

"What's that supposed to do?"

"Establish my bona fides."

"I just called Sturgis." The gate slid open. "Heard of him, but never worked with him. Must be interesting."

"The cases can be."

He studied me. "Sure. That's what I meant."

The condo was a second-floor unit toward the back, spotless, almost antiseptic. Two leather golf bags were propped in a corner. A portable bar sported good single-malt and premium gin. A dozen or so golf trophies shared a case with paperback books.

Crime novels, mostly.

Leibowitz saw me looking at them and chuckled. "You'd think busman's holiday, right? In the real world, we got sixty, seventy percent of the bad guys. These creative types get a hundred. Want something to drink?"

"No, thanks."

"I'm pouring Macallan 16 for myself. You sure?"

"You changed my mind."

Leibowitz chuckled. "Flexibility, mark of a smart guy." Removing a couple of old-fashioned glasses from the bar's lower shelf, he held them up to the light, took them into the kitchen, washed and dried, inspected again, repeated the ritual.

Through a split in the pine trees, the kitchen window offered an oblique sliver of stunning green. Atop a rolling hill, a figure in white contemplated a putt.

Leibowitz said, "Nice view, huh? I'm like that guy in mythology, Tantalus. All the goodies just out of arm's reach."

I said, "Rancho Park's not far."

"You play?"

"Nope, I just know about Rancho. After O.J. got sued, he went for the public courses."

Leibowitz laughed. "O.J. Thank God I never got near that one."

He brought over two stiff drinks, settled in a recliner. The first half of his glass went down in small, slow sips. He finished the rest in a single swallow. "Let's hear it for the Scots. So you want to know about Eddie Huckstadter—that's the name he was using back then. In terms of my case, he was one of the good guys, especially given his circumstances."

"What circumstances were those?"

"He was a bum," he said. "Excuse me, a 'homeless individual who should never be judged by conventional standards.'" Laughing, he reached for the bar, poured himself another finger of whiskey. "Truth is, Doctor, I *don't* judge. Not anymore. Once you get away from the job you start to get a different perspective. Like with Sturgis. Back when I started, you'd never get me working with someone like that. Now? He's got the chops? Hell, who cares about his outside life."

He studied me. "If that offends you, what can I say."

"No offense taken. Huckstadter left the scene. How'd you find him?"

"Sheer brilliance." More laughter. "Not quite. Hospital described him, I gave the description to patrol, a couple of our uniforms knew who he was right away from working the boulevard. Eddie was just another street guy. We picked him up the next day."

"He hung out on Hollywood?"

"Used to panhandle outside the Chinese Theatre and farther up, near the Pantages. Wherever the tourists were, I guess. Had his hair long, a pierced nose, the whole freak thing. That's what they were back then. Not hippies anymore. Freaks."

"Did patrol know him from prior arrests?"

"Nope, just as a bum. He was distinctive, that crooked mouth of his plus the limp."

He screwed up his own lips. The mustache went along for the ride. "They brought him to me, I questioned him, he gave the same story he gave the nurses at the hospital, but by that time he was irrelevant anyway. The case was closed, instant guilty plea by the bad guy—some scrotum named Gibson DePaul. Gibbie." Pronouncing the nickname with lingering contempt.

He sipped the refill. "Still, patrol goes to the trouble to follow through, I'm not going to make them feel they wasted their time. I rode cars myself. Ten years in Van Nuys, then four in West Valley before I decided to use *this*"—tapping his head—"instead of *this*." Doing the same for his biceps.

A brawny arm hoisted. Down went the rest of the second scotch. "I used to live in the Valley, back when my wife was alive—that's good stuff, they age it in sherry barrels. You don't like it?"

I drank. Savored the taste, then the burn. "I like it a lot."

Leibowitz said, "Huckstadter's become a serious bad guy? Sturgis told me, it almost knocked me over, I missed that completely."

"You didn't hear about it on the news?"

"Nah, never watch that crap, life's too short. Got a nineteen-inch in the bedroom, when it's on, it's tuned to sports."

"So Huckstadter didn't seem violent."

"Nope, but it's not like we spent much time together psychoanalyzing."

"Still, you're surprised."

"I'm always surprised," said Leibowitz. "Keeps you young—what I said before, flexibility."

"What was Eddie like back then?"

"Just another sad case, Doc. Hollywood's always full of them. All the glamour that isn't."

"He's got no adult record."

"Meaning he was a juvey offender?"

"He spent some time at CYA but the case was reversed."

"What kind of case?" said Leibowitz.

I described Huck's manslaughter conviction. "The crooked mouth's probably the result of a head injury while in custody."

"Well," he said, "I can see that making a guy angry."

"Huck seem angry?"

"Nah. Just scared. Like he didn't like being out in the daylight."

"Drug problem?"

"Wouldn't surprise me. Dope, booze, or being crazy is what gets people living on the street. But if you're asking did I see track marks, a raw nose, was he speed-talking or spaced out or hungover, the answer is no. No overt craziness, either. Guy was coherent, told the story logically from A to B. Most I could say about him was he looked depressed."

"Over what?"

"I assumed over the way his life had gone. Being homeless, it's easy to get beaten down, right? I wasn't there to be his shrink, Doc. I took the report, when he was through, I offered him a ride wherever he wanted to go. He said no thanks, he liked to walk. Now you're telling me he's serious bad news. That's disconcerting, Doc. My missing all the signs. Is there evidence he was strangling girls back then?"

"No."

"No, or not yet?"

"Not yet."

"Those marsh murders, they're definitely his?"

"Circumstances seem to point that way."

"Damn," he said. "Who'da known? I didn't see a sign of that. Nothing."

I said, "Maybe there were no signs."

"He was crafty, hid his dark impulses?"

"Yup," I said. "That's what I meant."

It took until nightfall to make contact with Milo's mobile.

I said, "Any interesting hot-prowls?"

"Only interesting ones were closed, the rest are simple burglaries—jewelry, stereos. No panty thieves, nothing creepy. And so far, Huck's avoided the real estate boom. He owns nothing."

"You might not want to spend much more time at the assessor's. Ten years ago he was homeless. Hard to see him building up enough equity."

"Hard to see him jumping from that to estate manager."

"Maybe the Vanders really do have tender hearts," I said. "Or by the time they met him, he'd turned his life around."

"Fine, but how would people like *them* meet someone like *him*?"

I thought about that. "Could've been through a temp job—Huck working as a waiter or a bartender at a charity function. Or just a chance encounter."

"He fools 'em into thinking he's re-formed? We're talking *mushy* heart, Alex."

"The same kind of idealism that might lead them to donate to the marsh?"

Silence.

He said, "Interesting."

"Unfortunately, I can't find any list of Save the Marsh contributors and Alma Reynolds claims there's no formal fund-raising group. Billionaire bucks fund the entire operation, which seems to be rent and twenty-five grand for Duboff's salary. I'm wondering if Duboff might've supplemented. As in the blond, plastic guy with the envelope that Chance Brandt saw."

"If that was a payoff, what was Señor Bondo getting from Duboff?"

"Don't know, but it's possible Duboff saved up some extra cash, despite a low salary, and Alma got hold of it."

I described the huge pearl Reynolds had tried to conceal, how she'd bought it shortly after Duboff's death, lied about its being a gift from him.

He said, "Or she splurged on herself and was embarrassed to admit it. Being a self-denying vegan ascetic and all that."

"She eats fish," I said. "Steak wouldn't surprise me."

"Hypocrite?"

"Holding something back. The minute she saw me, she tried to hide that pearl. Then she switched tactics and flaunted it, as if daring me to make a big deal out of it. But my seeing it clearly threw her. Instead of returning to work, she went home."

"Maybe the food didn't agree with her—okay, yeah, you might be on to some financial shenanigans, but that doesn't mean it's related to the murders. And if Duboff was hiding cash, it wasn't at his apartment. I went over the place myself. At some point I can brace ol' Alma, but not right now, too much going on. As in finding Mr. Huck. The airport fake-out may be stale but it works. Not a hint of where he is."

I said, "Maybe he'll write."

"Wouldn't that be loverly. Uncle Milo is soooo lonely."

CHAPTER

30

The next morning brought no callback from Milo or Reed, and neither detective was answering the phone.

I'd woken up warmed by sunlight and thinking about Travis Huck.

Petra and Milo were right: A single act of kindness meant nothing because psychopaths are great actors, and a façade of altruism lets them pursue the cruelty they love.

Public admiration feeds the lust for control and attention. The *look-at-me* tango. The marsh murders reeked of exhibitionism:

choosing hallowed ground for the dump site, calling the murders in, storing bones in a pretty box.

Why face four women east?

Not much had been made of that since the first day.

The only thing I could think of was geographic symbolism: Nadine Vander was Chinese American and her last sighting, before San Francisco, had been Taiwan.

Simon had flown in from Hong Kong.

Was all of this really revolving around the family?

Or were the Vanders just the crowning glory of a bloody orgy?

Destroy the rich and powerful and inherit their souls . . . if that was the motive, why not flaunt *their* bodies? But the only victim on display was Selena, an outwardly shy young woman who'd entertained at *literal* orgies before graduating to pain games.

However I tossed it around, the killings kept coming back to a sexual serial. And maybe the link to the Vanders was another young woman.

Had Nadine been Huck's target all along, as Reed had suggested? Lady of the manor, viewed from afar with lust and longing? Her husband and son, collateral damage?

Maybe Travis Huck was capable of all that, but his ten-year-old act of mercy hadn't been attention-seeking. Just the opposite, he'd fled the moment Brandeen Loring's health was confirmed.

Or maybe even back then Huck had dark secrets he didn't want exposed.

Raised by an alcoholic mother, locked up and abused until his rescue at eighteen. His life until the second rescue, by the Vanders, remained a mystery.

A lot could happen during a decade and a half on the streets.

I spent another hour on it, ended up addled and popping Advil to kill a massive headache. Shifting to robot-work, I cleared billing, straightened my office. Took a run and wound down by walking Blanche for fifteen minutes and stretching and showering.

I told Robin I needed to drive.

She wasn't surprised.

No sign of Alma Reynolds's yellow VW on Fourteenth Street. I phoned the doctor where she worked.

Out sick.

For all I knew, Milo had found the time to reel her in and she was sitting in a West L.A. interview room.

I tried him again. Still no answer.

Moe Reed's guess about Huck staying in his comfort zone made sense, and I wondered if the same applied to Alma when it came to buying jewelry. Looking up shops in Santa Monica, I found two that specialized in pearls.

The first turned out to be false advertising—a booth in an antiques barn that specialized in costume gems. The second, Le Nacre, on Montana, featured gray velvet cases of strands and solitaires, including the larger South Sea "marvels."

I studied tray after tray of gleaming orbs. White, black, gray, greenish, bluish, gold. No prices on display.

In a center case, I spotted a pendant that could've been the twin of Alma Reynolds's guilty pleasure.

The saleswoman, fortyish, frosted blond and fox-faced, wore a black Lycra-laced suit that screamed Torture At The Gym. She let me browse before gliding my way and pointing to the pendant. "It's beautiful, isn't it?"

"Beautiful and huge," I said.

"That's what you get with South Sea—size *and* quality. This one's a full seventeen millimeters. They can go as high as twenty, but you rarely see seven-teens with such excellent luster, shape, and nacre—that's the thickness of the outer layer. This one's a solid millimeter. Good shape and smooth. It's our last one."

"You had several?"

"We had two. They came in from Aus-tralia and the other one sold just a few days ago. Trust me, this one will also move fast. Quality always does."

"Lucky woman," I said. "Birthday or guilt gift?"

She smiled. "Which is your situation?"

"Birthday. But give me enough time and I'm sure there'll be guilt."

She giggled. "I'm sure you're right. No, actually, a woman bought it for herself. Said her mother had always worn pearls, it was time to treat herself to something nice."

"This is more than nice. May I look at it?"

"Oh, absolutely." As she unlocked the case, I received a mini-course on pearl grading and culture. "What's your wife's skin tone—is it your wife?"

Why quibble. "It is. She's got Spanish and Italian blood. There's some rose in her complexion but it's mostly olive."

"I can tell that you love her," she said. "When a man can describe a woman that easily, he's got deep feelings for her. Rose with mostly olive means this would work *perfectly* for her. The pinkish ones are even more valuable than the creams. We had one of those a few months ago, a sixteen, went out the door the same day it arrived. But pink doesn't work for everyone. Olive ladies do better with cream. I'm sure she'll adore it."

"How much?"

She flipped a tiny tag, examined a code. "Lucky for you, we bought well, so six thousand four hundred, including the chain, which is eighteen-karat and hand-crafted in Italy and has these adorable little diamond chips spaced perfectly. I'd definitely advise leaving it with the chain, they're a perfect match, we make sure of that."

I said, "People take them off? What would you do with a loose pearl?"

"Exactly, but people get ideas. The lady who bought the other one wanted only the pearl, said she had her own chain. I figured she meant something antique, from her mother. Then she pulls out a cheap, plated thing, real junk." She stuck out her tongue. "Saving a few bucks. It hurt me to see the pearl displayed that way, but people can be strange. She sure was."

"Had her own ideas."

"Not the type you'd think would appreciate something of this quality." She touched the chain. "So does your wife get to be ecstatically happy *before* you go do something naughty?"

"Any flexibility on price?"

"Hmm," she said. "For you I could take off ten percent."

"Make it twenty and you've got a deal."

"I'm sorry," she said. "Fifteen's the best I can do. When you consider what a large diamond costs, it's an incredible bargain."

"I don't really know much about pearls—"

"But I do and trust me, it's worth it. Seventeen off's the absolute rock bottom. You're lucky it's me and not my husband. At that price, there's barely any profit and when Leonard comes in and finds out what I did for you, he won't be happy." Touching my wrist with warm, smooth fingertips. "And guilt gifts for *him* are no picnic."

Robin's big brown eyes expanded like kaleidoscope disks. "What did you *do*?"

"Impulse buy."

"I'll say—it's gorgeous, baby, but *way* too big for me."

"Looks fine to me."

"When would I wear it?"

"We'll find an occasion."

"Really, Alex, I can't."

"Wear it once. You don't like it, back it goes."

"You are something." Several moments in front of the mirror later: "I love you."

"Fits your skin tone perfectly."

"It's so wrong for me . . . huge."

"You got it, flaunt it."

She sighed. "Darn."

"You really don't like it?"

"Not that kind of darn," she said. "Darn if I'm not going to make it *work*."

A long dinner at the Bel-Air, wine, and lovemaking K.O.'d me hard enough for a decent night's sleep. But memories of the pearl against Robin's chest brought me fully awake. Now the necklace was displayed on our bedroom dresser and when I peeked out the kitchen window, her studio light glowed.

I tried Milo again, finally connected to his cell, asked if he'd reached Alma Reynolds.

Instead of answering, he said, "Just got a call from my crime scene buddies. Travis Huck's room in the mansion was clean, but they found blood in his bathroom drain. Type AB. We've got no typing on Huck, so theoretically it could be his. But you know how rare AB is, what's the chance of two people turning up with it?"

"Who's the first?"

"Simon Vander. Medical examiner called Simone and got confirmation. Daddy was always getting hit on to donate. Reed also talked to Simone and she's going to give a DNA sample, see if that can be linked.

She's freaking out, pretty much over the edge. Wouldn't surprise me if Aaron Fox shows up, offering to help us poor dumb yokels. Meanwhile, I've got a call in to His Holiness. This should be enough to name Huck a flat-out suspect, get a full-court press on the search."

"No blood anywhere except the drain," I said. "Sink and shower?"

"Just the sink, Alex. Which is totally consistent with the bad stuff happening elsewhere, Huck spotting a stain on his clothes and deciding to wash it off. He was careful to scrub the sink itself. In fact, the level of clean in his room is just as suspicious as if luminol had turned the place purple. The place was gone *over.* What the bastard didn't figure on is our taking the plumbing apart."

"Is that routine procedure for the techies?"

"It is when I tell them to do it. I'm thinking the Vanders were lured to S.F., he picked 'em up at the airport, did them somewhere in Northern or Central California, buried the bodies, drove back to L.A. and kept up the loyal-employee façade."

"All those forests up the coast."

"Oh, yeah."

I said, "A lust thing for Nadine would explain facing the bodies east. Look to the Orient." His breath quickened.

"What?"

"I'm getting that feeling, Alex—stuff coming together. Listen, I gotta keep all my lines open in case Zeus calls from Olympus. If you want to help, see if you can come up with a hypothesis as to where Huck's hiding."

Travis Huck as Prime Suspect made the six o'clock news and the papers.

A renewed rush of sightings kept Milo and Moe Reed and two other detectives busy for the next forty-eight hours.

Nothing panned out.

I tried to work up a guess as to where Huck might be burrowed, looked at maps, drew blanks.

After two days of looking at her pearl, Robin locked it in the safe.

I drove to Alma Reynolds's apartment, spotted her VW, knocked on her door.

"Who is it?"

"Alex Delaware."

"You *are* stalking me. Go away."

"Six thousand bucks for a pearl," I said. "Mom would be proud."

The sound she emitted could've been rage or fear.

Silence said she hadn't taken the bait.

I sat parked up the block for nearly an hour. Just as I was about to give up, she hurried out of her building, got in the yellow Bug.

I followed her to a Washington Mutual on Santa Monica Boulevard. She stayed in the bank for another forty-two minutes, then drove to the ophthalmologist's office building but, after a brief pause, kept going, headed back to Pico, stopped at a Korean barbecue on Centinela.

Glass window in front, easy to follow the action.

I waited until her order arrived.

Massive plate of ribs, mug of beer.

I said, "Celebrating?"

She gasped and sputtered and for a second I thought it was Heimlich time.

Chewing furiously, she swallowed. Her teeth ground. "Go away."

"Just because the pearl's in a safe-deposit box doesn't mean you can keep it."

"I don't know what you're talking about."

"Mom might be proud of your taste in googaws, but would she approve of the financing?"

"Get the hell out of here."

"You put up with Duboff for years, see yourself as his rightful heir, and I take no issue with that. The problem is *how* he got the money. Even if it can't be linked to a crime, the IRS is sure to be interested."

She lifted a rib, and for a second I thought she'd use it as a weapon.

"Why are you doing this to me?"

"It's not about you," I said. "It's about four other women." I touched the rib. "Bones."

She turned a bad color. Shot up and ran to the bathroom.

Five minutes, ten, fifteen.

I went back, found both lavs empty. A rear door led to an alley that stank of garbage. By the time I'd returned to the front of the restaurant, the VW was gone.

CHAPTER
31

I parked three blocks from Alma Reynolds's building, walked back to her corner, and watched from behind an old, dusty coral tree.

Mr. Covert Operations. When I wasn't feeling ridiculous, my mind raced.

Forty minutes later Reynolds hadn't returned, and I figured I'd screwed up and caused her to run. I was sure she'd financed the pearl with payoff money Duboff had left behind.

Envelope passed in the parking lot. Donation or bribe?

Either way, nothing indicated a link to Duboff's murder.

I returned to the Seville. Drove a block before Milo called.

"Huck lawyered up."

"You got him."

"Not exactly."

Debora Wallenburg's law firm took up the top two floors of an ice cube on Wilshire, five blocks east of the ocean. Names crowded the door; Wallenburg was ranked second.

She was fifty or so, green-eyed and apple-cheeked, with a sturdy body packed into a gray cashmere suit. Platinum rings, diamond earrings, and a triple string of pearls bounced light in interesting ways. The pearls were pinkish silver, graduated in size; my slightly educated guess was ten to fifteen millimeters.

Good-looking woman, with the confidence to keep her feathered hair the same color as the suit. She'd deflected Milo's invitation to the station, insisted her office would be preferable.

Now she sat behind a leather-topped desk, listening to someone on the phone named Lester. Tiffany gilt-bronze pieces livened the desk's surface, including an elaborate lamp with a glass shade crimped to look like paper. The rear wall was devoted to a Mary Cassatt mother-and-child pastel, the perfect image of tenderness. The absence of family photos or anything kid-related turned great art into a prop.

Milo and Reed and I stood like supplicants while Wallenburg laughed at something Lester said. The décor was a thousand square feet of over-the-top: arterial red brocade walls, layer-cake moldings, copper-foil ceiling, teal-and-lavender Aubusson rug over teak planks. The fourteenth-story view was charcoal street, aluminum water, rust-colored talons of coastline scratching at the ocean.

I tried to figure out if the Vanders' house could be seen. Decided I was overreaching.

Wallenburg said, "You're kidding, Les," and turned in a way that directed my eyes to a side wall bearing Ivy League degrees and bar association awards.

She said, "Okay, thanks, Les," hung up. "Sit, if you'd like, gentlemen."

We arranged ourselves in front of the desk. Milo said, "Thanks for meeting with us, Ms. Wallenburg."

"Thanks for making the dangerous trek all the way from the wilds of West L.A." Wallenburg smiled frostily, glanced at her watch.

Milo said, "If you know where Travis Huck is—"

"Before we get into that, Lieutenant, I'm going on record: You're wrong about Travis. Couldn't be more mistaken. What evidence do you have to justify naming him a suspect?"

"With all due respect, ma'am, I need to be asking the questions."

"With all due respect, Lieutenant, I need to prevent a second gross miscarriage of justice. Step One in that process is clarifying what you think you know that justifies ruining my client's life. *Again.*"

"What's Step Two?"

"That depends on how One shapes up."

"Ms. Wallenburg, I understand your point of view, but disclosure will take place if and when Mr. Huck is charged with a crime."

"Sounds like you've already judged him."

Milo didn't answer. Debora Wallenburg picked up a Tiffany pen and suspended it between her fingertips. "Sorry for making you come out here for nothing. Do you need your parking validated?"

"Ma'am, if you're harboring Huck, you could be putting yourself in—"

"Now it begins. The veiled threats." Green eyes narrowed. "Give it your best shot, Lieutenant. I've already begun the paperwork on a massive civil suit."

"Step Two, already?" said Milo.

"I'm sure we're all busy, Lieutenant."

"Are you suing at Mr. Huck's request? Or is it your idea?"

Wallenburg shook her head. "You're not going to pry information out of me."

"Ma'am, this isn't the time for jousting. We're talking five known murders, with several more likely. Brutal, calculated slaughter. Do you really want to hitch your wagon to someone like that?"

"Hitch my wagon? I have no interest in publicity, Lieutenant Sturgis. Quite the opposite. For the last ten years, I've done corporate litigation because I had my *fill* of the sideshow mislabeled the criminal justice system."

"Ten years," said Milo. "Forgive me, but is it possible you're out of your element?"

"Or you are, sir," said Debora Wallenburg. "In fact, I *know* you are. Travis Huck is a decent human being and I am not some bleeding-heart, mushy-brained do-gooder who denies the existence of evil. I've seen plenty of evil in my day."

"Corporate litigation gets that nasty?"

"Witty, Lieutenant. Bottom line: I'm not harboring Travis, neither am I aware of his whereabouts."

"But you've been in contact with him."

The pen clicked. "I'm going to give you some free legal advice: Avoid tunnel vision and prevent a huge mess for all concerned."

"Any suggestions about alternative suspects, ma'am?"

"That's not my job."

Moe Reed huffed. If Wallenburg noticed, she didn't show it.

Milo said, "Huck fled. Not the behavior of an innocent man."

"It is when that man has been abused by the system."

"He called you because you saved him before. You advised him not to inform you of his whereabouts. Or his guilt. That way, you couldn't be subpoenaed to divulge. All legal, Ms. Wallenburg, but it skirts the moral issue. If Huck kills again, do you want it on your conscience?"

"Oh, please, Lieutenant. You should write screenplays."

"I'll leave that to disillusioned lawyers."

Wallenburg shifted her focus to me. Searching for the good kid in the classroom. When I didn't respond, she looked at Reed.

He said, "Huck will be found, tried, and convicted. Make it easy."

"On who?"

"Let's start with the victims' families," said Reed.

"Easy for everyone but Travis," said Wallenburg. "Nineteen years ago, he was hauled in like garbage, tried before a kangaroo court, tortured—"

"Who tortured him?" said Milo.

"His so-called caretakers. Haven't you read my appeals brief?"

"No, ma'am."

"I'll fax you a copy."

Reed said, "Whatever happened back then doesn't change the facts now. You're so sure he's innocent but you've got nothing to back that up."

Wallenburg laughed. "Do you really think you're going to pry facts out of me by insulting me? How about *you* deliver something in the way of evidence? Go ahead, convince me he's guilty. The only link you have is casual knowledge of Selena Bass."

Milo said, "He told you that."

Wallenburg said, "That seals it, you've got nothing. Why am I not shocked?"

Reed said, "You think we just picked his name out of the phone book?"

"I think you're looking for a quick and easy hook to hang your investigative hats on."

Milo said, "If I told you we had physical evidence, would that change your mind?"

"Depends on the nature of that evidence and how meticulously it was collected."

Reed laughed. "O.J., again."

Wallenburg said, "Think what you want, gentlemen. The fact is, even if I could be a party to this sham, I wouldn't."

Milo said, "This sham being—"

"Railroading Travis. Again. You really should've read my brief. He was beaten so severely that he incurred permanent nerve damage. And what got him in there? Pushing back at a bully. Coming up against wealth and power."

I said, "Why didn't you file a civil suit?"

Wallenburg blinked. "Travis wasn't interested. He's not a vengeful person."

Milo said, "Granted the first time *was* an outrage, you're the hero of the story. But that doesn't relate to the present situation."

"A hero? Don't patronize me, Lieutenant. All I did was basic lawyering."

"Just like you're doing now."

"I don't owe you any explanation."

I said, "Travis's life between his release and being hired by the Vanders is a blank. When he got out, you wanted to help him reintegrate, but he disappeared on you. Went homeless. All kinds of things can happen to a disabled young man living on the street. What makes you think he's the same person you saved?"

Wallenburg put the pen down, picked up a rocker blotter.

Milo said, "We're talking nineteen years with no legitimate identity. That kind of caginess implies something to hide."

"It implies nothing of the sort."

"What then?"

Debora Wallenburg plinked a long, silver nail against the blotter. "You have no idea," she said.

I said, "I think we do. He was traumatized, lonely, in so much despair he wouldn't accept your help in readjusting."

No answer.

"What part of the picture are we missing, Ms. Wallenburg?"

Her eyes lost lawyer-steel and turned human. Another quick blink restored them to flat, jade disks.

I said, "What happened to him during those hidden years?"

The phone rang. She picked it up and said, "Sure, put it through. Hi, Mort, what's up? That? I sent it yesterday, you should be getting it any minute. What's that? Absolutely. No, just taking life easy."

Making a show of relaxation, she sat back, chatted, did more listening, finally glanced our way.

Feigned surprise at our presence and kept talking.

A tall blond assistant in a suit almost as nice as Wallenburg's entered the office on lethal heels. "Gentlemen, the garage just called. Your car is ready."

John Nguyen said, "There's nothing I can do, Milo."

"Even if she's harboring a fugitive."

"Did she acknowledge that she was?"

"She claimed she wasn't."

"Do you have evidence to the contrary?"

"It's pretty obvious Huck reached out to her. I'm sure she's got an idea where he's bunked down."

Nguyen said, "You keep putting me in this position."

"What position?"

"Having to be Mr. Ice Bath. What you have doesn't mean squat, Milo, and you're too experienced not to know that."

We were at the Pacific Dining Car on Sixth, just west of Downtown. Nguyen was demolishing a surf and turf. Reed and I stuck with soda water. Milo had ordered but he had no appetite, which meant the world was coming to an end.

"Jesus, John, do you have any idea how high-profile this could get?"

"Seen the memos," said Nguyen. "Also heard rumors about your boss's slowing down the process."

"Well, now my bosses want everything sped up. I told Wallenburg I thought she'd dummied up deliberately and she didn't argue."

"Her situation, that's what I'd do, Milo."

"John, we've got a goddamn serial lust maniac out there and she can help us find him."

"Maybe."

"She's the hero of Huck's story, I'm sure he turned to her when he rabbited. Even without explicit knowledge of his where-abouts, she's likely to have a pretty good idea."

"Prove that she's harboring and I'll see if there's some way I can twist it in your favor."

"Surveillance on her would be—"

"Your choice, but I wouldn't be heavy-handed about it. Debora's going to be ready for you and if you overstep, she'll slam you with a civil suit."

"So lawyers get special privileges," said Reed.

"Hey, that's why we become lawyers." Nguyen forked a huge piece of steak. Reconsidered and sawed it in half. "What do you really expect to learn from watching her? She's not going to drive her Ferrari straight to Huck's crib."

"She's got a Ferrari?'"

"And a Maybach—the super-Mercedes," said Nguyen. "What's that, four hundred grand, excluding the gas-guzzler tax?"

"Crime pays," said Reed.

"I drive a Honda, don't make me cry. I knew Debora back when I was in school and she was teaching criminal law. She was a great lecturer as well as one of the best PDs in the city."

Milo said, "She make all that money shuffling corporate paper?"

"Not directly," said Nguyen. "Shortly after she switched to corporate, she was assigned to drawing up the contracts on a bunch of gazillion-dollar dot-com deals. Invested early and cashed out at the right time. I don't know why she bothers practicing anymore."

"Must be the thrill," said Milo.

"Ha ha ha." Nguyen dipped lobster in drawn butter, sipped his martini.

"John, if I asked you for a tap on her—"

"I'd say, 'So when are you opening at the Comedy Store?'"

"All those women dead, John. And maybe the Vanders—a kid, John, maybe with his hand hacked clean off."

Nguyen looked at his steak and sighed.

Milo said, "Public's gonna love us wimping out on this."

"You can't tap her, Milo. She's his lawyer, not his girlfriend."

Reed said, "Who knows?"

"You've got evidence of an intimate relationship?"

"Not yet."

"Find that—find anything that shows me she's behaved illegally."

Milo said, "If she's his girlfriend, she's the dumbest smart person in the world. His sexual partners tend to end up dead and dismembered."

"And facing east," I said, wondering if Nguyen would find that interesting.

He didn't. "I really wish I could help you, guys. Maybe you should forget about Debora and find Huck the old-fashioned way."

Milo said, "Meaning?"

"Shoe leather, interviewing street people—whatever you guys do that brings in the goods." He made a try for his steak. Chewed without apparent pleasure. "There's another reason not to piss Debora off. Once you do get Huck, we could be contending with her at the defense table. Then I'll be the one with the ulcer."

"You see her putting aside her corporate clients and taking him on?"

"From what you've told me, she believes in him," said Nguyen. "Even if she's not chief defense counsel, she'll play a role. I know Debora."

"Tenacious," I said.

"Beyond belief, Doctor."

"Ferrari, Maybach," said Reed. "She can afford to play Wonder Woman."

"Must be nice," said Nguyen.

CHAPTER

32

I've ridden in a few funeral processions. The drive back to the station had that same stunned, dispirited feeling.

Milo said, "Smart woman like that and she's taken in by his bullshit."

Reed said, "Like those losers who hook up with cons in prison. What's behind it, Doc?"

"Usually really low self-esteem and a desire for attention." Neither of which applied to Wallenburg, but why intrude on their resentment?

Milo rubbed his face. "All that dough,

but her life's empty so she wants to feel righteous again."

"Limousine liberals," said Reed.

The corners of Milo's mouth twitched but gave up short of a smile. "Haven't heard that one in a while, Moses."

"That's what my mother said my father used to call them."

Milo said, "Any suggestions about changing Wallenburg's mind, Alex?"

"With someone else, I'd try piling on the gory details—victim photos, autopsy shots, emphasize the suffering the women went through. In Wallenburg's case, it's likely to solidify her resistance."

"Because she sees herself as Iron Maiden."

"Saving Huck was a major event in her life, so viewing him as a vicious killer is too threatening. But if you do get some serious evidence—something that appeals to her rationality—you could crack her denial."

"That's what you were getting at in her office. Huck's not the same innocent kid, no fault of hers."

Reed said, "We've got blood in the drain."

Milo said, "I thought of telling her, didn't want to give her anything to work with. First thing out of her mouth would be 'ABO typing's not DNA.'"

Reed said, "We get a full confession, she'll probably still stand behind him. Poor little victim of the system." He shook his head. "Ferrari Debby."

Milo said, "Feel like following her, Moses?"

"Sure," said Reed. "Department paying for a Maserati? She gives me the slip, conventional wheels aren't going to cut it."

"Long as you can get it for thirty bucks a day."

"I could boost some hot wheels," said Reed. "But God forbid I should be heavy-handed."

Back home and away from their ill humor, I wondered if Debora Wallenburg had lied about not knowing Huck's whereabouts.

Smart people made foolish mistakes all the time; my profession thrived on that fact. But if Wallenburg had overstepped by harboring a dangerous fugitive, my guess was we'd never find out.

I thought about Huck, rootless, haunted. The cameo performance as a superhero.

Saving a baby.

Debora Wallenburg's initial act of kindness had created a long-term bond between her and Huck. What if the same was true for Huck and Brandi Loring's family?

No Internet hits popped up for *Anita and Lawrence Brackle* but *Larry Brackle* appeared on a three-year-old police blotter from the *Daily News.* Arrestee, age forty-three, a Van Nuys DUI bust.

No follow-up on that but an image scan brought up a two-year-old photo of Brackle celebrating the "Turkey Tenpin Fest of the Meadowlark Association Bowling Club" at a Canoga Park alley.

A dozen beaming keglers. Brackle had earned front-row center because size mattered. Even compared with the slight women flanking him, he was a small man—skinny, wiry, with black hair slicked back and sideburns reaching to his jawline.

I plugged in *Meadowlark Association* and came up with the homeowners' group at a condo development in Sherman Oaks.

Eighty-nine "deluxe" units on three acres north of Ventura Boulevard, just east of the 101 freeway. Prices ranged from mid-six-figures for a one-bedroom "Hacienda Suite" to nearly a million for "3 Br. 2 Ba. Rancheros."

High-def photos showcased white, red-roofed modules softened by ferns, palms, banana plants, and rubber trees. "Gracious path-ways for strolling," three pools, two with "whirlpool soaking spas," as well as a screening room, a gym "with sumptuous steamroom and sauna."

Nice upgrade from the Silverlake rental Brackle and his family had called home a decade ago.

I checked the names of the other bowlers. None of the women was Anita Brackle. Maybe she had no use for tenpins. Or Larry's drinking had continued, driving her away.

Along with Baby Brandeen?

I searched Brackle's face for signs of dissolution, saw only a skinny little bespectacled man happy to be among his peers.

Copying down The Meadowlark address, I told Robin I'd be stepping out.

She said, "This time it's not just rest-
lessness. You've got that heat in your baby
blues."

I told her about Brackle.

She said, "Huck helped the family, so
they're helping him?"

"I'm grasping."

"No grasp, no get." She kissed me. "Be
careful."

When I reached the door, she said, "Be
great if the baby's thriving."

The reality of The Meadowlark was white
stucco grayed by time and pollution, a pro-
fusion of plants in need of trim, a constant
overlay of freeway flatulence.

Security was mechanical but effective:
a deadbolted iron mesh gate. I checked
the roster of residents, failed to find Brackle's name, figured him for long gone, or a
sublet.

Then a listing at the bottom caught my
eye.

Ranchero Five. One of the high-priced
units.

I was deliberating whether or not to try
the direct approach when a FedEx guy
came charging through the gate. I caught

it before it could swing shut, made my way past the first two swimming pools, both unoccupied and leaf-littered.

The Haciendas were a collection of two-story units tucked into the northeast corner and segregated by a low wall of cut-out cement blocks.

The orange door to Five was nearly hidden by the broad leaves of a banana that had managed to thrive in the shade but would never bear fruit.

I rang the bell. A female voice said, "Larry? Forget your key again?"

I murmured something that could've been "Uh-huh" or "Uh-uh."

The door opened on a perilously thin, brown-haired, middle-aged woman wearing an oversized white jersey top and black yoga pants, and holding a cigarette. Bare feet, pink toenails, red polish for the tips of her spidery fingers. A gold chain rested on the arch of one varicose foot. A face perched on a long, graceful neck bore the aftershocks of beauty. Puckers around her wide, thin mouth gave her a capuchin look. Shadows under her eyes spoke of stories that could never be untold.

"You're not Larry." Smoker's rasp. Olfactory stew of Chanel and tobacco.

"Mrs. Vander?"

"Who's asking?"

I gave her my name and flashed the consultant's I.D.

"A doctor? Something happened to Larry?"

"No. I'm here to talk to him."

"About what?"

"Old friends."

"Well, he's not here." Kelly Vander began closing her door.

I said, "When's Mr. Brackle coming back? It's important."

The door stopped moving.

"Mrs. Vander?"

"I heard you." Behind her was a big bright, high-ceilinged room set up with a flat-screen and pink leather couches. A half-gallon bottle of Fresca stood on an end table. Music played. Jack Jones advising some girl to comb her hair and fix her makeup.

Kelly Vander said, "He went out for cigarettes."

"No problem. I'm happy to wait outside."

"What kind of old friends?"

"Travis Huck, for one."

"Travis," she said.

"You know him."

"Why wouldn't I? He works for my ex-husband."

"Are you and Mr. Vander in regular contact?"

"We talk."

"Have you spoken to him recently?"

She shook her head. "This has something to do with Simon?"

I said, "Did Larry help Travis get the job with Simon?"

She sucked in smoke. "I don't speak for Larry. For anyone. Give me your number, I'll pass it on."

"I'd rather wait."

"Suit yourself." The door edged inward another couple of inches.

I said, "Simon hasn't been heard from in two weeks. Same for Nadine and Kelvin."

"They're probably traveling. They do that."

"Two weeks ago, they flew from Asia to San Francisco. Any idea where they might be staying?"

"I wouldn't know. What's that got to do with Larry?"

"You haven't heard about Travis?"

"Heard what?"

I told her.

"That's insane."

"What is?"

"Travis doing something like that. He loves us."

"Loves the entire family?"

"Just about," she said. "Too bad about those women, that's really horrible. Really, really horrible. Jesus." Tugging the neckline of her top. "I'm sure they're okay—Simon and Kelvin. Nadine. Adorable kid, Kelvin. Plays piano like Elton John. He calls me Auntie Kelly."

"How often do you see them?"

"Not often."

"What did you mean by 'just about'?"

"Sorry?"

"You said Travis loved 'just about' everyone in the family."

"He loves everybody." Her cigarette hand shook. Ash fell to her chest. She brushed it off, created streaks on the white jersey. "Would you do me a favor, examine the label, tell me the laundering instructions."

Hooking a thumb to the back of the neckline, she pulled and bent forward. Provided enough slack for a glimpse of flat chest and puckered sternum.

I said, "Dry clean only."

"Figures."

"Travis loves everyone," I said.

"Who wouldn't he love?" She flashed brown, corroded teeth. The cigarette slipped through her fingers, landed atop her left foot, scattered ashes. It had to hurt. She stared at the smoldering cylinder, as if assessing her loss.

I bent and retrieved the cigarette. She snatched it, jammed it back in her mouth.

"Sorry to upset you," I said.

"Upset? I don't think so. Let me look at that I.D. of yours."

CHAPTER

33

Kelly Vander's pink couches were soft and yielding. Her condo had the after-thought look of temporary housing.

The seventy-inch TV was the source of the music; a cable or satellite station playing Singers and Standards. Jack Jones had given way to Eydie Gorme blaming everything on the bossa nova.

Kelly touched the soda bottle. "Fresca? If you want caffeine, there's Diet Pepsi."

"Nothing, thanks."

Inhaling her cigarette down to the filter, she ditched it in the kitchen sink, found a pack of Winston Lights, lit up. "Some people think diet is bad for you but I think it's better than all that sugar. Larry should be back soon."

She took something off the wall and brought it to me.

Framed, glassed newspaper ad. Full-color May Company spread, junior miss dresses and sweater ensembles on clearance. The date, thirty-one years ago.

"This is me." Pointing to a blond girl in a plaid jumper. Even without puckers, Kelly Vander's mouth had a simian cast and I would've picked her out.

"You modeled?"

She sat on a pink corner. "I'm five five now, used to be an inch taller before my spine compressed. But even with that, I was too short for the big time. In the beginning all they had me doing was kiddy wear. My boobs came in late because . . . soon as I got a chest, the agency pushed me straight into juniors and that's where I stayed. That's how I met Simon. He was in the rag trade, repping synthetic knits for a downtown manufacturer. There was a showcase for buyers, they set up a runway at the Scottish Rite, place squeaked like a haunted house."

"Over in Hancock Park," I said. "Near the Ebell." Wondering if Kelvin Vander's recital venue would draw a reaction.

Kelly Vander said, "That's the one. Karma." She poured herself Fresca. "Sure I can't get you any?"

"I'm fine. What was karma?"

"Meeting Simon. We girls were all lined up, they gave us outfits randomly. I just happened to end up with one of his company's suits. Blue, double-breasted. Metal buttons, like a sailor. I even wore a sailor hat." She touched her head, allowed herself a ragged brown smile. "Crappy poly, scratchy, I couldn't wait to get out of it. Simon came up to me later. He'd gotten a big order, thanked me. He was a little older than me. Seemed sophisticated . . ."

She exhaled smoke. Nicotine vapors wafted across her glass, gave the soda the look of a potion.

"You're a psychologist, huh? Known plenty of those. Some good ones, some not-so-good ones."

"That's better than no good ones."

"You work for the police?"

"I freelance."

"Must be interesting."

"It can be."

Big grin. "What was your most exciting case?"

I smiled back.

She said, "Can't blame any of them. The psychologists who tried to help me. What I had was resistant to change. 'Chronic eating disorder, resistant to change.' They told me if I didn't stop starving myself, I'd drop dead of a heart attack. That scared me, but not enough, you know? Like there's two parts of my brain, the thinking section and the *gimme* section. One of the doctors who helped me said it was a matter of developing new habits. He had me do exercises—mental, I mean. Getting the thinking section to dominate. That make sense to you?"

"It does."

"I'm okay now." Running her hands over her bony body. "I could probably still keel over from what I did to myself back then, but so far, knock on mahogany."

"You were healthy enough to have a child."

"You know Simone? She looks just like me . . . I should do my teeth. It's obvious, right? They're all rotted from bulimia, everyone says I'd look ten years younger if I did my teeth but I'm not sure I want that."

"To look younger?"

"Exactly," she said. "Every time I see myself in the mirror and cringe it reminds me of how I got that way in the first place. What do you think? Professionally speaking. Do I need that reminder?"

"I don't know you well enough," I said.

"*Ding.* Good answer." She pumped air, checked a wall clock. "Where's Larry . . . I finally got some insights. Third rehab's the charm."

"Did you meet Larry in rehab?"

She shook her head. "I don't speak for Larry. I own what I own and his emotional acreage is his. Speaking of which."

She glanced at the door.

I'd been listening for footsteps, had heard nothing. Moments later, the panel of orange wood swung wide open and sixty-three inches of sunglassed, aloha-shirted Larry Brackle charged in swinging a greasy white bag. A carton of Winston Lights was pinioned under his arm. "Got you donuts, honey. Those crunchy maple walnut cinnam—"

He removed his shades. "We got a guest, Kell?"

Kelly Vander said, "You do, Larry. It's *all* about you, baby doll."

Larry Brackle flicked ashes into a coffee cup. "You're trying to tell me Travis is some kind of Bundy? No offense, sir, but that's lunacy."

Kelly Vander said, "That's what I told him, sweets."

They sat next to each other, knees pressed together, smoking in unison, making their way through the Fresca.

I said, "The police consider him a prime suspect."

Brackle said, "Police thought that the first time."

"You know Travis's history."

Hesitation. "Sure. It was in the papers."

"Not the local papers."

Silence.

I said, "*The Ferris Ravine Clarion*'s pretty obscure, Mr. Brackle. Unless you know his story from some other source."

Brackle turned to Kelly Vander. Her face stayed blank.

He said, "Whatever, I heard about it."

"Travis told you."

"Whatever."

"Did you meet him in rehab?"

"Look, sir, I want to be a good citizen, but I don't speak for Travis. He owns what he owns and my shit is my own. No offense."

I said, "Speak for yourself then. Did you know him before he took Brandeen to the hospital or after?"

Brackle's jaws worked. Pint-sized man but his wrists and hands were thick and sturdy. "Man, I'm hungry." He sprang up, jogged to the kitchen, returned with a slab of pound cake on a paper plate. "Split, honey?"

"No, it's yours."

Brackle kissed her cheek. "It could be yours, too."

"You're so sweet but Ms. Tummy's full," said Kelly Vander. "I'll wait till dinner."

"You're sure? It's good cake."

"I am, sweetie."

"Okay. Let's have those steaks for dinner."

"You can have one, Lar. Little heavy for me."

"I'll cut them into thin strips."

"We'll see."

"You liked 'em that way before."

"Yeah, that was good, but I don't know, I'm kind of full."

I said, "I'm thinking you knew Travis before he found Brandeen. He went looking for her and Brandi in order to help you out."

"Now, c'mon, sir, don't be going off on some guessing game. Travis is a good man."

"I'm not saying he isn't. I know he didn't hurt Brandi."

Brackle's hands became glossy white fists. "Hell, no, he didn't. Everyone knows who hurt Brandi. *Sir.*"

"Gibson DePaul."

"Scum. They sent him up for life and he killed another inmate and got sent to Pelican Bay. Sir."

"You keep tabs on him?"

"We get that victim notification mailer they send us."

"'Us' meaning the two of you? Or you and your ex?"

"I can't say what *she* gets."

"Where is Anita?"

"You tell me."

"Lost contact?"

"Anita couldn't change herself. Didn't wanna try."

"What about the kids?"

"I see 'em on some holidays," said Brackle. "What's the diff to you? Why all this curiosity about my family?"

"Sorry. My main interest is Travis."

"Then you're spinning your wheels, sir. He didn't kill nobody. Not then, not now."

"Interesting," I said.

"What is?"

"The police consider him a prime suspect but people keep showing up who consider him a saint."

"Like who?"

"Debora Wallenburg."

Brackle and Kelly Vander looked at each other. Burst into sudden, strident laughter.

I said, "Must've missed the joke."

Brackle said, "Saints. There ain't no such thing, we're always talking about that. All there is, sir, are sinners of different degrees and what we all need is to learn to forgive ourselves, not wait for some preacher to do it."

I said, "So both of you met Travis in rehab."

No answer.

"It's not a secret that can be kept very long."

"Travis is entitled to his privacy, sir."

"Getting help's not something to be ashamed of, Mr. Brackle. On the contrary. He got himself together."

Kelly Vander said, "Okay, fine, that's where we met him."

I said, "Did you recommend him to Simon as payment for rescuing Larry's granddaughter?"

Brackle said, "You're a smart one. Why don't you use that brain on something important?"

"How long before Brandi's murder did you meet him?"

"Right before, okay? Six, seven months. I'd already decided to leave Anita because she refused to get better and I knew if I stayed with her, I'd be dead soon. Only thing that stopped me was the kids. Three of hers—including Brandi—and we had one together. That's Randy. He's in the service, over in Fallujah, got decorated."

"Randy's a wonderful boy," said Kelly, wistfully.

Brackle said, "We got a consensus on

that . . . yeah, that's where we met Travis, the three of us trying to get straight. His treatment was being paid for by that lawyer, Wallenburg. I thought it was damn nice of her and told him so. Told him he should take advantage of amazing grace and improve himself. *I* was using my own dough plus work disability, place cost a fortune."

Kelly said, "Simon footed my bill. Even though we were divorced."

"When was this?" I said.

"Twelve years ago, Simon and I had split up three years before but we stayed friends. I put Simon through a lot and he stopped loving me, but he still liked me. No matter what, I never raised my voice to him. Never tried to squeeze any extra money out of him even after he got real rich. I thought I deserved *not* to be loved so I made sure he stopped loving me. Simone was a teenager, the stress—I wasn't handling *anything,* Simon said give it another try, Kell, you owe it to yourself, we'll find a great place, all the creature comforts. He got me brochures. I liked the one from Pledges, lots of trees."

"Pledges in South Pasadena?"

"You know it?"

"Good place," I said. "Closed down a few years ago."

Larry Brackle said, "Great place. They got bought out by one of those corporations, bastards ran it into the ground."

Kelly said, "First day I got there, I met Larry. He liked me *and* loved me but it wasn't for years that he admitted it 'cause he was still married. And I wasn't in a receptive state—didn't see myself committed to anyone."

"How long have you two been together?"

Brackle said, "Officially, nine years. In here"—patting his heart—"from forever."

Kelly Vander said, "Instant friendship and acceptance, I never had that with a man. Simon's a good man, but I knew I was failing him constantly, and you can't live being a failure all the time."

I said, "The cops say Travis was a poly-drug user."

No answer.

"Rehab helped the two of you, but it didn't work for him. Two years afterward, he was homeless."

"That's where I saw him," said Larry Brackle.

"On the street?"

"Used to work in Hollywood, big apartment building, nice place west of La Brea, assistant super. On my way home, I generally took the boulevard, drove past the Chinese Theatre. One night I spotted Travis there, panhandling tourists. He looked real bad. Compared to when he was at Pledges, I mean. Stringy hair, beard, all hunched over. Not doing too good with the tourists because he wouldn't get in anyone's face, that's Travis, he don't confront. I drove around the block, pulled up, laid a twenty in his palm. He saw it was me, started to cry, said he was sorry for screwing up."

Kelly said, "Before we got discharged, the three of us made a promise to change and to reach out to each other when our thoughts turned bad. Larry and I stuck to it, that's how we succeeded. But we lost touch with Travis."

Brackle nodded. "I told him, 'No one's judging you, man. Come home with me for a meal and a bath.' He ran off and the next day, he wasn't there, same for the entire week. But then I saw him again, same deal, his hand's out, even worse-looking.

This time, he agreed to go with me. Anita was pissed off, said you see any extra room in this dump, genius? What with her, me, all the kids, we had a couple of dogs, too. I said I'd sleep outside in the backyard if that made it better. She said maybe both of you should. What ended up happening was Travis used this toolshed we had. I cleared away junk and put out a mattress and he'd come and go as he pleased. I got him a haircut. Once the hair was off, we saw all these pierces he had in his ears. Like a pirate. Especially with that limp, he was like a pirate. Kids loved the pierces, Anita hated them."

Kelly said, "But Anita came to like Travis."

"What changed Anita's mind was he was gentle with the kids. Soon she was letting him tell the kids stories. Then he was holding the baby, being real good with the baby. 'Course, Anita could be unpredictable, what with drinking and weed, so it wasn't always perfect. But mostly we had peace."

Deep drag on his cigarette. "Travis really liked that baby . . . man, it's been a long time. Now you're wanting to tell me

Travis is some kind of murder-monster? No way, José. I'm no shrink but I know people pretty good and Travis is *good* people."

I said, "Tell me about the night Brandi disappeared."

"She didn't *disappear,* sir. She went with *him.* That garbage we don't mention by name. Now, *that* one was evil from the get-go, his own family was scared of him. When Brandi didn't come back, we went right over to their place—Travis and me. His folks looked scared, said the little shit-face talked about visiting with Brandi and the baby, that's all they knew. Travis and me went searching the neighborhood. Travis took a bunch of streets, I took some others. He found the baby. Saw the blood and took her to the hospital."

"So he knew something had happened to Brandi."

"Brandi was hidden—that's what the cops said, off in some bushes. The baby was out in the open, he was thinking about the baby."

"Why'd he walk to the hospital rather than contact you?"

"Scared, wouldn't you be?" said Brackle.

"Going to jail once for something you didn't do, now there's a baby with blood? Not that he said it, it's just what I figured out. That boy's whole life was fear, I'd walk by the shed and hear him moaning, bad dreams. Daylight, there'd be this look in his eyes, what's the word—haunted. He was *haunted* by what they did to him. Anyone would be, way they beat his brain around. He probably got all freaked out the cops would blame it on him. But even with that fear, he wanted to make sure the baby was okay."

I said, "So you never talked to him about it."

"Nope. Travis disappeared after dropping Brandeen at the hospital."

"How'd you know it was him?"

"Cops described him. Asked if we knew who he was but we didn't let on. We were all crazy over what happened to Brandi, didn't want to complicate things. The main thing was find out who did it to her, and that we did tell 'em."

I said, "Travis took a two-mile walk in the cold."

"Travis was a walking man, sir. Filled most of his days walking."

"Where?"

"Everywhere," said Brackle. "But don't go misunderstanding, there was nothing crazy to it. He just liked to walk."

"It's the best exercise," said Kelly. "I used to do ten miles a day. I still do five."

The skin around Brackle's eyes creased. He forced himself cheerful. "Exactly, aerobic, boy wanted to be aerobic—nossir, he just liked to walk."

I said, "How did Travis hook up with Simon?"

Kelly said, "That was years later. We hadn't heard from him for a while, then out of the blue he called Larry to let him know he was doing better."

"Finally got himself some help that stuck," said Brackle.

"Where?"

"He didn't say and I didn't ask. He sounded good, I could tell this was different. I invited him for coffee with me and Kelly. He looked good."

"Clear-eyed," said Kelly. "Intelligent. That never really came out before because he was always so depressed. He said he was looking for steady employment, would do anything to make an honest buck. I knew Simon was looking for someone to manage his house. He'd been through a couple of flakes, needed someone reliable. He said sure, he'd try Travis out. It worked out great."

I said, "Did Travis talk about what he'd been doing since the last time you saw him?"

"No, sir," said Brackle.

"Where was he living?"

"I got the sense he'd been traveling."

"Any idea where?"

"We didn't get nosy with him," said Kelly. "We were thrilled he was doing well. It worked out great for everyone. Simon thanked me for finding Travis. Travis is gentle, he'd never hurt anyone. Now I *am* getting kind of hungry."

Brackle said, "Yup, dinnertime. We'd invite you to join us, sir, but we always portion for two."

I drove back to the city. A yellow VW was parked in front of my house.

Unoccupied, cold engine, no sign of Alma Reynolds.

My remark about her mother's pearls had scared her.

Maybe Robin had let her in.

As I climbed the stairs, a voice behind me said, "Now *I'm* stalking *you*."

She stepped out from the side of my house, came toward me carrying a green vinyl attaché case. Brand new, tag still tied to the handle, not much different from the one Milo uses when the murder books get thick. She wore a plaid shirt, jeans, work boots. Gray hair flew in all directions. Her eyes were hot.

"Here, take it," she said, thrusting the case. "We're finished."

My hands stayed at my sides.

The case touched my chest. "Don't worry, it doesn't tick. Take it."

"Let's talk."

She snatched it away, sprang the latches. Inside were stacks of twenty-dollar bills held together by rubber bands. Atop the money, a black velvet jewelry box.

She said, "Including the damn pearl. Satisfied?"

I said, "Going for the simple life?"

"Stop being nasty. This is what you wanted, I'm giving it to you."

"What I want is information."

"Doesn't *this* say it all?"

"It implies. Why don't you come up and we'll talk?"

"What? *Therapy?* Is there a *couch?* The psych board website lists this as your office. I'd think you'd be more careful, seeing as it's your home. What if I was a socio-path?"

"Should I be worried?"

"Oh, sure, I'm packing heat." She laughed, flipped her pockets inside out. Placing the case on the ground, she stomped to the VW, turned her back, slapped her palms on the hood. "Is this the proper position?"

"C'mon," I said. "Just a few minutes of your time."

She straightened and faced me. Her eyes were wet. "Sil taught me the position. He got used to doing it automatically at protests. Sometimes, the cops hit him any-way. He was a man of principle and look where it got him. So—but hell, why should *I* have anything nice?"

"I'm sure his principles were strong. That made finding his cash-stash doubly shock-ing."

"Look," she said, "I'm giving it to you, ev-ery bit of it, my hands are clean. Good-bye."

"Let's clarify a few things and that really will be the end of it."

"So you say."

"The way I see it, *you're* the person of principle," I said. "And I'm not the enemy."

Arms folded across her chest. She wiped her eyes, nudged the case with a work-booted toe.

"Oh, hell, I used to be Catholic. What's another damn confession?"

CHAPTER

34

Alma Reynolds bounced on my couch and laughed. "You've actually got one. If leather could talk."

I placed the attaché case on the floor between us.

"What's that," she said, "the altar of eternal truth? I'm supposed to see it and buckle?"

I moved the case aside.

"No matter what you think, Sil *was* a man of principle. He may have taken the money but he didn't spend it."

"The police went over his apartment carefully. Where'd you find it?"

"What's the difference?"

"He was murdered. Everything matters."

"Can't see how that does but fine, in his
car, okay? In the trunk, right out in the
open. Which is my point: It was nothing he
was ashamed of. There's no big mystery
here. People sent in minor cash donations
and rather than go to the bank all the time,
Sil saved them up so he could deposit
them in the marsh account."

"The small stuff."

"So you actually listen."

I said, "He told you about the money?"

"No, but it's the only thing that makes
sense."

"Sil controlled the account."

"Sil *created* the account. He *was* Save
the Marsh, I already explained that to you.
Every penny went to maintenance."

"Except for his salary."

"He never gave himself a raise, we're
not exactly talking rampant materialism.
Now that I've seen how *you* live, I understand why you can't seem to get that. *This*
place, all the Sunday supplement con-
tempo California living. I know what this
neighborhood costs, money's *your* thing,

but it *wasn't* Sil's. The fact that he left the case right out in the open is proof positive there's nothing corrupt about the money."

"How much is in there?"

"Fifteen thousand. Yes, I counted it. Who wouldn't?"

"Including the pearl?"

She flushed. "Keep the damn pearl, it didn't fit me anyway and it's obviously jammed a burr up your butt. Hell, give it to your wife, if you have one."

Thankful Robin worked in a separate building, I said, "The pearl's yours, why shouldn't it be?"

"Aw, gee, how *tweet* of you. *Forget* it. I'm washing my hands of the whole damn mess. Sil was right, filthy lucre does stain permanently."

I said, "The money could very well be yours, too, unless he left a will bequeathing it to someone else."

"Well, he didn't," she said. "Neither of us had wills. We made a joint decision to avoid pathetic attempts to control things from the grave."

"Then I'd say it's yours. You were his significant other."

"Are you dense or just being manipulative? I don't *want* it—and don't try to tell me the cops won't try to confiscate it. Isn't that part of the racket? The entire so-called-war-on-drugs is nothing more than a revenue scheme."

"The cops I work with are out to solve murders. And Detective Sturgis's skin tones don't go with the pearl."

"Oh, aren't you charming," she said. "Probably had a soft upbringing, always got your way because you were oh so cute. This is the last time I'm going to say it: I *don't* want the money and I *don't* want the damn pearl. Hell if I know what got into me in the first place. So stop harassing me—tracing me to that damn jewelry store, unbelievable. You're like one of those Homeland Security scammers."

"Alma," I said, "I'm just trying to figure out what happened at the marsh."

"*Tracing* me. That crack about my *mother*—you actually found that jewelry store?"

"Lots of motivation, Alma."

"Well, bully for you—if you must know, I didn't go in there intending to buy anything expensive. Just a trinket, something to remind me of Sil. Why the hell not? I was grieving." She sniffed. "He's so damn *gone* . . . you try filling hollow hours."

"I'm sorry."

"Like hell you are. You're toying with me right now."

"What I'm trying to do is figure out who murdered the man you loved. And a whole bunch of other people."

"Who says it's the same person? And even if it is, talking about the money isn't going to accomplish anything. It's what I said, small donations."

"Fifteen thousand worth," I said.

"It adds up." Less confidence in her voice.

"Are the bills of different denominations?"

No answer.

"It's easy enough to check."

"Twenties, okay?" she said. "It's all in twenties."

"Kind of a coincidence."

"So at some point Sil changed it into twenties . . . to make the count easier."

"If he went to the bank to change bills, why not simply deposit the money?"

She shot to her feet. "My hands are clean. Forget all that Catholic crap, I was never into self-flagellation."

I said, "Sil was seen taking an envelope from a man."

"What?"

"In the parking lot behind his office."

"Seen by who?"

"A witness."

"Who?"

"I can't say."

She smirked. "One of those 'anonymous sources'? Like the government always *happens* to find?"

"A witness with no motive to lie."

"So you say."

"It may not have been ominous, but it happened, Alma."

"Someone delivered a donation in person. Big deal."

I described the man with the blond hair and the reconstructed face.

She said, "Sounds like your typical L.A. guy."

"You have no idea who he is."

"Why would I? Good-bye, and don't spend it all in one place."

I said, "One more thing."

"With you people there's always one more thing."

"Us people as in . . ."

"Representatives of the state."

I said, "Everything's political."

"You'd better believe it."

"Does that include the knife in Sil's gut?"

Her arms turned rigid. "Oh, you're a beaut. Coming across all sensitive but there's a cruel streak you bring out at will."

"I'm trying to get to the truth. I thought we might share that goal."

"Truth is *bullshit*. Truth changes with *context*."

"Context is exactly what I'm looking for, Alma. If you want to canonize Sil, fine. But if you can open your mind long enough to consider an alternative, we might actually find out who murdered him."

If she'd walked out, I wouldn't have been surprised.

She stood there. "What alternative?"

"Consider the possibility that Sil was paid off. Nothing illegal, maybe just to bend the rules. I think whoever paid him also lured him—someone who knew the marsh and believed Sil had to be silenced."

"Rich bastards," she said. "Everything *is* political."

"Any rich bastards in particular?"

"How about those movie crooks for a start? Money corrupts and they have obscene amounts of money. They funded STM but I'll bet they've never stopped lusting for the land. Sil took their money but he despised them."

"Would Sil have gone out in the middle of the night for one of their lackeys?"

Silence.

I said, "Who did he trust, Alma?"

"No one. Sil wasn't a trusting person. I'm the only one he confided in and even then, he could be guarded."

"About what?"

"He was moody, could close up like a turtle, just be unreachable. But that doesn't mean he sold out. That damn bunch of mud was everything to him. Besides, what would anyone pay him off for?"

"I don't know."

"Well, neither do I. Good-bye."

I popped the case, took out the jewel box, pressed it in her hand.

She shook her head violently but didn't push it away.

"Depending on how things shake out, I may be able to get you the money, as well."

"I don't wa— why the hell are you doing this? Who the hell *are* you?"

"Just another guy with a soft upbringing."

She studied me. "If I was wrong about that, sorry, but it doesn't change facts on the ground. You're a government agent."

"Nothing to apologize for. I've been pressuring you."

"Yes, you have." Her hand closed around the box. "It's been hell, I need to get through it."

As I walked her out, she studied each room we passed. When we got to the VW, she said, "The only possible thing Sil could've been . . . no, that doesn't make sense. That wouldn't be worth fifteen thousand stinking dollars."

"Tell me anyway."

"There's another way into the marsh. Clear on the opposite end of the official entry, on the west side. It was intended as the original entry, but too many plants grew there and Sil insisted it not be touched. If it was up to him, the entire place would be off limits to visitors."

"Where on the west side?"

"Dead center, it's overgrown, impossible to see from the street, but if you push your way through, there's a gate. Sil kept it padlocked. He liked to go there—his secret place. Sometimes he took *me* there." Blushing. "It's beautiful, huge willows, high reeds, little brackish sub-ponds where tadpoles and frogs colonize. Lots of birds because it's closer to the ocean."

"How often did Sil go there?"

"I don't know. He only took me three, four times, always at night. We'd spread a blanket, be looking up at the stars, and he'd say, 'This is a billion-dollar view, if people only knew.' But that was rhetoric. Who'd pay fifteen thousand for a picnic spot? And why would that put Sil in danger?" She shook her head. "You're chasing your tail."

"Thanks, anyway."

"For letting my mind run wild?"

"It's called creativity," I said. "Lord knows, we could use more."

CHAPTER

35

I sped to the marsh and searched for the secret entry.

The preserve's western border was a dense block of eucalyptus and willows, a good twenty feet thick, fenced by four-foot-high metal pickets designed to look like wood. It took me three passes to spot the notch in the trees. Several yards of branches in my face before the second fence came into view.

Cedar stakes, padlocked, as Alma Reynolds had said. But only three feet high and climbing over was no big deal. Once on the other side, I endured another green gauntlet, holding back limb after limb as I treaded on uneven, leaf-strewn dirt.

Slow going, as I checked for evidence of human intrusion.

Ten yards in, I found it. Shoe prints, mostly blurred, but one crisp impression—a man-sized foot ringed by dots.

Foliage whispered above still water. Cattails shimmered as a great blue heron, huge, serpent-necked, with the dead-eyed mien of a prey-seeking pterodactyl, rose awkwardly, flapping its way to the ocean. By the time it disappeared, it had achieved grace.

Several seconds of silence passed before something scurried.

I kneeled and got close to the shoe prints. The dots seemed unusual but I was no expert. I took pictures with my cell phone, thought about what to do next.

All I could see up ahead was more green: trees tall enough to obscure the sky and shade the ground black.

Maybe this place *was* nothing more than a secret garden.

Fifteen thousand worth of clandestine picnic spot?

Not as absurd as it sounded. In places like L.A. and New York nothing stokes lust quicker than the threat of rejection. It's why the manufacturers of velvet ropes will never go out of business. Why costumed fools wait for hours on early-morning sidewalks, sweet-talking bouncers and risking junior-high humiliation in order to score overpriced drinks and brain-damaging dance track.

In places like L.A. some people fill their BlackBerrys—and their heads—with two lists: the places I go, the places I shun.

The part of the marsh I avoid because everyone goes there and it's so yesterday.

But there's this special spot, baby, way more gorgeous . . .

Chance Brandt remembered the blond man who'd paid off Sil Duboff from a fund-raiser. An affair populated by people who cared about the ocean or pretended to.

No reason to doubt Mr. Bondo's intentions; maybe the money would boil down to nothing more than a rich man's chump-change payoff for private nights beneath the stars.

But then why had Duboff been lured to his death?

Gutted and dumped, another body in the marsh. The public side.

I stood there, not sure if this beautiful place was malignant.

I'd print the shoe-print photos, e-mail them to Milo. For what it was worth.

The next morning at eight, his recorded voice was a drowsy greeting.

"Reed managed to follow Wallenburg but it didn't lead anywhere. We're lunching at noon tomorrow, the usual. If you have any sudden insights, I will save room for dessert."

"Get the photos?"

"Shoes," he said. "Probably Duboff's, but I'll send them to someone who knows about that."

This time, Reed kept pace with Milo, forking food into his mouth like a combine.

Career development.

When I sat, he put down his fork. "Wallenburg lives in a gated part of the Palisades, off Mandeville Canyon. Closest I could get was outside the gates. I thought

I might be on to something when she was still home at eleven. Then a rental Chevy followed by a Hertz van pulls up to the guardhouse and soon after the van leaves with two guys instead of one. Fifteen minutes later, Wallenburg drives out in the Chevy. I'm thinking she got herself a cover car, this is going to be interesting. She heads for Mar Vista, parks in front of a house that is definitely below her tax bracket, I'm thinking the bastard's crib *finally.* She uses her own key to get in, comes out ten minutes, drives away. Now I've got a choice. Knock on the door or keep tailing her."

He loosened his tie. "I go for the knock. No one answers. I try the back, same deal, drapes are drawn. Now I'm wondering if Wallenburg spotted me and played me, maybe it's just a rental property she owns and she's off to his real crib."

Milo said, "It was the right choice, kiddo."

"If you say so."

I said, "You're sure Huck doesn't live in the house?"

"Next-door neighbor says a family named Adams lives there, good people,

quiet. I showed Huck's picture—with and
without hair. No one recognized him."

He traced a four-sided figure on the table. "Welcome to Square One."

I said, "The Adams Family."

"How 'bout that. Another time, I might
be thinking it's funny."

"Any idea what size family?"

"I didn't ask. Why?"

"If a woman and a girl around ten live
there, it could be Brandeen Loring, the baby
Huck saved, and her grandmother, Anita
Brackle. And Huck could still be a guest,
despite what the neighbors say. No big deal
sneaking him in after dark. He keeps a low
profile, who's going to know he's there?"

Milo said, "What gets you from Point A
to Anita harboring a fugitive?"

"It's a theory and a minor one, at that.
But in some circles, Huck's a really popu-
lar guy." I recounted my talk with Larry
Brackle and Kelly Vander.

Reed said, "Wife number one, huh?
That clears up how Huck got the job with
Simon but not much else. You yourself
said Huck wasn't Anita's favorite person, it
was Larry who took him in."

"But Anita changed her mind about him. Conversion sometimes leads to the strongest faith."

Milo said, "Have to be more than strong to take him in with a kid in the house."

"A kid he's viewed as saving," I said. "For all we know, Huck's had regular contact with Brandeen—like that Chinese proverb, save someone and they're your responsibility forever. That's also probably a big part of Debora Wallenburg's motivation."

Reed said, "Everyone saving everyone. Meanwhile, we've got bodies. You really see Huck inspiring that kind of devotion?"

"Kelly and Larry are convinced he's a saint."

"Typical psychopath," said Milo. "Guy's ready to run for office."

Reed scratched his crew cut. Resumed eating.

I said, "Even if Ms. Adams isn't Anita, she could be someone else Huck knows from rehab. Misery loving company can lead to some pretty tight bonds. If Wallenburg wasn't playing you, she went there for a reason. The drapes could've been *drawn* for a reason."

Milo said, "If Huck's got a network of re-hab buddies, there could be safe houses all over the city."

Reed said, "Hero—" Something made him turn toward the restaurant's front door. He clenched his knife.

Aaron Fox walked toward us. Custom-tailored as ever, in a black, raw-silk suit, sea-green shirt, yellow pocket square.

Nothing jaunty in his step.

Reed got up and faced him. "Bad time, we're busy."

"No doubt, bro. But not too busy for me."

Fox sank down next to his brother's empty seat. His eyes were sharp but pink rimmed the sclera. He'd shaved carelessly, sported nicks and bumps in the tight, dark shad-ows below his jawline.

Milo said, "Long night, Aaron?"

"Lots of long nights. I could get screwed for talking to you," said Fox. "Might as well be monetary and not legal."

Reed said, "Got yourself in a bit of a professional fix?"

Fox frowned. "Is it my breath, bro? Yeah, it's a fix. Little conundrums are part of the job, but this is different. May I?" He reached for a water glass, drank greedily, poured another and finished that. Reaching for the *chapati,* he broke off a piece, ground it between finger and thumb. Repeated. Within seconds, he'd created a pile of bread crumbs.

Moe Reed feigned boredom as Fox smoothed the pile. Fox wiped his hand on a napkin. Plucked his pocket square and arranged it in three points. "When Simone Vander hired me to research Huck, she said it was her idea, period, I didn't have her permission to contact any of her father's business associates. I told her that's not how I usually work, she wants library science, she could do it herself."

Reed said, "Your mission, should you choose to accept it . . ."

"Give it a rest, Moses." Fox turned to Milo. "Simone said hiring me was more than wanting to know about Huck. She promised a much bigger job—rooting out a financial conspiracy against her dad. By his minions—her word. When I asked why, she said despite being a good businessman, he got taken advantage of all the time, a deep-pockets thing."

Milo said, "Which minions in particular bothered her?"

"Every one of Daddy's lawyers, accountants, and financial managers. She viewed them as leeches, falling over themselves to rack up billable hours. The lawyers, in particular, she thought were shady."

"Alston Weir," said Milo.

"Weir plus all his associates. She told me she wouldn't be surprised if the entire firm was in cahoots to loot the estate, maybe even with Huck."

"That sounds paranoid."

"A bit, but with mega-rich folk, you never know, the incentives are always there. I've seen plenty of predatory employees."

Reed said, "Did she suspect Huck of any specific financial screwiness?"

Fox shook his head. "With him it was more his creepy personality, worming his way into the family. Kissing Kelvin's ass, in particular. She claimed he spoiled the kid. Then, when Selena showed up dead, she got downright terrified and called me."

Reed said, "So far I'm not hearing much that's new."

"What's new, Moses, is she lied to me. Starting with there being another job.

Finishing with her deadbeating me. She hasn't paid a penny of her bill, shut me out completely—no e-mail replies, no return of my phone calls. *My* bad, I didn't take a retainer, figured it for a quickie. Which it was and we're not talking a mega-bill. Still, I like to be paid."

"So now we're your collection agency?"

Milo said, "How much are we talking about, Aaron?"

"Four grand, give or take."

"For Internet research. Not bad."

"The results of which I passed on to you guys. Then again, maybe you would have found it on your own."

Milo said, "We're grateful, Aaron. Is there a punch line approaching the horizon?"

"Oh, yeah," said Fox. "She annoyed me, which can be a *real* bad idea. My philosophy is go after every single penny. Really bulldog it, you can't have word getting out you're a pussy. So I go after her, starting with a records check. That turned up some interesting stuff: bunch of drug busts when she was eighteen to twenty-two, meth and weed, Daddy's lawyers got her off with probation."

"Anything since?"

"Not officially, but wait there's more, folks. She lied about more than the big job, lying seems to be her M.O. When I met her, she spun me stories about being a singer, a ballerina, a financial analyst for a hedge fund."

Reed said, "With us, it was just teacher."

I said, "Remedial teacher."

Fox said, "That, too. Supposedly, she just loves the tots. But her real love is 'the ballet.'"

Milo wiped his lips. "Tiny dancer, huh?"

"She claimed to have been in the *company* of the New York Ballet until she hurt her foot and lost a promising career. The *company* never heard of her."

He permitted himself a smile. "So much for my reading people. So now my adrenals are buzzing and I start watching her house, check out her garbage."

Milo said, "Fun part of the job."

Fox's grin took on wattage. "But oh so educational. What I learn is she lives on air, I'm talking diet soda and Special K—and not much cereal, at that. She also goes through a helluva lot of prescription decongestants and Ritalin. Now I'm thinking back to those meth busts. She just switched to legal speed."

I said, "Ritalin could fit with the special-ed fantasy. If she had learning disabilities, herself, maybe she fantasizes about a power role. The drug's also effective in weight control, if you don't mind the risks. Same for the decongestants. And she did have a role model for her eating disor-der."

"Who?"

I glanced at Milo. He nodded. I de-scribed Kelly Vander's struggle with an-orexia.

"Like mother, like daughter," said Fox. "When I met her I didn't think much of it. Skeletal is half the girls on the West-side. Yeah, sure, that all makes sense."

Reed said, "So she's an undernourished skank. What does it have to do with Huck?"

"I'm setting the stage, Moses. She's a liar and a possible addict, which says per-sonality problems, right? Which could explain what else I found in her garbage can: framed photo of her dad, her step-mom, and her brother all cut up, the glass all smashed."

He raised the water glass, as if toasting. "She trashed her family, guys. Literally."

I said, "Black ties for Dad and son, red gown for Mom?"

"That's the one."

"It was sitting on her coffee table. She called our attention to it. 'That's my brother, Kelvin. He's brilliant.'"

"Well, now he's brilliant and defaced," said Fox. "Literally. Sweet little countenance sliced up into confetti, like someone took a razor to it. To top it off, the damn thing was wrapped in toilet paper. Don't want to spoil your appetite, but not *clean* toilet paper. There's your glamorous side of the job."

Milo said, "The picture was a prop for our benefit. One happy family."

Reed said, "Now she doesn't need it anymore. Because . . . aw, Jesus. The Vanders haven't been heard from in two weeks."

Fox reached for another *chapati.* "But wait, there's more. Call in now and you get the Ginzu knife and the automatic vee-blefetzer. Given the real bad feeling I was getting from the little deadbeating bitch, I decided to keep shadowing her. First day, she did more of the usual rich-girl shit. Shopping, massage, more shopping. Which is weirdly carefree for someone who claims to be worried about her family. Second day starts off the same way. Neiman Marcus, little walk up Two Rodeo, she checks out the jewelry at Tiffany, Judith Ripka, buys sunglasses at Porsche Design. Then she drives two blocks— because she's an L.A. girl—to an office building on Wilshire and Canon. Lobby directory says it's the law firm Daddy uses. Same guys she bad-mouthed to me and she's visiting them. I sit across the street and wait for her to leave. When she does, it's not in her Beemer. She's a passenger in a Mercedes, some guy's at the wheel. They make a beeline to the Peninsula, Simone's pal tips the doorman big enough to leave the car in front. Two hours later, the two of them come out with that goofy, no-longer-horny look. Meanwhile, I've run the tags on the Mercedes—don't ask me how, okay?"

Milo said, "Perish the thought."

Fox said, "Comes back to Alston Weir, Attorney-at-Mischief. Such a greedy scumbag, she wouldn't trust him as far as she could throw him. Meanwhile he's her lunch-hour fuck-buddy."

Reed said, "Is Weir bald?"

"You think, Moses? Is there any other good reason to saddle himself with a big old mess of phony, piss-yellow fake-o hair? I'm talking Halloween, guys. Blond dust mop. What I find weird is the guy knows how to dress. Zegna suit, Ricci tie, Magli shoes. Threads like that and he blows it with a bad rug. Go figure."

"Maybe he's got an exaggerated self-image," said Milo.

"Meaning?"

"Thinks he's cuter than he really is, 'cause of all the Bondo in his face."

Fox frowned. "Yeah, that, too. So you know all this? I just blew off a client for nothing?"

No answer.

"Oh, that's just great. You guys sit there and let me spin my wheels." To his brother: "Having fun, Moses?"

Reed smiled. But no irony, no resentment. Maybe even something resembling brotherly affection.

"What?" Fox demanded.

"We knew a little, Aaron. You just made it a lot."

The four of us left the restaurant. Fox and Reed walked side by side, seemed on the verge of conversation. But neither brother initiated.

Milo said, "Did you happen to hold on to Simone's garbage, Aaron?"

"Lucky for you, I'm a bit of a pat rack, Milo. Moses can verify. His side of the room looked like some ashram, mine was beaucoup toys."

Reed said, "Beaucoup junk."

Fox said, "Shall I have it picked up or would you like me to deliver?"

"We'll come to you, Aaron. And thanks."

"Figured I had to, the girl's bad news. Any way to keep my part quiet?"

"We'll do our best."

Fox fooled with his pocket square and eyed his Porsche. "Meaning no."

Milo said, "You know how it goes, Aaron. Depends where it leads. Meanwhile, do us another favor and hold off on trying to collect your bill from Simone."

"For how long?"

"Until it's no longer an issue."

"Meaning never."

"Meaning until it's no longer an issue."

"Now," said Fox, "you're sounding like a lieutenant."

Pulling Alston "Buddy" Weir's driver's license took seconds. Forty-five years old, blond and blue, beta-carotene tan coating a heavy face that alternated between too-tight and losing the battle with gravity.

The bored, insolent expression of a man with better things to do than pose for the clerk. No one had questioned the biological authenticity of the Jan-and-Dean wig.

No criminal record, but a bar association complaint, still pending, had been filed two years ago over misappropriation of funds.

Locating Chance Brandt ate up over an hour.

We finally found the boy at the Westwood house of a friend named Bjorn Loftus.

Parents on vacation, gussied-up SUVs in the driveway, earsplitting music and marijuana fumes blowing through the doorway as Bjorn gaped.

He jabbered improbable lies until Milo

told him to bring Chance out *now.* Both boys staggered out moments later.

Chance smirked. "Again?"

Reed said, "Recognize this guy?"

"Yeah, that's him."

"Who?"

"Dude I saw giving the envelope to Duboff-jackoff." Bobbing his head and waiting for laughter that never came. "Mister look at me I'm all . . ." Chance's eyes clouded as he groped for a punch line.

"Sign your name to the photo," said Milo.

Chance's scrawl was unsteady. Reed had him repeat it.

Bjorn Loftus let out a dope giggle. "Now you're gonna have to *testify,* dude."

Chance said, "No way," and looked to us for confirmation.

Milo said, "We'll be in touch."

"Hear that, dude? You're gonna get *touched,* dude."

Chance said, "Not unless they're *gay,* dude," and lurched back inside.

Bjorn said, *"Dude."*

Milo studied the signed photo. "My head feels like it's gonna split open. Time for

Advil and a sit-down on what we know and what we don't."

I said, "My house is ten minutes away and I've got an ice pack for that neck."

"I said head, not neck."

"I was talking whiplash, from getting jerked around."

He and Reed laughed. "Yeah, let's boogie over to the White House. He's got a nice place, Moses. Cute dog, too. Maybe she can make sense of all this."

I said, "There's additional incentive. Fifteen thousand worth."

CHAPTER

36

Reed and Milo sat on the leather couch. No one bounced.

Blanche nestled in Milo's lap. She smiled; he didn't notice.

All eyes on the money.

Reed said, "When did Reynolds bring that to you?"

"Yesterday," I said. "I was about to tell you when Aaron came in."

Milo said, "Fifteen grand ain't picnic pay. Maybe it's time for the anthropologists. Death dogs, too." Blanche's ears perked. "No offense."

Reed said, "Weir and Simone have been

paying Duboff for access to the west side for something nasty? He finds out what their bribes are for and gets killed?"

"I doubt he knew, he'd have been screaming," I said. "But they couldn't risk his finding out."

"Guy has free rein to the marsh, if anyone's going to find it, he is. What if he did find out, then tried to make some extra dough?"

Milo said, "Leaning on a serial killer for more dough is pretty stupid. A *night*time meet, no less. I think the lure was just what Duboff was told: I've got something to make you a hero. And the caller had credibility because he knew about the secret part of the marsh."

Reed thought. "That makes sense, Loo. Duboff brought Reynolds because he wasn't expecting trouble. Guy started thinking he was the marsh god. But no matter what Aaron found, it doesn't let Huck off."

"Well put, Detective Reed. Okay, I'm gonna try to get some speed on that shoeprint analysis."

"Huck's the one who rabbited, Loo. More I think about it, more I like the idea of *all* of them being in on it."

"Three Nasty Musketeers? Then why would Simone hire Aaron to focus on Huck?"

"She and Weir used Huck but planned on ditching him all along."

"Weakest link," said Milo. "Criminal history, drug issues, frequents hookers. Yeah, that fits."

I said, "Killing hookers makes me wonder if they tailored the murders to Huck because he's a longtime john."

"That blood in his drain could be real, or a plant," said Reed. "But either way, he still smells dirty."

"Which leads us to another issue," said Milo. "If he's expendable, giving him a chance to split is a real bad idea."

Reed stared at him. "They didn't and we're chasing down a dead man?"

"Or Huck's a lone psycho killer and Simone just happens to be an angry girl with a penchant for lying."

Reed said, "Cutting up her family? Ripping off her brother's face. Doc?"

I said, "It's off-the-scale rage and the family is missing."

Milo said, "Okay, let's assume for the moment that Simone, Weir, and Huck did collude. The obvious motive would be getting rid of the Vanders."

Reed said, "Hundred million worth of motive? Hell yeah."

"Then how do the women in the marsh figure in?"

I said, "Like we said before, misdirects. If the Vanders were found murdered with no prior context, attention would've shot straight to the money. Meaning an unwelcome focus on Simone as sole survivor. But with Huck nailed as a lust murderer first, the Vanders could be seen as collateral damage—victims of a psychopath's final rampage. That fits the staging of the crimes: concealing the other bodies but making sure Selena was found, so she could lead us to the Vanders."

"That storage unit," said Reed. "Board games. We *are* being played."

Milo said, "Those bones being acid-washed and prepped means the other women were killed at leisure, maybe warehoused somewhere, then dumped sequentially."

Reed said, "For all we know, they were on dry ice in the unit."

I said, "One question: the evil bald guy. Huck or Weir minus his wig?"

Milo said, "You have any feelings on that?"

"Could go either way. But two guys who just happen to be skinned could be part of setting up Huck."

"Like Nguyen said, Alex, it's not that rare of a look. But the more I think about it, the more Huck's shaping up at least a partial patsy. If Huck murdered a bunch of people and was smart enough to leave no trace, why would he rabbit and make himself an obvious suspect?"

I said, "Maybe fear overcame good sense. Or he caught on that Weir and Simone had plans to end his future. With that much money at stake, he had to know he'd never be an equal partner."

Reed said, "Yeah, thirty-three million is a bit high for wet work. But he goes along with it anyway because killing is his thing."

"Or Simone seduced him."

"Another kind of three-way?"

"Why not?" I said. "But, Huck finally figured out he was expendable and ran.

Maybe he somehow learned about Aaron's investigation. Or he just got nervous when *your* investigation took on steam."

Milo said, "Simone heaps it on to Aaron: Huck's big-time weird, she's always been afraid of him. Huck doesn't help himself by actually being weird."

"I wouldn't be surprised if his corpse shows up at a strategic moment—apparent suicide, accompanied by a nice, neat confession note and a tipoff to where the Vanders are buried. A whole bunch of cases close simultaneously and Simone's one of the richest girls in L.A."

Milo rubbed his face. "Hundred million. Wars have been fought over less."

Reed said, "If Huck pulled a real rabbit, Weir and Simone have to be freaking out."

I said, "Maybe that's why Simone hacked up the picture."

Milo said, "Low frustration tolerance."

"If that's the case, she and Weir are working on Plan B right now. Get rid of any evidence that incriminates them, gussy up the case against Huck." My head tightened. "*That's* why Duboff had to die. He could link Weir to the marsh."

Reed said, "Oh, man. These people are from another planet."

Milo said, "We forgot something. If Huck was dead, Wallenburg wouldn't be shielding him."

I said, "Maybe she thinks he's alive. Anyone can send a text message."

"So who's the Adams family she just visited? Creepy and kooky folk Wallenburg just happens to know? Boot up your computer, Alex."

Reed was faster than Milo on the keyboard and he knew the access codes. Within seconds, he'd pulled up county records.

Anita Brackle née Loring had given marriage a third shot two years ago.

Civil ceremony in Van Nuys court. The lucky groom, Wilfred Eugene Adams, black male, sixty-two years old, home address in Mar Vista.

His name pulled up three DUIs, the final conviction six years previous.

Reed said, "Probably another rehab romance."

Milo said, "RDate-dot-com, there's a

business opportunity for you. Okay, let's check it out."

"We're holding off on the dogs and the anthropologists?"

"Not at all. Call Dr. Wilkinson." Tiny smile. "While you're at it, she can also check out the western edge of the marsh."

Reed's jaw dropped.

Milo said, "Goes with the job, kiddo."

"What does?"

"Long periods of futility livened by moments of chagrin."

Reed made the call as Milo and I waited in the unmarked. As he headed for us, he looked defeated.

Milo said, "Maybe she turned him down for a second date."

The young detective got in back.

"Everything okay, Moses?"

"Not in, left a message."

"Something on your mind?"

"Text messaging, I should've thought of that."

"What, 'cause you're the techno-generation and I'm the poster boy for horse and plow and just gave up on my Beta-max?"

"What's that?"

"A brand of buggy whip."

A Dodge van sat in the driveway of Wilfred and Anita Loring Brackle Adams's bunga-low. If Wilfred was home, he wasn't adver-tising the fact. Anita's voice was a gritty drill bit that threatened to pierce the locked door from behind.

"You go *away*."

"Ma'am—"

"I will *not* open my door and you can't *force* me to open it."

Fourth time she'd recited the mantra.

Milo said, "We really *can* return with a warrant."

"Then you'd really better *do* that."

Milo leaned on the bell. When he stopped, Anita Adams laughed. The sound was rocks in a tumbler.

"You see humor in the situation, ma'am?"

"You're playing the *bell,* like some sort of *brainwashing* tactic. Why don't you go get some of that *rap* music and blast it all over the *street.* See how *popular* that makes you with the *neighbors.* 'Specially

when it turns out you had no good cause
to . . ."

Milo and I returned to the unmarked.
Her taunts reached nearly to the curb.

"Sweet lady," he said. "Gosh, I wish she
was *my* mom."

We sat in the car and watched the little
frame house. I drank cold coffee and he
swigged Red Bull. Five minutes in,
he phoned Moe Reed. Liz Wilkinson and
three grad students interning at the bone
lab were on their way to the western edge
of the marsh. Insufficient daylight pre-
vented a comprehensive search but they'd
do a spot examination. Wilkinson suggested a helicopter sweep, and sure, the
dogs were fine.

Nothing back on the shoe print.

Milo clicked off just as a car pulled up
behind us.

Steel-colored Maybach. Debora Wallenburg got out and looked up and down the
street before approaching the unmarked.
Aqua Chanel suit, silver hair pulled back
severely, lots of diamond glint.

"Tired of the Chevy, Counselor?"

Wallenburg flinched but recovered
quickly. "You're following me. Charming."

"Have a chat with your elusive client recently?"

Wallenburg laughed. "Here goes the tape loop."

"What's funny, Counselor, is your viewing the situation as a yuk-fest."

"I view it as theater of the absurd."

"The way you claim to feel about Huck, I'd expect you to be taking it seriously."

"Your alleged case."

"Your client's demise."

Wallenburg's cheek muscles twitched. Courtroom training delayed her response. "What are you talking about?"

"When's the last time you actually *spoke* to ol' Travis?"

Wallenburg cocked a hip in a display of mellow. Tension around the eyes blew the performance.

"Just like I thought," said Milo.

"Is this the moment where your artful goading causes me to blurt out some crucial piece of information, Lieutenant?"

"It's the moment that I tell you I know Huck didn't call, you got a text message and assumed. No offense, Counselor, but maybe it's an age thing. Digital naïveté."

"You're mad," said Wallenburg.

"More like peeved."

"I meant in the mental illness sense."

"Insult registered, digested, soon to be excreted."

"My clients that concern you at this time are Mr. and Mrs. Adams," she said. "They request that you cease harassing them."

"Thought you were corporate," said Milo. "How does that get you to front for a couple of working-class alkies who just happen to know Travis from dry-out camp?"

"Oka-ay," said Wallenburg. "Now we switch to class warfare and denigration of people with the courage to recover."

"My dad's shirt was blue and I've known a few tipplers but the issue ain't politics, it's murder."

Wallenburg didn't answer.

"Hell," said Milo, "what's a few strangled women with their hands hacked off to a courthouse vet like you?"

"That's repellent."

"Thing is," said Milo, "you're not even doing good lawyering here. I'm not after your client as the prime bad guy. I'm figuring he was used and tossed. It's in both our interests to get to the real evil."

Debora Wallenburg shook her head. Diamond earrings swung. "You're talking nonsense."

"Then prove it. If Huck's still respirating, bring him in. He cooperates, everyone stays friendly."

Wallenburg clicked her tongue. "Hopeless. Stop harassing the Adamses, they're good people and you've got no reason to be bothering them. Last I heard the department's legal costs had climbed precipitously."

"A girl named Sue," said Milo. "What grounds?"

"I'll think of something." Wallenburg turned to leave.

"Huck's a foot soldier, Counselor. I want the officers."

"You people," said Wallenburg. "Everything's war."

"Or at least armed conflict. Prove Huck's alive by bringing him in."

"He's innocent."

"You know that because . . ."

Wallenburg began walking away.

"The key is timing, Deb. Once we get a warrant for this house, there's no telling."

"You're in Fantasyland. *Mile.* Talk about no grounds."

"Tell that to Judge Stern."

"Lisa was a classmate of mine."

"Then you know how she feels about victims' rights. And how she views attempts by officers of the court to meddle in extracurricular matters."

Wallenburg ran a manicured finger across her lips. "What a nice man you are."

She got in the Maybach and sped off.

I said, "When did you call Judge Stern?"

"Must be two years ago," he said. "Gang shooting, slam dunk, easy paper."

"The science of war."

"More like marching in the dark."

At four forty-seven p.m. an L.A. Unified school bus pulled up to the house. A blond girl in a red T-shirt, jeans, and sneakers got out and headed for the door. Ten or so, slight and stick-limbed, she labored under the weight of a mammoth backpack.

I said, "Baby Brandeen," more to hear the sound of it than to inform him.

"Makes me misty, lad. They grow up so quickly."

Before the girl reached the door it opened. A short, heavy, white-haired woman reached out and drew her inside. Instead of closing, she took the time to glare at us. A man materialized behind her, tall, black, bearded. Weary eyes, even at this distance.

Wilfred Adams said something to his wife.

She snapped back, flipped us off, slammed the door.

Milo said, "Maybe Huck *is* alive. She's sure protecting something."

His phone rang again. Moe Reed checking in a second time, from the marsh's western edge. No obvious signs of disturbance, but the same cadaver dog had arrived and was looking "interested."

"Pretty place," said Reed. "Got that Garden of Eden thing going on."

Milo said, "Find me the snake."

He lit up a cigar, had puffed twice when Debora Wallenburg's Maybach roared toward us from the north. The car pulled alongside the unmarked. A tinted window lowered silently.

Wallenburg's hair was loose. She'd refreshed her makeup, but couldn't hide fatigue.

"You missed me," said Milo.

"Oh, I pine. Maybe we *can* play nice, but first some ground rules: I know the law allows you to lie like a conniving, sociopathic bastard to a suspect. But I wouldn't recommend trying it with an attorney of record."

"The client being . . ."

"I need you to be straight with me."

"I am nothing if not sincere."

"What you said before—not seeing Travis as the prime evil. Was that utter bullshit?"

"No."

"I'm serious, Lieutenant. I need your assurance that we're operating in the same context. Plus, there can be absolutely no heavy-handedness."

"Heavy as in?"

"SWAT nonsense, property damage, scaring a small child. My pledge in return is full disclosure."

"Of?"

"I cannot specify at this time."

Milo blew a smoke ring, then a second that pierced the first.

Debora Wallenburg said, "You need to trust me."

He rested his head on the back of the seat. "When and where?"

"Those details will follow in due time. May I assume Dr. Delaware will be there?"

"Huck needs mental health consultation?"

"I'd feel better if he's involved. That okay with you, Doctor?"

I'd never been introduced. "Sure."

She said, "Mal Worthy and Trish Mantle and Len Krobsky belong to my tennis club."

Naming three heavy-hitter family lawyers.

"Give my regards."

"They all like you." To Milo: "So, we're on. I'll call you." Slow wink. "Or maybe I'll text."

CHAPTER

37

Travis Huck trembled.

Veins wormed across his temples, crossed his hairline, invaded the dense black stubble capping his skull. Eyes so deep-set they vanished in all but the strongest light stared at nothing. His cheeks could've been hollowed by melon scoops. The sag of his face was a history of its own.

Debora Wallenburg had bought him a brand-new shirt. Sky-blue, crisp cotton, sharp box-creases. He looked like a candidate for parole.

She'd had her desk moved forward

several feet, positioned Huck and herself behind the wooden barrier. Mary Cassatt's mother and baby looked down with jarring serenity. The kind lighting Wallenburg had choreographed failed to calm her client. He rocked in his chair. Sweated.

Maybe he'd fare worse under the fluorescence of a police interview room. Maybe nothing would make a difference.

It was four a.m. Wallenburg's text message had roused Milo at two fifteen and he'd called me twenty minutes later. A Sahara of silent streets turned the ride to Santa Monica into a motor-sprint. But for a hyphen of amber upper-floor windows, Wallenburg's office building was a granite spade excavating a starless sky.

As the unmarked pulled near the sub-lot, a mesh partition slid open and a uniformed guard stepped forward.

"I.D. please."

Milo's badge was exactly what the guy expected. "Elevator's over there, park wherever you like." Waving at a sea of vacant slots. The only vehicle in sight, a copper-colored Ferrari.

"Her sporty wheels," said Milo. "Hope it's not a game."

From the backseat, Moe Reed squelched a yawn and rubbed his eyes. "I'm ready to play."

Debora Wallenburg touched Huck's hand. He slid away from her. She sat up straighter, every silver hair in place, full-tilt makeup, diamonds.

Courtroom confidence wavered only when she glanced at Huck. He remained in his own world, had yet to make eye contact.

Wallenburg said, "Whenever you're ready, Travis."

A minute passed. Thirty additional seconds. Moe Reed crossed his legs. As if sparked by the movement, Huck said, "The only person I killed was Jeffrey."

Wallenburg frowned. "That was an accident, Travis."

Huck tilted his head away from her, as if offended by the characterization. "I think about Jeffrey a lot. Before I wasn't able to."

I said, "Before . . ."

Huck sucked in breath. "I used to live in a dream-state. Now I'm sober and awake but it's not always . . . good."

"Too many things to think about," I suggested.

"Bad things, sir."

"Travis," said Wallenburg.

Huck shifted and caught a faceful of caressing light. His pupils were dilated, his forehead an oil slick. Some sort of rash had spread around his nostrils, tiny berries sprouting in a pallid field. "Bad dreams fill me. I'm the monster."

"Travis, you are nothing *close* to a monster."

Huck didn't answer.

"How could you *not* feel stigmatized, Travis, with people prejudging you all the time?" Pretending to talk to him, but addressing the jury.

"Debora." His voice lowered to a whisper. "You're the rare bird who flies freely. I don't know *what* I am."

"What you are is a good person, Travis."

"The average German."

"Pardon?"

"Man in the crowd," said Huck. "Comfortable in his suit and his good shoes, oblivious to the stench."

"Travis, we need to concentrate on—"

"Dachau, Debora. Rwanda, Darfur, slave ships, Cambodia, melting deserts. Average man sits in a café and eats his cream cakes. He knows which way the wind blows, the stench blows into his nose but he pretends. You choose to fly freely, Debora. The crowd chooses a cage. *I* chose a cage."

"Travis, this isn't an issue of war and—"

Huck swiveled toward her. "It is, Debora. War breathes in all of us. Raid the neighboring pack, raze the village, eat the young. In a good world, to be human is to be *un*-animal. *You* made the choice to be human. I—"

"Travis, we're here for you to tell them what you know—"

"—sniffed the wind and stench blew through my head. I allowed it to happen, Debora."

Before Wallenburg could retort, I said, "You allowed the murders."

Huck clapped his hands on the desk, as if bracing for a fall. Long, knobby fingers pressed on leather, slid back, leaving snail-trails of perspiration. He worried his sagging cheek.

Wallenburg said, "Travis, you had absolutely noth—"

"I could've stopped it. I don't deserve to live." He bared his wrists, ready for shackles. Debora Wallenburg pushed one hand down. Huck grew rigid.

I said, "When did you know?"

"I—there's no beginning," said Huck. "It was just in here. Here. Here. Hereherehere." Slapping his head, his cheek, his chest, his gut. Increasing the force with each blow.

"You sensed violence was coming."

"Kelvin," he said. Lowering his head, he mumbled to leather. "I took him on walks. We didn't talk much, Kelvin's quiet. We saw deer, lizards, eagles, coyote. Kelvin likes listening to the ocean, says the ocean's a ground bass, the universe hums like a Gregorian chant."

I said, "And Kelvin is . . ."

Huck stared at me.

I said, "The family's dead."

Huck sobbed raggedly. A mustache of snot formed over his crooked lips. Debora Wallenburg offered him a tissue and when he didn't take it, she wiped him.

I said, "How do you know?"

"Where are they?" he wailed.

"You have no idea where they are?"

"I thought she *loved* them, I thought she was *capable* of love." One hand opened, as if panhandling. His palm was scrubbed clean, his nails gnawed stubby. When the fingers rotated, I saw scars on his knuckles—glossy, white, what appeared to be old burns.

I said, "By 'she' you mean . . ."

No answer.

"Who, Travis?"

He mouthed the word. Sound followed an instant later, as if digitally delayed. "Simone."

Moe Reed's eyes narrowed. Milo's were shut and his hands rested on his belly. To the casual observer, sleeping. I knew better; no snoring.

I said, "You're saying Simone killed the Vanders."

Each word made Huck shudder.

"That's your theory, Travis? Or do you know it for a fact?"

"It's not—I know—from what she—I thought she was vulnerable, not—because she hurt *herself.*"

"Hurt herself how?"

"Wounds you can't see unless . . . it's a secret game."

"Simone cuts herself."

Nod. "She tastes her own blood."

"When we met her, we saw no visible wounds—"

"She chooses the secret places." Licking his lips.

"You know that because . . ."

His head lurched forward. A cold, raw sound made its way past clenched lips.

I said, "You and Simone were intimate."

Strangled laughter. He supported himself on the desktop, again. "Stupid dream. She had other ideas."

Wallenburg prompted: "Tell them exactly what you told me about her, Travis."

Silence.

"Tell them how she *seduced* you, Travis."

Huck shook his head furiously. "That makes it sound romantic. It wasn't romantic, it was a . . . a . . . a . . ."

"*Tell* them or *I* will."

Huck pleaded, *"Debora."*

"I told them you'd give them facts, Travis. They won't believe you unless you give them facts."

Several moments passed. Huck said,
"I—it—she came over. To the big house.
No one was home. I'd been watching her.
Because she's beautiful. Physically. Talking to her was out of the question, she's
the daughter, I'm hired help. But *she* talked
to *me.* It was like she knew my brain from
the inside out. Being with her was like
opening a window."

I said, "Easy for her."

Nod. "She made herself small, we stared
at the ocean. She came into my room.
Rested her head on my . . . she showed
me her wounds. Cried into my shirt. It was
a revelation. The geography of flesh. Holding her as she cried." He rubbed glossy
knuckles.

"You knew about the geography of
flesh."

He stared at leather.

I said, "For her it's blades, for you it's
fire."

Crooked smile. "I used to need punishment."

"In jail?"

"After." Waiting for Wallenburg to scold
him.

She said nothing.

"I'm sorry, Debora. Being free brought back pictures of Jeffrey . . . I didn't want to worry you." To me: "I needed to feel *something.*"

I said, "What exactly does Simone use?"

"Everything. Razors, kitchen knives, a box cutter. She has guns, gifts from Simon. When he married Nadine, Nadine said please, no guns in the house. Simone holds them, talks about them, expensive guns, she puts the barrels in her mouth, makes believe . . . she put her hands down her throat to vomit. Sometimes she gives herself a sore throat, coughs blood. She loves her own taste."

Reed exhaled silently.

Milo continued to slump, barrel chest heaving. Wallenburg looked at him, then at me.

I said, "What else are you going to tell us about Simone?"

Huck said, "The first time she showed me fresh . . . stigmata, that's what she called them—the first time, I held her. Then we . . . she shaved my head, told me I was her priest, my bones were beautiful. I thought . . . the dream was thinking I could help her."

"How long did the two of you have a relationship?"

His eyes rolled back. Snapped back into
place like slot-machine cherries. "An eter-
nity."

I said, "Give us something more con-
crete."

Debora Wallenburg said, "Two months.
It ended around six months ago."

"That true, Travis?"

Nod.

"How did you learn Simone wasn't the
person you thought she was?"

"I stalked her."

Reed's shoulders bunched.

Milo didn't budge.

Wallenburg said, "Poor choice of words.
Just give them the facts, Travis."

Huck said, "I *stalked* her, Debora."

"You had concerns so you began watching her."

I said, "You followed Simone."

"I called for a week but she didn't answer. I was confused. The last time we
were together, she said . . . kind things.
Then all of a sudden, nothing? I started to
worry she was hurt. Then I thought, maybe
she's *waiting* for me. To do something

spontaneous. She told me spontaneous turned her on, I needed to loosen up. I was afraid to . . . improvise. Surprises aren't . . . I don't like them. Simone knew I didn't like to leave the script. So it would be a surprise."

"You made a spontaneous visit to her house?"

"Just once."

"When?"

"Three months ago," said Wallenburg.

Huck said, "Simon and Nadine and Kelvin were in Ojai for the weekend, they went because Kelvin wanted to meet Nikrugsky—the composer. The house was quiet, Simone wasn't calling back. The quiet turned into . . . old desires came back."

"For heat and pain."

"I found matches. Lit them but didn't broil myself. I called a sponsor. We talked, but not about what was really in my head. The quiet kept getting louder. I said go, go, go, be *spontaneous.* Drove to Malibu Canyon and picked flowers, made a bouquet, tied it up with grocery twine, poured grape juice into a wine bottle, wrapped it with a ribbon—black, her favorite color. I took water biscuits from the pantry. Two boxes. Havershams, from England, licensed to the royal family, Simone doesn't eat much more than water biscuits but when she does . . . I've seen her go through two boxes. Later she . . . expels them. Her throat bleeds, it looks like strawberry porridge."

I said, "You went over to her house."

"I wanted a loving surprise. She didn't answer my knock. I went out in back, Simone likes to be outside. All kinds of weather, she takes off her clothes . . . outside is where she bleeds herself. There are stains on her furniture. Teak furniture. It's a tiny backyard, overgrown, steep hillside in back, a little gazebo where she sleeps. Before I got there I heard it. Simone and someone. My brain understood but my legs kept moving. I found a stalker spot. Watched. There was no reason, I already knew what was . . ."

Catching his breath, he studied the ceiling.

I said, "What did you see?"

"Licking each other. Cats. Grooming, licking, licking, grooming." Moistening his own lips. "Licking, growling. Laughing, talking brutality."

"Simone and . . ."

Long silence.

"Who was with her, Travis?"

"The wig."

"Give us a name."

"Him," said Huck. "The-wig-the-smile-Weir-the-lawyer. A nightmare. She told me she hated him, he was corrupt, stealing from Simon, she was going to tell Simon, I shouldn't do it, she would do it, shit would hit the fan, teach those scumbags a lesson, then we'd be free . . ."

"But in the backyard . . ."

"Licking. No hatred. Except what they shared."

I said, "They shared hatred."

Silence.

"Hatred of who, Travis?"

Huck's breathing quickened. His eyes jumped.

"Who, Travis?"

"Licking laughing, that disgusting word."

"What word?"

"Gook."

"Nadine?" I said. "Because she's Asian?"

"They spewed it out like vomit gook-lover gook-sucker gook-fucker gook bitch slant-eyed gook scum-spawn." Clenched fists turned burn scars into pearls. "My head—hearing it, I wanted to burn myself up. Went home, found more matches. Soaked them in water. Called another sponsor."

Tears filled his eyes. "I never told Simon."

"Simone hates her family."

"More than hatred," said Huck. "It—she—there's no word for it."

"Had Simone ever shown resentment about Simon remarrying?"

"No, no, no, no, just the opposite. She *loved* Nadine, Nadine was smart, stylish, beautiful, not like *her* mother. I know Kelly, Kelly's good people, but she wasn't there for Simone, okay, I understand that, we all understand that, but . . ."

"Simone claimed she loved Nadine."

"She said she wished Nadine had *raised* her. They hugged, they kissed, Nadine treated Simone like a sister. When Simone came to the house, she played with Kelvin's hair. Beautiful hair, she always said. She kissed his cheeks. So *cute,* Travis. I *love* him, Travis. A *genius,* I *love* him, Travis. Hands of *gold,* I *love* him, Travis."

"Hands of gold."

"Gold, diamond, platinum, *magic* hands. She said his music was pure love and his hands went straight to his soul."

"No love that day in the backyard."

"My world flamed," said Huck. "I crawled back in my cage."

Wallenburg said, "You didn't say anything to the Vanders because you had no proof. Why would anyone believe you?"

Huck smiled. "Objection overruled."

"Travis—"

"I didn't say anything because I'm a coward."

"That's ridiculous, Travis. You have more courage than most."

I said, "She may be right."

Moe Reed arched a brow. Milo still didn't stir.

I said, "It *was* a tough choice, Travis. Lance the boil and hope you can dodge the pus stream, or pray that it stays at the verbal level."

"Excuses," said Huck. "Average German."

"Oh, for God's sake, Travis," said Wallenburg. "We're not here to be cosmic and philosophical, these are legal matters.

There was absolutely no way for you to know what they had planned and you had absolutely no obligation to divulge what you heard."

One of Milo's eyes opened. "Unless he was involved."

Wallenburg said, "Oh, please. Have you been *awake* for the last ten minutes?"

"Oh, yeah. Heard a good story."

Travis Huck said, "It's logical, Debora. I killed someone, I pay for sex—"

"Be quiet, Travis!"

I said, "Let's talk about the other victims."

Huck said, "Three women."

"Sheralyn Dawkins. Lurlene Chenoweth. DeMaura Montouthe."

No flicker of recognition. No tell, whatsoever.

Huck said, "I heard about them on the television. That's when I ran."

"Why then?"

"What they did for a living. I go to women like them. I started to feel I *knew* them. Maybe I *did* do something."

"Did you?"

"Sometimes it's hard to know what I do."

I repeated the names.

He said, "No. I don't think so."

Wallenburg's teeth clenched. "Travis. That is *not*. What *you*. Told *me*."

"Deb—"

Reed fished out three mug shots.

Huck studied them for a long time. Shook his head.

Wallenburg said, "He had nothing to do with it. He panicked and fled."

I said, "Have you ever picked up women near the airport?"

"No."

"Where do you cruise for them?"

"Sunset Strip."

"Why not the airport?"

"I have to stay close to home, in case Simon and Nadine need me."

"Need you for what?"

"Errands, takeout from all-night places— sometimes Nadine gets hungry late at night. Sometimes I get a CD for Kelvin at Tower Records on Sunset. Used to. It closed, now I go to Virgin."

Both stores were minutes from where Reed had found prostitutes who knew Huck.

"Twenty-four seven availability," I said.

"It's my job."

"Did Simone know you frequented prostitutes?"

Tiny smile, hard to decipher.

"Something funny?" said Reed.

Huck gave a start. "No—it wasn't *frequent*. I . . . I . . . occasioned."

I said, "Did Simone know?"

"I confessed to her."

"Why?"

"We were talking. Filling in dark spaces."

"Sharing secrets."

"Yes."

"What dark spaces did Simone fill?"

"Tasting her blood. Needing to feel. Wanting the perfect body, always feeling huge, hating the mirror, seeing lumps."

"What did you tell her about prostitutes?"

"I said before her there were *only* women like that. I said being with her was like landing on the moon."

"New life."

"New universe."

"So discovering her with Weir was—"

Huck clapped his hands together. "Crash-down."

I glanced at Milo. Back in shut-eyed repose.

"Travis, tell us about Silford Duboff."

Clouded eyes. "Who?"

"The guy who takes care of the Bird Marsh."

"I've never been to the Bird Marsh."

"Never?"

"Never."

I repeated Duboff's name.

Huck said, "Am I supposed to know him? I'm sorry."

"Let's talk about someone you do know. Selena Bass."

Huck seemed prepared for the question. "Selena is *how* I knew for sure."

"Knew what?"

"Simone's hatred didn't stop at words."

"You figured Simone murdered Selena."

"Selena *came* from Simone."

"Came from her how?"

"Simone *found* her. Said she did it for Kelvin. Simone brought Selena to the *house.*"

"Finding a teacher for Kelvin."

"Finding a friend who—guess what—is also a piano genius and a teacher."

"Simone called Selena her friend."

"They acted like friends."

"How so?"

"Happy skinny girls laughing," said Huck. "Those low jeans they wear."

"How do you know they weren't friends?"

"Simone told me. Later. Said she heard Selena play piano at a party. Selena had magic hands, golden hands just like Kelvin, she'd be perfect for Kelvin. Kelvin had a grumpy old teacher, wanted to stop his lessons. Simone told Selena she could make big money. I should've known there was more."

"More what?"

"The first time, I was bringing in groceries and Simone's car pulled up, she's got another girl with her, they're giggling. I went inside. They didn't. When I came out to get more groceries, they were looking at the ocean. Hands around each other. Simone's hand went to Selena's . . . her butt."

"Selena and Simone had a sexual relationship."

"Maybe."

"This was before you and Simone had a relationship."

"Yes."

"It didn't make you wonder."

"About what?"

"Simone's sexual preferences?"

Huck's eyes turned fiery. "I didn't care."

I said, "Later, after you were involved, Simone told you she'd met Selena at a party."

Nod.

"What did she say about the party?"

"Just a party."

"Tea and cookies?"

Silence.

He said, "Later, I had ideas."

"What kind of ideas?"

"In the backyard . . . after the licking, he got up and Simone stretched on the teak lounge and . . ." Wincing. "She had a razor blade. He came back, tasted her. He brought things with him. Ropes—beads— big huge plastic . . . I turned from that, didn't want to look, but I could hear. He said, 'Party time.' She said, 'Golden hands. Baby. All we're missing is her and the piano.'"

Huck shook his head; dripped sweat onto the desk. Debora Wallenburg saw it, let the spatter sit there.

I said, "Party time. Meaning . . ."

"Selena was into the same things."
Looking to me for confirmation.

"When you heard about Selena's murder, you developed a theory about what happened to her."

"A feeling."

"When we came to tell you about Selena, you didn't mention that feeling."

"I was . . . I didn't . . . you put fog in my head. Finally, it drifted out and I had the feeling. I didn't know what to do."

Without opening his eyes, Milo said, "You could've picked up the phone."

Wallenburg said, "And told you what? He had an intuition."

Milo favored her with an avuncular smile. "On whodunit cases, Counselor, we take anything we can get."

"Oh, sure. You would've believed him."

Huck said, "I was going to tell Simon. If."

I said, "If what?"

"I told anyone."

Reed said, "If. Longest word in the dictionary."

"I thought about it," said Huck. "Telling Simon. But she's his daughter, he loves her. I do errands."

"So you did nothing," said Reed.

"No, I . . . I phoned him, to hear his voice, maybe his voice would tell me what to do. He didn't answer. I kept trying. He didn't answer. I e-mailed. He didn't answer. I switched to Nadine's e-mail, she didn't answer. Then I started worrying. Then those other women got . . . I heard about them and said, 'Those are the women you go to.'"

I said, "So you ran."

"I *killed* someone, I pay for *sex*. I knew *Selena*. Everyone else is *rich*." Turning to Wallenburg. "You told me to come back, I disobeyed."

"Travis, it's not a matter of dis—"

Milo got up, walked to the front of the desk, focused on Huck.

"That the whole story, pal?"

"Yes, sir."

"Some yarn."

"Put me back in a cage, sir. I deserve what you want to give me."

"That so?"

Wallenburg shot to her feet, thrust her arm between Huck and Milo. "That was *not* an admission of guilt."

Milo said, "Selena, the hookers, one big setup just to frame you. Convenient."

"For God's sake, can't you see it?" said Wallenburg. "Superficially, he's the perfect scapegoat."

"Superficially?"

"Look at his core: a man who was railroaded but harbors no anger. Who's led a totally nonviolent life—who saved a *baby,* for God's sake."

"I didn't save her, Debora. I just lifted her from the sidewalk and—"

"Shut *up,* Travis! You've seen how Brandeen looks at you. If you hadn't found her, that bastard might've come back and beat her to death the way he beat her mother to death."

"Debora—"

"Don't *Debora* me, Travis. It's about time you got smart and started looking after yourself. You were stupid to run, stupid not to return when I told you to. Now you're being a total blithering *idiot.*"

"I—"

"Life sucks, fine, we all get that, Travis. But you are *not* to blame for this particular disaster and if you stick to the facts, the police will believe you."

Looking at Milo.

He remained silent.

Huck said, "I let it all *happen,* Debora—"

"You were their *gofer,* Travis. You are *not* a cosmic watchdog. If you'd said anything negative about Simone, you'd have lost your job and she would've remained free to charm her father and go about her plan."

"What plan are we talking about?" said Reed.

"A hundred-and-thirty-three-million-dollar plan," said Wallenburg. "That girl would never have been deterred. *Never.*"

Milo said, "Pretty precise figure."

Wallenburg's smile was icy.

Milo said, "If that's the case, we're talking about a real *long*-term plan. Killing prostitutes over a fifteen-month period, dumping them in sequence, just to set up the Vanders as a thrill kill?"

"We're *talking* about a hundred thirty-three million worth of incentive, Lieutenant. Selena's murder got you focused on the Vanders, which led you to Travis. The three women made all of it look psychopathic. That conniving little bitch *spoon-fed* you Travis. Given his history, she knew you'd put on your blinders."

"Garsh," said Milo. "Can someone tell me the way to Keystone?"

"A hundred and thirty-three *million,* Lieutenant. A year's worth of planning doesn't seem too much for that pot of gold."

"Be a great movie."

"Oscar for documentary, Lieutenant."

"We're supposed to buy it because of Mr. Huck's feelings. In here." Massaging the swell of his belly.

"You're supposed to buy it because it's true and it makes sense and you haven't a shred of evidence tying Travis to a single act of violence."

Milo flashed his happy-wolf grin. Bent over the desk and put his face inches from Huck's.

Huck licked his lips.

Wallenburg said, "There's no need for physical intimida—"

"Travis, I like your stories. Now tell me another one."

"About what, sir?"

"The blood we found in the drain of your bedroom sink."

Huck's Adam's apple rose and fell. "I . . . maybe I cut my hands . . . I go off balance. Headaches, maybe I got a cut and washed it."

"Got any scabs?"

Inspecting Huck's hands. "Nope, clean."

Huck said, "Put me in a cage, I don't care."

"What's your blood type, son?"

"O positive."

"AB's what we found in your drain."

Huck turned white.

Milo placed his paw atop Huck's left hand. Huck's fingers clasped Milo's, like a child wanting security.

"Tell us about AB, son."

"Simon," said Huck. "It's rare. He always gets asked to donate."

"Looks like he donated some to your drain. Tell me another story, son."

Wallenburg said, "Someone who'd slaughter people in a calculated manner would have no problem planting blood in a damn drain. Simone had access to that house—I'll bet Weir did, too—of course he did, given his relationship with Simone, all she had to do was give him a damn key and—"

Still gripping Milo's hand, Huck held out his free arm. "Put me in a cage."

"Don't say another *word,* Travis!"

Milo said, "Counselor, looks like we've come to a sort of consensus. Get up please, son. We're going to read you your rights and take you into custody."

"I agree," said Huck.

Wallenburg shot to her feet, clamped her hands on Huck's shoulders. "On what charges?"

"We'll start with a whole bunch of 187s, go on from there."

Her turn to tremble. "You're making a disastrous mistake."

Reed said, "You're really committed to this guy. What am I not seeing?"

Wallenburg's mouth formed a curse. "Lieutenant, our explicit agreement was—"

"That we'd listen," said Milo. "We did, now we're arresting him."

Wallenburg's mouth worked. "Oh, this is great, so predictable—I promise you it'll be futile, Lieutenant. And you'd better make damn sure he's not abused. The moment you walk out that door, I'll be drafting motions."

"I wouldn't expect anything less, ma'am. Please get up, son."

Huck complied.

"Please step around to this side of the desk." Out came the cuffs.

Wallenburg said, "Are you booking him at West L.A. or Downtown?"

"We'll hold him at West L.A. until appropriate transportation can be arranged."

"Everything according to procedure," said Wallenburg. "Talk about average Germans—you damn *well* better put him on *suicide* watch."

"I'm already dead," said Huck.

Wallenburg raised a hand, as if to slap him. Stared at her quivering fingers and let her arm flop.

"Thank you for everything, Debora," said Huck.

"*You,*" she spat, "are a first-class pain in the ass."

Riding the elevator down to the sub-lot, Huck said, "You really had no choice."

Reed said, "Why's she so devoted to you?"

Huck blinked. "Once she told me about

volunteer work she does. At animal shelters. She can't have children."

"You're her kid?" said Reed.

"No, but once you save an animal in the shelter, she said, you're responsible for it."

"You're one of her puppies, huh?"

Huck smiled. "I think maybe I am."

The door opened. Milo took hold of Huck's cuffed arm, propelled him to the car. "Anything else you want to tell us?"

"I don't think so. You don't believe me anyway."

"They teach you passivity in rehab?"

Huck exhaled. "Life's been long. Longer than I thought."

"So it's time to give up."

"When there's something to do, I do. At this point, there's nothing left."

I said, "Not necessarily."

CHAPTER

38

Milo stashed Huck in an empty West L.A. interview room, took his belt and his shoelaces. No booking, no printing, no mug shot. Just a tall cup of water, a coarse blanket, and a second pat-down that produced nothing.

The first frisk, in the hallway outside Debora Wallenburg's office, had produced lint, a seriously chewed blue Bic pen, three dimes, an LAX parking stub, a yellow Post-it with a Washington Boulevard address.

"Where's this, Travis?"

"Internet café."

"Mar Vista?"

"Yes."

"Your link to the world."

Silence.

"You don't have any cash?"

"Spent it."

"Debora was going to replenish."

No answer.

Milo said, "You travel light, friend."

Shrug.

"Where's your I.D.?"

"I . . . lost it."

"Sure you did."

"You know who I am."

"That we do." Milo waved the parking stub. "This gonna match to the one we found in Simon's Lexus?"

Huck said, "I'm sorry."

"For what?"

"Leaving it there."

"To mislead us. Kind of a stale scam, pal."

"Sorry."

"Your brilliant idea or Debora's?"

The too-quick reply: "Mine. I'll pay for the tow."

Reed and I watched through one-way glass as Milo stood behind Huck, then shifted face-to-face. Huck braced himself on the back of the chair.

"Sit, Travis."

"I'm okay."

"Sit anyway."

Huck obeyed.

"What else do you want to tell me, Travis?"

"Can't think of anything, sir."

Milo waited.

Huck said, "Really, sir."

"Okay, sit a spell—temperature okay?"

"Yes."

"Gets too cold, you've got the blanket."

"Thank you."

Milo left and joined us in the adjoining room. A milky patch marred the glass on the other side; dried sweat or some other body fluid. Huck's position placed the splotch directly above his head.

Man under a cloud.

We watched as he sat there. Finally, he walked to a corner and lay down. Placing one arm over his eyes, he curled himself smaller than I'd have thought possible.

Moe Reed yawned. "Nothing like an action film to start off the morning."

Within seconds Huck's mouth had fallen open and he was sleeping.

Reed said, "Pretty mellow for a guy supposedly all guilty and torn up."

I said, "Or he's escaping reality."

"Maybe he got duped, but you can't think he's totally clean."

"I think his mind works differently."

"Isn't that the point, Doc? He's a nut, easy to prime."

"I know the obvious suspect's usually the right one, but the way we were led straight to Huck via your brother always bothered me. Huck's account of Simone's hatred for her family fits the mutilated pictures Aaron found in her trash. Her lie about despising Buddy Weir also syncs with what Aaron saw, as does the fact that Simone and Weir are in a relationship."

"Blood and toys," said Reed. "Some relationship."

I said, "Sparse food in Simone's trash fits bulimia, so do her upbringing and her body mass. Overall Huck's account has the ring of truth. And minus his wig, Buddy Weir could be the bald guy Selena's caretaker saw. He's also a better fit than Huck to the charming, dominant man DeMaura

Montouthe described. After meeting her at a sex party, Weir could've known where Selena lived through dating her, or he found out from Simone. Either way, it would be easy to take her computer. But make sure to leave the toys he found in her drawer."

Reed said, "The bald guy could just as easily be Huck. The way he was talking about Selena—coming in with Simone giggling, low-cut jeans. To me that sounded like he lusted for both of them. Guy like that, doesn't get it unless he pays for it, coupla hotties show up, his mind starts revving. Finally he can't take it and boom. And one more thing, Doc, he's growing his hair out. Perfect if he was planning to disappear. Which is something he's good at."

"But he came in voluntarily."

"Because he knew we were closing in on him."

I said, "He says Simone shaved his head. Perfect move if she was trying to provide cover for Weir."

Reed rubbed his crew cut. "He says. Everything depends on us believing him."

Milo said, "Weir generally wears his wig. Had it on when he paid off Duboff."

"That's another thing," I said. "The pay-off. What motive would Huck have to kill Duboff? When I mentioned Duboff's name there was no recognition and I couldn't spot a tell. Weir, on the other hand, has a link to Duboff—passed him cash in the parking lot. Had to be payoff for access to the secret garden."

"Fifteen grand for picnics and Duboff's not suspicious?"

"Pure L.A.," I said. "The VIP room. Weir fit Duboff's notion of a major donor: Beverly Hills lawyer, backs environmental causes, Duboff figures the guy's racked up a lot of billable hours, is spreading the joy. Given Duboff's shoestring budget, he'd have been thrilled. And likely to trust Weir when Weir said he'd discovered something about the marsh murders."

"The west side," said Milo. "Okay, something turns up there, I'll adjust my attitude."

Reed said, "Exactly. Till then, I like Huck."

I said, "I can be fooled as easily as anyone, but I don't see Huck as sufficiently dominant. If he's been putting on a performance, why not spin it so he ends up in the clear? As in I Never Knew Anything.

Instead, he told us he suspected impending violence, didn't report it, feels guilty. The guy just about invited you to arrest him."

Reed said, "That could be another ploy. Setting up a double-jeopardy thing—we charge him prematurely, Wallenburg plays lawyer games, gets him out, we can't touch him ever again."

Milo watched Huck sleep. "I can see Wallenburg building a castle like that. Huck . . . I don't know. He really ain't no smooth dude, Moe."

"She coached him, Loo."

"No doubt, she did. But there's a limit. Something about the guy . . . he disappeared for years, could've evaded us a lot longer than he did. The question is, can we believe Simone's that bad of a girl?"

I said, "At the risk of introducing psychology . . ."

He smiled. "What?"

"A taste for pain—giving and receiving—is consistent with Simone's makeup."

Reed said, "She cuts herself. Supposedly."

"She cuts and starves herself, grew up with an impaired mother, had aspirations she couldn't achieve. That could lead to a seriously distorted body image and emotional numbness. Sometimes people like that need extreme stimulation."

"Feel no pain, feel no mercy, either?" said Milo. "We're talking big-time cruelty here, Alex."

"Aaron did find that photo."

Reed muttered, "Her not paying Aaron was a big-time mistake."

I said, "Let's say Simone met Selena at a party, ended up playing sex games with her and Weir, eventually introduced Selena to her family. It could've started out as finding a friend a job and earning her father's approval. But later, when she and Weir devised their plan, Selena was the perfect victim."

Reed said, "Lives alone, estranged from her family, maybe some secrets of her own . . . yeah, guess so."

"Whoever killed Selena used her as a lure. The first three bodies were concealed but hers was advertised, to the point of an anonymous call pinpointing her location. I'd sure like to see Simone's and Weir's phone records for the time of that call. Huck's, too. That would go a long way toward showing who's dirty."

"We have any grounds for phone subpoenas, Loo?"

"I'll call John at eight."

I said, "The bones in the box were another prompt. If you didn't find them, no loss. If you did, another step in the game."

"Also," said Milo, "playing with body parts coulda been fun."

"That, too."

Reed said, "You're saying Selena was basically a human flashlight, directing us to the Vanders."

"Who have vanished," I said. "Meanwhile, Simone hires Aaron to educate us about Huck."

Milo said, "With Huck in our headlights, we realize the Vanders are missing, start thinking about wholesale psycho slaughter with ol' Travis as Pol Pot. He obliges by rabbiting. Hell, even if he never gets found, suspicion doesn't fall on Simone and Weir and she steps into a hundred thirty mil."

"Hundred thirty-*three*," said Reed. "But who's counting. I can't even imagine dough like that."

I said, "I bet Simone can. Especially after Weir clued her in on the size of her father's estate. My guess is the plan was hatched over a year ago—maybe after they murdered and dumped DeMaura Montouthe in a bondage game that went wrong. That led to finding other street women and setting up the pattern."

Reed said, "Who's the boss, Simone or Weir?"

"I don't know. For Weir it's probably all about the money. Simone wants more."

Milo said, "A hundred thirty-three huge ones isn't enough motive?"

"Sure it is," I said, "but what makes things really satisfying for Simone is wiping out the competition. We're talking the ultimate plunder."

"The interloper who horned in on Daddy and his dough."

"Daddy, too. For abandoning her."

"What about Kelvin?"

"Competing heir and too damn talented," I said. "A genius who gives concerts, meanwhile Simone can't hold on to a job. Which brings us to the severed hands and the bodies facing east. Theoretically, they could also be misdirects—simulating a lust serial. But why choose those particular trademarks? We've got to be talking symbolic value."

Reed said, "Kelvin's golden hands."

"I can see Simone seething about that on long, cold nights. The right hand plays the melody, she's ending the concert."

Reed said, "And facing east is looking at Asia, like you said."

"If Huck's telling the truth, Simone's contempt has racial overtones."

Milo said, "The G-word. Lovely gal, our Simone."

Reed said, "If you're right and she's basically erasing the new family, any chance her own mother's in on it?"

"I don't think so. Kelly's sad but basically passive. And she adores Huck."

"Evil little girl," said Milo, "palled up with a greedy lawyer."

"Redundant," said Reed.

"You don't admire Ms. Wallenburg, Moses?"

"I admire her cars. How long before she starts pulling strings to spring Huck?"

"We book him on multiple 187s, forget strings, he's remanded." Milo peered through the smudged glass. Huck's mouth had shut but he hadn't shifted position.

Reed's cell phone chirped. A check of the number brightened his face but he squelched the reaction, turned almost comically serious. "Hi . . . really? Oh, boy . . . let me write it down . . . what's that? Sure. Afterward, yeah, good." Blushing. "Pardon?" Glance at Milo. "Depends on what the boss says . . . um, me, too. Yeah. Bye."

Milo said, "Let me guess. Dr. Wilkinson has nice news for us, plus she wants Indian for lunch, again."

Reed's blush deepened. "She got there early with her interns, they used spotlights." The color drained from his face. "Dogs found four more bodies, Loo."

"Who besides the Vanders?"

"Two adult Vanders plus two more sets of bones, lots of scatter, hard to say if they were turned in any direction and all the hands seem to be there. Probable females, one skull's definitely African American, other one's not clear. Simon and Nadine were easy to I.D. Not that much decomp, they were dumped far into the marsh but left on the banks with their clothes on, wallets and purses nearby."

He took a breath. "Missing right hands, facing east. Plus they found chicken bones, what looks like old potato salad, coleslaw.

Guess there *was* some picnicking going on."

"No sign of the kid," said Milo.

"Maybe someone had pity."

"Or just the opposite, Moses."

Reed winced. "Something even worse for Little Mister Golden Hands? Shit."

"Any way his body could be in the marsh and they haven't found it?"

"They're still probing, it might get easier after daybreak. They also got a second cast on that shoe print Dr. Delaware described, found a few others from the same footwear—looks like a sneaker of some kind but unusual, nothing domestic, may not be in the databases. Lab promises to have an answer, either way, by the end of today."

Clearing images of Kelvin Vander from my head, I said, "Lots of scatter could mean those other two bodies preceded the first three. No trademarks says it did start out as Simone and Weir playing bondage games, dispatching victims for fun. Once they got their rhythm, they adapted their methods for a huge financial scheme."

Movement on the other side of the glass

drew our attention. Huck had rolled so that his back faced us. He curled tighter, hugged himself.

Milo said, "What you said in the garage, Alex—maybe there's something he can do. You were thinking civic duty."

"If he's innocent, he might be open to it."

"Any point telling him about the Vanders? To gauge his reaction and give him additional motivation?"

"Not if you're seriously considering enlisting him," I said. "The emotional firestorm's too risky."

Moe Reed said, "Now we're *enlisting* him?"

Milo pointed to Reed's cell phone. "Get on the mini-horn, Moses."

"Who'm I calling?"

"Your brother."

CHAPTER
39

Subj: **you know**
8:32 a.m. PDT
From: rivrboat38@hotmail.com
To: hardbod2673@tw.com

it's me. i know all. can keep a secret. if can afford to.

Subj: **you know**
8:54 a.m. PDT
From: rivrboat38@hotmail.com
To: hardbod2673@tw.com

not there? you got another hour then . . .

Subj: **you know**
9:49 a.m. PDT
From: hardbod2673@tw.com
To: rivrboat38@hotmail.com

where r u

9:56 a.m. PDT
From: rivrboat38
To: hardbod2673

not important. find way to send $50 thou

10:11 a.m. PDT
From: hardbod2673
To: rivrboat38

ur kidding

10:15 a.m. PDT
From: rivrboat38
To: hardbod2673

don't hear LOL. do hear gook gook-fucker golden hands. also piano girl also whores for blame me. not nice. hmm . . . no fifty thou, 100 thou.

10:18 a.m. PDT
From: hardbod2673
To: rivrboat38

what?????

10:22 a.m. PDT
From: rivrboat38
To: hardbod2673

no big deal for you lotslotslots more $$$$ coming for you, you wont feel it. do it!!!

10:28 a.m. PDT
From: hardbod2673
To: rivrboat38

we need talk not cyber.

10:34 a.m. PDT
From: rivrboat38
To: hardbod2673

**don't think so LOL you do me like others?
you and badwig. now LOL see? i know.**

10:40 a.m. PDT
From: hardbod2673
To: rivrboat38

**u think u know u dont. we need to meet.
safe place for u. beachhouse?**

10:46 a.m. PDT
From: rivrboat38
To: hardbod2673

**oh sure your territory why dont you just
shoot me**

10:54 a.m. PDT
From: hardbod2673
To: rivrboat38

no more e trail im deleting w privacykeeper.
where r u some i-cafe???

10:59 a.m. PDT
From: rivrboat38
To: hardbod2673

100. do I need to repeat myself??? Ok 100.
100!!!

11:04 a.m. PDT
From: hardbod2673
To: rivrboat38

dont be parinoid beachhouse is good for u,
outside open sand, people all around what
could happen?

11:08 a.m. PDT
From: rivrboat38
To: hardbod2673

leave pch gate open by 7:30 that's p.m.
tonite!!! don't come till 7:45. leave garage

door open so I see you're not there first.
or badwig. low tide is around 8. come to the
tideline not later than 8:10. use big trader
joes bag. paper. wrap $$$ in saran for wet.
bring all of it!!!!

11:12 a.m. PDT
From: hardbod2673
To: rivrboat38

take time to get fiftyk but probly ok. if delay
can i reach u same eml?

11:16 a.m. PDT
From: rivrboat38
To: hardbod2673

fifty? LOL. hundred. no excuses.

11:21 a.m. PDT
From: hardbod2673
To: rivrboat38

ur being hardass. sixty best I can do cleaning

me out. not like u all hardass what's wrong???

11:29 a.m. PDT
From: rivrboat38
To: hardbod2673

don't like sixty. deserve more but ok i just want away what's wrong? you ask that? LOL. MEGA LOL!!!!

12:05 p.m. PDT
From: hardbod2673
To: rivrboat38

no LOL here. i care. take care of u.

12:11 p.m. PDT
From: rivrboat38
To: hardbod2673

best take care is $$$. no more talk.

12:14 p.m. PDT
From: hardbod2673
To: rivrboat38

talk helps everything will be ok promise we still good right?

Cybersilence.

CHAPTER

40

Moe Reed explained.

Sitting behind a rough-edged, smoked-glass-slab desk, Aaron Fox listened.

Fox's office was hermetically silent.

Milo had directed Reed to sum up the situation, maybe as part of training the younger detective.

Or, was there a chance he wanted to get the brothers talking?

No sense conjecturing; he'd never admit it.

Fox remained expressionless. When Reed finished, he said, "Murderous little bitch. I knew she was bad news but not that bad. You're sure Huck's up to it?"

Reed said, "We're not, but he says yes."

"And that's worth something?"

"He's what we've got, Aaron, and we'll be watching, okay? She's the one suggested the beach, it really is an open spot."

Fox said, "It's open all right, but what's to stop her from paying him off, then having him followed?"

"If she does, we'll be ready."

Fox tamped down the collar of a white-on-white silk shirt. "Another possibility is Weir positions himself on the deck of the house with a nightscope rifle and nails the poor sucker. Shots synchronize with the incoming tide, noise wipes out the sound."

Reed said, "We'll be watching Weir's office and the house. He shows up there, we reevaluate."

Not mentioning Robin's call to Weir's office, claiming to be a prospective client. The secretary taking her bogus name and volunteering that Mr. Weir was in meetings all day, she'd be sure he got the message.

Fox said, "Reevaluate as in call it off?"

"Reevaluate as in reevaluate."

"La Costa's private sand, Moses. How're you going to get access?"

Reed's neck swelled. "All of a sudden you're Dudley Downer?"

"I'm a realist, bro. Leads to longevity."

"We got access from a neighbor. Our watch car'll be stationed across PCH. Everything's covered. This is the plan, Aaron. Up to you."

Fox ran a finger around the circumference of a silver-disk desk clock. "It's already four, what's to say Weir hasn't gotten there and hunkered down?"

Milo said, "We're on it, Aaron."

"Okay, okay . . . Malibu neighbor, huh? You guys have the right friends. Anyone I might have heard of?"

Reed said, "Someone Dr. Delaware knows."

Fox stretched. Onyx cuff links gleamed. "Sounds like Dr. Delaware and I need to get better acquainted. Okay, I'll go get the toys."

After he left the room, Milo said, "Nice work space, sure beats civil service."

Fox's place was on San Vicente near

Wilshire, the southeast corner of Beverly Hills. The décor was skinny Italian leather seating, charcoal felt walls, chrome and brass and glass and cubist lithographs. The building was a twenties duplex, one of the last carryovers from the street's former life as a quiet residential byway. Now the structure shared space with commercial and professional buildings.

Fox's "Workland" had once been a master bedroom. Big and bright, with a rear view of a cactus garden, soundproofed padding beneath the felt. Playland—his living quarters—was on the second story, accessed through a teak spiral staircase, probably salvaged from a yacht.

Reed said, "He probably writes the whole building off. Aaron needs his deductions."

Fox returned with a brown suede carrying case, settled back behind the glass desk. Fishing out a black box the size of a cigarette pack, he laid it down, added what looked to be a pen, then a tiny white button attached to a cord and a pin-jack. Similar wires spaghettied from the other components. The whole kit could fit in a trouser pocket.

Fox's mocha hands passed over the equipment, like a battle priest blessing armaments. "One-stop shopping, gentlemen."

Milo said, "That's all of it?"

"Plus my laptop. Feed's programmed to interface, one keystroke and we've got DVDs for posterity."

"Cute."

"Private enterprise."

Milo pointed to the little black box. "That's the recorder?"

"Recorder and transmitter," said Fox. "This here"—touching the white button—"is the camera. Don't ask me what it cost. We're talking high-def infrared, cuts through the dark like a knife through trans fat." Deft fingers rolled to the pen. "Decent mike, but truthfully, not spectacular. Manufacturer claims a two-thousand-foot range, I've found one thousand to be closer to the truth, and sometimes it blanks out. High-tech industry's like Congress, promises more than delivers. For best results, have your mope stay no more than ten feet from her. I've got another one, a little more reliable, but it's embedded in a jeans jacket, if he gets hugged hard enough, it could be detected."

"How much wiring of our mope do we have to do?" said Reed.

"Recorder goes in his pants pocket, we cut a hole in there, run one cable up to the pen in his shirt pocket, I substitute the button for one of his and install the video feed. Any of you guys sew?"

Silence.

"Great, so now I'm your tailor. Be sure he's wearing a shirt with a pocket and that it already has buttons the same color. And don't even think of asking me to donate one of mine. There are limits."

Reed said, "He's wearing a blue button-down with white buttons. Brand new, courtesy his lawyer."

"Wallenburg," said Fox. "I thought she was corporate. What's her connection to him anyway?"

"It's complicated," said Milo. "Ever work with her?"

"I wish—hey, maybe if this works out, you can put in a good word and she'll send me some of those Enron-Worldcom cases."

Reed said, "Maybe *if*?"

"I wish you the best," said Fox, "but hardware's one thing, the human factor's another. When *I* play with these toys I'm in charge—wearing it myself, or rigging up one of my freelances. My people usually have SAG cards. You're working with a guy with mental problems."

"He's motivated," said Reed.

"Good intentions, and all that?"

Milo said, "Road to heaven."

"If you say so."

Travis Huck's reaction to the plan had changed his demeanor. Evaporation of fear, a smile almost broad enough to hide his lopsided mouth. I wondered if his concept of heaven included early arrival but said nothing. What would be the point?

Aaron Fox said, "You're sure all you want me to do is sit on my ass and check the feed?"

"That's it," said Milo.

"Aw, shucks."

"You want action, Aaron, you can always come back to the real job."

"Gee, why didn't I think of that. I guess billing for my time on this—not to mention having the department insure my gear—is a fantasy."

Milo said, "I'll guarantee full coverage of

the hardware on my own ticket. And who knows, everything works out you might get the dough Simone owes you."

"Oh, I'll get it," said Fox. "One way or the other."

CHAPTER

41

Seven fifty p.m., La Costa Beach, Malibu.

The world has compressed, its boundaries the black-rimmed rectangle of a nineteen-inch laptop screen.

Green-and-gray world, tinted by infrared illumination. In the background, waves roll in a lazy, almost sexual rhythm.

A man stands by the tide line, motionless.

I sit at a long table of ancient pine. My seat affords me an oblique view of the screen. Milo faces the laptop, moves his face close to it at times, then he retreats, polishing off more Red Bull.

Aaron Fox is positioned to his left. He drinks sparingly, almost daintily, from his personal bottle of Norwegian Fjord Spring Water. In between swallows, he chews cinnamon gum.

Moe Reed stands in a corner and watches the ocean.

The table is a seven-foot trestle, waxed and knotted and crisscrossed with scars that look calculated. It fills most of the dining space of a house ten lots north of the late Simon Vander's beach escape. Like Vander's place, this residence is a smallish two-story box on battered, creosote-coated pilings, worth eight figures. Unlike Vander's wood-sheathed bungalow, its walls have been stuccoed whale-belly blue, its windows upgraded to copper-tinted, rust-resistant double-hungs. The interior is cozy, under a beamed ceiling, wired for concert-hall sound and cutting-edge video. The walls are dead-white diamond plaster, set sparingly with the type of art that gets people cracking wise about their kids being able to paint just as well.

The furniture's at odds with all that, a carryover from the house's former life as a "rural beach cottage." Rattan and wicker and chunky easy-use wood pieces, many of which resemble the thrift-shop discards they are, are set up carelessly over faded machine-made Oriental rugs slightly soured by mold. The kitchen is barely big enough for two people to stand in. A stainless-steel Sub-Zero and purplish granite counters overachieve.

Décor doesn't matter, tonight. I suspect it never matters much, with a western wall of sliding glass offering a fine view of the Pacific.

The doors are open, the ocean shouts, I catch glimpses of stars above the overhang of the deck.

My eyes return to the screen.

The miniature world remains inert. I touch the smooth, waxed surface of the table. Nice; maybe it really was "rescued" from a monastery in Tuscany, as the house's current resident claims.

She's the sister of the owner, sponging happily. Her brother is an expatriate British rock star, now on reunion tour in Europe. Moe Reed gave me credit for finding the place but the real connection was Robin, who'd worked on the star's guitars years ago, when he had to pay her on the install-ment plan.

The beach house joins four other resi-dences in his real estate portfolio: Bel Air, Napa, Aspen, a pied-à-terre in the San Remo on Central Park West.

The sister is a fifty-three-year-old self-described "production assistant" named Nonie who doesn't bother to tell us her last name, as if we don't deserve more than the minimum. Tall and white-blond and sun-seamed; her midriff blouse re-veals a navel that should never have been pierced. She works hard at looking thirty, hasn't labored at anything else for years. Her attitude is imperiously clear: Police work is one step above septic-scrubber and Milo and Reed and Fox and I should be genuflecting every ten seconds for the privilege of using her borrowed space.

Her brother would not approve of such frost. Terming her "an insufferable mooch" when Robin reaches him in Lisbon, he agrees readily to donate the house.

"Thanks, Gordie."

"Sounds exciting, luv."

"Hopefully it won't be."

"What—oh, yeah, of course. Either way, it's yours for as long as you need it, luv. Thanks for cleaning the bridge pickup on the Tele. Just played it in front of seventy-eight thousand people and it *sang.*"

"That's great, Gordie. You'll tell Nonie we'll be showing up?"

"Did it right off, told her to cooperate fully. *She* gives you any trouble, tell her there's always her own pathetic dive."

Gordie's call notwithstanding, Nonie chooses to be cranky. Milo adopts a more diplomatic approach than that suggested by Gordie, listening patiently as Nonie drops name after name, flicks her hair, drinks brandy, struggles pathetically to bask in her sibling's reflected fame.

When she stops to take a breath, he gets her talking about the table from Tuscany, applauds her good taste without laying it on too thick. Despite the fact that she's never actually come out and claimed she found it.

She peers at him suspiciously, but is eventually won over by his persistence and her own need to feel important.

When the time is right, he gives her a hundred dollars and asks her to leave for her own safety, have a nice dinner on LAPD. The money comes out of his own pocket. Nonie looks at the cash. "The places I go, this might cover drinks."

Milo peels off more bills. She accepts them with a look of great personal sacrifice, fetches her Marc Jacobs bag, puts on her Prada shawl, stomps toward the door on her slingback Manolos.

Moe Reed walks her outside to her Prius. Remains with her until she hangs a reckless right turn onto Pacific Coast Highway, narrowly avoids collision with an oncoming SUV, speeds off amid a chorus of horns.

Before Reed returns to the house, he gazes south, though he has no hope of spotting Detective Sean Binchy a hundred fifty yards away, stationed in an unmarked sedan in front of a shuttered pizza joint. A cheap laptop sits on the passenger seat, programmed to stream the same feed Aaron Fox has rigged into his computer. Getting the "inferior piece of crap" to cooperate has turned out to be the biggest hitch so far, with Aaron Fox cheerfully demeaning civil service "snitware" before finally succeeding. Even after the connection is made, transmission is spotty, sound obscured by the traffic on PCH.

Binchy received the laptop from Milo at six p.m., has already been watching the Vander house for an hour when we arrive at Gordie's. No one has entered or exited and the garage door has been left open per Travis Huck's instructions.

Huck stands in the sand.

Eight o'clock arrives. Passes.

Eight oh five, ten, twelve . . . we wonder if this will fizzle.

The garage door left open is a positive sign, and we cling to it.

Eight fifteen. Huck seems undisturbed. Then I remember he's not wearing a watch.

It finally happens at eight sixteen, sudden and jarring as a heart attack.

Moe Reed is the first to notice. He points at the screen, nearly levitates from his seat.

Simone Vander has materialized on the beach. From nowhere.

The camera in Travis Huck's button captures her willowy frame floating forward.

I think of a mermaid rising from the ocean.

As she gets closer, the bag in her hand takes shape. Large, paper, Trader Joe's logo. Everything right on course, so far so good.

Simone's clothes are dry, maybe a walk-on-water miracle?

So-thin girl, dry hair fluffing in the breeze. She walks along the beach. Bare feet mold to the sand. Walking with confidence, a rich girl accustomed to private silica, ambling, loose-limbed, swinging the bag, not a care in the world.

Huck stands there.

Milo says, "Where the hell did she come from?"

Aaron Fox says, "Don't know. Camera is great for up close but past a certain point, you lose clarity in the long image."

As if in illustration, Simone steps within fifteen feet of Huck, stares at him, stops, and her facial features clarify. Maybe a bit more tense than her easy walk had suggested. Green overtones don't help. Bones sharper than I remember.

But still, a pretty girl.

The outfit she's picked is SoCal Cutie

101: sprayed-on, low-riding jeans, dark middy blouse revealing a drum-tight belly, bangle bracelets, big hoop earrings.

Two pierces in her navel. The breeze blows dark hair away from her left ear, revealing a solitary diamond glinting from cartilage. The feed is that good.

Huck doesn't move and for several seconds, neither does Simone.

"Travis." The sound's a bit grainy and her voice seems high, distant, muffled. As if she's talking through a mouthful of whipped cream. Or blood.

"Simone."

"Where will you go?"

"Not important."

Simone smiles, steps closer, swinging the bag. "Poor Travis."

"Poor Kelvin."

Simone's smile freezes. "Your little buddy."

"Your little brother."

"Half brother," she says.

"Gook brother," he says.

She gives a start, her eyes narrow, backtracking, trying to figure out where he got that.

She says, "Didn't know you were a rac-ist."

"I heard you say it, Simone." Something has changed in Huck's voice. Deeper. Tighter.

Fox catches it. "Sounds like he's working himself up. He goes for her, we're too far to stop it."

No one in the room answers him.

Simone Vander says, "You stalked me."

"I did."

She laughs at the shameless admission. "I fuck you four times and you can't get over it."

"Five."

"Four. Loser. The first time was a joke. You have to actually put it *in* before you *spooze* to call it fucking." She laughs harder. The tail end of her cruel mirth is softened by the fizz of an incoming wave.

She walks closer to Huck.

"You are such a dickbrain *loser,* Travis."

"I know."

His flat agreeability enrages her and her eyes turn to surgical incisions. She stops, sinks into the sand a bit, shifts position and finds higher ground. The bag swings wider. "You think you can escape your loser self by admitting that you're a loser? What's that, some rehab bullshit?"

Huck doesn't respond.

"You're a loser, a retard, a dickbrain preemie burnout. So don't go thinking you can mess with me, Travis. Only reason I'm here is because I feel sorry for you, okay? And guess what the first thing you're going to do when you've got my money?"

Silence.

"Take a guess, retard."

Silence.

Simone tosses her hair, holds the bag in both hands. "The first thing you're going to do—and you're going to do it soon—is take every penny I give you and shove it up your nose or shoot it totally into your veins. Maybe we'll both be lucky and you'll totally O.D. What do you think, honey? Wouldn't that be a good solution for every-one?"

Huck doesn't answer.

The ocean rolls.

I wonder if he's sweating. Moe Reed is. Milo is. Dark circles have spread under the armholes of Aaron Fox's white-on-white silk shirt.

My scalp is sodden, my mouth is dry.

Another wave comes in, a big one, crashing.

Simone says, "Just do it, Travis. Like Nike says. O.D. yourself and put everyone out of their misery."

"Why'd you do it, Simone?"

She laughs. "Why did I fuck you? Good question, Brain-Dead."

"Why'd you kill them?"

Simone doesn't confess, nor does she deny. She appears to glance past Huck, as if expecting company.

The four of us tense.

Moments pass.

Huck says, "All of them. Kelvin. How did you get yourself to that point?"

Simone's laughter is sudden, shrill, unsettling. "You know how neat I am, honey. Comes a time, dirt has to go."

Huck doesn't speak. Maybe stunned. Or smart enough—with enough experience as a therapy patient—to use the silence.

Simone swings the bag. Arches her

back, appears to be flaunting whatever chest she has.

Aaron Fox says, "She never stops. First time I met her, she was all sex."

Simone says, "Catching up's been fun, stud, but let's just do this."

Huck doesn't answer. Simone appears distracted by the ocean. "Now you're a dickbrain dumbie, too?"

Silence.

Fox says, "Say something, dude, keep her stringing along." His jaw is tight and all his insouciance is gone and I catch a sense of what he was like working homicide.

Simone steps closer to Huck, just out of arm's reach. A steady button-camera says Huck remains still.

He hasn't budged since we planted him on the sand.

"Just like that," he says.

"Like what?"

"You pay me, you're free of sin."

"Sin?" says Simone. "What the fuck is that?"

"Sixth Commandment."

"What's—oh, thou shalt not yadda yadda yadda."

"All for money," says Huck, with sympathy in his voice.

"Nothing sweeter."

"It was more than that," says Huck. "You're jealous of Kelvin. Always were."

"Jealous," she says, as if the word is foreign.

"He's got talent. You've got issues."

Simone stares into the camera. Her chest heaves. She smiles. "You know what my issue is, Travis? Being here with a dick-brain like you so I can give you money so you can go shoot it up your arm or jam it in your nose. So cut the talk—you always wanted to talk."

"You were nice to me so you could set me up."

"Nice to you?"

"Pretending."

"Sweetie," she says, "you are so set-up-able."

"So you could clean house."

"Sweep, mop, polish," she singsongs.

"Your dad gave you everything, Simone. You could have everything without killing them."

"Really?" she says. "Everything for me and nothing for her? You *are* retarded."

"There's enough to go around, Simone."

Simone thrusts the bag at him. "Take it and shut the fuck up."

She grows smaller in the camera's eye. Huck has retreated a foot or so.

"Take it!"

Milo slants forward.

Moe Reed mutters, "Go, go, go."

Huck says, "All because you wanted the gold for yourself."

Simone smirks. "I've *got* the gold. Loser."

"A kid, Simone. You hugged and kissed him and played with his hair. You hugged Nadine. Now they're gooks?"

"They were always gooks—"

"You *kissed* them."

Simone laughs. "Like in the Mafia—*The Godfather.* You get kissed before you get blown away."

"Was it easy, Simone? Did you look in their eyes—did you look in Kelvin's eyes?"

Simone laughs louder. "What's the big deal? Everyone dies the same."

"Keep talking," says Milo.

Huck says, "You looked into his eyes."

"The eyes change," says Simone, and her own orbs illustrate by taking on a dreamy look. "It's like watching the light go out. There's nothing like it." Arching her back again. "I watched the light go out in *her* eyes and I *came.*"

Milo pumps a fist. "*Got* her!"

She drops the bag on the sand. "Here's what you want. Have a bad life."

The camera doesn't falter.

"What, you think I'm punking you, loser? C'mere, look."

"What did you do with them, Simone?"

"Ate 'em," says Simone. "With fava beans and Chianti . . . what did we *do*? We jammed dynamite up their asses—who cares? Take this and crawl like the maggot you are."

She bends toward the bag, inserts her hand, comes up with a bound wad of bills.

Tosses it.

Huck doesn't budge. The money lands on the sand.

Simone stares at it. *"What?"*

"It's fine," says Huck. "Leave it and go."

Simone studies him.

"Leave it and go," Huck repeats. "Have whatever life you think you deserve."

"What's that, a curse, some kind of hex?" says Simone. "From you, a curse is a blessing."

She turns to leave. Stops, rotates. Jams her hand into the bag and comes up with something that isn't money.

Long and thin; she holds it aloft.

"Oh, shit," said Fox, as she charges Huck.

The camera captures her eyes, hot and frigid simultaneously. The blandness of her face as she thrusts the knife.

Huck's hands shoot out into the camera's eye as he grabs for the weapon.

Simone lunges, twists, grunts, blood spurts.

Huck says nothing as she continues to stab him.

Milo runs toward the deck stairs that lead to the beach, Reed races on his heels, overtakes him.

Aaron Fox gapes at the screen.

I catch the look on his face as I run after Milo and Reed.

See him right now, and you wouldn't know he was ever a confident, elegant man.

The sounds from the screen, wet, thumping, insistent, fill my ears as my feet hit the sand and I'm well out of range and hearing is no longer relevant.

CHAPTER

42

When we get to the spot where Simone Vander has attacked Travis Huck, he is sitting on the sand, cross-legged, like a yogi. His face is calm as he watches blood rain from his hands and arms and chest.

Simone is stretched out several feet away, inches from the water's edge, flat belly exposed to the moon, twin pierces winking.

The knife protrudes from the side of her neck. Long-bladed, wooden-handled kitchen utensil. Her body is twisted as if in escape. Her eyes are white and dull.

Moe Reed stoops on the sand, like a

baseball catcher. Checks, needlessly, for a pulse.

He stands up, shaking his head, joins Milo at Travis Huck's side.

The run has left Milo panting. Struggling to keep up with Reed, he managed to call for an ambulance.

He and Reed attend to Huck, tearing off their shirts to use as tourniquets. Within seconds Milo's undershirt and Reed's broad, bare chest are slathered with blood.

Huck seems amused by the fuss.

Two bound packets of money lie on the sand. Later, we'll discover both are bundles of singles covered by twenties at both ends.

Seventy dollars each.

Aaron Fox shows up, surveys the scene. Approaching Simone's body, his look says she's something alien and slimy, washed up by the tide.

A wave rolls over her, leaves a coating of foam on her face that dissipates as bubbles burst in the warm night air.

No lights have gone on in the neighboring houses. This is a haven for weekenders. By sunrise all blood will be laundered by the ocean, but now the sand is gummy.

Fox and I stand around as Milo and Reed, working silently, in perfect concert, reduce spurt to seep. Huck turns pale, then an odd off-white, begins to nod off.

Milo braces him and Reed holds his hands. The young detective says, "Hang on, pal."

Huck looks at Simone's corpse. Moves his lips. "Uh-ah-uh—"

Milo says, "Don't talk, son."

Huck's eyes remain fixed on Simone. He shrugs. Leaks.

"Don't move," says Moe Reed.

Huck mutters something.

"Shh," says Milo.

Huck's head sways. His eyes close.

He forces himself to form words.

Says, "I did it again."

I'm thinking about that as movement from the beach house grabs my attention.

Brief flash of activity below the house, where a bulb fastened to the bottom of the deck casts weak light on the pilings and the bulkhead beneath the main structure.

Something shifting. No one else notices. I go over.

A Zodiac raft hangs on chains from a rafter. Behind the boat is a door, slightly ajar, cut flush with the plywood that veneers the bulkhead.

No lock, some sort of storage space, it probably blew open.

But no wind, tonight. Maybe it's been that way for a while.

I make my way between the pilings, smelling salt and tar and wet sand. Enter the cave-like space created by the overhang of the deck. The Zodiac is fully inflated. Other things dangle from the rafters, like sausage at a deli. A small metal rowboat, two sets of oars. An old Coca-Cola sign, rusted beyond easy recognition, nailed to a listing, warped crossbeam.

Things go better with . . .

I approach the door. Barely wide enough to squeeze through. No movement, no light from within, and unlikely to be deeper than the few feet allowed by the bulkhead.

Blown open, who knows how long ago.

I swing the door open, just to be sure.

Come face-to-face with a black figure eight.

Double shotgun barrel. Above the lethal tube, a face, slack in spots, unnaturally taut in others.

Hairless. No eyebrows, no lashes.

A visage turned mask-like by the tickle of indirect light.

Bald head, pale eyes. Dark T-shirt and sweats, dark running shoes.

Big diamond ring on one of the fingers gripping the trigger.

What I can see of the shotgun's stock is shiny and burled. Engraved metalwork elevates the weapon to art. A whole different level from my father's bird-slayer.

One of the pricey weapons Simon Vander got rid of when his new wife asked him to.

Buddy Weir's diamond ring bounces as his finger tightens.

"Easy," I say.

Weir mouth-breathes. It's his turn to sweat.

A soft-looking, slope-shouldered man, stinking of sulfurous fear.

More dangerous than if he'd been angry.

Pale eyes look past me at the scene on the beach. He seems about to cry.

The ring bounces again. The barrel moves closer, stops inches from my nose.

A strange, wonderful numbness takes over as I hear myself speak.

I say, "Wrong eye."

Confusion freezes Weir's hand.

"You're right-handed, but you might be left-eyed. Close one, then the other, see which one makes my face jump more. Also, you need to stop fighting the gun, guns don't like to be wrestled with, lean in, embrace, be part of it—go ahead, blink, test your eyes."

Weir's look is scornful, superior, but his eyes effect unconscious compliance and the shotgun wavers.

I duck, hit him hard as I can, low in the gut, follow with the most vicious kick I can muster, connect with his groin. He gasps, doubles over, the gun points upward.

Thunder.

Wood shreds.

Weir is still in pain as I put all my weight into a two-handed blow to the back of his neck.

He crumbles to the sand. Still holding the shotgun.

I stomp his arm, break some bones, free the weapon.

Lovely trap gun, probably Italian. The burl is glorious walnut, the metal engravings scenes of Renaissance hunters stalking mythical beasts.

Weir moans in agony. Later, I will learn that his ulna shattered like glass, will never be the same.

I watch him writhe, allow myself a moment of satisfaction that I will never disclose to anyone.

Milo has heard the shotgun go off, arrives with his nine-millimeter in hand.

He flips Weir, uses plastic ties to bind Weir's wrists and ankles, just as a Malibu EMT squad arrives.

One squad, one stretcher. Travis Huck gets priority.

Weir suffers.

During a brief pause in his wails, I hear something.

From the bulkhead.

Faint, bashful knocking. A higher tide would've obscured it.

Milo hears it, too. Keeping his gun in hand, he points at the doorway, stops, peers in, vanishes.

I follow.

The boy is propped against cement block. The stench of feces and urine and vomit is overpowering. He has been wrapped in black garbage bags, bound with loops of nylon cord, like a pot roast. The blindfold over his eyes is black muslin. The rubber ball in his mouth is bright orange. His nostrils are unobstructed but snot-smeared. His head has been shaved.

He kicks small, bare feet against the front plywood wall of the storage area.

Six feet square; convicted murderers live in bigger spaces.

Milo and I hurry to free him. Milo gets there first, calls him by name, tells him he's safe, everything's okay. As the blindfold is peeled from dark, almond eyes, Kelvin Vander looks up at us.

Dry-eyed.

In another world.

I touch his cheek. He screams like a trapped raccoon.

Milo says, "Everything's fine, son, nothing to worry about, you're safe now."

The boy's eyes bore into his. Acute, studious. His cheeks sport finger marks, welts, small cuts.

He has both his hands.

Milo says, "You're gonna be okay, son."

Tilts his own face away from the child's.

Hiding the lie.

CHAPTER

43

Case closed. Big case. The police chief was happy. Or some reasonable facsimile of such.

A.D.A. John Nguyen's work was just beginning, but he was also smiling. For all their scheming and planning, Simone Vander and Buddy Weir had left a lovely evidentiary chain: over a year of phone calls and another rented storage unit, this one in the heart of West L.A., paid for faithfully each month with Weir's personal check.

Inside were more box games and paperwork attesting to Weir's national rankings in

Scrabble and backgammon and bridge. Credit card records documenting monthly trips to Vegas, often with Simone. Weir's blackjack and poker winnings appeared to exceed his losses—though Nguyen's staff, still digging into Weir's finances, hadn't unearthed all the details.

One nice detail: The shoe prints at the western side of the marsh matched to a pair of six-hundred-dollar Legnani driving shoes found in the closet of Weir's Encino home.

Three polished wooden boxes were also found in the bin, not unlike the cache that had held the finger bones. Each receptacle offered up a trove of photos.

Weir and Simone in full S&M regalia.

Women, five of them, partially clothed, then naked. Three of the subjects were easily matched with mug shots of Sheralyn Dawkins, Lurleen "Big Laura" Chenoweth, and DeMaura Montouthe. The remaining two were phenotypically consistent with the bones found on the west side of the marsh, but took longer to identify. With help from Vice, Milo and Moe Reed finally I.D.'d them as Mary Juanita Thompson, twenty-nine, and June "Junebug" Paulette, thirty-two, prostitutes known to work the airport stroll. The news didn't grab a single second of media interest, nor did the department choose to issue a press conference.

The depiction of each victim's involvement with Weir and Simone spelled out a sequence so stereotyped it had clearly been scripted: initial exchange of cash, smiling participation, a gradual morph into gagged, bound terror, death by strangulation. Postmortem close-up of a pair of green-handled garden shears, sometimes in Weir's hand, others in Simone's.

Bones.

Milo was too smart to think in terms of happy endings, but a call from the chief's office to review five more cold cases sent him off to ponder and grumble.

Moe Reed applied for transfer to West L.A. but an executive order to get something done on the Caitlin Frostig disappearance kept him in Venice.

He called and asked if I could help.

I agreed to meet to review the case, but my attentions were focused elsewhere.

One day, driving to the station to deliver my proofread statement on the marsh murders,

I spotted Reed walking hand in hand with Dr. Liz Wilkinson. Both of them laughing. Up to that point, I'd never seen the young detective crack half a smile.

That night, I took Robin out to dinner at the Hotel Bel-Air.

She wore her pearl.

Travis Huck spent two months at Cedars-Sinai. Most of his stab wounds had sliced muscle and a few had damaged nerves, leading to residual weakness and soreness. Deep gashes in his left arm would probably render the limb useless and prone to infection. His doctors raised the specter of amputation somewhere down the line, a possibility confirmed by Richard Silverman, M.D., director of the E.R.

Rick, asked by Milo to keep tabs on Huck's progress, said the patient was healing physically.

"But I don't have a feel for him psychologically, Alex. Kind of inappropriate affect, no?"

I said, "The smiles."

"Exactly. No matter what. Even after refusing painkillers."

"For him it could be the best choice."
"Guess so, but it's got to hurt."

When I visited Huck, I found him at peace, his face so slack and serene that most of the droop was gone. The nursing staff voted him their favorite patient. On a busy ward, that translates to compliant.

He watched a lot of TV, read and re-read all seven volumes of Harry Potter, ate some of the fruit and candy Debora Wallenburg messengered over, gave most of it away.

Wallenburg volunteered her services in the prosecution of Buddy Weir. John Nguyen declined respectfully. Confided to me that he'd probably "screwed my chance of going corporate."

One time I approached Huck's room and encountered Kelly Vander and Larry Brackle leaving. Seeing me flooded Kelly's face with shame and she hurried past. Brackle held back, seemed to want to talk.

I smiled.

He ran after Kelly.

The hospital security guard who sat near Huck's door when time permitted hustled over. "Hi, Doc. When she gave me her name, I didn't want to let them in." Crooking a thumb. "Mr. Huck said it was okay, so I searched her purse, nothing iffy."

"How long were they in there?"

"Twenty minutes," said the guard. "I was listening, Doc, no problems whatsoever. Once I took a peek, they didn't see me. She was holding Mr. H.'s hand. Toward the end, she cried a bunch and I think he was asking her to forgive him or something like that and she was saying no, it was she who needed forgiveness. Then there was a whole bunch of crying."

"What did the other guy do?"

"Just sat there."

I thanked him and cracked the door.

Huck was on his back, sleeping peacefully. He hadn't roused by the time I reviewed his chart and chatted with his physical therapist. I left and drove to another hospital.

At the Inpatient Rehab Center at Western Pediatrics, Kelvin Vander lived in a private room sentried twenty-four seven by private eyes subcontracted by Aaron Fox. A third of every billable hour the freelancers submitted was deposited directly into Fox's bank account.

Kelvin's new lawyers were happy to pay. Their own hourly billings were drawn upon a seven-figure account attached to the Vander estate. The estate had been valued at over a hundred and seventy million. A family court judge assigned to protect Kelvin promised to keep an eye on the boy's money. If things got out of hand, he'd cap the attorneys' annual draw at a million or two.

Over a three-week period, I spent over a hundred hours with Kelvin, would eventually send my own bill, but had other things on my mind.

When I showed up, the boy looked straight at me.

One month later. Still not a word.

I tried drawing, games, just sitting there.

My own benevolent silence.

At my wit's end, I called the judge and made a request.

He said, "Hmm. Kind of creative, Doctor. You think it'll work?"

"I thought he'd open up by now, no predictions."

"Know what you mean. Went to see him, myself. Cute, but like a little statue. Sure, I'll authorize it."

The next day, I was in Kelvin's room when a spinet piano and matching bench were delivered. In the bench drawer were folders of sheet music I'd retrieved from the Steinway grand gracing the boy's ocean-view bedroom in the house on Calle Maritimo.

I removed some of it, fanned it on his hospital bed.

He closed his eyes.

I waited awhile, left his room. Was charting at the nurses' station when the music began, first tentative, then louder, streaming through the door and perking up the private cop on shift.

Everyone listened.

"What's that?" said a nurse. "Mozart?"

I said, "Chopin." One of the études, I was pretty sure.

Over and over.

I drove home and dug out a box of CDs.

Ten minutes later I had it: Opus 25, number 2, in F minor.

Technically challenging, sometimes sprightly, sometimes sad.

Later, the nurses told me he'd played it all day and well into the night.

ABOUT THE AUTHOR

JONATHAN KELLERMAN is one of the world's most popular authors. He has brought his expertise as a clinical psychologist to more than two dozen bestselling crime novels, including the Alex Delaware series, *The Butcher's Theater, Billy Straight, The Conspiracy Club,* and *Twisted.* With his wife, the novelist Faye Kellerman, he co-authored the bestsellers *Double Homicide* and *Capital Crimes.* He is the author of numerous essays, short stories, scientific articles, two children's books, and three volumes of psychology, including *Savage Spawn: Reflections on Violent Children.* He has won the Goldwyn, Edgar, and Anthony awards, and has been nominated for a Shamus Award. Jonathan and Faye Kellerman live in California and New Mexico. Their four children include the novelist Jesse Kellerman. Visit the author's website at www.jonathankellerman.com.